The Ghost of Bridgetown

ALSO BY DEBRA SPARK

Coconuts for the Saint
Twenty Under Thirty, editor
On the Tail of the Dog Star

The Ghost

of

Bridgetown

Debra Spark

Graywolf Press

SAINT PAUL, MINNESOTA

Publication of this volume is made possible in part by a grant provided by the Minnesota State Arts Board through an appropriation by the Minnesota State Legislature, and by a grant from the National Endowment for the Arts. Significant support has also been provided by the Bush Foundation; Dayton's Project Imagine with support from Target Foundation; the McKnight Foundation; a grant made on behalf of the Stargazer Foundation; and other generous contributions from foundations, corporations, and individuals. To these organizations and individuals we offer our heartfelt thanks.

Published by Graywolf Press
2402 University Avenue, Suite 203
Saint Paul, Minnesota 55114
All rights reserved.

www.graywolfpress.org

Published in the United States of America
Printed in Canada

Lyrics from Mac Fingall's song, "Big Belly Man," from the CD *One More* by Red Plastic Bag and Mac Fingall, are quoted with the permission of Rick Howell at Jumbie Music (ASCAP).

Material from Abraham Joshua Hershel's book, *A Passion for the Truth*, © 1973, is reprinted with permission of Farrar, Straus and Giroux.

ISBN 1-55597-352-3

2 4 6 8 9 7 5 3 1
First Graywolf Printing, 2001

Library of Congress Control Number: 2001088661

Cover design: Steve Rachwal

Warm thanks to Colby College and the Corporation of Yaddo for their generous support during the writing of this book.

Portions of this novel were originally published, in a slightly different form, in *Ploughshares* and *Green Mountain Review*.

You are accompanied through life . . . not only by the beloved
and accusing departed, but by your own ghost too,
also accusing, also unappeased.

—A. S. BYATT, *Angels and Insects*

The Ghost of Bridgetown

Charlotte Lewin

May/June 1997

⌁

N O ONE HAD SEEN THE MENORAH IN YEARS. The Massachusetts congregation almost said they didn't have it when the letter came. But then someone remembered, and there was a search of the synagogue's single locked closet, and there, behind ancient phylacteries, a stack of unusable sky blue yarmulkes, and a crumbling square of matzoh wrapped in a linen napkin, was the item. It didn't look like a menorah. It looked like a companionable elephant walk: eight golden elephants with barbaric, purposeful grins, all linked trunk to tail. Their backs were hollowed out for candles. Two red stones—no one had bothered to figure out if they were rubies—adorned each head. These were the eyes, of course, as if elephants and flash cameras had always coexisted. The tusks were real ivory—that was the rumor, which grated with its irony. Who'd kill an elephant for an elephant? You needed a magnifying glass to make out the letters etched down one beast's leg and up the other. The rabbi translated the Hebrew: "He crept under the elephant and slew him; the elephant fell down and there he died." The "he" was Eleazar, a Maccabee. "Okay," the gathered nodded. Everyone knew that Hanukkah celebrated the Jewish Maccabees' victory over Antiochus, the Syrian ruler who wanted Jews to worship Greek gods. Someone said, "Not too swift, that Eleazar." There was a bit of laughing agreement while the rabbi swathed the animals in plastic bubble wrap. He didn't seem inclined to explain the elephants' significance further. Perhaps he didn't know anything more.

Charlotte Lewin was charged with accompanying the menorah to Barbados. No reason for it to be her exactly, save that she was the surviving grandchild of Howard Weinstein, who was the lawyer for Temple Sinai. The Massachusetts synagogue had held the menorah—never used it, never wanted to—for almost forty years.

This is what happened:

At the turn of the century, a synagogue in Barbados was deconsecrated. "Really?" Charlotte said when Howard told her. Deconsecration sounded so exotic. What was it, a bordello in the basement, tabs of acid lining the rabbi's prayer shawl? But Howard shook his head, offered up only that most prosaic of facts: nonattendance. There'd been a thriving community of Sephardic Jews in Barbados. And then there wasn't. Conversions to Anglicanism, emigration—who knew what else accounted for the sudden lack of faith? The synagogue's effects were sent away, little orphans gone to board at the homes of foreign relatives, places better equipped for their care. Which meant, for the most part, Bevis Marks. Most of the belongings went to that famous synagogue in London. But a distant relation, a Yankee tourist, *someone* managed to claim the menorah, and when he passed on, the piece went to a fledgling synagogue in Westford, Massachusetts. It was barely a synagogue, really. The congregation met in an old church meeting hall, but they had a locked closet, rarely opened, and, in 1997, a good lawyer.

And then Jews started moving to Barbados again. Ashkenazic Jews this time, chased out of eastern Europe instead of Brazil, the country from which the original group had been fleeing. Now there was a small community on the island: Polish Jews, Canadian Jews, German Jews, Guatemalan Jews, Ethiopian Jews, Chinese Jews. Howard hooted as he related all this. "Chinese Jews," he said. "I kid you not." Charlotte shrugged. Why not? She was ready to believe anything.

The Barbados synagogue had weathered decades of insults. Its cemetery had been used as a parking garage, then as a dump. The temple itself had been made to house hardware supplies. Next door, a madwoman squatted in what (she claimed) had been the rabbi's quarters. At night, she bathed in the trickle of water that spilled from the nearby Montefiore Fountain. But that was all in the past. The building had been restored, the grounds cleaned, and there were regular services on Fridays. A letter arrived at Temple Sinai, documenting all these improvements, and explaining that it was time to return the menorah.

Howard wanted to send Charlotte because she wasn't dead. Her sister had died and she hadn't, and this was the limitation of gifts, his means of expressing affection: you could only convey them to the living. Howard's gift to Charlotte was a trip to Barbados, but she didn't want to go. Or at least this is what she told him as she drove him home from the hospital. They'd gone for pre-op tests. Howard was getting prepared to say goodbye to his stomach. The half of it that was cancerous would be removed the next day. His mind, though, seemed to be on other matters. "This menorah," he started then stopped to remind her, "the one I want you to take with you on your trip." Charlotte kept her focus on the road. The day's rain had blurred everything, save neon signs and headlights, into a uniform gray. Up ahead—over a sign that read, "Come on In to the Chicken Sha," (the "ck" had blown out)—a chicken's wing opened and closed, opened and closed. Howard went on: there had been a second letter about the menorah. Not from the Barbados synagogue this time, but from the director of a museum on the island, a place called the Bajan Institute. The menorah belonged to him, the man wrote, to him and his museum, and he'd made a persuasive case. Charlotte couldn't listen to the details. *Cancer*, she was thinking. *You, too.*

But not in the brain, she reminded herself, and not in the body of a young woman. It was important to make distinctions: what was dreadful, what was not so bad. This was a new belief; before she'd only been impatient. She'd hear the word *cancer* and think, *If it is going to happen, let it happen fast.*

Two years earlier, when Charlotte found out Helen's cancer had gone to her brain, she'd wished Helen dead. Now, Charlotte couldn't untangle which part of that wish was love, which part fear, and which part selfishness, though she chided herself for the wish a thousand times. Not that she imagined it made any difference. If wishes mattered, the other, stronger wish would have had to win out. Her sister would be alive today, getting set to celebrate her twenty-seventh birthday; she would be leaning forward from the backseat to carp about Charlotte's bad driving.

Charlotte inched forward at a red light. Of course, there was no protest, because twenty months after Charlotte made her terrible wish, it came true; Helen sputtered to an end. No more Helen, though she'd been everything before. Suddenly, everyone was released from hospitals and doctor visits. Friends turned their attention to Charlotte's family, as the family had once turned their attention to Helen. The principal victim had changed. And yet now, four months after her family had buried Helen, Charlotte was shuttling her grandfather home and imagining herself tomorrow. She'd make her grim-faced way up the dismal stairs at Mass General and envy everyone turning right—right for prostate cancer; a relative cakewalk, she couldn't help but think—instead of left for bone marrow transplants and the who-knows-what of her aging grandfather's stomach ailment.

When she visited Howard after the operation—not the very next day, when he was uncharacteristically self-pitying, saying, "Look, Charlotte, look what twenty-four hours has wrought," but two days later—he was almost giddy.

"Charlotte," he cried from his bed. "Come into the greenhouse." Behind a curtain, in the dim hospital room, he was surrounded by plants skewered with gift cards and unwrapped fruit baskets. It put Charlotte in mind of her own panicked unwrapping and storing of grapefruits and oranges during Helen's *shiva*, her sense that she had to take care of all this quickly, and her disgust at herself for being pleased at receiving some smokehouse almonds. Sometimes, she'd come to realize after that first horrible wish, you let yourself think the most inhuman things to test how dreadful you were. It was a way, of course, to make yourself cry, as if you didn't already have enough to cry about.

"So," Howard said, his eyebrows doing quick, inquisitive push-ups, "how are you?"

"I'm all right," she said and busied herself finding a water pitcher for the flowers she'd brought. "Hope you like tulips."

"Red," he cried. "My favorite color."

"Oh, yeah," Charlotte said. "That's right."

For Helen's *shiva*, Howard had sent scarlet anemones, the largest bunch Charlotte had ever seen, but after the funeral, when Charlotte asked him how often he thought of his own brother, who'd died forty years earlier in a car crash—the great event, as Charlotte understood it, of his life, the reason he drove so dangerously slow on highways—he'd said, "Never." And then he'd said something so startling that Charlotte supposed she misheard him. "I haven't thought of him since the day he died."

Now Charlotte slumped into a chair at the foot of Howard's bed. "Can you see me here?"

"Well," he called out and pressed a button that raised the head of his mattress, "now I can." He hit the button again and said, actually said, "Whee!" She looked up, and he explained, sheepishly, "Like a ride at the fair."

Charlotte considered his IV. What sort of mood-altering drugs were dripping into him? A huge purple bruise bloomed from the needle at the back of his hand, but he seemed to have made his peace with whatever pain was there.

She sighed once. Howard deserved her grief, but it was all gone, drained by Helen. She'd brought twenty minutes of false cheer with her, and she could see he didn't want it any more than another fruit basket. It would be wrong, too, to ask him how he was. Even now, the last thing Howard wanted was comfort, so Charlotte offered a question: "What was that you were telling me the other day? About the menorah?"

"Oh," he gestured to a file on the nightstand. "I was planning to tell you again. It's essentially a repatriation case, so I knew you'd be interested."

"Oh, I am."

She listened carefully this time, and Howard spoke slowly, as he always did when it came to matters of business or finance. The director of the Bajan Institute—a "museum without walls," devoted to island culture—had written to Temple Sinai, protesting their decision to return the menorah to the Barbados synagogue. The Institute's director wanted the piece for his museum's collection. It was an early example of island artisanry, of metalsmithing. There was a contract between the Barbados synagogue and Temple Sinai, but that didn't make any difference, the director claimed. The menorah had been made by Nigel Jones, a slave whose history the Institute was just beginning to unearth. You couldn't have a contract over stolen property, and the work had been stolen from its makers.

"So," Howard tapped the *New York Times* at his side. His fingertips were dusky, still ink-stained from his thorough perusal of the paper. "You see the question. Give it to the blacks or give it to the Jews."

"My least favorite dilemma," Charlotte allowed.

"Well, it's yours," Howard said. "Your case now. I'm hiring you as my assistant."

"You know I'm not a lawyer." Charlotte gave half a laugh. As a girl, she'd noticed how pleased adults were when you said you hoped to grow up to be whatever they were. Surely she'd claimed an interest in law once, along with medicine, journalism, computer programming, political action, and reading to the blind. That about covered her family. But not her. She was assistant director of education at Boston's Museum of Fine Arts, relegated, lately, to children's programming, which hardly made good use of her Ph.D. "Toney baby-sitting," she told friends.

"But this is like what you were telling me about," Howard insisted. "The Indian graves."

"Yes," Charlotte said, "the Native American Graves and Repatriation Act." They'd been talking about it over dinner just a week earlier, when Howard had been reading a *New Yorker* article about Kennewick man, the hotly contested skeleton that anthropologists wanted to study and Native Americans wanted to bury. Charlotte had tried to explain that for art historians, the issue of returning objects to native tribes, or plundered countries, wasn't a new one. "There's the Elgin Marble in the British Museum," she'd started, but Howard had waved her quiet. He knew all that.

"Well," Howard coughed now. "I have to study the contract for this menorah, which is potentially ambiguous, for a number of reasons that I don't need to bother you with. Presuming we *are* in a position of ownership—which we may not be—I want to be prepared to make a decision. I want you to go to the island and . . . what is it you told me last week?" He feigned vagueness but then repeated her words exactly, "To comply with the 1990 Act, the object should go to the group most culturally connected to the object, and you need some proof that the person with whom you're dealing is, indeed, authorized to represent the group."

Charlotte gave his IV another appraising glance. "But this isn't a Native American object."

"No, but I think that Act suggests the terms on which we might proceed."

"Well, the Act specifies that it goes to the group most culturally connected, not the person who made the object."

"But that doesn't necessarily negate the blacks' claim of cultural connection."

"Let's discuss this later," Charlotte said, and a nurse's arrival cut off Howard's protest.

But the very next day, when Charlotte dropped by after work, Howard pressed his case. And why not? A lawyer. He never questioned, but badgered, even when he meant to be kind. "I've given up answering," Charlotte once told Helen. "I've taken to abdicating." Which meant that in college she'd once told him, "You're right. You're right. I don't know why I'm studying art history. It was an idiotic decision," and he'd looked hurt—one of the rare times she'd seen him chagrined—and said, in a small voice, "No, no, I just wanted to know what you were thinking." And then it was Charlotte's turn to feel ashamed. She hadn't thought he'd be interested in her *thoughts*. Her relatives, the elder generation, at least, didn't they like—in the warmest way possible, of course—to help her understand her terrible inadequacy? "Silly girl," they chirped affectionately. They delighted when she pulled a door that clearly said "push." Such a silly girl. Charlotte wanted to tattoo her resume on her cheeks. She had gone to Columbia, then Yale as a graduate student. She'd spent summers working at the Museum of Modern Art before returning to Boston to join the Museum of Fine Arts. Yet when her mother got in earshot of one of her friends, the story she most liked to tell was about how Charlotte, at age two, had used the contents of an unflushed toilet to wash her hair.

"Honey," Howard interrupted her thoughts, "how long can you go for?"

Charlotte smiled and shook her head. She wasn't in the mood for travel or abdication. What was a relative's illness if not months of abdication, a slow abandonment of your desires. "Ohhh," you said whenever you heard bad news. It was a gift, that little breath, almost of wonder. You gave yourself a two-letter word and a comma-length pause, the whole substance of your hopes hanging on the sound, before you said, "Okay." She wanted to be through with it. And even so, Charlotte couldn't refuse Howard exactly, because accepting his gift was a way to be good to him.

"A week? Ten days?" Howard prompted. He had a new, thumbprint-shaped bruise under his right eye. What did they do here? Beat you up while you slept?

"Why not longer?" Charlotte asked, almost imagining she was in earnest.

But she wasn't. Black-Jewish conflicts made her squirm. Her guilty liberalism in the ring with her familial attachments? No, thank you. Not for a week, not for a day. And the whole dilemma seemed fabricated. Why would Temple Sinai want to involve itself? Couldn't they simply give the menorah back to the Barbados synagogue and let them deal with this request from the Bajan Institute? "Good point," Howard said, in the condescending, congratulatory tone of an elementary-school teacher. But then he launched into a muddled lecture on contract law, which ended with Charlotte agreeing to peruse the colorful travel books at Barnes & Noble. That's what Howard wanted anyway, for her to go on a trip, not do research for him. And Charlotte *had* built up a lot of vacation time. If she didn't take it soon, she'd lose it all in December.

And yet she couldn't quite accept his offer. She knew Howard interpreted her hesitation as a form of politeness, but she had no interest in the Caribbean, had never understood people who took trips there. Europe was a vacation. Africa and Asia an adventure. Beaches and fruit drinks were a waste of time. Plus she burned easily. The whitest of white girls, she told friends, and it was true. They said, "Ivory skin," and Charlotte loved the compliment, but the truth was she was not the whitest of white girls. She was the bluest, her veins, particularly when she was cold, mapping her with startling clarity. She was her very own *Gray's Anatomy*. "Here's how it fits together," her body seemed to be telling her at all times. And her mind, wanting balance, offered back images of how her sister's body *didn't*—how it sent blood clots up her legs and gave her a seizure; how it wouldn't let enough oxygen through her lungs.

While Charlotte waffled about the trip, Howard pushed forward with his plans. From his hospital bed, he booked a flight and then a hotel room. Evenings, Charlotte visited, but he never let her stay long. He'd report, eagerly, on what he'd done for her that day and then he'd say, "You go now. Go have fun."

"Okay," she'd say, guiltily slinking back out the door.

Weeks passed this way. The plan was for Howard to be transferred to rehab but problems kept cropping up—a tear in his esophagus, a blood clot in his legs. Charlotte learned all this from the nurses. Howard only said, "The beaches in Barbados are like pure silk," and he made a gesture that suggested he was smoothing his hands over fabric. "And pink," he'd tell her. "Pink beaches. From the coral."

Charlotte weakened. Why not go if it would please him? She showed up, late one unseasonably steamy afternoon, with her own gift: she had arranged to take a week off from work.

"And why not bring your young man?" Howard said, not content to give her a gift she could accept but having, now, to make it more lavish. "Summer is the downtime for Barbados. Hurricane season. No one goes, so everything's two for one. If your young man can swing the plane fare— and we can get it for him at our cost—you can bring him along."

"Oh," Charlotte said, "a holiday with the gentleman friend." She and Lawrence had broken up then un-broken up so often that it seemed embarrassing to admit that they'd broken up again. For good, this time, since Lawrence had started dating someone new.

"Exactly," Howard said, still trying to set the world right. Illness hadn't changed him. This had always been a matter of ignoring the trouble at hand and finding an expensive gift, a pricey dinner, a particularly rich cookie to present to "the girls" in his life: his assistants and grandchildren. His wife, before she died. It wouldn't do to protest on the grounds of a diet or to advise him that fifty-year-old secretaries might like to be referred to as women. His world had stopped in the 1930s. Even his small office was a relic, with its frosted-glass partitions, rotary phones, and teletype machine.

But, of course, in the thirties, proper girls didn't travel with their lovers. It was a shock to be asked to invite Lawrence along. Still, Charlotte felt it was important to complete her abdication. Life had a what-does-it-matter-now feel. "A traveling companion," she gushed. "Grandpa, that would be great!" If she were the nurse, currently fiddling with the

Hickman below Howard's collarbone, she'd have thought, *That's just the kind of woman who pisses me off.*

"Howard," Howard said and gave the nurse a smile. "Grandpa makes me feel old."

"Howard," Charlotte said, slowly, trying to deepen her voice into the gravelly, considered notes of sincerity, "thank you."

The night before her flight to Barbados, Howard called. "Bon voyage," Charlotte expected him to say, but he was almost curt. Mad, she wondered for a second, because in the end she said she couldn't use a ticket for Lawrence? "Listen, Charlotte. I got another letter today."

"A letter about?"

"Same thing as before. From the Bajan Institute. The menorah belongs to them. A slave artifact. Etcetera, etcetera, etcetera." Howard sounded weary of the whole matter. "You can read it yourself. Pat'll bring you the file."

"Okay," Charlotte said.

"And, by the way, you're staying a second week. I already made the arrangements. You can take another week, can't you?"

"From work?" Charlotte said, suddenly furious. "Well, no, I have to. . . ."

"Yeah, work," Howard interrupted. He sounded vague, as if his focus were elsewhere—on the evening news or the *Times* puzzle.

"Are you okay?" Charlotte asked.

"Of course." He cleared his throat into the phone, "Bye-bye, honey."

An hour later, Pat—Howard's longtime secretary—stepped into Charlotte's apartment with the files. "Here's a photograph of the menorah."

Pat held out a Polaroid. In it, the elephants' backs were encrusted with stones or colored glass—the red-yellow of an apple, the creamy blue-gray of a spruce tree, the speckled green of frog's skin—all arranged together in neat little squares and draped over the elephants' spines like miniature Persian blankets. Charlotte turned the snapshot over. On a sticker, someone had typed: "*Menorah.* Bridgetown, Barbados, 1810 (?). Silver, repoussé, cast, engraved, parcel gilt, precious stones, glass."

Pat said, "He's decided against sending it down with you. I guess he'll have an art handler take it later. Actually, you know more, I'm sure, about how all this works than he does. There's the contract and a few letters.

Folders of history. Who knows what he wants you to do? I mean beyond have a daiquiri."

Charlotte nodded.

"And you can take the extra week?" Pat said.

"Yes, I arranged it, but he really put me in a position."

Pat shrugged, a you-know-him lift to her shoulders. She turned to go.

"And how's he feeling?" Charlotte said.

"You didn't hear?"

Charlotte shook her head.

"He's been throwing up blood."

"Oh, my God."

"But don't call him," Pat said. "Whatever you do, don't call him. He'd want you to just go on the trip. Have fun and find out some things for him."

"Yes," Charlotte agreed. She knew Pat was right. She shouldn't call. She wasn't even sure what—once she was in Barbados—he'd want her to do. Figure out the menorah's lineage, she supposed. How else did one determine cultural connection? Meet the Jews concerned. The blacks. Ask them what the menorah meant to them. Ask the people at the synagogue why they thought *they* represented Jewish interests, as if the answer wasn't perfectly obvious. Ask the Bajan Institute why they thought *they* represented the island's interests. She could do all that. But, then what?

Lawrence had agreed to drive her to the airport. And then they would never see each other again. Charlotte felt prescient. How did she know that? They had had so many recreational breakups, what made her think that now, at this perfectly wrong time, five months after her sister's death, in the throes of her grandfather's illness, as she was about to go alone to an island where dim-witted North Americans took a dermatologic nightmare of a honeymoon, they were, nonetheless, going to end even their friendship? The air inside the car practically shimmered with the unhappy fact. That and the gamey smell of roasted chicken. "What's that? Were you eating something weird in this car?" Charlotte asked. The beginning of the end. It wasn't weird, Lawrence said. It was fried poultry. Did she always have to criticize, and when he was doing her the favor of driving her to the airport?

"In my car," Charlotte pointed out. "This is my car, and I'm loaning it to you for the two weeks that I'll be gone."

"Just stop," he said.

"I just wish," Charlotte said, "you could do me a favor with some good grace. Just do it because it's nice to do things for other people."

Lawrence huffed as if she was being impossible. They rode in angry si-lence till Charlotte said quietly, "Just park the car in the lot when you're done and mail me back the keys."

"Fine."

They were quiet, and just at the point when Charlotte would normally say, "No, I didn't mean that," she concentrated on her closed mouth, how it felt to have her tongue play behind her teeth. They passed over Haymarket Square, then turned into the ugly yellow of the tunnel that led to the airport. "Tunnel radio," she wanted to command. Helen always had, when they went through the tunnel, and Charlotte would invariably find the appropriate radio station just as they emerged from underground. "It's D," she said, finally, letting Lawrence know where he was to drop her. He pulled up in front of the terminal and popped the lid to the trunk. She stepped out and hefted her bag—weighty with books on silversmithing and West Indian slave plantations—to the sidewalk. In her purse was a third volume, *Life is (Still!) with People: Life and the After-Life for the Post-Holocaust Jew.* She leaned her head back into the car and said, "I didn't mean what I said. We'll figure out the car when I get back."

"Yeah," he agreed tersely.

"Please, let's not . . ." She wanted an amicable parting—just like she wanted not to go to bed mad, like she didn't want him to storm out of her apartment in the midst of an argument then fail to call for days—but he pulled away from the curb before she could finish her sentence.

"I . . . ," Charlotte started, then looked down. Her eyes started to tear, but what she felt was relief. It was shameful. She'd felt this very emo-tion—just for an instant, she promised herself, a second that didn't really count—when her sister collapsed for the final time, in the bathtub: the pleasure of the end. She looked up at the taillights of her car as it merged into the traffic that led away from the airport. Then she bit back a smile. It was over.

CHAPTER TWO

Wayne Deare

June 19, 1997

↵

PROBLEM #1: THE JOB DIDN'T PAY ENOUGH. Which led to problem #2: the things he did to pick up extra cash. Exhibit A: his weekend plans. For two hundred dollars, he'd agreed to jump out of a plane as
part of a Sunday-afternoon party stunt. Which had him more frightened
than he'd imagined he'd be when he'd blithely agreed to some surfer's
beachside proposition. "Kind of a joke. For my folks," the man had said.
"Thirty people jumping out of a plane for my parents' thirtieth anniversary." The man—white, probably no more than a few years Wayne's
senior—had sighed, apparently at the stupidity of the idea, then said
flatly, "I'm paying everyone who does it. Two hundred dollars. For two instruction sessions and then the jump."

And ever since Wayne had shrugged an okay, these dreams of falling
and falling. Of hitting the earth and not stopping, of accelerating to the
earth's core, getting hotter and hotter till he woke, sweat puddling above
his collarbone and the hollows of his throat, the remainder of the night
spent weighing his fear against the size of his phone bill. But last night his
boss, Frank Elcock, had called with talk about a bonus—details to be dis-
cussed in the morning—and Wayne imagined that the extra cash might
be his salvation.

As it stood, since shortly after college and his return to Barbados, Wayne
had worked—but only part-time; jobs were so hard to come by, even with
a degree—as director of public relations for the Bajan Institute, a new museum devoted to celebrating island culture. It was a museum without walls,
which meant that, though the Institute had offices and a small collection

relegated to a storeroom, its exhibits were held in different venues. The idea was to get the work out and to the people, as Wayne's own letters put it. Earlier in the year, a display of whips, leg irons, and other equipment used to punish slaves was shown at the Leeds' sugar plantation. Around the equipment, the curator had hung exuberant tourist advertisements for the island's "gracious" plantations. It wasn't a subtle exhibition, of course, but that was, Wayne was coming to realize, how public art worked; everybody had to get it, even if they already got it.

Wayne believed in the museum's fundamental goal, but public relations wasn't his forte. He wasn't good at selling, and as he saw it, his job required him to produce a sophisticated version of a child's chant: *Look at me. Look at me.* He spent most of his day writing letters of entreaty or thanks. He lived now in fear of repeating an early error. In his first week on the job, he had finished off a note to a bank sponsor by writing, "I hope you enjoy our pogrom. Sincerely, Wayne Deare, Director of Pubic Relations."

If, as Deirdre—his best friend from college—liked to say, all typos mean something, what did these mistakes signify? And was this the sort of mistake you were supposed to apologize for? "Dear Sir, Our programs are not pogroms. In fact, they're quite life-affirming. I have no pubic relations. Thank you again for your generous contribution to the Bajan Institute."

A bonus sounded good. But not so good that he skipped the early-morning instruction session for the jump. A bird in the hand, and all that. So by the time he got to work, it was well after nine. Then, soon as he cleared the office door, Deirdre called, and they resumed their constant conversation as of late. It was, as Deirdre called it—she named their conversations, she said, so she could put herself on autopilot when they got into one of the regular ones—When You Gonna Leave?

As always, he told Deirdre that his stay was still practical, that he couldn't come north till he sold the family house, dealt with the lingering peculiarities of his father's will. Deirdre told him that this was bullshit, that there was something seductive and easy about the island, and it was what kept him there: the promise of not having to continue. No more exams or tests—of the student or professional or personal kind. It was like stepping away from the lines of the playing field into the no-nothing pasture that surrounded the goals.

"But," Wayne told Deirdre, "I couldn't do it any other way. I mean I had to come back here."

"Of course." Deirdre gave a laugh.

"Why are you laughing?" Wayne said, disgusted.

"Nothing, nothing, you just sound so sad."

Oh, that's a riot, Wayne thought to say but kept his mouth shut. More and more these days, he and Deirdre failed to connect. Wayne cleared his throat as Deirdre waited for a reply. She had gotten hold of a free phone line, so she'd called before their normal time. They'd agreed on Tuesday nights, trading off who called who, though Wayne would have gladly paid the cost of all the calls for the feeling they gave him: that he was still tethered to the world by something he cared about. What was that if not proof that Deirdre had completely misread his stay?

"I'll never find a job," Wayne whispered to Deirdre in case Frank, who occupied the neighboring desk, was listening.

Wayne could almost hear Deirdre roll her eyes. "Would you just shut up? You've got a job. Where am I calling you anyway?"

"Listen," Wayne said, "I gotta go for just that reason. I only just got back from the airport."

"The airport?"

"Yeah, it's a long story. I'll talk to you Tuesday."

"Okay." Deirdre sighed—she hated to pass on the free phone call— and said good-bye.

As soon as Wayne hung up, Frank looked over. "What that?" he barked, waving at the phone.

"Nothing," Wayne muttered.

"Huh. I don't have anything against an occasional personal call," Frank said in such a way that it was clear he did.

Wayne knew better than to start an argument, though he sensed Frank longed for combat, atavastic habit of his (now abandoned) profession. What bred in *his* bones. He'd been a prosecutor in Guyana before he decided to stop putting brothers in jail and start working for black uplift. Not that the decision made him friendly to the brothers and sisters with whom he actually worked.

"We've got to talk about that menorah," Frank said. He had a funny voice, as if someone had cut out half his tongue. He made up for the muffled sound by speaking precisely but with a peculiar, staccato rhythm that had him stopping every third word or so, as if for breath.

"What menorah?"

"That menorah we're trying to get for our permanent collection."

Frank never explained things unless pressed. At first, Wayne thought this was a form of self-absorption; Frank assumed you knew what he was talking about, because he imagined everyone's thoughts were in accord with his own. But, soon enough, Wayne realized this couldn't be, for Frank always had an edge, as if prepping himself for a challenge.

"Frank," Wayne said. "I have no idea what you're talking about."

The secretary, Janice's, typewriter clattered noisily across the room. As if to frustrate their conversation further, she turned her desk radio to a staticky station of pop music.

"The Bajan Institute," Frank began, and Wayne steeled himself. Early on, he'd noticed that he responded to Frank's weird breathing by holding his breath while Frank talked. Any long explanation was bound to make him feel lightheaded. ". . . is trying to acquire some early examples of metal-smithing for our permanent collection as well as our upcoming exhibit. There's a menorah in the ownership of a synagogue near Boston that's about to be returned to the island. Done by Nigel Jones. Heard of him?"

"Yes," Wayne snapped. Everyone at the Institute knew who he was: a slave on the old Dundidge sugar plantation. There'd been a forge there. Over at the Barbados Museum, there was a bowl and a creamer, probably crafted by Jones, who'd disappeared—escaped or died, the records were unclear—during the slave revolt of 1816. His name was found along the handle of a serving spoon and in slave registries of 1810 through 1815. But nothing more was known about him, and in 1816 the Dundidge forge closed down.

"Well," said Frank, "we want to secure the piece."

In the background, a voice from Janice's radio sang out, "I ain't dancin' with no big belly man, big belly man, big belly man. Don't you touch me with your big belly man, your big belly man, your big belly man."

"Apparently, a representative of the synagogue has arrived on the island to decide who to give it to, so we need to make our claim."

"Wait," Wayne said. "Who does it belong to?"

"No matter if you're fat or thin," the radio insisted now, "we ain' gonna stop this par-tee-ing," and Janice's keys fell to the rhythm of this verse. The Bajan Institute had a computer, but Janice refused to learn how to use it.

"Well, that's the question," Frank said. "We say it belongs to Nigel's descendants. The Bridgetown synagogue has a contract with the Boston synagogue, so they think it belongs to them. Only the contract is with the Jews of this island, not the Bridgetown synagogue per se."

Wayne swallowed some air, then said, "Well, it sounds like it's going to be pretty hard to convince the Jews that we should have it."

"I don't care about them. I don't have to convince them. I have to convince this representative, and if not her, a judge. And the contract is for property that has been stolen." He stopped, then added, "Plus there are black Jews on this island. Over at the whatzit-called, the Holy Temple of Sheba. *Their* interests aren't represented by the Bridgetown synagogue."

"Well, do *they* want the menorah?"

"They haven't expressed an interest as of yet, but if they're fully apprised of the . . ."

Toni, the Institute's curator, came up behind Frank and interrupted him to say, "It really is a beautiful piece. Elephants."

"African elephants," Frank said.

Wayne arched an eyebrow into a question.

"The menorah," Toni said. "It's of elephants, linked trunk to tail." She hooked her pinkies together by way of demonstration. Of the four of them in the office, she was the only one with an art background, and everything—her concerns, her style—reflected this. Her hair, dyed a gentle red, was straightened and pulled back today into a large black band.

"It's ours," Frank said.

"What he's not saying," Toni reached through her red T-shirt to readjust the waistband on her white leggings, "is that, of course, we'd lend the piece out to the Jewish community for the holiday of Hanukkah."

She gave Wayne a smile. Her unofficial job: mediating between Frank and whomever he was frightening. Just recently, Wayne learned that, twenty years ago, she'd made a clumsy exit from a roundabout and smashed into another car, killing her boyfriend in the process. The accident put her champion-the-underdog goodness in context. And she was genuinely good, in a way that Frank—"Sir Frank," they called him behind his back, "His Royal Heiny-Ass"—would never be. She was atoning.

Forever. Now she slipped herself into a chair by Wayne and tucked her legs girlishly up under the pillow of her ass. If he could get past her plumpness, he'd be in love with her. But he could not. And yet he regularly judged women who could not get past his height: all those girls who failed to return his phone calls or said, "I don't think so," when he'd suggest an evening out. *Bitches,* he thought at night, half-serious, in post-jerk-off despair, *bunch of bitches.*

Toni said, "It's eight days a year that the menorah is in actual use, so we don't feel that it compromises anyone's religious beliefs for the piece to be restored to the people of the island for the remainder of the year."

Wayne nodded. "Okay."

"So you'll go?" Frank said.

"Frank," Wayne said, "is it too much to ask you to start at the beginning of your thought?"

Frank gave Toni a what's-the-matter-with-him? look.

"Go where?" Wayne said. "What're you talking about?"

"Oh," Toni laughed. "He wants you to go talk to the representative. Tell her about the Bajan Institute. General PR before anyone starts talking legal action. Save her from this hothead here," Toni clapped Frank's shoulder.

"There's five hundred dollars in it for you, if you can secure the piece for us," Frank said.

"It's really quite valuable," Toni explained. "The materials and the craftsmanship. It'd be worth a lot to us. To have, and then to sell, if we needed to, to keep the Institute going."

Frank turned back to the papers before him at his desk as if the conversation were over.

"Come," Toni stood and motioned Wayne toward the front door. "I need a smoke. I'll tell you all about it." She was a short woman, and as they walked out, she arched her neck to look up the length of Wayne then pivoted to say to Frank, as if she were merely mocking herself and not her companion, "I feel like his lunch."

"Yeah," Frank said, "with an Oreo cookie for dessert."

Wayne flinched. It was the most overtly hostile thing Frank had ever said to him, but when he turned to respond, Frank was dialing his phone as if nothing had happened. "Don't," Toni commanded. "Don't say a thing. He's just being an asshole."

As soon as they stepped outside, though, Wayne erupted. "Who does he think he is? I'm the one who's from here. He doesn't know anything about what Barbados is." He felt stupid, even as he said this. Since he'd been back, he'd felt that the island—his hometown, after all—was eluding him. There was a new, harder edge to things. Jobs, always scarce, were virtually nonexistent, and without work to structure the day, people seemed to have collapsed into the sort of depression that means suicide—if only one weren't too tired to select a knife or to find a bottle of pills. How Wayne knew this, he couldn't say, for it wasn't anything obvious, just the way men slapped their dominoes at the rum shop, that little extra force, or the number of boys' bikes upended on the beach, like giant metal crabs, even during the work or school day. One day, he saw a guy sitting on the harbor bridge's rail, peeling and eating a mango—something he'd seen a thousand times when he was young, but this time, Wayne swore it looked like murder, the stripping of the skin, the slow chewing of the flesh. There were more Rastas around than before, and more people joking about "going up to Black Rock," the island's mental hospital, for a permanent visit.

Things hadn't always been like this, or not in the form—slightly menacing and altogether impotent—that they seemed to take now. The fact was that in the last few years, with his schooling up in Boston, Wayne had done everything he could to prevent himself from knowing—knowing through experience, at least—what the island was about, what people were feeling. Still to admit this—to Frank or even Toni—would be too close to accepting the criticism that was always leveled at members of the black middle class. You were supposed to lift yourself up, then, as soon as you did, your family patted you on the back, told you how proud they were, while everyone else acted like you'd betrayed your race or lost your rights to membership, become a house nigger, an Anglo-Saxon, a mouthpiece for white values and beliefs. And, Wayne thought, he wasn't even there yet, was still just a student, or an ex-student, an ex-well-funded student whose stipend was running out.

"Oreo, shit," he said to Toni.

The sidewalk in front of the office was narrow, really just a glorified gutter. A Pepsi truck chugged noisily by before Toni could say, "It's got nothing to do with you. He just got his divorce papers today."

"He's married?" Wayne said. "That's news." Frank had always struck Wayne as one of those people who had no personal life. It wasn't that he was unattractive. He was a slim, somewhat stylish man with his mustache and goatee. There was even something about his personality, his determination, that turned what might be physical flaws in another man—a bald head and cheeks pockmarked with old acne scars—into virtues. Still, Frank didn't seem to do anything but work. He kept long hours and if he went to the beach or out on a boat, it was only to pursue a contact.

Toni duplicated his schedule but took an hour each week to talk to a therapist. "Maybe," Frank once told her before she left for her appointment, "*I'm* the crazy one, but when you commit to work, you should commit to work." Wayne, who'd been making press packets that morning, had wanted to stand up and grind his stapler into Frank's smug face. And this was the fantasy—out of character in its violence—which possessed him now.

"Well, he's not married anymore," Toni said, lighting up a cigarette and taking a single long drag. "And catch this: she was white."

"No shit!"

"No lie," Toni said and laughed. "But"—she cleared her throat—"it really *is* a bad situation. He's freaking. There's a kid—they're both still in Guyana—and she's saying all sorts of shit about him to prevent him from getting visiting rights."

Wayne couldn't work up any sympathy for Frank. He thought about slipping a copy of Franz Fanon on black men and white women into his mailbox.

"Listen," Toni said. She bent a knee, placed her foot against the wall behind her and leaned back, as if for a long conversation. "The menorah. What you've got to do is call this woman. Go have a drink with her, tell her about the Institute, feel her out about what she's gonna do. Frank just wants to know what's going on.

"The problem is the representative—her name is Charlotte something-or-other—Frank's got it written down inside." She jerked her hand back over her shoulder as if Wayne might have forgotten where that was. "I think she's just in for a week or so. You should probably try to meet her on Monday."

"Why don't I call her right now?"

"I don't think she's coming in till the weekend." Wayne frowned. He would have no sense of his chances for the $500 bonus till after Sunday's jump.

Toni was quiet for a moment, then she said, "What's the matter?"

"Nothing's the matter. Why're you asking me what's the matter?"

"Because you look like you just lost your mother."

Wayne gave Toni a hard stare. She knew his mother was dead.

Toni held up her hand. "Poor choice of words. Still. What *is* it?"

"I was thinking about *The Autobiography of Malcolm X.*" Toni was the only one these days with whom he could talk books. Even if he found one of his old Combermere friends, they'd talk D. H. Lawrence, or some such crap.

Toni smiled. Wayne always suspected she found his bookish interests cute, as if he was only just discovering what she'd long grown out of. "Never mind," Wayne said.

"No, come on. Tell me," Toni said and pulled out another cigarette. "Make it last the length of this smoke."

"Well, there's this section where Malcolm talks about the degradation of a black man going to conk his hair, or a woman going to straighten hers. Internalized racism is what got you under the iron, but then you have to think, that smell of burnt hair is something tinged with nostalgia. A family memory. I mean, not for me, no one in my family did that, but for some folks. And it turns out to be something good. That smell. Like slavery is horrible, of course, but there's something to be said for us all being over here now. It's a better world for us getting off the African continent and mixing things up." Wayne couldn't remember why he had brought this up. He had written a paper on this topic during his freshman year at Tufts and hoped he wasn't offering this extended *non sequitur* because he wanted to sound smart. It did have something to do what he'd just been thinking; he just couldn't remember what. "Not that I'd say all this to our friend inside," Wayne added.

Toni waved her hand. "Well, you listen. The menorah. It's not just one of his dumb-ass projects. We *should* have it back. It means something to reclaim the fruits of our labor, to take back what's been stolen. And it'd be like money in the bank. Something to sell if we go too far into debt."

Wayne nodded. The Bajan Institute wasn't just a nonprofit, he liked to tell Deirdre, it was an against-profit. "Yeah, I'm not disagreeing, but you wouldn't take a cross back, would you? You can see why someone might object."

"Well, no one's objected yet, since we haven't really put it to anyone. And anyway, a church uses a cross every day of the year. Come on"—she gave him a shove—"you just have to make a good case. Five hundred bucks, okay?"

"Yeah, yeah," Wayne said. He was thinking about his future, ruling out yet another profession—lawyer; he'd never manage to do anything that involved persuading others. "Whatever."

CHAPTER THREE

Charlotte Lewin

June 21, 1997

⟋⟍

A DUPPY BY DEFAULT, HE WAS DROWNED, but he came out of the sea. *Never dead,* he said, though who would believe him? *Life raft,* he explained, but his employers—a graying pair, nondescript Anglicans who already spoke of the Will of God to describe his disappearance—now spoke of that same Will to describe his appearance.

He was an unlikely, sunburned ghost, white-toothed and island-bred. At the request of the local clerics—and for the general benefit of the public—he was installed on a stool and behind a bottle at the Breadfruit Bar. The whole arrangement—bar, stool, man, bottle, beer—sat on Farhall Street. By day, the Breadfruit was a failing bar, an eye in the storm of activity of the street. By night—who knew? The place had a reputation, and each evening, it earned its changeable identity, only to be scrubbed clean in the morning of peanut shells and beer, events and personality.

Charlotte was standing in the airport customs line when she first heard of the good-willed ghost. She craned her head back to eavesdrop on two women, huskily whispering about a man who spent his evenings laying hands on the ill and blessing children. Apparently, he would tell the story of his life, his time at sea, only if you told your own story, whatever that might be, first. He accepted payment in cigarettes and liquor and an occasional flying-fish sandwich.

Charlotte turned to hear more, but the woman speaking gave her a look, blank with hostility, so she swiveled her head back around and pretended to be deeply engaged in a "You Are Welcome to Barbados—Drugs Are Not" sign.

Later, Charlotte's youthful cabdriver continued the story. "The ghost's age," he started. No one could guess what it was, though his parents, or so the reports went, had specific numbers to offer. He seemed to be, alternately, craggy sage or soft-lipped infant, and sometimes both at once. If you slit your thumb open on a knife, he might heal the wound with a wisp of the tobacco smoke he blew from his mouth.

Charlotte, already wilting in the day's soggy heat, nodded at this. Around her, the island sped by: coconut palms, bamboo, hibiscus. She couldn't name the other trees: one covered with gaudy orange-red blooms, another dark and feathery, smudged against the sky like a charcoal drawing. There were goats tethered to posts, cement-block homes painted pink, turquoise, or peach but weathered into colorlessness, the flat hue of decay. Everywhere, rusted galvanized tin was pieced together to form crooked backyard fences, and there were bars—really no more than shacks built over counters—with reveal-nothing names like Hideaway or T&P. And churches. Moravian. Church of Christ. United Church of Holy America. Salvation Army.

The road the cab was on narrowed and angled toward the water. The first sight of it was a shock, such a vibrant turquoise, and Charlotte allowed herself a pointless exclamation: "Oh, the water." Yes? There was a pause in which the driver waited to hear more. Charlotte offered the required sentence: "It's beautiful." And it was, though otherwise the landscape—both Third World and all too familiar—disappointed. The taxi passed two strip malls, filled, as malls with sixties and seventies architecture were invariably filled, with unglamorous banks and Laundromats. The street's gutters were rivulets of papery trash, highlighted with the signature yellow of M&M wrappers.

At a stoplight, three bare-chested men wearing crocheted wool caps, puffy as popovers, crossed in front of the cab. "Hey." One waved to the driver. "*Hey.*" The driver stuck his arm out to grip his friend's hand.

"I telling her about the duppy." The driver gestured with his thumb to Charlotte.

"What duppy?"

"Ah, you don't know, mahn?" the driver said, but the light changed color, and he had to wave good-bye without enlightening his friend. It was hard to tell if the exchange was meant to mock her in some obscure way. The pure embarrassment of being white, Charlotte thought, especially here, where it was clear white people were tourists and black people had real lives.

"You don't believe me about the ghost." The cabdriver laughed. "The ghost a Bridgetown."

Charlotte was about to answer, *Sure I do,* when he interrupted to say, "But it's a fact."

Charlotte smiled and sank deeper into her seat, hugging her arms, as if that might hide her skin color from the general observer. *I'm here on business,* she wanted to explain. But Charlotte's true purpose hardly mattered; she'd have said anything to convince the driver she wasn't who he took her to be. "For Christ's sake, why do you care?" she could hear Helen say. And she'd be right to ask. This desire to be above reproach was dumb for a thousand reasons. But even Helen—breezy, loud-mouthed Helen—had felt it. In the hospital, at the end, she kept saying to their mother, "But I'm a good girl, aren't I? Aren't I?"

Inside the Paradise Hotel, Charlotte's room—pleasantly cool with air-conditioning—was standard issue with a few tropical touches: a bamboo headboard on the bed, a gift basket of fruit on the dresser, a sliding glass door that opened onto a small concrete patio overlooking a white, spacious beach. Below, black women wearing brightly colored headdresses dunked themselves into the sea. There was something oddly ritualistic about their play, as if they were actually baptizing one another. As a girl, Charlotte had been on family vacations that seemed to require the same stupefied glee as this hotel. Disneyland, she recalled, had made her sick with grief, a guilty depression padding after her as she shook Pluto's hand and pretended to enjoy riding a little boat through a world of singing dolls. The only fantasy that could engage her was of *working* at Disneyland, sitting in an overheated booth and dispensing tickets, daydreaming about boys from Space Mountain stopping by to flirt. Even now, only work—or the illusion of it—appealed, so she stepped back out of her room with a self-imposed assignment: she would find the synagogue before dark.

She walked along the crumbling edge of a road into Bridgetown. Narrow, toy-like cars chugged past her. At intervals, a white van—some sort of bus?—gave a double-noted beep, and a black man, early twenties at the oldest, emerged from a passenger-side window to make a *Ride?* gesture with his forefinger. She shook her head, No and No, but came to regret it. The heat only increased with her distance from the hotel. After ten minutes, her clothes—none too roomy in the first place—were slicked to her. And what with the sunscreen she'd slathered over herself, she felt filthy. Even with the lotion on, she darted from one side of the street to the other, keeping, best as she could, to the shade from the second-floor porches that hung over the narrow sidewalks. Occasionally, one of the buildings would open on a small market selling little more than soda and chips, but most of the places she passed were sealed up. On the buildings' second floors, signs stuck out like file-folder tabs: Bayview Jazz, The Club, 'Round Midnight. Once things got dark, she supposed, the street would be hopping. "Don't," the hotel's desk clerk had warned her, "walk back here at night." And Charlotte saw how all this could feel seedy without sunshine: something about the slight sag of the buildings and the semisecrecy of an upstairs club, the vague feeling that what *really* went on here happened in places that were hard to find—there being no clear map to the illicit.

Eventually, she came to a harbor and then a bridge, which led to the rush of activity that was the city: New York's Fourteenth Street meets the tropics meets St. Moritz. She passed a glittery watch store, then an alley littered with cardboard boxes and coconut husks. A familiar, greasy smell wafted past her. A Kentucky Fried Chicken.

She was ambling, but heading—more or less—toward the synagogue, though the building eluded her. Finally, Charlotte stopped at a stand to ask for directions.

"What you like?" prompted the vendor.

"Oh, nothing, nothing," Charlotte said, then noticing the sudden darkness of the sky, continued on. A few fat drops fell on her head, and the wind whipped up, furious bursts rattling loose traffic signs and sending plastic bags hurrying down the street.

Charlotte jogged to a cluster of vendors, their stands covered with graffiti: pictures of lions and instructions to Lively Up Yourself. She was headed for the cover of shops across the way, but already it was raining too hard for her to get there without being soaked. At her right, an older woman had taken shelter in an abandoned stand. Charlotte stopped and considered joining her, when the woman called out, "Well, git in here, mahn. Come on."

"Okay," Charlotte smiled and stepped in.

"It ain' so bad. A roof ovuh yuh 'ead."

"It's that, all right," Charlotte allowed, shouting slightly under the roof's noisy clatter. The air had the tinny smell of new rain.

"Ah forget me parasol."

"Well, me, too. Obviously."

The woman hugged a straw purse to the hill of her belly. A matching hat was squashed down over what had to be a wig, for a tuft of white sprang from under a dark curl by her ear, and her eyebrows were a chalky gray. A butterfly-shaped discoloration—several shades darker than the rest of her black skin—spread itself over her nose and cheeks. She wasn't pretty, even without the discoloration, but she had the sort of long-lived-in ugliness that flips back on itself and becomes its own sort of beauty.

Outside, everyone had taken cover save two boys, soaked beyond caring, who ran by the stand, calling back and forth in an amiable way, as if they were reciting a nursery-school rhyme:

"Fuck you."

"And your mother, too."

"Fuck you."

"And your grandmother, too."

"Hmmph," the woman said. "This use to be a real sweet island, you unnerstan what I'm saying?" Charlotte nodded. She loved the island patois. It struck her as heartbreakingly beautiful in its rhythms, though it *was* hard for her to decipher. Still, perhaps because the woman was talking directly to her, she caught most of what she said. "Real *sweet*, mahn. Las' few yea', eve't'in' change. Lord, Je-sus, it ah shame."

"What happened?"

"Drug, mahn."

It was funny to hear her ending her sentences with the "mahn" Charlotte associated with . . . well, men, young men.

"And crime. Jesus say two for two and all. You murder a man, you should be hanged. Rape. You see that in the paper? Rape a child? An' dey say dey wanna help da man. Help da man become ah betta man. Ah tell you, mahn. Should pruh-teck de child. Yuh see chillen, you should pick 'em up and hug 'em, you unnerstan' what I'm saying?"

"I do. I do," Charlotte was easily a foot taller than this woman and she felt enormous next to her. "You know," she began, "I was wondering. Have you heard anything about this duppy that everyone's talking about?"

"Duppy. Sure," the woman said. "Dat's obeah."

"Yes, I know, but I was wondering if you'd heard about this specific person, this duppy who just . . ." Charlotte let her sentence trail off. She had no sense that she was making herself understood.

"Duppy's a ghost. Like yuh gotta ghost," the woman explained. "Maybe an obeah man git yuh hair or yuh monthly blood, yuh unnerstan' what ahm saying? An' den da duppy git yuh sick."

"So a duppy is bad?"

"Bad? Ah, no."

Charlotte asked her if she'd ever seen one, and the woman laughed. She started to tell a long story about a summer of her childhood when she'd been sent to the east side of the island for a holiday with her aunt and her cousin Melony. Melony had long, dark hair. And she used to let the woman—then a girl of six—comb it. After she brushed her cousin's hair, she would sit in her lap, and they'd look at the ocean. Melony would tell her things: why the men put tires on top of their fishing boats, or why they painted the tops of their boats yellow (it was so they could be spotted if they were lost at sea). Melony taught her how to make a spoon out of a young coconut, so she could eat the jelly. When the vacation ended, she asked her mother when she'd next visit with her aunt and cousin. Her mother gave her a strange look and said, "Soon." For weeks after, she asked how her relatives were doing. But she never returned for another visit. Finally, on her twelfth birthday, her mother asked if she remembered that summer with her aunt. She said she did. And did she remember asking after Melony? That she did, too. Then her mother told her what she felt she had been too young to hear six years earlier. Melony was dead. She'd died six months before that summer when the woman had gone to visit her aunt. In fact, the only reason she'd been sent was to distract her aunt from her sorrow.

"Je-sus," Charlotte said, not that she fully believed the story, only that the woman believed it. "And you're sure it was her?"

The woman said she was. Even now, the feel of that girl's hair on her palms was more familiar to her than her own.

"Oh," Charlotte said. Given the wig, how much was this saying?

"Look," the woman nodded toward the street. The rain had lightened, as fast as it had come.

It seemed wrong, once she'd breathed a "Jesus" in response to the woman's story, to ask for directions to the synagogue, so Charlotte was soon lost again. Not that she didn't know where she was; she knew exactly where she was. According to her map, she should have been within arm's reach of a stack of yarmulkes, kissing distance from a Torah. But she wasn't.

Of course, Howard might just have neglected to mention that this particular synagogue was invisible. As a girl, Charlotte had had a recurring dream about an invisible clubhouse, a place that only revealed itself once you went inside, but then you discovered it wasn't a place where you wanted to be; it was strewn with the remnants of a desperate fight, clothes and broken furniture and, most horribly, a chunk of someone's hair with a bit of scalp still attached.

"Miss," a voice called as Charlotte stepped off the curb. Charlotte turned to see a straggly fellow with one of those never-trimmed beards that makes a man look insane. Was he talking to her? Apparently sensing an opportunity in her hesitation, the man rocked forward, like a clown-punching balloon. "Can I have some money?" he said, bobbing back.

"I'm sorry." Charlotte turned abruptly and crossed the street, but the man followed, coming right up to her ear and pleading, like any disappointed child, "Please. Please. Pllleaasse." He was so close, a drop of his spit landed in her ear. Charlotte stopped short, slapped at her ear, and said, firmly, both words quick and hard, "Sir, no," before she walked on.

Behind her, the man whined, in a hurt, baby voice, "You don't have to be so sell-fish."

At a different point in her life, Charlotte might have considered the charge, but now she turned and said, "You don't know anything about my life. So fuck off, mister."

But the man was already out of earshot.

A vendor, sitting in a sagging lawn chair under a blue umbrella and beside a cart lined with plastic syrup bottles, looked up and said, "Don't trouble yourself. He a bad man. These people," he gestured with his chin in the direction of the beggar, "there's a greediness to them. They eat too much and beg too much. Just enjoy yourself. Enjoy your time in Barbados."

Charlotte flushed. This was somehow worse than the beggar. "Okay," she said, "I'm sorry," and hurried away.

Back on Broad Street, the city's narrow main thoroughfare, she stopped for juice in a tiny, overly air-conditioned mall. Inside, a line of men were waiting to play something that looked like the Lotto. Her creepy drink in hand—sorrel juice; she shouldn't have experimented—she sat on a slightly sticky bench and studied her map, trying to figure out where she'd been. Her eye settled on a street name. Farhall. Why was *that* so familiar? A cigar brand? But then she remembered: the street which housed the Breadfruit, the bar which claimed the duppy each night. It was only a few blocks away. Why not abandon the search for the synagogue and pay a visit?

True, Charlotte wasn't a believer, never had been, but ghosts. They . . . attracted her. Or belief in ghosts did. What enticed her was the metaphysics of the matter. Wouldn't it change your sense of what death was? And why didn't people ever talk about *that*?

Charlotte shivered. Her juice was repulsively cold. She looked for a place to toss it, but there were no bathrooms anywhere, so she placed the full cup on top of a garbage can. As she turned to leave, a young man called to her.

"What?" Charlotte said.

The man stepped closer to repeat himself. It was the beggar from before! He brought his face so near that Charlotte thought he might kiss her. She jumped back. His lips were chapped and bleeding. Was he reproving her for buying a juice she didn't even want instead of giving him her change?

"Don't be scared of Barbados," he laughed, darting his face toward her again.

"I'm not," she said, jerking her head back and walking purposefully out the door and into the early evening warmth, a comfortable blanket after the chill of the air-conditioning.

Everyone, she thought foolishly, as if a horde had just descended on her, *leave me alone*. She was on the edge of tears, not because the fright from the man had been so serious, but because she felt dreadful for still being capable of fear. The worst had already happened. What right did she have to flinch at anything else?

The sun was starting to lower. Charlotte checked her watch. It was only 5:20. Back home, it wouldn't darken for hours. So, Farhall. Charlotte didn't need to believe the duppy story to check it out. It wasn't clear that anyone—save those women back in the airport—did. *Rumors, rumors:* they entertained but didn't persuade. This was an Anglican island, after all, and in these first few hours meandering the streets, Charlotte saw that there was a reserve to people here. They didn't meet your eyes, and save for those to whom she *had* talked, they seemed to have the kind of British propriety that Charlotte associated with the eminently sensible. Still, she couldn't help but want to find the people who weren't, those who really did believe, even if they were, like palm readers in Manhattan, a slub in the regular fabric of island life.

She pushed down the street, past Amen Alley, a tiny passage cut off from the light of day. Charlotte could just make out two men filleting fleshy fish on a lopsided wooden table. The image pleased her into wishing she was the woman waiting to receive those fillets, to fry them up. A simple dinner, the end to a simple day. But then a spider hit her arm, and its frantic scramble as she brushed it away depressed her. Fish, bugs: everything wanted life. No surprise there, but still she didn't want to be reminded. Only last night, while she was half watching late-night TV, the hysterical cowering of some bad guy in front of a gun made her feel like disintegrating.

The streets led to increasingly narrow roads till she came to Farhall. She walked the length of it, but no Breadfruit Bar appeared. How irritating to be stumped twice in one day. But she was also relieved. The city's atmosphere had changed perceptibly in the last half-hour: things closing up, groups of men clustering around sidewalk domino games. And all the stores, as if by some agreement with the hour, seemed to have become betting places or bars, each an entirely male province. But then, as she was turning for the harbor, she looked down an alley and saw a pile of sand. So the bar *was* on Farhall, but on the alley side of the street.

Earlier, Charlotte's cabdriver had told her that every morning locals came with plastic buckets and created a virtual sandbox in front of the Breadfruit's door. A duppy, he explained, wouldn't enter a building without first counting all the grains of sand at the door, and, math whiz or no, your average duppy couldn't do that before daybreak, the hour when all duppies are due back at their graves. But the ghost of Bridgetown—apparently, he hadn't so much as flinched at the sand. He'd stepped right over the pile and into the bar. He'd ordered himself a beer and insisted, once again, that he'd never died.

Charlotte hesitated before entering the alley; it felt too private, like someone's backyard, though halfway down, there was a blue "Open" sign poking out like the flag on a trick gun. Below it, a child's shovel, fluorescent green, was upended in the ineffectual sand hill. The toy gave Charlotte courage, but then at the bar door she faltered again. Perhaps the "ghost" wouldn't be around? And what did she want from him, anyway? Some confirmation that her skepticism was faulty, that death was a pleasure, and that the community of the dead was so chummy that when he returned to the grave, he'd be able to greet Helen? Stupid, Charlotte thought, and yet she peeked into the bar with something close to expectation.

It was a single room, unadorned save for a handful of wooden tables to the right and a bar to the left. It didn't seem to be a frightening place, which is to say it looked more like a sandwich shop than a place for hard drinkers, honeymooners, or men on the make. At one table, two women fanned their babies with menus.

Charlotte pulled a *Time* magazine out of her bag, thinking she'd pretend to read while she eavesdropped, but she didn't have to wait long for information.

"It's the duppy," the bartender said as soon as she took a stool at the bar. He gestured to the room's only other white person, a man sitting two stools away.

"Oh, really?" Charlotte lifted the damp hair from the back of her neck. Above, a ceiling fan turned sluggishly, offering no real relief.

Next to the white man, a black patron with a closely cropped beard, linen pants, and narrow red suspenders leaned back on his stool to call over to Charlotte, "He's no duppy."

The white man reached up to pluck at one of the red suspenders, as if it were a bass string. "Sit down, Greg," the white man said cheerfully. "Sit down and shut up." He rolled his eyes at Charlotte, as if she were in on the joke.

Charlotte smiled and looked back at her magazine. Greg came over to see what she was reading. "News," he said dismissively. "I'm a reporter," he added, swallowing a burp. "And I'll let you in on a secret. I'll give you a lead. Here's news." He pointed at the white man. "It's the Will of God." He laughed once derisively.

"Just call me Will," the white man said, rolling his eyes once again, as if he'd already identified Charlotte as someone who could appreciate foolishness without engaging in it.

"Will. Hi." Charlotte greeted him quickly, then turned to the bartender. "Could I get a . . . ?" She pointed to a glass of whiskey someone had abandoned at the bar, and he nodded.

She tried to take Will in without appearing to look. There was a delicate roundness to his face, a cap of dark hair. He was a handsome man, almost pretty in that long-eyelashed, slim-bodied way that some men had. "You're?" he asked.

"Oh, sorry," she said, as if waking from a doze. "I'm Charlotte."

"This is Greg," Will offered, pointing to the reporter at his right, "and Winston," gesturing to a third man, silent all this while, sitting next to Greg. Charlotte nodded a hello. Greg offered a goofy, absentminded grin, but Winston did nothing. Reserve or hostility? Charlotte couldn't read his studious silence, so at odds with his dress: black pants and vest, a white shirt open to just above the navel. He seemed about Will's age— somewhere in his twenties. Greg had to be older. The hairs at the bottom of his beard had begun to whiten. He almost looked like an elf who'd dipped his chin in a vat of milk.

"What *you* looking at?" Greg barked, his fingers playing quick little trills on the bar top as he waited for an answer. The question didn't seem rude, exactly, but some mixture of authoritative (*he* knew what was going on) and ironic (he knew what he thought about what was going on).

"Nothing," Charlotte said. "Sorry," and then she took several quick sips of her drink.

She glanced down at her magazine then back up at Will. It seemed clear that all the stories about the duppy were a joke. Anyone could see he was no sage. He was a kid, despite the patch of hair thinning in the back and the high rise of skin at his temples. She guessed he was a fisherman or a day laborer, because he had the body for it and also the clothes, the nondescript blue jeans with the plain blue shirt.

"I heard you were a duppy," Charlotte offered tentatively. She still wasn't sure she wanted to get drawn into conversation. "But you look— what can I say?—decidedly corporeal to me."

"It's a case of mistaken identity," Will shrugged and slipped a cigarette out from the cuff of his shirt. "Like one? They're wrinkled, but . . ." He palmed one over.

She took it but said, "No, no, I don't smoke," and turned the cigarette over, tapped the wood of the bar with it. Her head hurt slightly from the day's sun, and she felt a little odd, as if she were playing at being sophisticated.

"Okay." He reached over to take the cigarette back, carefully returning it to his shirtsleeve. Charlotte thought of someone replacing a vein. He was Frankenstein, building himself up after the temporary loss of a body part.

Charlotte couldn't figure out where to put her eyes, so she looked back down at her magazine, tried to find a hard-news article to read, though normally she worked her way from the gossip through the arts before pushing herself through the economic and political news.

"Hey," Greg shouted, and Charlotte looked over as if he were going to reprove her again for staring, but his words were directed elsewhere—at a second white man, just entering the bar. The newcomer sported a broad-brimmed cowboy hat and a leisure-suit jacket, both a pale eggshell brown. He had a substantial "generosity," Charlotte's ex-boyfriend's term for the prominent belly that some men wore like a pillow strapped under their belts. Tourist, she guessed now. Off one of the cruise ships.

"Hi, all," the man said.

From Texas, Charlotte decided. There was a slight twang to his voice. The man called out to Will. "So you're back from converting the heathen."

"You know I was just along for the ride," Will said. He used the thumb of one hand to move across the back of the other, cracking each knuckle along the way. "Nothing wrong with a little gainful employment." He turned to Charlotte and explained, "I was a cook for some religious people on a charter boat. I had a little accident and now I'm okay. That's why everyone's saying I'm a duppy."

"Where are they?" Charlotte said. "I mean, the other people from the boat."

"Oh, they weren't on the boat at the time of the accident. Just me and the big, bad sea."

"But you've seen them since?"

"No," Will said. "I've only been back for a little over a month." She must have looked some way she didn't feel, for he added, in a consoling voice, "They put in a call. 'Glad to hear you're alive,' and so on."

"I'm sorry," Charlotte said.

"What's to be sorry about?"

Charlotte shook her head. He seemed, suddenly, very young to her, perhaps because he appeared so unaffected by his brush with death. It made her think she'd better be going. There was nothing to learn here.

"Hey," Will started, as if something had just occurred to him. "Do you play poker?"

"Sometimes."

"Fantastic, then we've got a game," he announced to the men surrounding him.

"Let's do it." Greg slapped the bar then stepped unsteadily to the back of the room. Charlotte watched him disappear through a wood door.

"We were going to play," Will explained to Charlotte, almost apologetically. There was something odd about the way he was talking to her, as if she weren't a stranger, but someone whom he had in his care for the evening. "We set up a little table on the patio." He cocked his head toward the door.

"Oh," Charlotte began, gripping her magazine to indicate that it was something she needed to get back to, "I'm not much of a card shark."

"Why don't you play anyway? Game's starting, and we'd never forgive ourselves if we left you to these jokers." He tilted his head in the general direction of the barroom floor, as if it were filled with randy truck drivers. "You can quit whenever you want."

Charlotte considered this for a moment. She had come for Will's story, yet here she was hesitating. For a brief while in college, she had thought she'd be a journalist, but it was this very sort of timidity that stopped her.

She knew she'd always be too frightened to get the scoop. But what was there really to be frightened of here? Or anywhere? she reminded herself, thinking of the man with the bleeding lips and then of Helen, lying in the ICU and noticing, for the first time, a huge bloody bruise that had been on her arm for days. Helen had started when she'd seen it, apparently shocked by how painful it looked, then nodded back into sleep.

"Okay," Charlotte said. Perhaps she had decided too hastily that there was nothing to learn here. Didn't her first impressions tend to be untrustworthy? And anyway, it wasn't late. She could play a few hands without destroying her plans for the evening—which were to sleep, so she could get an early start tomorrow. "Why not?"

Out on a weedy patio with peach-colored walls, Greg was turning over a bucket to use as a table. He could have dragged out any one of the tables from the barroom floor, but, Charlotte supposed, this made the card players feel makeshift and grubby in a way that proved they were men, stubborn people with no use for arrangements.

"Let's leave this open," she said and slid a rock under the door to the bar. If she was going to be the only woman on the patio, she wanted easy access to those inside, particularly the middle-aged mothers rolling dewy Coke bottles over their foreheads, the ones with T-shirts that proclaimed "150 Years of Witness: Greenbay Moravian Church."

Silent Winston and the man in the hat stepped onto the patio. "This is Edward," Will said. The man in the hat gave a half bow.

"What this?" Winston pointed his chin at Charlotte. "I don't want none of this."

"Put a cork in it," Edward snapped, his Texas twang even more pronounced than before. "Put a couple corks in it."

"I don't want none of you no neither, brother."

Charlotte looked at Will, but he was busying himself with the poker chips. Charlotte supposed she should get angry, not on behalf of herself but on behalf of her sex, but she didn't feel like a worthwhile representative of her sex at the moment. She wasn't very good at cards. She wasn't going to upset any stereotypes about women with her hard-assed poker game.

"Don't pay him no mind," Greg said.

"I think we should let her play," Will suggested, almost sweetly. "What do you think, Winston?"

" 'Kay," Winston said sullenly and slid into one of the five chairs that Greg had drawn up to the bucket. " 'Cause she friends with the duppy."

"He isn't a fuckin' duppy," Greg said.

"Thank you," Charlotte offered, ingratiatingly.

"Cut," Winston said and placed the pack of cards in front of her. Charlotte took the chair opposite him and did as he said. Winston leaned back and ran his fingers along a gold chain that he had fished out from under his white shirt.

"Let me sit by the lady," Edward insisted and installed himself between Charlotte and Greg. At her right, Will smiled. It was a suspicious smile, and Charlotte suddenly wondered if she'd been drawn into an elaborate con, but then that seemed stupid. It wasn't as if they were going to get any money out of her. She'd fold if she didn't think she could win.

Will started dealing the cards, quickly shooting them into five stacks.

"Let's see, let's see," he said. "Seven-card stud. High-low. Deuces wild."

"This a joke?" Winston snapped.

"No joke, sir."

"The woman and now this."

"He thinks," Greg said, by way of explanation, "the wild-card crap is for sissies."

Winston gave him a long look and said flatly, "He read the mind."

"My deal. We'll play my way. Your deal, we'll play yours. How's that?" Will said.

Winston shook his head and looked at the floor, mumbled, "Some duppies is rude, mahn."

"Okay, okay," Greg said edgily, "I give the sun only about ten more minutes till it completely disappears." He gave an appraising glance up at the square patch, the blue-gray ceiling, that capped the patio. "So, let's go."

As they played, Will talked up the hand. "Looking like two sweet cousins, two jack of all trade for my friend here," he chimed once Greg had two face cards up. And later: "Those cousins still leading. You going to make your bet?"

"Yeah," Greg said and lit up a cigarette. The chips went in, clink, clink, clink. Charlotte was used to playing for peanut M&Ms with Helen and her parents, back when she was a kid and always stayed in the game if only to be a good sport, to make it more fun; back when the loser wasn't the worst player but the person who couldn't keep from eating the profits.

The first hand went to Will.

"Hmm," Charlotte said as Will gave her the pack of cards. Her deal. "It'll be five-card draw."

"No fun," said Will.

Winston just snorted, and Edward said, "That's the way."

Charlotte shuffled clumsily. When she was ten, it had been enough to simply scramble the cards all over the table, then gather them up. "Look at that," Edward said now as she awkwardly smashed the two halves of the deck together.

"I know, I know," Charlotte nodded. "Let's see . . . most people could do it better with one hand, right? Most people could do it better with two feet? How's that?"

"Couldn't have said it better myself," Edward allowed.

Charlotte took a sip of her drink. She was feeling a little drunk and grateful for the feeling. Already she could hear herself back home, at some party, bragging about joining the locals in a poker game.

They played a few hands in relative silence. When there was conversation, it focused on the game. Finally, a gap-toothed woman with the round, too-large head of an infant came out and placed a candle on the ground by the bucket. Ominous shadows licked Will's face. "Ah, I can see the cards now," he smiled at the woman. A spidery blood clot floated in the white of her right eye.

"I'll sit out a few hands," Charlotte said, and when no one acknowledged her words, added, "I need another drink." She could see it was the only acceptable explanation for getting up. Inside, she paid the bartender and asked, "How do I get a cab?"

"Oh," he said, waving his hand, "no trouble. I call you one." He said he'd let her know when it came.

Back outside, in the candlelight of the patio, Charlotte tried, unsuccessfully, to bluff a hand. This made the men hoot with laughter.

"She keep the straight face," Winston punched Will to say.

"Oh, shut up," she said, exasperated.

This was even funnier. "She tell me to shut up the mouth."

Charlotte brushed a fly from her ear. A bath would be nice right now. She tried to focus back in on the game. Who was winning? Who losing? she wondered with little concern. Then a pattern seemed to be developing. Was it or was it not true that Will won every hand he dealt? Surely, Charlotte couldn't be the only one who noticed this.

"What you want?" Winston suddenly demanded.

"What?" Greg said.

"Drink," Winston spit.

Greg tapped his temple and said, "Okay. Okay. I'm drinking gin." He palmed over a large bill.

Winston hadn't touched a drop of liquor all evening, but he seemed to have a fascination with making sure others had what they needed.

"You?" Winston asked Charlotte. It was the first time he'd spoken directly to her all evening.

"I'm through for the night," she said.

"I'll come with." Greg stood.

"Yeah, Winston can't be trusted with change when he's losing," Edward said and followed the other two men into the bar.

Will pushed his chair toward Charlotte's. The inside of his knee knocked against hers. Accident or not? she wondered and left her knee pressing his. Her cab would be here soon. She could do what she wanted.

"Let me teach you something while they're gone," he said conspiratorially. Charlotte thought she'd like him better if he faltered a bit when he spoke, if his hair were longer and fell sloppily in his eyes.

"I *know* how to play," she said.

"Oh, I know you do." He shuffled the deck slowly.

"I just have bad luck." It was true; she never won at games of chance.

"And I"—he fingered the deck—"have good luck."

"I don't need your kind of luck, thank you," Charlotte said.

"What's *that* supposed to mean?"

"Nothing," Charlotte breathed softly, willing herself all the courage to spit out the word *cheat*.

"Don't you believe in luck?" he said.

"No, I guess not. Not really. Unless it's bad." She laughed, though she was thinking that she reminded herself of the sort of cynical women who sit late at bars, talking of ex-husbands, old hurts, who sit and lick their wounds. A contest. Whose wounds went deeper? Who could add cancers and rapes, muggings and untimely deaths, peculiar accidents, exploding pumpkins and crazed, man-eating guppies to the rest? In fact, Charlotte had never met a woman like this. And yet she was driven by fear of becoming one. The whole cartoon catalogue: shrying bitch, whore, ice cube, prima donna, just-one-of-the-guys girls, fag hag. Stupid terms, all of them. She knew that, but it didn't matter.

"No, no, I'm serious," Will was saying. Where *was* her cab? "I'm talking about luck. Do you or don't you believe in it?"

Charlotte shrugged. Maybe *this* was what she'd come for.

"It's a matter of concentration. Let me tell you a story. When I was a kid, I could fix broken clocks. All sorts of clocks. Grandfather, cuckoo. I'd just concentrate and . . . there it was. One day, I'm sitting in the backseat of my dad's car. He's driving around with this lady in the front. I still don't know who she was. We've got this clock in a paper bag that we're taking over to the Salvation Army."

Charlotte wondered for a moment what it could possibly be like to have a childhood on this island.

"I'm thinking, 'Sure, we'll have to fix it right up or the army won't want us.'" He laughed. "I don't know what I was thinking. I was a kid. So, I set to thinking about fixing that thing and soon enough, there's a tic-tic sound along with the steady hum of the motor, and this woman in the front starts screaming, 'What're you doing? What're you doing? How'd you do that?' And then I see that what I've done is out of the ordinary, and that very knowledge . . . it's like a loss of innocence, if you see what I mean. I couldn't do it anymore."

Charlotte nodded politely

"You believe me, don't you?"

"Well, I . . ." She hesitated. "I guess I don't. But I believe that *you* believe."

"Oh, well, *that's* flattering." He pushed his chair back a few inches. Charlotte looked down at her hands. "Well," Will leaned forward again, "don't you believe that there are things we humans don't know about?"

"Of course." Charlotte straightened up in her chair. "Obviously, I know we're limited by our way of perceiving the world. We've only got our eyes and ears and hands to go by, and, who knows, if we had something else, there probably would be a whole other world, a whole thing outside even our limited notions of worlds or . . ." Now she was getting lost in her own thought; she tried to start again. "If we didn't need our bodies to receive all this data for us . . ."

"I didn't *go* to college," Will interrupted. "What I'm asking is"—he paused—"don't you think there are unspoken forces?"

Charlotte felt an old panic. *He's asking me to go to bed*, she thought. But then that seemed ridiculous.

Before she answered, she twisted her long hair into a rope and pulled it across one shoulder. "I don't think you can make a clock work by concentrating . . . or win poker, for that matter."

"But, come on. Don't you think sometimes, there's just this thing." Will looked up and searched the sky, now freckled with the night's first stars, for the right thing, or word.

"I'm sorry," Charlotte said, and she was—sorry she couldn't agree with him, or pretend to agree. His enthusiasm, his desperation for convincing her—there was all that to appreciate. And if she could honestly assent, the world wouldn't be what she thought it was; Helen would somehow be okay, deeply okay. In the afterworld, having a ball with all the virtuous dead: her grandparents and a childhood friend who'd died of leukemia. But who could buy this?

"Come on," Will whispered now.

"Let's stop this," Charlotte said, almost frightened.

"No, wait." His chair screeched against the floor as he moved it near again. "Don't you believe that there are forces between people? Don't you? And you can't see them? And you can't hear them, but they can make things happen?"

"Yes, but . . ." He looked at her. "Emotions aren't magic," she said flatly.

"So, you do admit it, that there's something there?"

Charlotte was quiet.

"Or maybe you don't believe in it?"

Love, she thought he meant now. It was hard to hold onto what they were talking about. *Passion*. Or maybe, *You're one of them*. Senseless virgins—that's what she'd have to avoid seeming like now.

"Don't you believe in *that*? Don't you?" he whispered one final time, then snapped back into his chair. Winston, Edward, and Greg had returned.

Charlotte pulled at the edge of her lower lip. He was saying, *Don't you believe in love? And passion? Don't you? Or maybe you believe I didn't fix that clock in that car?* But it was an either/or situation. She was Dickens's Miss Havisham, Faulkner's Rosa Caufield. Or a believer. There was no in-between.

"A cab came for you," Edward said.

"Oh," Charlotte started to stand.

"Sit, sit." Winston patted the air, as if it contained an imaginary dog.

"We told it to come back later," Edward said innocently. There was no apparent sense, on his part, that this might be read as a hostile, even threatening action.

"I need to go," Charlotte said, dropping into her chair.

"No trouble," Winston said.

"It'll come back," Edward coughed. "When the game's over." He placed a whiskey in front of her. "For you. It's on me."

"God," Charlotte said. "What time is it?" Her watch—she knew she'd checked it earlier—wasn't on her wrist.

"Early still. We're almost through," Will said.

"I'm going to sit a few more out," Charlotte decided. But no one seemed to care much. For a while, she thought about phone calls she might make tomorrow, then she tried to concentrate on the game. Will had folded, so he looked up, raised his eyebrows, then reached behind the bucket to drum his index finger lightly on the back of Charlotte's hand. She looked down. He was pointing, very slightly, to her left. At once, Charlotte saw what he was trying to show her. The ornate, ivory handle of a handgun was peeking out of Edward's suit-jacket pocket. Charlotte started.

Helen, if she were here, would whisper, "He loves it. Thinks it's a second dick. You should see how he's decorated the first one."

Responding to Charlotte's movement, Edward looked up and smirked. "Ever been to Montana?" he asked.

"Once, yes," she said. "Once I was in Bozeman." This was a lie, but Helen had been. Charlotte found herself doing this a lot lately, appropriating Helen's life. Only last month, she'd cut her finger while slicing a carrot. At the emergency ward, squeezing her hand in a dish towel and answering the intake nurse's questions, she'd given her age, automatically, as twenty-six, then said, "I mean, thirty." The nurse had given her a queer look. "Wishful thinking, I guess," Charlotte grinned queasily.

"Well," Edward folded his hand and turned purposefully to Charlotte, "Bozeman, that ain't real country. Where I'm from is real country. Up in the mountains. Bozeman . . ." He turned from Charlotte and spat at the floor.

That, Charlotte hoped, would say it all, but then he turned back to her and said, "You can hear mountain lions up there. Ever hear a mountain lion?"

"No, I guess I haven't."

"It sounds like a woman screaming, if you know what I mean, just like a woman screaming, if you see what I'm saying."

Charlotte looked at her knees. Her skin felt too sensitive. Yes, she knew what he was saying.

"What I mean," he said, in case it was not entirely clear, "is it sounds like a woman screaming at the height of passion. You see?"

"Ante up," Will said in a disapproving voice. It was his deal.

And then a shot fired out in the street; Charlotte jumped at the sound, imagining she could hear it even after the initial shock, ringing through the narrow passageways outside, bouncing from building to building and never once finding the sky to escape.

"My God," Charlotte said, tears springing embarrassingly to her eyes. *I want to go home*, she thought. *Right now.*

She picked up her drink to hide her reaction but her hands were trembling, so she set it immediately back down. She'd had way too much, and her drunkenness descended on her quite suddenly, like some dirty, gauzy garment she now had to wear.

"It's only a firecracker," Will said.

"Some festival," Greg explained. "It starts at midnight. You walk backward into the water for good luck or to clean your soul of sins or something like that. A religion thing," he added dismissively.

"I've never heard of that," Will said.

"I saw some people," Charlotte offered, and tried to talk very carefully, clinically, to prove to herself that she wasn't drunk. "Outside my hotel room? They were doing something in the ocean. I mean, it looked like they were baptizing people in the ocean."

"Probably the Tie-heads," Greg said. The reporter. He would know. "Colorful clothes?"

Charlotte nodded. Too broadly, she thought, and pulled her chin to a halt.

"The Spiritual Baptists. I think they do that. Right?" Greg turned to Will.

He shrugged. "How the hell would I know?"

Water made Charlotte think again of a bath. How nice it would be to get clean. She really felt terrible now and had that vague sense of her skin as being insufficient, as if she couldn't count on it, not tonight, to hold her together. If she stood, who knew what organs might drop to the floor?

"Okay," Will said. "Another game of seven-card stud." Charlotte didn't even look at the cards Will dealt her. "I'll be right back," she said to no one in particular. "Nope, nothing there," she heard Will say as she stood.

She knew she had to step carefully now. How had this happened? Greg had brought her a third drink, and she'd sipped it, even though she hadn't wanted it, because she couldn't figure out what to do with her hands. Or had it been a fourth?

Inside, she again asked the bartender to call her a cab. "Please don't let him leave," she smiled. She wondered if he could tell she was drunk. She felt suddenly exhausted by everything—the traveling, the conversation with Will, even her own embarrassment.

"Bathroom?" she asked, and the bartender pointed to a door in the corner.

It was small and old, but, she was glad to see, clean, with those brown paper towels that smelled so horrible when they got wet.

She set the water running. Her face, in the tiny mirror above the bathroom, was pale and unaccountably peeved. *You don't have to be so sell-fish. Oh, God*, she thought and leaned her forehead against the wall and started to cry.

When she stopped, she looked reflexively at her wrist, having forgotten already that her watch wasn't there. Where might she have lost it? She burned herself when she went to test the sink's water. The short, sharp pain almost set her to crying again, but she added cold water, and when it felt right, she scrubbed her face with a small bar of white soap.

Okay, she thought. She was settling down. *Okay*. This was how she always ended her crying jags, with the sense that she'd just retreated from a fistfight and found, despite her breathlessness, that her wounds weren't so bad.

She stepped back to look at herself in the mirror. Her top was pasted with sweat to her breasts, each nipple clearly outlined in white cotton. She groaned and pulled the fabric off her chest.

The door to the bathroom cracked open. "Someone's in here," Charlotte called, but the door continued to open, and she quickly brushed the back of her hands over her cheeks, as if some tears might still be there despite her fierce scrubbing. It was Will, pushing the door open with his blue-jeaned hips, then elbowing it closed behind him.

"You okay?" he asked. "You all right?"

Her eyes had started to tear again. She turned from the mirror, and, in that watery space between them, it seemed he was swimming to her.

"Are you all right?" he asked again and put his arms on her shoulders. "We're all your friends here. Don't worry."

"Thank you," Charlotte sniffed and crossed her arms over her breasts.

"It's okay," Will said. Next to her, he was just her height, smaller than he'd seemed before, and she found this frightening. How could she have expected answers from someone who was so negligible in the flesh?

"Thanks, Will," Charlotte said cheerfully, to undercut the intimacy of the situation. She should ask him to go.

Will laughed. "I've got a real name. That Will thing is just a joke. I'm really Henry."

The water was still running in the sink, and Henry reached behind her to wet his hands. He rubbed his palms over his face. "This what you're doing? Washing up?" Charlotte nodded. He dipped his hand into the water again and said, raising a corner of his mouth, "I could help."

"Oh," Charlotte said. So he had been flirting with her after all. "I," she started, leaning her hip against the edge of the sink. She felt flattered. Naïve, Charlotte knew, but there it was. Maybe her problem was that she wasn't a female type but a male type; the guy who thought a beautiful woman on his arm signaled his own attractiveness.

"This okay?" Henry said, and she nodded her head yes. He moved toward her. "You're really . . . you know, you're . . ." He waved his hand. She saw that she was supposed to fill in the blank with a compliment. So what? Beautiful? Special? Vertical?

Charlotte laughed. "You, too."

"Me?" Henry said, placing a wet hand on her neck. "Naah. I'm a dime a dozen."

He leaned in to kiss her.

"Um," Charlotte said, pulling back. "What's your last name?"

Henry smiled, and before he answered, she let herself imagine their life together, self-deception of this sort being her prerequisite for sex. The future, as she saw it, involved an alarming amount of sunburn.

"Lazar," Henry said.

Jewish? Charlotte wondered. That might be awkward, given her reason for being here. But he didn't *look* Jewish.

"Well," she said, mock satisfied, "*now* I know everything." He leaned forward again to kiss her, placing his warm lips on her own and his tongue, quickly and deeply, into her mouth. A kiss that wasn't a prelude to sex so much as an assumption of it. Charlotte felt this was the moment for a decision on her part, but all she thought was that she probably tasted like alcohol, even though her earlier dizziness was subsiding. Tomorrow, she wouldn't be able to blame this on drink.

She felt her blouse being pulled from her skirt. And then Henry's warm hands, his chapped fingers, moving on her waist, her stomach, and finally under her bra, damp with the day's sweat, and onto her breasts. His palms were slightly scabby, as if they'd been cut up by fish lures.

Henry edged her around to the side of the sink, then pushed her carefully back over the porcelain, so she was lying over the sink cabinet. "Cold," she said and almost giggled.

"Condom?" she thought to add.

"Oh, yeah, yeah," he said, reaching into his back pocket, and Charlotte flashed on the day she'd thrown out Helen's diaphragm. She'd been squatting on the bathroom floor, going through a cabinet and pitching Helen's lipsticks and headscarves into the trash. When she came to the diaphragm, she felt compelled to open the case. The diaphragm itself was virginal, never used. Charlotte already knew that. She'd spent much of the past year reassuring Helen about the man she'd eventually meet, the one who wasn't going to care about her lumpy reconstructed breast. One night Charlotte had even said to Lawrence, "Well, you wouldn't, you know, care, if it was someone you loved," and he'd said, "I hate to be horrible, but sure I would." "Wrong answer, bucko," Charlotte had said, then pulled her pillow out from under her head and clobbered him. She had thought of all this as she had clicked the diaphragm container shut and tossed the whole thing in the bathroom's plastic waste bucket, registered the light thud of plastic hitting plastic, and then—and then nothing. That was that.

Once Henry had the condom on, he pushed into her with such ease that Charlotte imagined she had been doing this all her life, wandering into rest rooms and having men she wasn't even sure she had been flirting with follow her.

She felt she was going under, and she was, sort of, slipping sideways over the low sink as he rolled onto her. Her feet, crossed at Henry's back, left her toes to tickle the string of a light cord, her hair to graze the dirty linoleum. Henry whispered, for no apparent reason, "Oh, hey, I'm sorry." And then, "You believe me. Don't you?"

She didn't answer. His skin was lovely. Perfect, smooth, save for a spot where it was peeling at his back. Why hadn't his days in the lifeboat done more damage? She envied the hardness of his thighs against her own. *God*, she mouthed, blood rushing to her head. Lawrence had never been this—this what? "Yes?" Henry said, as if she'd spoken aloud.

"Just, just," she stopped. "Do it"—dumb pornography, the truth was she relied on it—"as hard as you can."

He smiled, as if he'd figured her out and said, "Oh, so it's like that, is it?" But he did what she wanted, saying—and she winced at the words— "Here you go." And then the liquor she'd been drinking took another lap through her circulatory system. She felt woozy, her brain—for once, for once—abandoning her to her body, only she was completely aware of that abandonment. The bathroom cartwheeled around her, and then she thought, as if she were a third party in the room, an outside observer, *Hey! I'm doing it with a spectral being.*

Henry reached around her side to turn off the faucet, to stop the water from streaming below her. "No," she closed her hand around his. "Leave it." Everything was so unlikely that she assumed, in a distracted way, that this was it; she was finally having the nervous breakdown she craved. The release of a collapse. Didn't all grievers want that?

Water swooshed under her. "Okay," Henry whispered, while Charlotte imagined the drain stopping up, the sink filling and then water running over the lip of the sink, building up on the floor, crawling up Henry's legs, over his hips, then reaching her back and rising further. She couldn't help it. She was one of those women who liked a flood.

CHAPTER FOUR

Josh Lazar

June 21, 1997

⁓

T OMORROW WAS THE THIRTIETH ANNIVERSARY of the Lazars'
marriage, and Josh Lazar—up late, unable to sleep—had organized a
party for his parents. A big party. An extravagant, embarrassing affair that
he had no interest in attending himself. Indeed, an affair to which, he suspected, no one wanted to go; it would smack of what Jews were reputed to
be, not what, Josh hoped, they were. It would be—he knew it, he knew it
in every pound of his own Ashkenazic flesh—a Shylock-fest. The whole
thing made him sick. Lying in bed, fifteen hours before the actual event,
he could already feel hate streaming from the bartenders and girls,
dressed—he had arranged for them to be dressed—in foolish island garb.
Hibiscus flowers twisted over their left ears, the waitresses would hand
him a conch fritter and he'd smile—hoping they'd read sympathy into his
grin—and they'd offer that blank, bored look he'd seen so often on the island, that you-pay-me-but-if-I-smiled-you'd-own-me-so-I'm-not-smiling
look, and he'd start to babble about his own economic troubles, a gross
play for equality, and they'd humor him, and he'd just want to go home
and die.

But his parents, they had wanted a party to mark the occasion. He had
to do something. Not that they had explicitly asked for the celebration.
Still, it was clear they wanted a party, because they'd given lavish shindigs
for *their* parents to mark the various milestones: the birthdays, the wedding anniversaries, the anniversary of the Lazar clan's arrival on the island, which, as far as Josh was concerned, was an anniversary for vomit.
(The real reason his Polish grandparents had disembarked at Barbados instead of continuing on to Brazil as planned was that Sadie, his paternal

grandmother, was seasick.) Actually, now that he thought about it, a lot of the family's anniversaries centered on regurgitation. Certainly any celebration of the family's business came back to it. There was no gathering of Lazars where the famous story wasn't trotted out and told as if the assembled hadn't heard it hundreds of times before. The tale—no doubt apocryphal—was this:

In 1943, Saul, Josh's paternal grandfather, sat down to a midday meal with his family. They were at the Atlantis Hotel in Bathsheba, so it must have been a Sunday afternoon, and their thighs must have been sticking to the dining room's white porch chairs as they watched fishermen come in with their morning booty. The fishermen jumped off wooden boats that weren't visible from the porch and swam, underwater, with their catch. It meant that from the Atlantis you could look out on undisturbed water then blink and see, as if by magic, men emerging from the sea, fists up above their heads and fish streaming down their arms like so much seaweed that had clung to them on the journey to the surface.

That lunch. Flying fish, pickled bananas, maybe someone had managed to find some greens, and there was definitely bread. Not, by the way, that Sadie wasn't a good cook. She made her own gefilte fish from the day's saltwater catch. There was no one in the Southern Hemisphere who made a lighter knaydl. But they liked to go out on Sunday.

What no one said, but Josh suspected, was that they were trying to be WASPs, going out for a big Sunday meal and all, but when he'd suggested this interpretation to his mother, she'd given him a dismissive look, said, "What is it with you? Why do you have to make everything ugly?"

So on that Sunday, they'd eaten. "Delicious," Saul had pronounced the bread. Apparently back then Saul was slender, but Josh always pictured the man he knew when he was a child, a man who put on weight in womanish ways; his face and chest remained thin while his hips and thighs ballooned up. His lips were unnaturally red. "What," Saul had said, taking another bite—he was pleased, the epicure—"is *in* this?" Beyond, of course, flour and water. He wanted to know what made the bread so good.

"Lard," offered the waiter. He'd been asked before.

Saul coughed and spat the bread onto the table. A kosher Jew. They'd brought their own plates and silver for the meal. Figured they could excuse the kitchen any history of mixing milk and meat as long as they weren't mixing anything at the meal. But pork fat? You couldn't excuse that away.

And so that was it. The oft-repeated legend. Food came flying out of a Lazar's mouth, and the next thing you knew, family history was being made. On the spot, Saul decided to open a bakery and make his own delicious, untainted bread. At first, it was just a small operation, something he ran out of a closet in the back of his fabric shop, but soon that wasn't enough to meet the growing demand for his kosher mixes. Before long, he'd moved into a larger shop and then into an abandoned bus depot, just north of Bridgetown, a place near the water and within a mile of the flour mills.

The Lazars had come to the island as paupers, but when death forced Saul Lazar to leave the island for a cemetery plot in Poland, he was a rich man. (What Bajan hadn't heard of Lazar bread? What mother hadn't dumped an aggressive-smelling diaper into the plastic sheath the loaves came in?) Saul's death was another anniversary the family now noted with due pomp, which is to say they read his name out loud during Yizkor and looked sad. For them, that was pomp enough for death. They liked to keep to happier matters when they gathered in groups. But they didn't forget that Saul Lazar had made them lucky people, wealthy beyond their needs, that he was smart enough to get out of Poland, to feel where things were going before it was too late.

So, tomorrow's party. The thought finally pulled Josh from bed, sent him to the bathroom for an aimless consideration of his three-day-old beard. Not that the party would *really* celebrate the wedding anniversary. It would be an excuse to acknowledge the island's Jewish population. His mother had made a big deal about the guest list, but in the end, she invited the usual suspects: a small community of transplants from Europe, that cadre of real estate agents and lamp harp manufacturers who gathered once a week at synagogue, referred sporadically to the horrors of Hitler, and peppered their speech with Yiddishisms.

From the start, Josh had known he would give the party, just as he had known his parents would finance the celebration. Josh was a twenty-six-year-old surfer; what kind of event could he bankroll on his own? Rum punch on the beach? A round of Banks beer and, hey everybody, don't forget to bring your volleyballs? It wasn't as if his older brother, Henry, had remembered the event and returned home to help with the planning. Eight months ago, he'd gone off to cook for some Jesus freaks on a charter boat, and for seven months, no one had heard from him. There hadn't been a letter, a phone call, or anything. After four months, his parents had started to worry; after six, they had made efforts to track him down, but nothing had come of them. Still, no one had panicked. Henry had always been a disappearer. The quotidian—that's what he couldn't stand, and he simply vanished when a Sunday afternoon dragged on or neighbors suggested a dinner party.

Josh hadn't worried. He knew Henry would return if something dramatic happened. He'd return and adopt a manner of priestly concern: Mom's frail heart—how to help? Dad's fights with the truck union—hadn't they exhausted him? Then everyone would collapse into praise of Henry: the way he noticed things, took such care. An unusually sensitive boy, and that wasn't all. He was so talented. Hadn't people always said he could have been a screen star? Or gone professional with the tennis? The praise would lead, it always led, to the year of the Queens Park riot. Henry had covered the story for the *Advocate*. "And he was just a boy," Josh's mother would say. "Just a boy and he wrote the whole front page." But Henry hadn't been just a boy; he'd been a college student with a summer internship at the paper. "It was Crop Over," Josh's mother would begin in the hushed voice of someone telling a fairy tale. "And everyone had gone out for the parade. Henry was the only one in the newsroom, the only one, and he had to write that story."

And then, of course, Josh had been right. Henry had returned, only not *for* something dramatic but *as* something dramatic. A Jewish duppy, if that didn't beat all. You had to hand it to him. He had a knack for putting a positive spin on things. He blew off his family, wrecked his employers' boat, spent a day on a life raft, and instead of being a sunburned fuck-up with the good luck to be fished out of the ocean, he was a miracle, back from the dead.

Josh had spent a whole boyhood with his brother, but lately, during his increasingly sleepless nights, the years distilled themselves to this one image: Henry showing up in his convertible for Josh's bar mitzvah. He'd arrived, then walked into the house—the Bridgetown synagogue hadn't been restored then, so they used a private residence for services—and he'd waved at the gathered, Queen Mother-style, hand rotating on the pole of his arm. A blue party hat, black yarmulkes, the faces of Josh's female class-mates all flitted across the lens of Henry's mirror sunglasses. He neglected to remove them until he'd settled into one of the white-and-blue lawn chairs, erstwhile pews for the makeshift house of worship. ("Holy of holies," Josh used to think in those days and look about the room, antici-pate the Coke and Manischevitz and Plus soda that would be offered after services. He was convinced, even then, that nothing in his life would ever feel right.) And Perle, Josh's aunt Perle—the one everyone said was so mad—had given the still-waving Henry an appraising look then muttered into Josh's ear, "Is he for real?" Josh had given her a conspiratorial smile and felt, perhaps for the first time, as if he did have an ally in this family.

Outside of the family, of course, people had their own ideas about Henry and what had happened to him in his months away. Josh heard it all on the beach. Just yesterday, he'd even heard it off the beach and in the water. Someone shouted a guess to him as he paddled out to the waves—mushy, not worth much—that surfers caught this time of year over a coral reef off Bathsheba. The unlikely rumors all tended in the same direction: Henry had been learning to swim with a school of sharks; Henry had been smuggling drugs, then hiding out till it was safe to return home; Henry had been buggering grade-school boys in Trinidad. Who knew? Henry, with his smooth good looks, had always been a mystery to Josh. All he knew was that the months of his brother's absence made it clear that it fell to Josh, the *de facto* only child, to celebrate his parents' anniversary in the style to which they were accustomed: late twentieth-century bloat.

And so: the jump. A $6,000 stunt, when all was said and done; $200 for each skydiver. His parents didn't like his daredevil side—the surfing, the skydiving. But it was a way to make *his* mark on the event. He could never get over the notion that his parents were the colonial oppressors, controlling him with their money, the very cash which, for years, he as-siduously refused but which he'd finally taken to prove himself a good son, to make the party. But he, the oppressed, had found a way to get back at them, even as he met their demands. He could do that, after all. Could, say, call his mother "the tzarina" behind her back. Not that he did, but it was a thought.

So far, it had been a virtually sleepless month. And Josh—never a reader, never a student, never even an indoors person—had spent his nights boning up on Freud and Marx, perusing the few books he'd acquired during his one semester at the University of the West Indies. It was the insomnia—it doubled Josh's hours and doubled his sense of what he might do with his wakefulness. But it also made him feel as if he'd lived longer than he, in fact, had. By morning, he always felt as if he were creeping toward middle age. He'd even developed the habit of putting his right hand, protectively, over his heart, as if to quell a sudden pain there.

But Josh didn't feel up to the books tonight. Instead, he stepped around a stack on the floor and flopped back into bed. He drew a sheet—icy from the air-conditioning—up around his neck, then sighed theatrically before he turned off the light. A minute later, the light was back on, and Josh was huffily kicking at his covers and reaching for a book. He read several pages before he started to pay attention. The master, the book informed him, needs the slave just as much as the slave needs the master. *Okay,* Josh thought and tried to puzzle out what this might mean, but it was a sleeping pill of a sentence, drawing Josh away from the very contemplation it invited. He let the book drop into a tent over his chest. Out the window, a horse trotted by on the beach. *Riderless?* Josh wondered, and before he could answer his own question, it was dawn, and he was deep in a dream in which he and a giant, joke-cracking lizard rode a single enormous wave from Barbados to Brazil.

CHAPTER FIVE

Wayne Deare

June 22, 1997

꧁

O N THE GROUND, NO ONE KNOWS WHAT'S GOING ON. Up in the air, everybody knows, though their knowledge is based on such a partisan view of those below that, at first, no one objects when Desmond Croney leans over Trevor Deare's shoulder to speak of maraschino cherries being stuck up football-sized noses, of jewel-bedecked women tucking snacks into napkins to bring home as a present for the hired help. No one protests, but then no one chimes in. Still Desmond persists. Nose flattened against one of the plane's windows, he peers out, then turns back to report what he cannot possibly see. "Booze almost gone." He grins at no one in particular. "And when it all gone . . ."

"We jump," Wayne Deare says emphatically to his brother Trevor, a late recruit, sitting, at the moment, in Desmond's lap. "After the drinks, we go."

Wayne and Trevor Deare are pressed, with twenty-nine other men, into an aircraft making wide circles at the edge of the ocean. When Joshua Lazar gives the signal, they will fly the half-mile to the Garrison Savannah. Then, because they've been paid handsomely to do so, they will parachute into the midst of an anniversary celebration. Their mission—a foregone conclusion; if they're at this altitude, they've chosen to accept it—is to stall the dinner hour with a calypso.

"This a mistake," Trevor says good-naturedly, his new gold front tooth flashing brightly before his tongue starts to toy with the design—an unlucky, three-petaled shamrock—cut into the metal.

"He scared," Desmond, Trevor's partner for the jump, proclaims. It's noisy in the plane, but that hasn't stopped the skydivers from carrying on a constant conversation. Ever since they hooked themselves together—the novices' butts lying in the experts' crotches, all thirty men ready for the tandem jumps—things have been pretty pornographic. Worse for men like Trevor, who are sitting in their partners' laps, but none too pleasant even for Wayne, who is standing with his hips and back nestled against the torso of his partner, Taz. Wayne is six-feet three-inches tall—at least, this is what he tells people—and not about to sit in any man's lap.

"He scared," Desmond repeats. "Scared for—" Desmond sticks his arm out from behind Trevor, then reaches around to drop his hand suddenly so it slaps against Trevor's leg—"scared for splat," he says, his fingers splayed around the curve of Trevor's thigh, the embarrassing Day-Glo pink of the silk jumpsuit. Wayne finds the turn of the conversation from butt fucking to accidental death a relief. Still, he says, in his brother's defense, "Scared of a cappella calypso music."

"That's right," Trevor points at Wayne to agree, then gives a little shudder of horror, though Wayne suspects he doesn't know what a capella means, probably thinks it has something to do with the Jews.

"A capella means music without instruments," Wayne offers.

Behind him, Taz thrusts his pelvis forward into Wayne's thighs, then chants, "Yes-sir. Col-lege boy."

"Fuck off," Wayne snaps in an automatic, emotionless way, and with those words he senses he's finally succeeded in alienating himself from everyone on the plane. He has been back on the island for almost twelve months, and still everything he does or says seems to piss somebody off.

"I see it now," Desmond cries, as he peers back out the window. He has the insistent, broad mannerisms of a stand-up comic, daring the audience not to find him funny. "The Jew got the drink, got the cherry in the drink, and nobody like the cherry. How you gonna snack with a cherry in the hand?"

At length, Josh Lazar, silent all this while, rises to the defense of his family below. "Listen," he says, but there's no energy in the reprimand, "it's my signature on your check. Right?"

"Too late. You already done sign," Desmond says, cheerfully, then adds, "I don't have nothing against Jew, understand. But they does have big noses." Desmond looks around, as if to solicit the agreement of others, but they're not interested. A few roll their eyes. Or try, despite the limited space in the plane, to turn their backs to Desmond. A foreigner, after all. A rude Jamaican. A wannabe Rastafarian. The evidence: his dreadlocks, though he arrived at yesterday's training session with a beef patty in one hand. So: a carnivorous Rastafarian—oxymoronic as any Jew for Jesus, emphasis on the moronic—not given to bathing in water (pure or otherwise). In fact, there's a sour stench to Desmond that makes Wayne wonder if he's been living on the beach instead of with (as he claims) his mother.

"Where you live?" Wayne asks him now.

"St. Andrew. I told you, brother," Desmond insists, though he has done no such thing. " 'Course I come down here to par-tee." He balls his hands into fists and rocks his shoulders, in a two-second parody of his drunken, dancing self. Trevor is forced to bob with him, slipping right then left off Desmond's thighs. "After Dark. *You* know it." Wayne does, though he's never been in the place. Nightclubs aren't his style. "St. Andrew, man. I have a hangover. I go back home. I drink, maybe, eight or ten coconuts and I'm fine."

Wayne nods, having nothing to offer as a response to this, and Desmond starts up again. "I say," he chants, as if it's a song he'd like to sing, a pointed calypso instead of the pap that they'll probably hear when they hit the ground, "how you gonna snack with a cherry in the hand?"

"It's not funny," Wayne finally says. "Okay?"

Desmond coughs out half a laugh then tells the others, "He vex with me." After which, he *does* start singing, "Happy Han-u-kkah. Have a har-mon-ica."

Wayne looks over at Josh, who doesn't seem to be listening. His hand lingers over his heart, and his thumb makes quick circles there, as if he's fingering his own nipple. The gesture makes Wayne think of a "spirituality" seminar his college friend, Deirdre, once dragged him to. "This will be," the instructor had said, "a class about learning to love ourselves."

"Oh," Wayne had said, mock eager, "will it be a hands-on experience?" No one had laughed. Deirdre had whispered, "You jerk." Even now, the memory makes Wayne smile, and Desmond takes his grin for encouragement.

"Hap-py Han-u-kkah. Have a har-mon-ica."

"It's offensive, man," Wayne says, pronouncing the words slowly, as if spelling things out for Desmond, though, in truth, he has no idea what this harmonica tune is supposed to mean.

"Yeah? Well, it's oh-fen-sive," Desmond looks at Wayne, then turns, abandons some of his rum-shop Bajan to say to Josh, one of only two white men in the plane, "that they're no black folk at that par-tee down there."

"Shut up, Cappuccino," someone calls from the front of the plane.

"Hiii yella," someone else barks, and Desmond, a mulatto, sensitive about little but the lightness of his skin, is silent at last. He turns to pout elaborately at the window, while the plane takes another stomach-churning lap around the edge of the ocean.

Wayne feels briefly sorry for him. After all, he doesn't want candy-ass politeness—he doesn't want that—but he does, for Christ's sake, he does want something like decent behavior. No reason to tempt the moral universe when you're jumping out of a plane. Right?

"Right?" he wants to say to his brother, Trevor, but Trevor is otherwise engaged.

"Sure," he is saying to Josh Lazar, "sure you got the good chute."

There'd been a fuss, back on the ground, when no one could find the key for the closet where all the single packs were kept. So Josh is wearing the same hulking 45-pound pack that all the men are wearing. Only it's not the same. He sent someone back to his home to get a tandem pack he had there.

"The good chute," Trevor repeats.

"What're you talking about?" Josh says with a bit of a whine. Like most of the men on the plane, Josh is young and fairly athletic, but he doesn't look it. And it's hard to figure out why. His stomach is flat, though it looks like it's dreaming of paunch. His hair, now hidden under a leather helmet, is full but seems poised to depart and expose the pink top of his head to the worst of the afternoon sun.

"In truth. Look'ee here," Trevor says and reaches behind him to pull on Desmond's arm. Then he starts pointing at the seams of Josh's pack.

"I used to be a skydiving instructor," Josh says.

"For about two weeks," someone whispers in Wayne's ear.

"So," Josh continues, oblivious to this bit of criticism, "that's why I've got my own pack."

"Oh, yes, the good e-quip-ment for the Jew-boy. But no matter what *we* got," Desmond says. The ugliness in his voice is unmistakable. His joke is a real complaint, but Desmond, as far as Wayne knows, has no personal history with Josh, and no extended contact with the island's insular community of white Jews. They're filthy rich, of course, reason enough for anger, but Wayne doesn't imagine Desmond knows the Jews well enough to be able to identify (as Wayne can) the particular West Coast mansions where they live, the five-million-dollar homes where their North American brethren winter. "No one care if a black man make the pancake on the ground, but if the . . ." Desmond cuts himself off abruptly and looks at the others; he's finished his part of the song, the chorus can begin. But no one, no one save Trevor, picks up on this line of accusation.

"Yeah, how come you got that one?" Trevor asks as if Josh hasn't just offered an explanation. But then Trevor's hearing is bad; there's no telling what he's actually picking up. "You so special. What make you so special?" Trevor gives a half-laugh then addresses the others on the plane. "*He* sure ain't going splat. Not with that protection."

"All the chutes are safe," Josh turns back to say flatly.

"That so," Trevor says. "Facts is facts? Well, give us yours then. A trade here and now."

"Oh, please," Wayne groans, purposefully jostling against his brother. The plane is already too crowded, and Wayne takes this as a personal afront. The cramped interior, like any low ceiling, has spoken: *You are a freak.* And if Wayne had any doubt about this, he has only to consider his family: Trevor is five feet, nine inches, and his parents are under six feet (in both senses, having died in recent years.) "The last thing we need is your arms flailing around."

"O-kay, time," the pilot shouts. The plane dips slightly with his words, and Wayne tastes curried potatoes—today's last-minute lunch, a chicken and potato roti from Chefette—at the back of his throat.

"We heading over," the pilot adds, and Wayne and the other passengers rearrange themselves for the jump, standing if they've been sitting or simply moving away from the door out of which they'll jump.

The pilot signals one of the men to open the door, but Josh calls out abruptly, "Wait. Wait. Do another circle." The pilot does as he says, heading, once again, back out toward the ocean. "I want to switch parachutes with you," Josh says, using his chin to indicate Trevor, but meaning, of course, Desmond, who wears the parachute for the two men.

"Awright, man," Trevor says, "let's do it"

"Oh-ho-ho," Desmond says, "gonna see how da pee-ple live."

"Will you just shut-the-fuck up?" Josh says, so harshly that even though no one likes Desmond—Desmond is too stupid to like—a voice calls out, "Okay, you all. Lighten up. Lighten up." Some heads, sheathed in leather helmets, bob up and down in agreement. They look, it occurs to Wayne, less like war pilots or daredevils than so many versions of Snoopy the dog.

"Come on," Wayne says loudly and gives Trevor the hard, you-asshole stare that generally presages a fight between the brothers. Trevor doesn't give a shit about Josh's fancy parachute; Wayne knows that. Back on the ground, when they'd gone to suit up, Wayne had said, "What's this? The supply closet for midgets?"

"Someone's scared," Trevor had laughed.

"I'm not scared," Wayne declared, edgily, but even at forty-five pounds, the packs were so unimpressive—like a hiker's backpack and bedroll. He'd kicked one and asked, "This is supposed to hold a man up?" Trevor had laughed again, then looked pointedly at his own crotch, and said, with pretend panic, "Oh, bro', you think size's the thing?"

Now Trevor says, as if the parachute exchange had been Josh's idea from the start, as if Wayne is the last, ungreased joint, standing in the way of the world's smooth operation, "Let the man have what he want."

Not that anyone needs Wayne's permission. Trevor and Desmond are already unhooking themselves. Josh has his parachute off and at his feet. To give them room to complete the swap, the others press closer together, and just when Wayne fears there will be a return to the earlier conversa-tion, everyone hooting about men-lovin' men, Josh tightens Trevor's—now his—parachute and calls, "All right, the door," and the pilot starts back for the Savannah.

With the door fully ajar, the plane's cabin is a rush of sound—wind and machinery, an angry racket to which the men respond by pressing against the plane's walls and giving each other high fives. The air, Wayne notes, smells faintly of eucalyptus and brine, even up here, at 9,000 feet.

"Alleyne. Christopher," Josh shouts the surnames of the pair who are to step to the door.

Those who want to freefall the longest are going first. Earlier in the day, Taz had decided that Wayne and he would only freefall for fifteen seconds, about 4,000 feet. "Good," Wayne had said, not wanting the optional extra five seconds. Too dangerous, he reasoned, though lately even ordinary things have felt fraught. A dead child by the side of the road will prove to be, on closer inspection, a sack of trash. A six-foot spider leg sticking out of a sewer grate will be a twisted pipe. Just yesterday, at the training for today's jump, Josh Lazar had raised his hand—he had a question about whether all the men could fit in one plane—and Wayne saw that his wrists bore the pale, worm-like scars of a substantial bloodletting. Then Josh twisted his elbow and the scars disappeared. It had just been a trick of the light.

"So long, baby," Alleyne yells before he and Christopher disappear into the air. Wayne gives an involuntary shudder that he turns into a coughing fit, so no one will accuse him of fear.

"All right?" Taz calls from behind him.

The plain fact is that Wayne's scared of heights—not pathologically so, not like his friend Deirdre, who couldn't stand on a table and look down without starting to shake, but sensibly so. Like: he wouldn't use a balcony ledge as a balance beam. Like: he would never leap out of a plane without a partner and a large cash incentive.

Trevor, who has never shared Wayne's fears, is next. It's hard for Wayne to believe he's related to his brother, who is currently standing by the door and bouncing, lightly, on the balls of his feet, a sign of excitement left over from childhood. Or perhaps it is all too easy to believe they are related, for their virtues and vices are so neatly split, like a nation-state divvied up so no one has too much power. The republic of intelligence and hard work goes to Wayne, while Trevor is the despot of good looks and charm. An equitable distribution—that's the idea, but no one has enough to rule with. Wayne's twenty-four and still hasn't had a woman. What he has had, as Trevor will be the first to remind him, is too much studyication. Also, as Wayne will be the first to remind Trevor, too much growth hormone. Although when Wayne complains, Trevor always pooh-poohs him, makes some crude joke about the length of his spine and the inches of his manhood. But Trevor doesn't know what the doctor in Boston discovered. He has grown three inches since secondary school. Three inches! Who is still growing in college? Wayne still goes around saying he's six feet, three inches. But he's not. He's six fucking six. Holy Jesus, he sometimes thinks, he's never going to stop. Someday it will be a legitimate fear to be frightened of looking down at his toes. And Trevor? Trevor is small for a man. He's never finished secondary school, never been off the island. Isn't even interested in the possibility. He can't keep a job or be good to the women who flock to him. He can't quite stay away from alcohol either, and there's no one with any foresight who doesn't see where his bingeing is going to take him. There's something more to it than the couple of beers everyone puts away in the evening.

"He gone," Taz says and Wayne looks up to see that his reverie—he spends long hours every day in this sort of agitated filial comparison—has made him miss the actual moment of his brother's jump. "Four more," Taz shouts. Four more pairs, then it will be Wayne's turn.

When the time comes, Wayne and Taz position themselves next to the door. "Like brother, like brother," Taz calls over the rush of air and gives Wayne a pat on the shoulder.

Wayne wags his head, rejecting this equation, but Taz doesn't seem to notice.

"Ready?" he calls into Wayne's ear.

Wayne nods broadly. He has already surmised that Taz is mean-spirited, given to ruthless jokes about women and gays. Still, he does inspire confidence. He has thick, lumberjack arms, and now that he isn't mock fucking him, Wayne's glad Taz is plastered to his butt. Taz is not going anywhere, so Wayne takes hold of the door frame and considers his next move. Wind whips at his face, but instead of seeing the sky, Wayne flashes on a room at the Old Terminal, a place used for folding chutes and storing uniforms. The skydivers, a group with no apparent sense of irony, had decorated it with photographs of dead jumpers.

" 'Kay," Taz says, "ready."

Wayne ducks into the wind to wrap his hands around the strut of the plane's wing. There is the cold against his face and a strange feeling in his bladder, as if fear is a thing, a balloon in his loins. He has no intention of letting go of the strut. Indeed, he feels a curious absence of thought, certainly no inclination to make the decision to loosen his grip, but then Taz nudges him, so he turns and—stupidly, he thinks, the balloon inflating further—bellyflops into the air. Right away, his head starts to tumble toward his toes, and there is an oceanic roar, a sound accompanied by a feeling Wayne remembers from going off a high dive into a hotel pool—ohmigod, ohmigod, ohmigod, no. The drogue, a miniparachute, pops up and rights Taz and Wayne, but it doesn't—it isn't intended to—slow the fall, so Wayne can't help anticipating the slap of the ground underneath him, as if the land will be like that long-ago swimming pool's water, a permeable surface, something he'll sink himself into with relief. Anything to stop the hollow-torso feel that he associates with fear. Then Taz taps the altimeter at his wrist and pulls the rip cord. There is a sharp tug at Wayne's crotch—"It'll be," Taz had explained when they were still on the ground, "like the wedgie of a lifetime"—and indeed, for two unbearably painful seconds, Wayne gives up his dream of fatherhood as his balls are yanked toward his throat. Then the roaring subsides, and both men rise, or so it seems, abruptly in the sky.

For a moment, it is as if they have stopped moving altogether. A pause, a glitch—gravity's on holiday for a single, glorious second. Then, when they resume the trip to the ground, it is at a slow, almost leisurely pace. Wayne recognizes that he isn't going to die, not today, so he lets himself look down at the island, a muttonchop of land on the blue platter of water below.

After the brief terror of the freefall, the floating seems like a ride at the fair, almost cozy. The men pass dreamily through a cloud. Inside, it is completely quiet. Wayne considers his hands, the pink arms of his jumpsuit and the pure white of the atmosphere. *This is just me*, he thinks, having not a clue what he means, though he feels that he must be stumbling into profundity, that such a dramatic displacement of his physical self ought—it was only fair, wasn't it?—to be accompanied by spiritual revelation. *Just me*, he thinks again and observes that even here, even this high up, his stomach has its signature cramp. His body will never, never release him from its claims. Then Taz and Wayne are out of the white, and the land is beneath them again.

Taz says, "Where are we?"

"It's there," Wayne shouts, pointing at a yellow-and-white tent. Behind him, he feels Taz tugging at the chute, directing them toward the grassy center of the Savannah's racing track, and pulling, in the process, a memory out of Wayne. It is of flying a Chinese dragon kite in the Savannah. This must have been—so long ago. Perhaps the very year that Wayne hit his head falling off the back of a flatbed truck. Now—maybe because of that fall—Wayne remembers little of his youth. So the kite memory is a true surprise, though there's nothing much to it. His father had gotten the thing off the ground, and it had made a victorious flapping sound before careening away from the track and into a tree. Months later, at a cricket match, Wayne had seen the dragon's red cellophane, still wrapped like a bandage around one of the sandbox trees on the east side of the Savannah. Now, Wayne looks down for a glimpse of red in one of the trees, but he doesn't want to see anything, not really, now that his father is gone.

At the end, the ground seems to rush toward them. At Wayne's back, Taz energetically jerks the cords and finally flares the chute, so they'll come down slow, land, if possible, on their feet. But the concluding moments are clumsy. Wayne hits on his ass and is dragged several feet through grass then onto the dirt of the racing track, before Taz is able to pull in the chute.

When they stand and unhook the cables from their suits, Wayne feels awkward, almost dizzy. He looks around as if the Savannah is new to him, eyeballing St. Anne's—the fort his friends call Red Dick for its brick, phallic-shaped tower—and closer by, the track's ramshackle bleachers.

"Thanks, man," Wayne says, but he doesn't hear his own words.

The jumpers have all been warned about the possibility of deafness. Sometimes the ears get clogged from atmospheric changes. They're to gather outside the tent and start the performance anyway. Soon enough, they'll start to hear what they're doing. A few yips and encouraging shouts are all that's required.

Now Taz nods at Wayne, says something.

Wayne nods back dumbly. Who knows what he's assenting to?

Then Wayne thinks Taz says, "Every dog's got 'e's day." It's just a guess, though. (This is Wayne's first attempt at reading lips, and he doesn't expect success, mostly because Trevor—who's inherited their father's progressive deafness, along with the old man's stubborn insistence that his hearing was fine—is so good at it.) If Wayne's right, he wonders what Taz's words are supposed to mean. Perhaps they are Taz's admission of his limitations—*this* is all he does, gives men a brief bit of confidence for this odd sport—or perhaps he's talking about Wayne, saying *now* Wayne's finally done something.

With their chute folded, Taz and Wayne push toward Trevor, Desmond, and the others who have landed. They are all standing on the tent's periphery. Inside, the predominately white guests are either crowded around tables or standing in sociable clumps, busily engaged in conversation. So far, only a few have turned to remark upon the jumpers.

A guy who everyone's been calling Mighty Marty is the only white skydiver who has landed. He's already peeled off his suit and is dressed for the performance in stiffly creased white pants, white bucks, and an old man's zipper-front blue shirt. *Jewish calypso*, Wayne thinks, with a shake of his head. The world really is mad. For his next gathering—not that he's likely to have one—he should find a hip-hop klezmer band.

Back at the hangar, Josh had said Mighty Marty should begin once a third of the skydivers landed. The idea is to make plain, as soon as possible, that this is a stunt, a joke, not (if you are prone to thinking in these terms) a terrorist action.

Mighty Marty has a microphone, and when Taz and Wayne join the group, he nods at them and starts to sing. Some guests turn their heads to see what's going on, but they don't step away from the tent, as if, despite the relatively late hour of the day, they need its shelter.

Wayne admires Marty's fluidity. At least he moves like a real calypso singer. Despite the salt and pepper of his hair and the dated get-up, Marty's in great shape—the kind of guy who would have been a racquetball player at Tufts, a tense, competitive young man used to being the best at everything. And Mighty Marty's not bad looking. There's some story about his wife from Trinidad, but Wayne can't remember what it is, just that the woman's supposed to be gorgeous.

"Bra. Seal," he thinks Marty is singing.

"That's right," Wayne adds, as required, his own bit of punctuation to Marty's words. "Bra-zil," Marty seems to mouth now. Maybe it's a song about Recife. The first Jews on the island were refugees from Recife, coming to Barbados because Oliver Cromwell said they could.

Wayne feels—still doesn't hear—the soft thud of more skydivers be-hind him. "Yessir," he calls out and wonders how loud his voice is.

Next to him, Trevor taps his chest. Angina, Wayne thinks for a brief, panicked moment—the very thing that plagued their mother—but that's stupid. Trevor is only trying to tell him that he still has his card. Once everyone's on the ground, each of the jumpers will present a card to Abe and Hannah Lazar, the anniversary couple. Thirty cards in all, extending best wishes and love from the community. The last card, the thirty-first—the one to grow on—will be from Josh, who will wait till the thirty other skydivers are down to make his own jump.

It isn't immediately clear how they're supposed to find Hannah and Abe Lazar among the guests, who have finally realized what is going on and have edged toward the performance. It's a party that seems to be thriving on good humor. Wayne can see these people are willing to make fools of themselves; they rock back and forth with Marty's music, or drum their fingers on their thighs. A few must be singing along. Their mouths are moving, at least.

Finally, some guests push Abe and Hannah to the front of the crowd. Abe's partially balding and completely white-haired, with the kind of open face and easy smile that makes his excess weight seem jolly, high-spirited, instead of slovenly. Despite the heat, he's wearing a substantial blue suit, and Wayne can see he's of the generation that only uses T-shirts for layering under a dress shirt and tie. Hannah's his obligatory opposite—a thin, somewhat horsey-looking woman. The slabs of her cheeks are rouged in an unfortunate, theatrical way. She has a wide-mouthed laugh that seems a bit forced; this cannot be her preferred facial mode. Perhaps for this reason, Wayne imagines her shrieking.

As the Lazars grin obligingly at Mighty Marty's performance, each of the skydivers dances forward to present his card. This is the moment that pains Wayne. He is a terrible dancer and the slow rocking he does now is only because it's so queer not to move when there's music all around you. But his considerable size makes him, even in the best of situations, hunch over.

Still, he's supposed to make his presentation on the heels of his brother (card number 24) and Taz (card number 25). He recognizes most of the other guys who are starting to hand their cards over to the couple.

It's a parade of the unemployed: surfer friends of Josh's, beach boys, rum-shop layabouts, and Wayne, the panicked college graduate. You'd have to be hard up to agree to do this.

Trevor dances ahead. He presents his card and gives a quick bow to Abe and Hannah. Wayne thinks that this could possibly be more frightening than jumping out of a plane. He reaches into his chest pocket for his envelope and moves forward, his arm extended. The Lazars, who have been smiling throughout the presentation, look confused. Hannah's Cheshire grin collapses into a slack-faced gape. "Wi-ah tie," Wayne thinks he hears from behind them. Wayne keeps moving forward, his arm still extended, but the Lazars now seem startled. Hannah grabs Abe's shoulder, and Wayne starts to shake his head, as if to comfort her. It's okay, he could reassure them about his large, loping self, and then the very impulse makes him hate them. There's nothing wrong with me, he thinks. As he draws closer, he notices, with some satisfaction, a cold sore that's spread around the corner of Hannah's mouth. It's oozing just slightly, and she's scraping her bottom lip with her teeth, so the crust of the sore is giving way to blood. The earth shakes once beneath Wayne, and he jerks his head, as if to free water from his ears, but it does no good. He's still basically deaf. Abe turns to Hannah, but Hannah doesn't look at him. Her eyes are trained straight ahead and then Hannah's face is all panic, and she isn't retreating from Wayne, as he thinks, for a moment, she might, but running toward and then past him. Before Wayne even has time to turn, the people at her sides have also started running. Wayne hears some more words from Mighty Marty's microphone, but he can no longer place the singer. Perhaps he has moved under the tent? "Mil-lie gone. . . ." The words crackle in his ear.

You're kidding, Wayne thinks, for he only needs two words to know what song Marty is singing, an old Afro-Barbadian folk song—not Jewish at all—about a man who murdered his common-law wife, then told the police she'd gone to Brazil. Why would *he* sing that song? And why would he sing it *here*?

Trevor grabs his arm and pulls him around. "The jump," Trevor calls into his ear and points to the far side of the Savannah, where everyone is running.

"Wha? What?" Wayne says back and then, in an instant, his ears clear and he hears everything. Trevor shouting, "Josh. The chute never open," and behind him, Mighty Marty, still apparently unaware of what has happened, chanting:

> Oh Lawd, poor Millie.
> Wid de wiah tie up she wais'
> An' de razor cut up she face.
> Wid de wiah tie up she wais'
> An' de razor cut up she face.

CHAPTER SIX

Charlotte Lewin

June 22–23, 1997

⁓

T HE HOTEL FELT ABANDONED. There were people in it, to be sure, but they felt leftover, the detritus of a storm, or perhaps just the opposite, the daft folks who'd ignored warnings of impending disaster, foolhardy desk clerks and long-term guests who'd decided they'd stay put for the hurricane, no matter what the radio broadcasts said. Charlotte's fifth-floor room opened on a courtyard. There didn't seem to be anyone staying in the neighboring rooms, and on the far side of the courtyard, the doors were all boarded up with plywood. Outside, the pool was drained. A reddish soot danced across the cracked bottom. Downstairs by the patio, a sign insisted that meals were available all day. A line of silver chafing dishes seemed to confirm the fact, but the restaurant tables went unoccupied. A lone waiter in a red vest and black pants stood by the buffet. He gave a listless stir to a gray stew. A pink item—a pig's foot?—rose to the surface, and Charlotte coughed, a gagging sound that couldn't possibly be mistaken for irritation, but the waiter looked up quickly, as if he'd been accused.

"Can I get something to eat?" Charlotte hugged a yellow envelope to her chest—the files Pat had given her two days earlier. Knocked into sleep by Dramamine, she'd been unable to read them on the plane.

"Yes, please," the man said flatly, and Charlotte wanted to mumble, "Oh, never mind," retreat to her room, fish some guava juice out of the overpriced bar, and leave breakfast at that.

"Just some juice," she said, as she sat down. "And maybe some toast."

"Coffee?"

"Yes." Her voice rose into a servile, little-girl squeak. "And coffee."

She would read the file over breakfast, then compose her Tolstoy list. Back in college, someone had told her that Tolstoy made a list of what he hoped to get done each day, and ever since, Charlotte had done the same. So: Find synagogue. (Not that this errand felt all that necessary. In the matter of the menorah—now that she thought about it—what possible difference could her perceptions of the building make?) Place phone calls (to residences). Organize phone calls (to businesses) for Monday morning. Take last night and—she had a fantasy of the previous evening as so many sheets of paper—take last night and tear it up.

She wrapped her arms around herself and stuck her fingernails into her ribs. Short of having the events to rip up, she might as well go at herself. *You are*, she thought, *the biggest idiot*. But something about this felt false. Inauthentic self-flagellation. Now *there* was something worth reproach. The truth was that all morning she had been remarking on her blankness. On waking in her startlingly bright room, she took her emotional temperature, checked her heart, and found nothing there. She imagined a doctor by her bedside, the crisp snap of his wrist as he shook down the mercury on a thermometer. "It's just as I suspected," he'd confess. "No inner life."

Dressing, too, she had been relatively sanguine. She had a sour stomach but surprisingly little remorse. Or happiness. Or shame. Or pride. Perhaps later, emotion, like some clown with a frozen trout, would step out of a closet and clop her on the head, but for now she just felt tired.

Last night, she'd stiffened when the sex was over, then kept her distance as she'd parted from Henry. Henry Lazar, an altogether earthly creature, after all. What had she thought? That he'd vaporize in the middle of the act, save her from dealing with the embarrassing aftermath? "I'll call you," he'd said, and she had actually responded with a sarcastic, "Yeah. Right." If he was earnest, it was a dumb, mean thing to say. But this interpretation didn't occur to Charlotte, not as she neatened herself up in the bar bathroom, not later. Instead she was thinking that, with men, there was always a contest for aloofness, a competition which she regularly lost by caring about what happened. Why not avoid the game altogether? After all, it was her strategy for softball. Just Don't Play. So, a one-night stand. Charlotte's first. Or the first where she understood, right away, that was all it was. She was changing or—an unpleasant thought, one that made her abandon thoughts of reading the folder by her plate—adopting some of her mother's characteristics.

Weeks earlier, her mother had said to her, "Sometimes I don't know what it is. I just don't feel *anything*."

"Shock," Charlotte said.

Her mother waved this away, and Charlotte realized that her mother meant she didn't feel anything about anything other than Helen. The world had contracted into one tragedy: hers. A protective device, Charlotte knew, a reasonable enough way of handling tragedy, but not Charlotte's way, not a way that she ever wanted to be hers.

At least this was what she was thinking while she drank her tepid coffee. Then she shook it off—her family wasn't here, after all—and turned to the archival material about Barbados Jews in the eighteenth and nineteenth centuries. She could feel a world emerging from the papers spread across her breakfast table. And what could she do but marvel at the emotion—it was a sort of love—she felt for its denizens? Shadowy, long-bearded figures stood behind her bamboo chair and laughed, confirmed the record of their exploits. True enough, they'd sacked their own temple during a wedding. Yes, they'd shipped in rabbis, like any old wholesale goods, during Sabbath and High Holy Days. They'd turned the ocean into a ritual bath and done an emergency bris with a coconut shard. They came to Purim carnival costumed as sharks and flying fish, as Esther with her pet green monkey.

If Charlotte could have turned and talked to any one of these phantoms—nee 1700—she'd have been happy. The tone-deaf cantor. The Kaballah-dabbling merchant in short pants. The crabbed inhabitant of the rabbi's house, that arthritic squatter who boarded so close to the temple she didn't bother with services, she could hear them in bed, and she liked drifting off to the prayers. And there were others: the peddler of thread. The silent immigrant who worked in the sugar-boiling house. He had a single, lachrymose eye, but if you asked after him, expressed concern at his lopsided weeping, he'd have you bend over and taste the tears that were dripping down the left side of his nose, and you'd step back, stunned. They tasted like sugar.

It took the impatience of the waiter to pull Charlotte back from this world and make her pay her bill. As she waited for change, a small brown bird perched atop the chair opposite her. There was something weirdly human about the way he eyed the leftover toast on her plate. Charlotte shooed him away, but he hopped right back.

Charlotte pulled the twentieth-century part of the file from her envelope. Howard had placed it in a separate folder, perhaps to remind Charlotte that her world bore no relation to the one she'd been reading about. Not that she had any doubts. As Charlotte passed through the hotel lobby for the beach, a white girl—her hair plaited with pink plastic beads—skitted past. Then a younger girl, hampered by a frog-shaped flotation device, stumbled by in pursuit, calling miserably, "Karen, wait up. Waaitt up."

Charlotte took off her sandals, then walked onto the beach, past a stand of coconut palms, and away from the hotel. Before her, the land was as orderly as a flag. A blue stripe for the ocean, a white for the sand (not pink at all, as Howard had promised) and a yellowy green stripe for the scraggly seaside trees, their wispy leaves like so many tendrils of fine, wind-tossed hair. No one was out, though after a stretch she passed a single middle-aged black man, dressed in yellow swim briefs, legs spread apart. His head and arms bobbed to one knee then the other. Some sort of yoga exercise.

"Hello," Charlotte nodded, and he said, "Aw right," in a tone so friendly it seemed a blessing. All the ways people lived in the world. What could *his* story possibly be? When she felt she was a polite distance away, Charlotte sat down, dug her feet into the hot sand, tented her dress around her ankles, and started to page through a synagogue newsletter. This month's, conveniently enough. The publication wasn't anything formal, just a couple of pages, Xeroxed and stapled together, with community news, appeals for money. Details of the accomplishments of various children. Which amounted, as best Charlotte could tell, to leaving the island for college in Toronto or London. She flipped the pages quickly, was about to set the newsletter aside when the salty wind off the ocean fanned the remaining pages, and her eye caught on the word "Lazar." Charlotte turned to the newsletter's final page.

Abe and Hannah Lazar.

She jerked her head as if she'd been slapped.

Of course, Lazar was a Jewish name, stupid to have tried to convince herself otherwise. Even worse was where she saw the name: under the heading "Menorah Committee." The news was this: a four-member group had just been formed to represent the synagogue in a contest for the item. In fact, they'd be meeting later today, after the Sisterhood meeting, at 141 Shore Drive, or "Abe and Hannah's!" as the newsletter proclaimed with chatty intimacy.

Charlotte hadn't often been forced to consider the consequences of her bad behavior. When she thought about previous humiliations, she'd think of how she'd been voted "Most Polite" in junior high. Most Polite. Good God. She came to her misdeeds so late. In college, at a party, she'd danced on a piano, then felt like a fool. She had once, exuberantly, put her hand over a male professor's while they were talking, and had known how he must have taken it, when she hadn't meant it that way at all. In the private realm, there were larger crimes: emotional scenes with boy-friends, a period when she scratched herself regularly, scratched till she bled, because she was so frustrated with something minor—her weight, her performance at work. But, in the end, these were small things. So Charlotte had wandered into the waters of desire. She'd never taken a true swan dive off the dock of good-girlhood. Maybe because she had a sis-ter, always around, always ready to call her on any smug attempt at sophis-tication. ("Sure, I smoke," she could imagine her adolescent self saying, and then, even in the moment of picturing this, there was Helen's elabo-rate laugh, her readiness to say, "Smoke? She can't even light a match un-less it's one of those foot-long things for the fireplace.")

Charlotte put her papers in her bag, then ambled down to the tur-quoise ocean. She bunched her dress up by her thighs, walked out into the clear, warm water and curled her toes into the soft ocean floor. So much more appealing than a rocky New England beach or the slimy, leafy muck she had trod over in the lakes of her youth. She probably should go to that meeting, that Menorah Committee meeting, scheduled for 7:45 this evening. Or maybe she shouldn't go, maybe she should call Howard and say she'd accidentally gotten embroiled in . . . but what would she say? To Howard, of all people? (And Howard, she thought: was he all right? She'd gone two whole days without wondering how he was.)

She glanced at her wrist, but it was bare. Of course. She forgot; she hadn't found her watch last night when she'd returned from the bar. But she didn't want to purchase an overpriced Timex at some tourist shop. A matter of pride with her: *not* shopping.

Back toward the hotel, a second person stood in the curlicue surf. Charlotte started to slosh over, then angled up to the sand. As she drew closer, something felt off in her vision, then she realized what it was. The man was eating a stick. *Oh, please*, she thought, *the things people have to deal with.* She should buy a watch. Help the general economy. Do her part. But in the space of time it took her to have this thought, she drew closer and saw that the man wasn't starving, he was using his teeth and tongue to peel and greedily lick a stalk of sugarcane.

By the time she was at the elevator, she felt frantic. True, she wasn't here on formal legal business, but she *was* representing her grandfather. The doors of the elevator closed. She looked into the round mirror at the ceiling's corner, said to it, "Very good. Really, that's very good, Charlotte. Having sex with a stranger in a bar." She distended her jaw into a grimace, "Very attractive, very attractive. Very fucking attractive." She grabbed her stomach and pinched at the extra flesh there. "You big, fat idiot." By the time she was back in her room, her stomach was a pattern of half-moon-shaped cuts—her fingernails doing their work—and she was weeping. *I can't do anything*, she thought. But there was something she could do. She could go to sleep.

She woke to a strange image: the sun projecting the balcony door onto the adjacent wall, so that next to the TV was a shadow door with a distinct three-dimensionality. It looked as if it would open, happily, readily, to a room with a shadow bed and dresser, which would lead in turn to a shadow hall and a whole shadow hotel and island. Charlotte got up quickly, pulled the curtain. The shadow vanished, replaced by a memory—perhaps because she had been dreaming about it?—of herself in sixth grade, on the day of the placement exam for junior high. For weeks, her homeroom teacher spoke of the importance of the exam. In previous years, there had been no test; Charlotte's teachers had known she was smart and simply put her in the most advanced classes. What if she did badly now? Her fear of being placed in a slow class was somehow connected with her homeroom teacher's accounts of junior-high bathrooms. Walk in, and people would stick needles full of drugs into your arms.

Could he possibly have said this? Or shown them, as Charlotte remembered him doing, a film of a woman who'd torn her eyes out on a bad trip? But Charlotte knew he had, just as she knew that all she could think about during the exam were the LSD trips she'd be forced to take. Her hand trembled over the test questions. "Book is to library as cow is to . . ." Who knew? Music raced through Charlotte's ears. Sometimes she heard this same music when she was eating breakfast cereal. It was repetitive and insistent, like a skipped record, only it was silent, a song of impending doom or, Charlotte now suspected, low blood sugar.

So she faked a headache, secured a hall pass for the infirmary. While Charlotte waited for her mom to fetch her, she chatted with the nurse. After some time, Charlotte—so used to confiding in adults, convinced she was grown-up herself—confessed she wasn't really sick, just scared of the exam. The nurse told her she'd have to go back to class then. Charlotte refused, said, "You don't understand anything." When her mother arrived, the nurse told her Charlotte was a rude little girl, that she'd even had the nerve to call her stupid. Charlotte told her mother the true story on the ride home, but—like the nurse; all adult compassion was on holiday that afternoon—she said, "Well, you've learned an important lesson. People never remember what you do right. They only remember what you do wrong. 'The evil that men do lives after them, The good is oft interred with their bones.' Marc Antony in *Julius Caesar*." Then, she added, "I didn't learn it myself till I was in college." Charlotte knew she was supposed to be flattered by this confession. She was learning grown-up things and having grown-up emotions.

Charlotte had wanted to go and apologize to that nurse, but her mother wouldn't let her. Sometimes undoing a fault was as bad as doing it, she'd explained. You had to know when to leave things alone. But this was surely not a skill that Charlotte had developed. Once she was fully awake, she set about proving (for herself, of course; for Howard, too, on some level) that Henry Lazar was no relation to Abe and Hannah.

But no one was home. It took Charlotte too many phone calls—to Hoffman, Goldstein, and others—to figure out the reason. They were all together, at a party for the anniversary of Abe and Hannah Lazar. "Lazar?" Charlotte said weakly, twisting the sticky hotel phone cord around her fingers, "Aren't they . . . ?" and a maid or secretary filled in the blank with some bit of information. Finally, she gave up on the calls. There was no point in trying to reach any Jews today, not even to ascertain whether the Menorah Committee still intended to meet after the party.

There was no getting around it: last night was a doozy, a grand-slam breach of professional ethics. Henry Lazar *was* probably Abe and Hannah's son. If she advised Howard to give the menorah to the Jews, and if people found out about her behavior, she'd be accused of the most slimy sort of favoritism. Of course, who would ever know about her liaison? She didn't think Henry was the type to talk about his sexual exploits. But— well, she didn't know, she didn't know. She stared around her room, its comforts—the large bed, the humming air conditioner, and giant TV—a momentary distraction. It was nice to be in a real hotel room, not the Motel 6s she opted for when she was footing the bill. Still: what now? No Jews to talk to, and she couldn't call anyone at the Bajan Institute or visit the City Archives till business hours. So the synagogue. She would pick up where she'd left off yesterday and try to find the building.

This time, she took a taxi into town. At first, it seemed the elderly cab-driver—a Jehovah's Witness, inclined to an impromptu backseat conversion—wouldn't have any more luck than she in finding the place. He affably suggested other houses of prayer that might serve her as well. Charlotte insisted she had business with this particular edifice and finally handed the driver a tourist flyer with the address. "Deednfait," he confessed, looking at the paper with deep skepticism. "I wouldn't trust such a thing." But a few minutes later he deposited her by the synagogue's wall.

It was different from what she imagined. Smaller and incongruous, perhaps because it was separated from the city by architectural style, as well as by a wall and three scrappy graveyards. The building looked as if it were divinely constructed, not built from the ground up, but descended from the sky. Only there had been a mistake. It had been intended for elsewhere—for a Spanish colony—but as the building fell to earth, there had been a sudden, last-minute twist of the planet, so it ended up here, among Anglicans and Africans.

The synagogue itself was a creamy after-dinner mint of a building, constructed of pink stone with white trim demarcating the floors and highlighting the windows. On the second floor, lancet windows—they looked like popes' hats—topped square-faced frames.

Negotiating the brittle, paltry weeds that thrived in the graveyard's gravelly dirt, Charlotte slowed her pace, as much to combat the heat as to look around. She'd supposed a tropical graveyard would be full of gaudy blooms, but the land here was as unadorned and exposed as a parking lot. Before her, flat, coffin-sized slabs paved the ground. Hurricane-proof headstones. The virtue of Jewish markers: they couldn't be blown over, because they already hugged the earth. Which meant there was a true record to be found here, though not a clue to the menorah's lineage, of course, and even if there had been, it wouldn't have been an easy history to read. Black fungus bloomed from the center of each stone.

Still, Charlotte felt surprisingly reverential, as if she'd come to where she was supposed to be, the place of her forebears, though this was patently not the case. Charlotte wasn't even a Sephardic Jew. In fact, as a girl, in Hebrew school, she'd been jealous of the Sephardic Jews, their elegant Mediterranean looks as compared to her trademark face—the overbite and receding chin (subsequently corrected by orthodontics), the large, pointy nose that she had eventually grown into.

From her morning reading, Charlotte knew that mourners left pebbles as calling cards on these tombstones. But now there were no telltale pebble piles, and there were no flowers. A buff-colored dust coated everything. The graveyard itself seemed dead.

Not that Charlotte usually paid much attention to the commerce of grief and remembrance in Boston cemeteries or, indeed, at Helen's grave. The treatment of the body after death seemed insignificant, though Charlotte sometimes thought of the day when she'd gone with Helen to buy the dress in which she was later buried. This was after Helen's mastectomy but before her cancer spread. The dress was a black knit with royal blue bands at the hemline, neck, and sleeves. A lovely dress, and Helen looked terrific in it, though she only wore it once, to a party for Howard's birthday.

A few weeks after Helen died, a friend told Charlotte that Jews bury their dead in shrouds, since, in the end, everyone is supposed to be equal before the Lord. Charlotte had actually shuddered at her friend's words. A terrible oversight: they had dressed Helen inappropriately for the here-after. (Helen at the Baltimore Symphony, shepherding her family through the audience, stopping to put the back of her hand over her eyes and nod at a garish evening gown in the crowd. "Fashion Don't," she'd said.)

Below Charlotte, everyone in the Barbados soil was dressed for the oc-casion. Fashion "Do's," Charlotte was sure of it. For no particular reason, they felt like friends, all of them, even Benjamin Massia. "Underneath this tomb," his stone read, "lies the earthly remains of Benjamin Massia. . . . He had been reader of the Jews Synagogue for many years without fee or reward and performed the office of circumciser with great applause and dexterity."

"Great applause." Charlotte loved that. She could almost imagine the deceased, under the ground but still enthusiastic, sitting up in their as-signed spots and calling out their praise for Massia's steady hand.

Charlotte guessed that the synagogue would be locked—what with the Lazars' party—but, as she got closer, she saw the front door was ajar. She stepped in hesitantly—wary about trespassing—and her eyes ad-justed reluctantly to the light leaking through the shuttered windows. A stack of tourist pamphlets sat on a small table near the door, but who knew if this meant the place was officially open?

The synagogue had been so pink outside, Charlotte wanted it to feel pink inside, but there was a decided brown cast to everything. The place felt both elegant in its appointments and consciously straining for ele-gance. A balcony overhang, with green latticework, was a disappoint-ment, as was the faux marbling of the supporting pillars. Still, it was cool, cooler than the impossibly hot graveyard.

"Any questions, dahr-lin'?" a voice, throaty and ruined, floated down to her.

Charlotte started, for the room was empty. But then, from the far side of the ark, a hefty white woman padded toward her, feet shushing over the floor's black-and-white squares of marble. She was sixty, perhaps. A squat nose punched into the dough of her face. Thin gray hair pulled back into a bird's nest of a bun. She wore an orange and yellow caftan and a pair of terry-cloth slippers with two smiling chickadees embroidered on top.

"You're . . ." Charlotte didn't think it was polite to ask if she was praying, so she stopped herself. "You're visiting? Or do you work here?"

"Oh, work here, sweetheart. Well, some mornings. We take turns, ever since the restoration." The woman leaned a palm against the back of one of the highly shellacked pews. She seemed to have some respiratory problems or to be struggling with the heat. Her ankles were thick, and her feet, splayed in her slippers, looked as if they were melting.

"I thought everyone would be at the party for the Lazars."

"Oh, sure, dear. Everyone is."

"But, you?"

"Oh, no," the woman shook her head forcefully. "I don't go to parties." She heaved once. Her breasts seemed monumental, how breasts had seemed to Charlotte when she was a girl; edifices that counted for one-quarter of the space a woman took up in the world. When had women changed? Young women didn't seem so heavily burdened anymore, as if within the space of the past two decades, the species had adapted for the rigors of professional life, crowded subways, and pants with suspenders.

The woman coughed, a long, rattly effort. "And you? Why aren't you at the party?"

"Oh, I'm . . . I'm just visiting on business. I heard about the party, but I don't know the Lazars."

"Don't know the Lazars," the woman repeated, as if this were not possible. "You're?"

"Charlotte Lewin. I'm from Boston."

"Oh, Boston," she echoed, as if she knew all about it. Then she collapsed into a doughnut-shaped cushion perched at the end of one pew. "Perle."

"I'm sorry?"

"I'm Perle. Just so you know." There was something brusque in her friendliness.

"I have met Henry though. Henry Lazar." Charlotte almost clocked herself on the head. What was this impulse to say the very thing you didn't mean to say? But that was a disingenuous question. She knew what it was. Despite herself, she wanted to know more about Henry.

"And Josh. You've met Josh?"

"No," Charlotte shook her head. "Who's he?"

"His brother, of course. Hannah and Abe's kids. Josh and Henry. They're not bad kids." Perle added this last bit as if she were contradicting the conventional wisdom.

Perle fished a cigarette holder out of the pocket of her dress. Charlotte had never actually seen one, save in old movies. "Don't worry," Perle said as she placed a cigarette in the holder. "I'm not going to smoke. I'm just going to *dream* about smoking." She pointed the unlit cigarette at Charlotte, "And I thought *you* were from a cruise ship. But, *no*, you must be the one I read about in the whosits, that newsletter, the one who's got the menorah."

Charlotte nodded. "Well, not *with* me."

"Ridiculous," Perle said. Charlotte must have looked offended, because Perle added, "Not you. The types."

"Well . . ." Stuck for something to say, Charlotte gestured to the *bimah*, the reader's desk, and then to the stained-glass Star of David above the highly varnished wood of the ark, "it's a beautiful place."

Perle, apparently weary of compliments about the building, ignored her. "Services are at seven on Fridays. I'm not saying we'll have a minyan. Plenty of times, there's no minyan."

"Well, maybe I'll come," Charlotte offered. "I've been bat mitzvah-ed."

"Oh, they don't care. They won't count women. You can give it a try, but I don't think they'll care."

"Oh," Charlotte nodded again. "Do you know if the Sisterhood is meeting this evening? At the Lazars?"

"You should give it a try," Perle said, ignoring her. Or perhaps she hadn't heard the question. Charlotte noticed the tan plastic comma of a hearing aid nestled in her ear. "I'd like to see that. See how they handle it. Male chauvinist oinks. That's what I call them. Oinks." She coughed, then sucked in air. "It's nice to see a girl who still goes to *shul*," she added, in a softer tone, then leaned over to pat Charlotte's thigh. "Well, you'll come for dinner." It was more of a command than an invitation.

"Oh, that's kind, but I . . ."

"You'll meet Hannah and Abe. You need to meet Hannah and Abe."

The idea of meeting Henry's parents at a social event did sort of appeal. The exhausting flip-flop of her feelings. "Thank you, but I was thinking I might meet them tonight. After the Sisterhood. And I really wouldn't want you to go to the trouble . . ."

"It's not going to be fancy," Perle said sharply, as if Charlotte had assumed far too much. "I'll pick you up. Where are you staying?"

"The Paradise."

"Then, when? Tomorrow? You can come tomorrow? At seven?"

"Seven," Charlotte smiled uneasily. "It'll be a pleasure."

Charlotte felt Perle was dismissing her with the invitation, so she pulled her sunglasses from her straw bag and headed reluctantly back into the heat of the day. A couple, dressed in citrus-colored T-shirts and weighted with shopping bags, ambled toward the synagogue. "Le-on," the woman whined, as if the name were her oldest complaint; would he just hurry up? To avoid them, Charlotte headed to the graveyard that ran along the synagogue's right. There were newer graves here. One looked like a black marble tub filled with cement. Three gray pebbles and half a brick sat on its rim. "Hillel Schumann," another grave read. "Born in Moscow, escaped the Russian Revolution and Nazi execution. Fell asleep on June 17, 1967." Hillel had died the day Charlotte was born. How strange that she should have picked his headstone, out of all of them, to read.

"Sweetheart," she heard Perle call. She turned to see the older woman coming round the building, her body bent painfully over. She was holding out a piece of paper. "Here," she said. "You want to see this?" Perle handed Charlotte a photograph of a young woman on a ship deck.

"Is it you?" There was something about the figure in the picture, the slim-faced woman with the serious expression and incongruous, large flower in her hair, that reminded Charlotte of her grandmother.

"It's me the day I arrived. From Poland. I didn't know a thing. I got off the boat, and everyone was barefoot. I didn't know where I had come to. The Lazars took me in."

Charlotte couldn't quite figure out why Perle was showing her this photograph. Was she trying to establish herself and the Lazars as original settlers, good people with the right to have a menorah where they worshipped?

"How did you know them?"

Perle pulled her head back. "What do you mean how did I know them? My sister. How did I know my sister?"

"Hannah's your sister?"

"Of course, who else? Abe? You think Abe's my sister?"

Charlotte laughed. "You know," she said, "you remind me of my grand-mother." But Perle refused to be charmed. She shrugged as if to say, *What's that to me?*

"Well, then," Charlotte handed the photo back to Perle. "I'll see you tomorrow."

"Now I don't live in some fancy area," Perle said, the aristocratic tone of her voice making it clear that she could if she wanted to. "So you don't need to dress. Just come in whatever."

"Okay," Charlotte smiled then turned toward the alley that led to the main street.

By the time she reached the road—Jews' Way, it apparently used to be called—her dress was plastered to her back with a V of sweat. She started to cross for a taxi, its rolled-up windows a sure promise of air-conditioning, when a white truck abruptly turned a corner and clattered past, just miss-ing her toes. Charlotte jumped back, composed herself in time to read the truck's logo: Lazar Bakeries. The truck skidded to a stop at a light. Painted on its rear door was a grinning loaf of bread with stick-figure arms and legs. Two curls—to indicate heat or fresh aroma—emerged like worms from the loaftop. "Lazar!" the writing on the truck said. "It's the freshest!" And in the exhaust dirt that had stained the bread black, someone had written, "Eat shit!"

Back at the hotel, there was a package for her: the elephant menorah in a sea of Styrofoam squiggles. Charlotte's fingers swam through the pastel packing, but she could find no letter of explanation. "How-ard," she groaned. Charlotte didn't want the menorah here. It was like traveling with anything of value—the anxiety of worrying about, say, where you were going to store your pearl necklace, wasn't worth whatever pleasure you got out of adorning yourself.

Once she had ferried the elephants downstairs to the hotel safe, Charlotte called her grandfather. As the phone rang, she thought of the time, back in high school, when she'd interned at his office. One day, Howard had called her over for one of his purposeless meetings. He seemed to have a real obsession with detailing the obvious on a large chalkboard, a gray slate so worn with use that Charlotte could never make out the writing on it anyway. His mouth had been chalky that day, and for several days prior to it, two dusty white lines had bisected his lips. Charlotte imagined he had been kissing his own words. But then Howard reached under his desk and pulled out a bottle of Mylanta and swigged. "Ulcer," he burped. Charlotte had said, "Your lips," and he'd pulled out a white handkerchief and wiped his mouth.

"Char-lotte," Pat cried into the phone. "Is it wonderful there?"

"Oh, yes, it's great. Listen, is Howard there?"

"Howard, Howard," she said, as if she were patting down a desk, trying to find an errant piece of paper named Howard. "One sec." She came back and whispered, "By the way, he's doing *much* better."

Then Howard's voice burbled onto the line. "Honey," he said. "Are you enjoying yourself?"

Charlotte said evenly, as if this made sense as a response, "I got the menorah, but I think you forgot to pack a letter."

"Oh, no," Howard said. "No letter. Listen, are you calling from the hotel? The rates are ridiculous. They add on extra charges."

"Well, I'll be quick. I just needed to know what was going on."

"Nothing's going on, sweetheart." Charlotte could picture him: phone pressed between ear and shoulder, one hand on top of his pigeon-gray hair, the other stroking his paunch, lovingly calling attention to the feature that most embarrassed him. "We just thought if we sent you the menorah, you could make the decision about who to give it to, and once you've done that, you could begin to enjoy yourself. No reason to make this all business."

"I can't do that. You know I have no power to do that."

"I give you the power."

"Now I didn't go to law school," Charlotte began, her voice a jokey reprimand—it was too hard to be straightforward with him—"but I'm pretty well certain you can't do that."

"Honey," Howard said, "it's like you said from the beginning. We should just give it back to the synagogue and let them deal with the request from this museum that isn't even a museum."

"It's a museum," Charlotte said. "It's just without walls. One of my best friends directs one in Baltimore. It's perfectly legit."

When Howard didn't respond, Charlotte added, "You know, I *do* enjoy myself when I'm working."

"Oh, sure, sure," Howard allowed, "but everyone needs to relax now and then. In fact, Pat . . ." He coughed, then called out again, "Pat, come tell her what we've arranged."

Charlotte heard a receiver being lifted, then both Pat and Howard's voices faded. "We rescheduled your return flight. To give you another week there. The hotel room's booked through. So you can really vacation after you do your work."

"I don't think," Charlotte said tightly, "that's necessary."

"And your folks send their love," Howard called. "Listen, I've got to go. Have a piña colada. They have great piña coladas there. Or maybe that's Puerto Rico. Well, anyway . . . just telegram us with what you decide, we'll pass the word on to Temple Sinai, and as far as we're concerned, you're through there and can start spending time at the beach."

Howard clicked off. The pleasure of quickly tying things up: perhaps this was what had been behind his saying that he never thought about his brother after he died. *How completely idiotic*, Charlotte thought, and the thought felt like an embrace, as if she were hugging her sister, saying, as she had in fact said in that final hour when the family decided to go—one by one—into her hospital room for a good-bye, "I will think about you every day of my life." Of course, by that point, Helen couldn't hear her— she was never going to hear anything ever again, Charlotte had to keep reminding herself; the simple fact was too impossible to absorb—so Charlotte was really speaking for her own benefit, promising herself that there was still a way that she could do right by Helen, Helen who was doing that breathing—Cheyne-Stokes—that people do before they die. No breath, no breath, no breath, huge breath, so Charlotte found herself holding her own breath and praying that things would just stop already. *Don't go*, Charlotte had thought, and then, in virtually the same moment, *Go. Please, just go.*

"Pat," Charlotte started her objections to this new plan but then realized Pat had hung up, too, and that her voice sounded—as it always did when there was no ear, save her own, to receive it—strange, both wan and eerie, as if it was only another person's body that made her real.

But after a nap—a post-Helen indulgence; she'd never been able to sleep during the day before—Charlotte had a change of heart. True, she didn't like Howard's meddling, but ringing her boss to say she'd be taking an extra week off? That seemed rather grand. *Oh, hold my paycheck, if you like. I've got some business to finish up.* And what would he imagine? That she was in the CIA? Unlikely, but still, the pleasure of creating a mystery, and then just the pleasure of being here, a place where everything was interesting, even if it wasn't pleasing, simply because it was new. And this sense of engagement—even with small things—stayed with Charlotte for the rest of the day, attached itself first to the almond tree by the hotel's entrance—she'd never seen almonds *growing* before!—and then to the cab driver who ferried her from the hotel to the Sisterhood meeting. (He kept quoting a tour book—one that Charlotte had, in fact, read—as if he weren't a man but a tape recorder, and when she said, "Oh, yes, wasn't the Hyde Mill plantation where the Federation Riots started?" he got confused, stopped, then rewound himself till he found a different portion of his interior tape.) And then it attached itself to the Lazars' neighborhood, a gated community of colossal mansions, each with private gates—there not being enough locks, Charlotte supposed, to keep the unruly natives away. She overtipped, in her embarrassment about her destination—no amount of awareness about the island's slave history could make up for this—then started to wonder about Henry, for at the far end of a circular drive, his parents' large Georgian home belied the workingman's manner he'd affected at the bar. So who was he, anyway? (For hadn't he swaggered last night the way people do when they've truly known hard labor?) And finally, as she walked down the dark drive, sandal heels faltering over the impractical white rocks that served as pavement, she allowed herself to be intrigued by the group at the Lazars' front door.

There were three in all, standing in a pie wedge of yellow light. An athletic-looking man (midforties, intense eyes, a Philip Roth-type, handsome actually, but dressed in foolish white bucks and a leisure suit); a woman in a white jumpsuit, substantially bejeweled with clunky bracelet and earrings, a hefty gold belt cinched at the waist and accentuating the bulge of her belly (did she have to be Jewish?); and a short, tan man, dark-haired but balding, a business-like roll to his shirtsleeves as if he'd just come from doing dishes or drowning cats. The three seemed to be departing—two cars, one with the driver-side door open, were parked nearby—though they all faced a figure in the door. From a neighbor's yard, a wolfish chorus of dogs started up, so Charlotte could not guess at the group's conversation till she was upon them.

The woman said, "She should just take the pills." She was holding a prescription bottle toward the door.

"There aren't pills for everything," said the short man by her side.

"Don't I know that," the woman said, not unkindly, then called toward the door, "Abe. Just to sleep, just to sleep, and . . . oh, Jesus Christ . . . we'll come by in the morning."

Through the screen door, a heavyset man in a dark blue suit wagged his head then said, "Thank you, but it's not necessary."

The athletic man was the only one who seemed to note Charlotte's arrival, but he gave her such a reprimanding look as she approached that Charlotte almost stepped back. "I think I've made a mistake," she said, when she was within earshot, though she knew she hadn't. She had heard the woman use Abe's name.

"Can I help you?" the athletic man offered brusquely. Some sort of fluorescent pink fabric was draped over his arm like an oversized waiter's napkin.

"I was . . . I was going to come to the meeting of the Menorah Committee, after the . . ."

"Oh, no," the man said, more gently. He touched her elbow lightly to indicate she should step with him, away from the entrance. "You're?"

"Charlotte Lewin," Charlotte said. "I'm from Boston, from Temple Sinai . . . well, sort of."

"Oh, yes," the man smiled. "I'm sorry for my manner. I thought you might be a reporter. *They'll* be here soon enough, sniffing around. But listen, I'm Marty Berkowitz." He seemed to think the name should mean something to her. He extended his hand to shake hers, a strange bit of formality given he'd already put his hand to her back to guide her further from the door. "I'm afraid there won't be any meeting this evening. There's been a bit of an accident."

"Oh, God," Charlotte said, her sense of panic immediate.

"Their son," Marty said.

Oh, God, I can't, a voice started in Charlotte's head, *I can't.* "Henry," she said.

"No, the other one. Terrible, and well, you know . . ."

"Of course," Charlotte said, "I'm so sorry, I . . ."

"Well, you couldn't know," he whispered, then explained everything. There'd been an accident at the racing grounds. Josh Lazar had parachuted into his parents' party, only his parachute had never opened. He was dead and everyone was in shock. They were just leaving now, having tried unsuccessfully to give Hannah some tranquilizers.

Behind Marty, the wedge of light narrowed and disappeared. The front door closed. Charlotte and Marty would have been standing in darkness if not for the car with the open door, the faint illumination of its interior light. The other two came over.

"I guess we should go," the woman said.

"You did what you could," said her apparent husband. He smiled, then quickly corrected his mouth, as if he were ashamed to have allowed himself a smile at a time like this. Marty quickly explained who Charlotte was.

"Just," the woman said, "just when it seemed he was finally getting himself together, you know?" She shook her head.

Her husband put his arm around her shoulder, then pulled his hand back so he could cover his face. He let out a fast sob. "Jesus Christ, Jody, he wasn't, you know that. He wasn't getting anything together." He wiped his palm over his face, then said, "So . . . if I can find Henry, I'll . . ."

"Right," Marty said tersely. He turned to Charlotte to explain, "The brother. He doesn't know yet."

There was a discussion of who would try to find Henry, and through it Charlotte made out that there had been a fight between the brothers, and Henry—perhaps as a result—hadn't attended his parents' party. No one knew where he was. The woman said that he might have left the island, that he often took unplanned trips, but Marty insisted he hadn't.

"Maybe he's still a duppy," Marty said. "You must have heard that story that's going around." No one spoke, and he added, weakly, as if embarrassed, "Going around with the folk." He waved his hand toward the street, as if "the folk" were all out there. "Mostly," he added, his voice dropping to a sheepish whisper, "going around the bars."

"I think," the husband said flatly, his disapproval apparent, "that Josh is the duppy now."

⌐

The next morning, Charlotte woke to a phone call, and in her brief moment of clarity before she croaked out a froggy hello, she thought, "Let it be Howard."

"Who is this?" a female voice demanded, and Charlotte replied, archly, "Who is *this*?"

"It's Perle Bachman. Charlotte?"

"Yes," Charlotte softened her tone immediately.

"Charlotte, of course, now we have to do dinner another time. Okay?" she demanded.

"Of course," Charlotte agreed and started to say how sorry she was about Josh but Perle cut her off.

"Okay, dear. I'll call you," she promised, then said, as she had the previous day, "You'll have to meet Abe and Hannah. But not now."

"No, of course not," Charlotte agreed, and Perle hung up.

But Charlotte had already met them. The previous night, Marty Berkowitz had offered her a lift back to the hotel, then he'd patted his pants down and realized he'd left his keys inside. So Charlotte had ventured—though no farther than the foyer—into the Lazars' home. And they'd come over, of all things, to greet her.

"I'm terribly sorry," Charlotte had said as she shook Abe's hand, damp with tears, or maybe just sweat. He was a plump man, formally dressed, red silk handkerchief in suit pocket, gold cuff links winking under jacket sleeves. Most of his hair on top was gone, revealing a skull patterned with freckles and moles. There was no likeness at all to pretty-boy Henry.

"Yes," Abe said frankly but with a broad, sociable smile, "we're grieving." He looked down at the floor, bobbed his head a few times.

He was in shock, Charlotte assumed. She wasn't about to judge him for his strange response. But then he pulled Hannah forward. She was thin, flat really. It was almost as if he'd made her materialize, magician-style, from the space behind him. Charlotte imagined their meals together, how she'd fuss and fuss, and then say, after two mouthfuls, "I'm stuffed. You have mine." Her gray hair curled at her ears in small, girlish locks. How surprised she must have been to reach old age; even her neat chin and long, aquiline nose seemed to say how peculiar it was, how she had always been so much younger than this. "Say hello," Abe commanded. Hannah's face was ruined with tears. A cold sore wept at the corner of her mouth. Charlotte couldn't make herself speak. It seemed an invasion even to look at her.

"I've got them. Found the keys," Marty called from somewhere within the house, and Charlotte turned immediately toward the door, as if haste were a politeness under these circumstances.

"I'll get the lights," Abe offered, referring to the white globes that lined the driveway. "So you can see out." Charlotte turned, smiled a thank-you as Hannah flicked a switch behind her husband. Nothing happened.

"They're broken!" Hannah cried tragically. "Now there's something *else* that needs to be fixed." Her voice was half-whine, half-accusation: the impossibility of keeping things up in this godforsaken place.

Abe reached behind her and hit another switch. The white globes came on, lighting the path like a model's runway. Abe rolled his eyes at Charlotte, as if his new acquaintance must understand how it was, how it was to live with someone as stupid as Hannah.

The bit of rudeness stayed with Charlotte all night, after Marty had dropped her off at the Paradise and even into her sleep, where she dreamed not of Abe, but of Henry, rolling his eyes at Helen, who ate cocktail peanuts—bags and bags of them, salt crusting at her lips, fingers slippery with oil—on the wing of a plane. Henry's self-presentation didn't seem so puzzling now. Why not try to be the very thing your parents weren't?

After the early morning call from Perle, Charlotte showered quickly, poured the better part of a bottle of sunscreen over herself and headed downstairs for breakfast. Rejecting an unappealing buffet of cinnamon rolls, limp pancakes, and browning fruit, Charlotte settled into a chair and asked for a cranberry juice.

She stole a newspaper from a neighboring table, and there, on the front page, was the story of Josh Lazar's accident. She read, repelled by her own interest. She was looking, she knew, for what she didn't find: Henry's name. And in lieu of that, some details that Marty hadn't divulged last night. But there wasn't anything, save the newspaper's odd decision to mention that the stunned guests were being served mini-quiches and rum punch at the time of the accident.

A sullen-faced waiter put a glass of juice in front of Charlotte. She looked at him, then grimaced at the paper; she felt some need to have someone else's reaction to the tragedy. But the waiter wasn't getting involved. Charlotte, compelled to say something, asked for a scrambled egg.

Oh, Henry, she thought. She should get in touch with him, express her sympathy, but, of course, she had no idea how to find him. And who knew if this desire was about his needs or her own? She wanted to be able to say, "Actually, my sister . . ." But then Charlotte cut short this line of thinking.

My brother died twelve hours ago. It seemed an impossible thing to have to know, even though Charlotte had once been twelve hours away from Helen's death. Last night, while Henry might have been absorbing the news about his brother, Charlotte was in her hotel room, getting loaded on rum punch. The drinks they'd sent up from the bar had been incredibly strong, and she'd used her brief buzz to garner the courage to call Lawrence, who, luckily, hadn't been home. Then she'd taken off all her clothes, stepped onto the hotel balcony and lay down on the still warm concrete and wept to the regular heave and suck of the ocean. She didn't think anyone could see her. You'd have to be a farsighted flying fish to get a gander, and who cared, anyway, she thought, as she rolled on her back, cupped—it was a habit now—her hand over her right breast, and imagined it gone. The left breast was staying with her—she had a real sense about this—but the right already felt like a detachable part, like Mr. Potato Head's nose.

Now, last night's tears seemed debauched—more so than the drinking and public nudity, if you could call it that. She should pull herself together. Here Henry had a tragedy even more immediate than her own, though thinking that didn't make the tragedy any less, of course, for Helen, who was still dead. That was the impossible thing about grieving. You could (supposedly) resolve your grief, but that didn't bring anyone back. The dead person still had no chance to get over her own death.

A waiter slipped an egg in front of Charlotte. Immediately, she realized she couldn't possibly eat it. Certain foods which she thought she liked—eggs, tuna fish, bananas—would, every now and then, make her feel like retching. She signed the bill and headed back to her room, still thinking she should do something for Henry. But what?

In junior high, Charlotte had a pseudoboyfriend—Steve Myers—who she'd never kissed, but who always asked her to dance during the square-dancing segment of gym class. He was the smartest boy in class, and Charlotte was the smartest girl, so they were competitive in a flirty way. Steve was a popular boy, because he had what Charlotte didn't have—good looks and athletic skill to go along with his intelligence. There was something heroic about him; he had a princely way of defending Charlotte against school-bus teasing—once even punching a boy who'd been shooting pins through a straw at her. One day, and without warning, his father died. Steve was out of school for days, and when he returned, Charlotte did what she always did when Steve missed classes: she collected his homework assignments. This time, she presented them to him with a stack of puzzle books. She had biked to her small town's drugstore to buy them. The ones he liked: word jumbles, crosswords on grayish, insubstantial paper. Choked up, she'd handed them to him and said—she didn't know how to say she was sorry about his father—"I got these for you." It was science class, and the room felt like *it* was breaking into elements. He held out his hand to receive them silently and never spoke to her again.

Remembering Steve now, Charlotte felt the same slap of pain she used to feel, all through high school, when she'd pass him in the halls. He was dating Carrie Loudon by then, and dances were evening affairs that no one with any self-respect attended. She still thought what she used to think when she'd bike by his house and see him shooting hoops alone in his driveway: *I am never going to get over anything.*

CHAPTER SEVEN

Wayne Deare

June 23, 1997

✎❍

T HERE WERE A LOT OF HUMAN WANTS Wayne didn't understand.
The urge to surf on a refrigerator door, say. Or to wear a T-shirt that
said, "A little pussy never hurt no one." But the desire that most eluded
Wayne, the one that made him feel it wasn't enough to get off the island,
he was going to have to get off the planet, was the desire to look at car-
nage. Not that he hadn't checked out a roadside or two when he was traveling, but he did this to reassure himself that nothing bad had happened,
that no one had been hurt, however much their day had been ruined by all
that smashed metal and broken glass.

It was a womanly trait, Wayne was coming to think, this hope that
others weren't expiring in colorful ways. Men, or the men he knew, rev-
eled in the gruesome. Over beers, Trevor and his friends delighted in describing inexperienced scuba divers whose lungs had exploded or bathers
who had exited life as shark food. It was a TV-induced hard-heartedness,
something like disassociation, or it was resignation; if bad things were
going to happen, you might as well have a little fun with them. Either way,
Wayne wasn't interested.

Yesterday, Trevor had run with the others to the corner of the Savannah where Josh fell, but Wayne had held back. Why run if you couldn't
be of help, and if a man fell out of the sky, how much assistance could you
offer? The reports, quickly trickling back from the accident site, made it
pretty clear Josh Lazar had taken care of his future needs. Which is to say,
he'd hit the ground with such force that he'd furrowed out a grave for
himself.

Christ, Wayne had thought yesterday, *Christ Almighty. Don't tell me anymore*. But Wayne wasn't going to avoid the gory details today, for as he and Trevor drove back out to the airport, his brother was eager for confidences. "Oh, you should have seen him, man. Just like a jelly doughnut tossed against the wall."

As the wind through the open windows rat-a-tat-tatted at some bleached newspapers in the backseat, Wayne considered this. Had he ever seen a pastry in just such an unfortunate position?

Trevor said, "His brain coming right out the ear, just oozing out like the . . ."

"What the fuck's the matter with you?" Wayne reached behind him to slap the newspapers down. "I mean . . . it could have . . . it could have been you." Last night Wayne had finally acknowledged this fact: if Trevor hadn't gone along with Desmond's stupid teasing, Josh would never have changed parachutes. If not for that last-minute switch, Wayne would be coffin shopping now.

Trevor shrugged, then said, "Just fall out of the sky like a . . . just fall." He shook his head.

"Did you even hear what I just said?" Wayne asked.

"Man, where you get that?"

"Hello?" Wayne reached over and knocked on his brother's skull. "The switched packs?"

"Oh, I tell you," Trevor swatted at his arm, "if *I* was using that pack, there'd be no problem."

"Right," Wayne said. "On your first jump, you'd have fared better than an expert."

"*And,*" Trevor added, as if he weren't contradicting himself, "you didn't want me to switch. 'Member?" He poked Wayne's arm. "*You* said all the packs was the same."

Last night, in thanks for his brother's life, Wayne had made the customary promise to God: from now on, he would love and appreciate what he had. Now it was all he could do not to start on a litany of complaints. "Well," Wayne said, eager to stop a fight before it started, "a good thing you didn't listen to me." Their mutual jealousies were deep and probably unresolvable. Yet they did have moments when they strayed into something like friendship. At any rate, it was best to be civil. "So, what do you think they'll want to know?" He was talking about the police. Wayne was using a late lunch hour and Trevor was missing an afternoon shift at the hotel so they could drive back to the airport hangar. Everyone who had been at yesterday's jump was supposed to show up.

Trevor shrugged, sullen. When Wayne next looked over, Trevor was pressed up against the car door, his arms crossed, his face contorted with rage. "What you say to him?" their mother used to scold when she found Trevor pouting this way. It made Wayne want to scream. An act, it was all an act with Trevor, an act made easier by the natural contours of his face, for despite his good-time personality, Trevor appeared perpetually forlorn. His irises were oddly placed, too high in the whites of his eyes, so that at rest Trevor had a soulful, hangdog look. It was what, Wayne knew, drew women to him, and each year, there was a new girlfriend, good-hearted and eager to help, ready to get Trevor on track with a job and regular meals. Not that things ever panned out. When their mother was still alive, the girlfriend *du jour* eventually ended up in the family kitchen, listening to her say, "I love him, but, honey, you doing yourself no favor by staying with that boy. He his own-way child." The first time Wayne heard her say this, he'd been shocked, as if his mother had revealed a tightly held secret: the ties between women were stronger than blood.

"I wonder," Wayne said now, "why they didn't just ask Desmond and the pilot. Seems like a waste of time to talk to us all."

"Whatever." Trevor made a show of staring out the window.

Wayne huffed once angrily but kept himself from voicing his deepest complaint, from reminding Trevor that he hadn't come home much during their father's illness.

At their father's funeral, Trevor had said, "Ain't it enough that I here *now?*"

But it wasn't. It was too late. It was worse than too late, for at the ceremony, Trevor, handsomely dressed in his single suit, had made a show of being the good son, seating people and dispensing Kleenex. He'd come for the performance, not the bedpans, and though Wayne knew that this was not laziness or hard-heartedness as much as a well-warranted fear of his father's deathbed disapproval, he couldn't forgive his brother. You only had a person's lifetime to make things right, and Trevor had waited too long.

"You shoulda let me drive," Trevor said.

"Right," Wayne said, tight-lipped. "That would have been a real good idea." Six months ago, Trevor's license had been suspended for driving under the influence. Now, he biked everywhere, and Wayne drove the car that had once been their father's through Barbados's narrow streets.

"Oh," Trevor snapped, "so you going to bring *that* up."

Wayne lifted his hands from the wheel, as if to say, *Okay, you win.*

"Just drive," Trevor commanded, and when Wayne next looked over at him, at the slightly superior attitude he wore as he gazed, purposefully, at the highway's blacktop, he thought, *God, I hate you. I hate, hate, hate you,* and then, with an emotion that owed as much to desperation as to love, *He's the only one I have left.*

Sitting in the same folding chairs they'd occupied on the previous day, the jumpers were subdued. Josh Lazar wasn't inexperienced—one of their own had gone down—and the atmosphere inside the hangar was funereal. Already someone had tacked a Polaroid snapshot of Josh to the wall, and his photo had acquired the same air as all the pictures of the fallen, as if the irony of their early ends was a scrim behind which they had always stood. Cy Lythcott, the owner of the skydiving school, a fit, ex-military man—who kept reminding everyone that the meeting would begin at "thirteen hundred hours"—was getting set to make an address. The group was identical to the one that jumped yesterday, save for the addition of two police officers, standing by the wall, and a single, seated man in a light blue suit, probably from an insurance company.

Lythcott stood and cleared his throat, though there was no hubbub that needed to die down. "We've asked you back today to help us figure out what went wrong yesterday, to help us answer the question that is on all our minds." He paused, then started up again in a tone that was almost ministerial. "How could this have happened?"

The audience answered with something like a communal shrug. Then people piped up with their sense that it couldn't have happened. The equipment had been checked, and, Lord knows, Josh had jumped often enough.

Was there, someone wanted to know, a way to tell if it had been an equipment malfunction? And what about the reserve chute—the parachute that always popped open when the canopy, the main chute, didn't? Why don't you, a different person suggested, examine the parachute?

"Right, man," Trevor whispered, mixing a heightened island patois with a feigned spaciness, a voice he generally reserved for mocking Rasta-farians. "Why I no think that?"

Wayne laughed and stuck out the tip of his tongue and crossed his eyes. It was his I'm-a-bonehead face, an invention that was now two decades old.

Lythcott interrupted the stream of questions to tell what he knew about the accident. This wasn't a case of the reserve parachute and the canopy getting tangled and causing an accident. "That, after all," Lythcott said, "was what killed these men." He paused and pointed to the photographs around him, then shook his head. "It's not an uncommon problem." Wayne noted that he had neglected to mention this yesterday when he was assuring the novices about the safety of the sport. Technically, Lythcott went on, even if Josh had passed out when he jumped from the plane, even if he had been unable—or, for some reason, unwilling—to pull the ripcord, the safety should have floated him to the ground. But neither the original chute nor the reserve had released from Lazar's jacket. "So you have two things that went wrong here," Lythcott explained.

Wayne could see how desperately Lythcott wanted the *sadness* of the death to be separate from the *problem* of the death. If he could make the issue a technical one, emotions wouldn't enter in here, even though some of the gathered men must have been Josh's friends.

"Cy," one of the jumpers raised his hand to ask, "what I want to know is how safe is this operation anyway?"

"Very safe," Cy said quickly. "We're licensed by the . . ."

"I don't care about all that," the jumper interrupted. "How'm I sup-posed to feel safe after this?"

Taz, Wayne's partner from yesterday, joined in. "No disrespect," he said. "But we can't trust this equipment now."

The audience assented and the conversation slipped away from Cy, with each of the regular jumpers expressing their fears.

"This is," Cy said evenly, "a safe operation. It has always been a safe operation."

The talk, which seemed to be sliding toward the hysterical, was all about protecting the self from future harm. Not that this was supposed to be a memorial service, but it made Wayne wonder about the group. Had they all just been chance acquaintances of Josh's?

"Check out the hour," Trevor said. Wayne looked down at his watch. If they didn't leave in five minutes, he'd have to stay late at work. He willed people not to ask more questions, but they went on, repeating, in essence, what had already been asked.

Finally, one of the policemen stepped forward to announce that he'd be taking statements from everyone who had participated in yesterday's jump.

"I gonna," Trevor whispered to his brother, "miss my shift."

Wayne nodded sympathetically. It was their first moment of agreement today, a result of Trevor's almost pathological distaste for authority, an uneasiness that predated his own problems with the law. In the world according to Trevor, hypocrisy and power were one and the same. If you were a teacher, doctor, or policeman, you were constitutionally incapable of telling the truth. You were also probably fat.

"I get a dinner shift if I at the hotel by three." He looked at the long line of men already clustered around the police.

"At the Sands?" Wayne asked.

Trevor nodded.

"So what?" Wayne wanted to say. No one ever ate at the Sands; Trevor was hardly losing tips. "Well," he offered instead, "we can't just run off."

"Why not?" Trevor said. "Who notice?" He jerked his head to the tables. The skydivers were blocking the authorities' view of the brothers.

"Still and all," Wayne said, not wanting to seem like too much of a good boy.

"Give me the keys."

"Are you crazy?" Wayne cupped his hands over the pocket where the keys were, a gesture that struck him, even as he made it, as slightly obscene, as if he stored his balls there. "We'll be out of here soon enough."

"No, we be gone now." Trevor looked like he might stomp his foot on the ground. Did he act like a schoolboy around friends, too? Wayne could imagine him in his school uniform of old, the khaki short pants and matching shirt with maroon highlights at the pocket. Six, maybe seven years ago, at end of term, Trevor had used a black Magic Marker to draw a penis and some grizzled balls on the front of his shorts. Then he'd paraded down Bridgetown's Swan Street, where he had his first run-in with the law: a constable gave him a thorough dressing down, made him go into the bathroom of a Barbecue Barn, turn his clothes inside out, then head home with his seams showing and his pants held up with a piece of rope.

"Come on," Trevor hissed in Wayne's ear.

"No, *you* come on," Wayne said, moving toward the tables where the interviews were taking place and pushing Trevor, lightly, at the back so he would follow.

"This don't business me." Trevor shook his brother's hand away and chucked Wayne in the chest, before he stepped out the room's back door.

Wayne wanted to slug him. Wayne always wanted to slug him, and if he had to confess his life's purest moments of release, it would be those times, in childhood, when he knocked his brother to the floor, straddled him, and repeatedly slapped his face. Not that he didn't feel guilty about this, even today. Wayne's one recurring dream—the only ones that really mean anything, Deirdre insisted—was of a beating session that ended with Trevor's head caving in like an overripe melon.

Now Wayne resolved not to go after Trevor. Instead, he took his place at the end of the line, his mind drifting—to the call he'd make about the menorah if Toni had remembered to leave the phone number he needed on his desk, to the saltfish he should have soaked for dinner—till it occurred to him that Trevor probably knew how to hot-wire a car. His face tightened in anger. What was it to Trevor if they answered a few questions? And then, of course, he saw what it might be: his brother might have something to hide.

Wayne pressed his hand to his gut. *You make me sick*, he wanted to tell Trevor. And he'd mean it. His stomach always seized up when Trevor misbehaved. Mistakes weren't allowed, not for his brother, who was already out of prison on a conditional discharge. And, of course, if Trevor went back to Glendairy, he wasn't going to the section for first-time offenders, as he had two years ago.

Wayne looked about, made as if he were going to the bathroom, then stepped through the back door. Outside, Trevor was sitting on some crumbling steps, his back against a turquoise wall. "Are you in trouble?" Wayne asked.

Trevor dug his heels into the dirt below him, threw up his hands, then said, as if to a member of his audience, that invisible group who held Trevor in such high esteem. "He usually accuse me of something."

"I just want to know what's going on. Why you can't stay in there."

"I told you. It don't trouble me, and I got a job."

True enough, Wayne thought, and that was its own sort of achievement: Trevor had a job and felt some pressure to get to it. "Okay," Wayne walked toward the car. He was probably overreacting. If Trevor had something to hide, why would he come to the hangar in the first place? "You'd let me know if something was going on. Right? I might be able to help."

"I haven't done one earthless thing," Trevor insisted. "I want to go to work so that the Sow Pig don't let me go." Wayne gave a half-laugh, a snort of air through his right nostril. "And she one sow pig. Butt down to here." Trevor bent over and karate-chopped his own ankle.

"I thought the Sow Pig worked at the Imperial," Wayne said.

"She does."

"But you told me you're working at Co-Co Sands today."

"Yeah?" Trevor said and gave him a hard, what's-it-to-you? stare.

"Never mind," Wayne said and walked toward the car. Why was he lying? "Well, come on then," he added, for Trevor was still sitting slumped against the concrete wall.

Trevor stood and ambled over to the car, as if he felt no urgency about the hour now that he'd won the argument. "What's today?" Trevor said over the roof of the car.

Wayne looked at his watch. "June 23rd."

"That's what I thought," Trevor said. "I only got two shifts this week anyway. Two shifts in town. One shift at Imperial." He held up his hand as if to say, *You see. You see how important it is that I work.*

June, Wayne thought, *when had that happened?* Last time he checked, it was May and he was telling himself to get out before hurricane season. But now it was June, the month when the St. Lucy girls' Panama hats, part of *their* requisite school uniform, always mildewed. It had taken him years to figure out why anticipating the end of school was linked, in his memory, with the damp, fungal smell. He realized, with something close to regret, that this was the first June since he'd been a toddler that the month smelled as sweet as the rest of the year.

Wayne had never intended to come back to the island after college, and if his father had been well, he wouldn't have.

After he graduated, Wayne lingered at Tufts, serving as a resident counselor for a year while he took classes in urban planning at MIT. "Your High-ness," the grad students called him, good-humoredly, and it didn't offend, didn't bother him the way schoolyard epithets had. At St. Lucy's Primary, in the years before he'd been admitted to Combermere, Wayne's academic skills had combined with his other unfortunate physical feature—a large birthmark in the center of his forehead—to make him the Swami. The refrain of his childhood: "Let's ask the Swami." For the answer. For the homework. Wayne still sat, à la *The Thinker*, forefinger pressed to his head, though he'd had the birthmark, now a large frown of a scar, removed during his freshman year at Tufts. "What's that?" he remembered schoolmates asking him about the birthmark. He'd laugh as if they were impossibly stupid. "Some fudge got stuck to his face," a boy once said, only to be contradicted by another who'd said, "That's not fudge. That's shit."

Deirdre went from Tufts to MIT, too. She was studying business at the Sloan School. "MIT," Deirdre liked to say, "where the nerd world meets the Third World." It was a more or less accurate description of the school, but not the two corners where Wayne and Deirdre had landed. They both steeled themselves for the comment—if not spoken, surely thought—that they'd only been admitted because of quotas. When the post-college year was up, Deirdre continued on with her degree, while Wayne turned down an MIT scholarship and a paid internship at Boston's Redevelopment Authority. He'd spent a year angling for both, but as soon as he got the offers, his father's lung cancer made its own claims.

Wayne packed his bags, put his futon in storage, and went home to care for his dad. For the whole of the plane ride to Puerto Rico, then Barbados, Wayne heard his father's phlegmy cough and allowed himself to resent the man for smoking all those years. Then, passing through customs, he ordered himself to turn that thought, like the last drop of self-interest sneaking through the faucet, off.

For the stretch of the illness, Wayne struggled to summon up the appropriate emotion for his father, who had never married his mother and who hadn't been around much when Wayne was young. His absence had always seemed ordinary enough. What was strange was the whiny loyalty he'd developed in the wake of his illness and how he'd conscripted Wayne and Trevor's friends to his project of demanding reciprocal feelings from his sons. Now, someone like Deirdre would call and Wayne's father would commandeer the phone, tell her how proud he was of Wayne, knowing that Deirdre would repeat his words later, couple them with some fondness for the father who was able to speak so frankly of his emotions.

Indeed, one night, Deirdre did tell Wayne, "You know, your father really loves you." Then she'd said into the silence of the phone, "Well, maybe he's already told you that."

"No," Wayne said, "he's never said that."

"Well, that's good he finally said it. I mean," Deirdre slowed herself down, "how does that make you feel and all?"

But Wayne hadn't answered. It was impossible to explain.

Wayne's father had lingered into the first months of the new academic year, then died in January. By that time, Wayne felt thoroughly derailed. He couldn't say the idea of school seemed appropriate any longer—how to figure dorm food after spending afternoons making saltfish and mashed breadfruit for his dad?—nor could he imagine talking about the placement of a walkway in relation to a building's windows after he'd watched his father slowly choke to death. Even the Boston internship seemed wrong now, like more of a delay, something preventing him from getting where he really wanted to be—not that he was quite sure, anymore, where that was.

Still, Wayne's vision for himself flickered at the edge of his consciousness. And he was certain of this: he wanted to live in a big city, and Bridgetown didn't qualify.

Once, at Tufts, when he and Deirdre were just walking around the streets by Davis Square—they liked to look into the lighted windows and imagine everyone's life on the basis of their furnishings—they'd ended up at the White Hen Pantry for an evening's supply of junk food. On the walk back to campus, turning off Massachusetts Avenue, a car whizzed by and someone shouted, "Why don't you go back to Africa?" It was shocking, Wayne supposed. People didn't say that sort of thing in Cambridge. Certainly didn't say it in Barbados. But Wayne wasn't shocked.

"Hey," Deirdre said, before Wayne even had a chance to offer a response. "It's Marcus Garvey."

Wayne laughed. "You get that often?" he'd asked, and she'd answered with a story that seemed entirely to miss the point.

"Well," Deirdre said, "once I was on this very corner with Charlie." Charlie had been her sophomore-year boyfriend. Wayne had struggled not to hate him, then had been thrilled when he and Deirdre had broken up. From the beginning, Wayne had loved Deirdre. A problem, since she was never going to love him. And why should she? You could make a cast of Wayne, put two Deirdres inside, and still there'd be room leftover. You didn't want to be so overfleshed in a relationship. It was disgusting. "And we were, you know, kissing." Deirdre kissing Charlie—an entirely unhappy thought. "And a car whizzes by and some frat boy or something shouts out, 'Fuck her or walk.'"

Wayne grimaced.

"Actually," Deirdre said, as if she were reconsidering the whole issue, "it kind of turned me on."

Wayne nodded. He was willing to go wherever she wanted with this. It kind of turned him on, too. He'd wanted to put his palm to her neck, lean down for a kiss. Instead, he said, "Can I have a chip?"

But clearly she hadn't understood why he'd asked her about the "Go back to Africa" comment. In Barbados, one of the constant projects of conversation was to characterize your place, to say something about the island and its inhabitants, to make distinctions between Bajans and Jamaicans and so on. It was the fallout from colonialism or, perhaps, a result of tourism—all those efforts to describe your home for outsiders.

At college, though, people didn't think this way. Everything was a personal anecdote and the project—even when talking about putatively larger things—was self-definition. Another reason Wayne wanted to go back north to a city: the luxurious permission a city gave you to be self-involved.

He has, every now and then, the need for a city. That was what Wayne was thinking as he drove Trevor back to Co-Co Sands in Bridgetown. The line was from Italo Calvino's *Invisible Cities*, a book he'd read twice since he'd returned to the island. In it, Marco Polo tells Kublai Khan of a city where colored threads run between people, describing their attachment: red for anger, blue for love. Or something like that. Wayne had recently dreamed of such a city—its citizens woven into immobility—and could no longer recall if the city he remembered was in the book or from his dream. Nor could he recall whether there was a color to describe the emotion that informed his current silence. But then there would be no point in pushing Trevor for information. He'd only flare up, especially at Wayne's inevitable question: "What have you done?"

So, with a laconic "Later, bro," Wayne dropped Trevor off at Co-Co Sands. Afterward, as he headed for the Bajan Institute, everything he passed felt like a rebuke, a reminder of failures, big and small. Outside the gates of Harrison's, he thought of how disappointed he'd been not to be admitted. Shonya, his first friend at Combermere—a girl; he'd always had a talent for friendships with the opposite sex—had felt similarly disappointed, though she claimed her regrets had nothing to do with Harrison's prestige. The rule: prime ministers went to Harrison's, cabinet members to Combermere. Go to Harrison's and you'd become a doctor or a lawyer. To Combermere, you'd be a businessman. Shonya wanted to be a teacher, so she couldn't have cared less about all that. "I just *hate* Combermere's uniforms," she'd said, and it was true that the girls' lower-school uniforms—stiff khaki dresses with zippers up the front—flattered no one. Shonya was in London now. As was skinny Jude, with his little fuzz of a mustache. His old best friends.

Wayne's car edged along Queen's Park, then passed a house where he and the other fourteen Barbados Scholars had gathered the summer before they left for college. There was something exultant about that fête, unhampered—as even the best graduation parties were—by a sense of sorrow about the future. In those days, Wayne had been jealous of himself. He really had. He'd needed to cut himself off, even from close friends, so he didn't feel so guilty about getting to go to college. He wished he hadn't now. It would be good to hang out with any of the old Combermerians, even to accept their teasing about where school had gotten him. *They'd* done all right for themselves, even without college. He saw John Leeds was reporting for the paper, and Ena Harewood had some administrative job with the government. He'd like to see *her* again. They'd fooled around once, during a class outing to Farley Hill Park, when they'd wandered away from the picnic, through the grand mansion—gutted by fire, a big gray carcass in the middle of woods—and out to a bench that overlooked the eastern hills as they fell away to the ocean. She seemed to accept his advances out of mere curiosity. She was politely distant the next day at school. The only one who ever flirted with him back then was mannish Sara Ishmael, and she flirted with everyone. Only Samuel Sayers, one of the younger teachers, reciprocated. "Oh, sir, sir." Wayne could hear her now, her edgy, insistent mocking. She *was* kind of funny, not that Wayne could remember many of her jokes, save her repeated insistence that if the school would only install a helipad by the cricket field, she'd open a lucrative college for drug pushers. And why not? It was hard to make money on the island.

When he got to work, the peeling front door of the Bajan Institute was a reminder of just how hard. One day, Wayne had offered to paint the door for twenty bucks, and Frank had said curtly, "Don't have twenty extra bucks in the budget." An outright lie. If there was truly no money, where was the $500 bonus going to come from?

"Janice," Wayne called, as he slid behind his desk, "did Toni put that number ... "

"Yes, yes," Janice said. "I *told* you I'd remind her."

Frank and Toni had gone to petition a Parliament member for arts funding. Normally, Janice used their absence to call her boyfriend, but now she was paging through a fashion magazine. She looked up. "Some work! Go have a drink. How come I never get those assignments?" She stood reluctantly and handed Wayne a piece of paper. "Menorah!" it read. "Charlotte Lewin. The Paradise. 654-7894."

Janice pointed to the paper. "Maybe she'll be cute." Wayne smiled involuntarily. "Oh, yes. You're hoping so. Sure enough."

"No, I'm not," Wayne said weakly. He felt as if he were thirteen. Janice was teasing; why did he feel he had to answer? Still, her words made him nervous. He picked up the phone and dialed. "Hi, I'm ..." Janice winked as he tried to explain his purpose to the voice at the other end of the line. But Charlotte Lewin made it easy. She agreed to meet, and to meet early, over at her hotel.

"Sure, a drink. I've been doing research all day, so that'll be a welcome break." She giggled. She sounded like *she* was thirteen. "How will I recognize you?"

"Oh," Wayne coughed, conscious of the low rumble of his voice, "I'm quite tall, so it'll be easy."

"Good," Charlotte said. "That gets me off the hook of trying to describe myself. I hate that."

Me, too, Wayne thought, as he hung up. *Me, too.*

From a distance, The Paradise loomed up like an elegant beachfront highrise, but up close, the famed hotel was a surprise. A big, concrete eyesore, weeping water stains. Everything about it suggested the staticky world of old black-and-white TV shows. There had to be a grand ballroom, elegant as a gym, tucked away somewhere. And institutional china, worn gray at the rims with use. Wayne loped over the red carpet, a long tongue of a welcome mat, and into the lobby, with its sunken lounge and mildewing sectional couches. Modern updates, they were, something to bring the place into the present—the present being, for the hotel's purposes, three decades in the past. Wayne expected to find (*did* find, later) a mirrored ball in the bar. But not before he lingered in the gift shop, among vacation necessities: Alka-Seltzer, Tylenol, gift boxes of rum. He thought to buy a sugar cake, dyed a pistachio red, but his stomach seized at the idea. Sweets. Maybe that was his problem. He should give them up for a week, see how the perpetual cramp in his stomach fared. As soon as he made the resolution, the urge for the sugar cake overwhelmed him. "You're weird as a woman about food," Deirdre once told him after he'd confessed his thenprogram: only juice till dinner.

"It's my stomach," he'd said, hoping she didn't translate stomach, as he did, into bowels. "It gets upset."

"Help you?" a woman behind the cash register offered.

"Just looking." Wayne smiled, and to give force to his claim, he took out his reading glasses and turned to the magazine rack. The volcanic eruption in Montserrat. All the magazines were still running articles on it. All save *Dear Heart.* "Pay My Bills and Have All the Sex You Need" its headline offered. Wayne checked his watch. Five more minutes.

"You sure I can't help you with something," the clerk repeated. It wasn't a question. Wayne could, of course, explain that he was passing time while he waited for someone, but, irked, he looked up, smiled, and shook his head. He fingered a candy bar as if waiting for her to look away, so he could stuff it up his sleeve.

Finally, two minutes before six, he walked upstairs to the bar. It was an extension of the restaurant porch, a roofed-in peninsula that jutted toward the pool. Inside, gray barrel chairs—they would be hard for him to sit in—clustered around the room's low tables.

The exhaustion of a new introduction was upon Wayne as he placed his reading glasses in his pocket and stepped forward. Off to his left, a white woman with long brown hair stood by the bar. A great figure, Wayne could see that right away. She was slim, long-legged, big-breasted but slouched into herself, a posture suggesting lassitude or her crustacean heritage. She was curled as a shrimp. Still, he felt a surge of interest in this encounter.

Before he was two strides into the room, the woman turned and stuck out a hand to introduce herself, but Wayne saw, as her face came into focus, that he already knew her.

"Charlotte Lewin," she said.

"Yes," Wayne stuttered and forgot to offer his own name. "Haven't we met?"

"I don't think so," she said, then blinked, confused, as if she *did* recognize him. "I'm sorry."

"Well, actually," she began, at the same moment that Wayne said, "No, I guess I made a mistake."

They hadn't met. Not really, and there was no guarantee that Charlotte had ever noticed Wayne the way he had noticed her. She was part of the cast of characters in the Mass General waiting room, his ersatz study quarters during the final months of his one-year tenure as dorm counselor. One of the guys on his floor, Paul, had leukemia, and in the weeks before he was transferred to a California hospital, Wayne visited dutifully.

Wayne had barely known Paul before he got sick, but the blowhards on his floor turned cowardly in the face of the illness. They were willing to stand at the edge of the dorm roof and urinate onto the grass below, but they weren't willing to take a subway ride to see their newly bald classmate. Wayne peed indoors and had a tough-skinned, steel-jawed feeling about illness, an emotion that bordered on dispassion. Illness was something you did, like walking and sleeping, but it was also a social activity. Like going to a party. You had to do it right, and so did those around you. This meant that when Wayne showed up at Mass General to find Paul asleep, he couldn't just leave an "I was here" note. So he'd go hang out in the floor's small waiting room. He'd always been good at blocking out noise, and he could do his homework there as easily as at school.

After a few waiting-room stints, Wayne realized what he'd stumbled into: a three-act tragedy suddenly extended to a fourth, then a fifth and sixth act. This went on ad infinitum, as if the performance were a baseball game going into endless extra innings. Things couldn't end till the matter of winners and losers was resolved. Someone had to die or in a clear, unequivocal way, not die.

Family members would drift in and out of the waiting room with their miniature cans of soda—stolen from a refrigerator at the end of the hall. He couldn't help but listen to their stories. Everyone had given up the whispery voices that Wayne associated with bad news.

Charlotte—he hadn't known her name back then—was one of the regulars. A well-groomed, professional-looking woman. The first time he'd seen her, he thought she was an intern, sans lab coat. She was telling someone about a special radiation procedure at the Brigham. After that, he'd see her alone or with her parents or, on occasion, a man whom he took to be her husband before he noticed she didn't wear a ring. There were two others, a generation older than Charlotte's parents—perhaps a great aunt and uncle? Wayne had never been able to pick up all that much about them. What he'd noticed, though, was that Charlotte was eavesdropping, too. Unlike him, she didn't try to conceal her listening. It was as if she thought all talk within earshot was, in some way, related to her. Strangers had a habit of finally addressing her, describing their situation. But when she was drawn into conversation, she had a bird-like manner, a nervous way of trying to console others that could be, he thought, no consolation. There was too much of her own anxiety in it, too much of her need for others to be okay.

Wayne might have forgotten all about her if not for a man he couldn't help but notice. Although the waiting room wasn't used much by patients, occasionally a person tethered to an IV pole would push down the hall to page halfheartedly through the room's ancient *National Geographics*. One day a black, unusually tall man appeared. He had a British accent, but there were traces of the Caribbean—he was probably from St. Kitts—under his Queen's English. Perhaps for this reason, he seemed to

Wayne like a version of himself, but one that had been subject to a child's eraser. A ghost, really, with his bald head and thinned-down frame. Not that there weren't plenty of differences between the men. The patient had clearly been athletic—maybe a basketball player—since he was always being visited by a slew of ceiling-scraper, muscle-laden men. And he was relatively light-skinned, with a round, soft-featured face, unmarred by a scar or the sharp cheekbones that made Wayne look, he was convinced, like the drag-queen version of himself, like Nothing Brancker, since, as Deirdre, aka Pumpkin Johnson, had told Wayne, your drag name was the name of your first pet—and Wayne had never had a pet—followed by your mother's maiden name.

Wayne had nicknamed the patient Me-Self, and when he saw him in the hospital halls, he'd think, *There goes Me-Self*. Me-Self seemed to have been granted Wayne's earliest wish: to be sent to London for school. Wasn't this the unaffordable carrot held out to tempt bright island boys into studying? You were the kind of kid who lined his T-shirt with examination books, padding against the lickings that punctuated your day, or you were the kind of boy whose eyes were on that most elusive prize: the foreign scholarship. Me-Self had had Wayne's early life, the one he was meant to have, and now he was dying so Wayne could finish things off. Once this murderous fantasy was in his head, Wayne couldn't get it out, and he watched Me-Self carefully, without ever making the tautological, or narcissistic, mistake of addressing him.

One day, Wayne, Me-Self, and Charlotte were in the waiting room. A friend (Me-Self's Deirdre?) had been visiting with Me-Self, but she had left the room, and now Me-Self was leaning back in a chair, arms to his chest, as if he were holding together the sides of a smoking jacket. There was something haughty yet elegant in the way he stretched his legs, crossed at the slippered feet, out over the carpet, in the studied way he acted as if he were alone in the room, as if he couldn't be bothered with the polite nod visitors and patients gave each other before they sank back into their own desperate thoughts.

At length, Me-Self stood, apparently ready to make his way back to his room, but the tubing to his IV got stuck under the wheels of his stand. Just as he started to struggle with it, Charlotte stood and said, "Want me to get that?"

The man looked at her with no kindness and said, "I'm not dead yet."

"Sorry." Charlotte sat quickly back down.

You gave the ill their anger. Wayne knew that, even before his father's cancer. Still the remark seemed unusually cruel, perhaps because it assumed Charlotte didn't know anything about it. *It* being illness and death, though, of course, you didn't get to this particular wing of the hospital unless you were well-acquainted with the humiliations of illness and the pain of dying or watching someone die. Did he think she just liked to come here on her lunch hour?

After the man had untangled his IV and left the room, Wayne had wanted to turn to Charlotte and say, "Fuck him," but when he looked over at her, her hand was over her face, and she was crying silently into her palm.

He decided to act as if he had no idea she was crying. "Who are you visiting?" he inquired, though he'd already figured out it was her sister.

"My sister," she said, quickly smearing tears off her face and looking up. "And you?"

"A friend," Wayne said. Then: "That guy was just an asshole."

"Oh, well." Charlotte threw her hand down as if to wave his concern away. It was as if the interchange hadn't bothered her at all. "It's hard to have people *at* you all the time."

Wayne had agreed but thought, *It is?* For that was his wish: to have people, or really a person, at him, at least some of the time. He wanted the claustrophobic feeling that he was loved. Once Deirdre had told him that as far as she was concerned, he didn't want to be loved, he wanted to be under surveillance.

In the hotel bar, Charlotte, perhaps embarrassed by her failure to remember Wayne, played host.

"So, what?" she said, wiggling her fingers playfully. "What should we do?" Her eyebrows raised. "Have a drink here?" Her voice was high and girly. Wayne remembered being surprised the first time he heard it, by how the relative intelligence of her speech was undercut by the voice and a slight lisp. There was something unaccountably slutty about the combination, and it was duplicated in her appearance. Her dress was sophisticated. Right now, she was wearing the sort of slim sheath American women bought at fancy stores—the kind of dress a Bajan woman could sew up for pennies, not that a Bajan woman would go for so unadorned a frock—but she had clipped the front of her long hair back in such a way that it poufed up on top like a little beehive, and the result reminded Wayne of those white girls at Tufts who could make messy hair look like sexual invitation. He didn't think black women had the same latitude. At least he'd always been drawn to women with their hair in neat cornrows, the orderly march of the braids around their heads.

"Or if this isn't good, we can go," Charlotte started.

"No, no, here's fine," Wayne said, and he settled uncomfortably into a chair. He knew—well, he'd been told—that he moved gracefully despite his size, but he always doubted the compliment. He'd snorted with derision when, early in their friendship, Deirdre had said, "Tall's good in a black man. Gives you that sexy, basketball-player kind of thing."

The bar's chairs were so low that Wayne's knees rose awkwardly above him, like a cricket's haunches. He fidgeted, trying to find a place for his shins, then said, "Mind if we sit at the bar?"

" 'Course not," Charlotte said, and they moved to the bar's long-legged stools, trading a view of the water for a view of the bartender.

Not that he wasn't something to look at. All the other hotel employees were wearing standard waiter garb—the black bottoms with the white tuxedo blouse—but the bartender wore baggy pants, and over his broad chest, a yellow and black dashiki. His hair was cropped short and perched on it was a yellow, green, and red cap, patterned with maps of Africa.

Wayne had seen places like this before, where the bartender was a celebrity and, as such, not subject to the same dress code, or even rules, as everyone else. Trevor sometimes talked longingly of owning his own rum shop, a dream that had always seemed, to Wayne, to be about free liquor. But now, as he studied the bartender's hat, Wayne thought perhaps he should reconsider Trevor's hope. Perhaps it was noble, really, a dream of independence. The same, in effect, as Wayne's dream for himself, one that he'd formulated at Combermere when he'd first read William Blake's "Jerusalem"—"I must create a system, or be enslav'd by another man's."

As Wayne was thinking all this, the bartender gave him a quick, complicitous smile and under the shelf of the bar formed an O with the fingers of his left hand and plunged his right forefinger into it. Wayne scowled and turned away. Charlotte, scanning a menu, appeared not to have seen any of this.

"You guys want," the bartender paused, as if trying to think of what he could offer, "something to drink?"

No, Wayne felt like saying, we're here to play rounders.

"Just let me know what you'd like, folks." In the corner, a waitress was dropping bits of batter into hot oil. There were no other customers in the bar. "And help yourself to the fritters and hot sauce. There'll be a run on them later."

Both Wayne and Charlotte bobbed their heads in something like compliance, but neither of them stood. Instead, Wayne used a stiff, unfriendly voice to order—a beer for him, a soda water for her.

When the drinks came, Wayne told Charlotte about the Bajan Institute's mission, then made his pitch for the menorah. A replay of Toni's words from the other day: reclaiming the fruits of Nigel Jones's labor, sharing the candelabra at Hanukkah, and a well-maintained, temperature-controlled storeroom for the object when it wasn't on display. (A lie, that storeroom, but what were the chances she'd look into it?) Charlotte listened attentively, revealing nothing, saying only that she was glad to have the information.

"Any questions?" Wayne asked.

But Charlotte had none, only said that Dundidge sounded like it should be the name of a jam, then, in a rather poor British accent, added, "Oh, have you triiiied the Dundidge plum? I like it even better than the marmalade." Wayne didn't laugh, and in the uncomfortable silence that ensued, he considered telling her how he knew her, bringing up the hospital or asking how her sister was doing, but he held his tongue. He recalled that after they'd talked in the hospital waiting room, he'd felt a passing sexual interest in her. Underneath her black shirt, her nipples had been erect. The room was polar, the air-conditioning on high. Wayne didn't flatter himself, or even Me-Self, so much as to suppose she'd had any feelings for them. Still pressed into the corner of the couch, he entertained the possibility of asking her to join him for a cup of coffee. He might have done it, too, if Charlotte's mother hadn't called from the hall, "Come on. She's awake."

Now, Wayne, stuck for how to continue the conversation, said, "I went to college in Boston." He had the idea their meeting should last thirty minutes, even though their business had only taken five. And, anyway, she might feel favorably about the Bajan Institute's case for the menorah if she was reminded of their connection. Out beyond the porch, a boy was dragging beach chairs into some sort of storeroom below the restaurant. The scrape of metal against concrete offered its own message: day closing down, time to go home.

"Oh, really? Where?" Charlotte asked. But before he had a chance to answer, she said, "So it's there. Maybe we met up there, you think?"

"I was at Tufts, then MIT."

Charlotte nodded. "Oh, I know people who went there." She paused. "But I think I'm a little older than you."

Her words certainly placed her: economically, socially. During Wayne's first days at Tufts, he hadn't understood why, at freshman parties, everyone seemed already to know one another. Or, if they didn't know one another, they had friends in common, even though they hadn't been educated in the same place. It was their prep schools, or the sports leagues they competed in, or their fathers' careers that put them all, sooner or later, in the same place at the same time.

Charlotte threw out a handful of names, all of which rang no bells. They switched to talking about restaurants they liked in the Cambridge area, then movie theaters. It was the same bland conversation Wayne used to have in the Tufts dining hall. A terrible conversation. At its root was the unhappy admission that you and the other person had nothing in common except for a mouth and a pair of eyes.

They were both warmly agreeing that they liked Thai food when Charlotte said, "I *do* know you, you're right. I just can't . . ."

"Could it be . . . I was thinking, Mass General Hospital?" Wayne suggested, as if it was only now coming to him

"You . . ." She hesitated, then Wayne could see her remembering. "Oh, God, yes, *yes*. You were so nice to me that day in the waiting room, when some guy—I can't remember, he snapped at me or something—but, yes, thank you. *Thank* you. I remember being so touched. How could I have forgotten?" She tapped his forearm quickly with her hand.

The bartender interrupted to ask if they'd like anything else. "A white wine," Charlotte said and shifted in her chair to face Wayne more fully, the skirt of her blue dress crawling, as she moved, back along her thighs. Behind her, the bartender winked, once conspiratorially and then elaborately, as if he'd gotten a hair stuck in his eye. Wayne felt in need of a coach. Someone to tell him how to proceed. The setup was all here. They needed to talk. Why not in her room? She'd take him up, fumble with the key, fail to find the light when they entered, turn back (accidentally on purpose) into his arms.

Charlotte interrupted this fantasy to say, "You heard about the accident at the racing grounds?" When Wayne said yes, that he'd been there, that he'd been one of the skydivers, Charlotte wanted to know all about the jump: what had it felt like? had he been scared? Wayne answered with what details he could, omitting only the prejump, swapping-parachutes conversation, which might, if disclosed, turn his petition for the menorah into something it wasn't: an aggressive act against Jews instead of a positive move for his people.

"And the boy who died . . ." Charlotte began.

"Yes," said Wayne. "It's a shame." Wayne could see she was disappointed he had nothing more to offer. Sometimes Deirdre acted the same way: frustrated because Wayne wasn't getting to the heart of the matter, the juicy part of the story that anyone else would tell.

Just then the bartender came over to say, "That accident you're talking about?"

"Yeah?" Wayne said.

"Well, back in the kitchen," he pointed toward the hotel, "on the radio, they're saying it was no accident. They're saying it was murder."

"Excuse me?" Wayne pushed the lobe of his left ear forward, a habit he'd picked up from his brother.

"They're saying someone tampered with that guy's parachute then gave him the old heave-ho."

"Jesus," Charlotte hissed.

"What?" Wayne said, incredulous. "Wait! How could *that* happen? He was the only one in the plane when he jumped. Except the pilot. The *pilot* killed him?"

"Well, I don't know," the bartender allowed. "We'll catch the news." A small TV was perched to the right of the bar's liquor bottles. "Mind?" he said as he turned the set on.

"No," Wayne said, "of course not." The TV sputtered on to a story about the Greenland dump controversy before switching to a piece about Crop Over, then cutting to an *ad* for Crop Over. ("Sweet fuh days," Wayne had been singing to himself for weeks now, adopting the festival's slogan as "the test pattern of his consciousness," a phrase Wayne had picked up from a John Barth novel and one which struck him as pointedly accurate for his own brain, which seemed drawn, at rest, to advertisements for foodstuffs).

"Missed it," the bartender said, going to switch the TV off when the story *did* come on. "Oh, oh," he said, pulling his hand back from the on/off switch, "here you go."

"Murder at the Savannah?" asked a box behind the anchor's left shoulder as the newscast's theme music died down.

"Josh Lazar," the anchor began, cleared his throat, said, "Excuse me," grinned nervously at his error, then stumbled on, "son of prominent local businessman Abe Lazar, was killed two days ago in a skydiving accident. Police are just now beginning to suspect foul play."

The face of Mighty Marty, the party's calypso singer, came onscreen. "Sure," he said, head bobbing at some invisible questioner, "there was some unpleasant conversation on the plane, just before the jump. And two men—one fellow named Trevor, a known ex-con, and the other, I can't say what his name was—but they insisted on switching parachutes with Josh. It's a terrible business, all around."

Wayne put his beer down on the bar. A known ex-con. "Oh, please," he said.

"What?" Charlotte said, but he waved her quiet.

"There had been reports . . ." a reporter started to say, in the crisp, over-enunciated way of her trade, and then her face popped onto the screen. It was Sheri St. John. She'd been a star student, a few years ahead of Wayne at Combermere. ". . . of a fight on the plane." The screen cut to one of the jumpers. Wayne remembered the man, because he'd smelled of patchouli oil, and he'd never known a man to smell of the fragrance. "I wouldn't call it a fight exactly. More like ribbing, you know? All in good fun. One guy teasing another. No problems."

"But," said Sheri, the camera panning back to make it clear she was standing in the Savannah, "some say it was *more* than *good* fun, that Josh was subject to anti-Semitic *slurs* before his un*time*ly death."

A white man came on the screen. Nasal voice. "I heard there was talk of big noses. Stuff like that." His own nose was a honker.

"Well, who's *this* guy supposed to be?" Wayne asked. No words at the base of the TV image identified him.

"Was Josh Lazar's death an anti-Semitic attack?" Sherri asked the TV viewer, and Wayne flashed on the earnest frankness with which (six years ago!) she'd given her valedictory speech, "Christ is as Christ Does," how she'd teared up at her own incomprehensible words. "The police are just beginning their investigation into"—the camera panned portentously over the dried grass of the Savannah, then past the track's rickety bleachers and up to cotton-ball clouds—"what happened two days ago in the skies above the Savannah."

"See," the bartender said, switching off the TV. "Murder."

"That's crazy. Why would anyone want to murder him?" Wayne turned to Charlotte and said, "He was kind of a nothing."

"A nothing?" Charlotte asked, her voice edging into accusation.

"I mean"—Wayne turned to the bartender—"I can't think of anyone who'd want to hurt Josh Lazar."

"Well," the bartender shrugged, "the Lazars," as if that explained it.

"Bro," Wayne said, hands open. An appeal, as if to an old friend, an old friend too feebleminded to have noticed Wayne's earlier archness. "What don't I know?"

"I don't know anything you don't, but that the Lazars own a lot of property, and no one's going to accuse them of being good landlords."

"Um . . . I don't think that's right," Charlotte put in, her manner an odd combination of tentative and know-it-all. "I think they're just in the food business. Bread and flavors."

The bartender seemed surprised she'd add anything to the conversation. He gave her a disparaging look. "Flavors?" he said, as if she were not worth addressing.

"Yes," Charlotte said, apparently unaware of his tone. "Vanilla, chocolate. You know. What you might put in ice cream or pudding."

"I don't know where you get that," the bartender said.

Before Charlotte could respond, Wayne asked, "Well, did the radio say something more than this?" He waved his hand at the TV. "I mean, did they suggest a motive?"

"Yeah, they found something that looks like a swastika in the plane."

"Come on," Wayne said, uncertain if the bartender was simply bull-shitting him now, perhaps getting back at him for his earlier high-handed manner.

"Well, they're not sure. They said it looks like that. But it could just be a dent in the plane."

Wayne laughed. "It could be a swastika. It could be a crack in the side-walk. It could be a flying fish. Who's saying it might be a swastika?"

"Well, the Jews, of course. You think a black man would accuse an-other black man of putting a swastika somewhere?"

Charlotte said, "Well, it could have been a white person who sug-gested it just as easily as . . ."

"Aside from the Jews, there are, maybe, two white people on this is-land," Wayne said, too sharply.

"Well, *that's* a bit of an exaggeration," Charlotte said, and Wayne had to nod, because she was right, and because his shortness had less to do with her statement—even though it did strike him as a stupid thing to say—than with his concern for his brother. *Could* he be mixed up in this?

"So, do they have suspects?" Wayne thought of the way he and Trevor had skipped out on the questioning at the hangar earlier in the day.

"Who you think I am?" the bartender said. "The po-lice?"

"Well, did the radio . . . ?" Wayne began, insistent. He needed *some*one to help him out here.

The bartender shrugged even before the question was out. "Well, it'd have to be someone who was on the plane, no? But the radio talkin' 'bout conspiracy."

Wayne paused. The bartender's slight slip into island dialect, what was that? His real self coming through or sarcasm? Wayne couldn't inter-pret the bartender's story without knowing the answer. His own speech became even crisper. "On whose part? And how did they figure all this out?"

The bartender did a little drum roll on the bar top and said, "I told you all I know," before stepping backward for a ringing phone.

Charlotte turned to Wayne. "You're good with the questioning. Ever consider the law?"

"No, never," Wayne said quickly, thinking of the word *conspiracy*.

Could that parachute exchange in the plane—could it have been some sort of setup? Desmond trading away a chute he knew to be faulty? If so, how much trouble would Desmond have denying everything and pinning the blame on Trevor, a man who'd already done time?

Trevor was not, Wayne knew, capable of murder, even though he'd once put a gun to a man's head. That was what got him sent to prison, two years ago. He'd tried to scare a man into paying the money he owed on some drugs. But Trevor had used an unloaded gun. That's why his sentence was so short. And because he agreed to sober up, though whenever Trevor called Wayne—collect from prison—he always said, "First thing I do when I leave here is have a beer." Still, he'd stayed off drugs, and as soon as he left Glendairy, he found the two restaurant jobs. In the twenty months since he'd been free, he'd worked regularly and kept, more or less, away from his old group of friends, the ones who dragged him into "dis bad business" in the first place.

The bartender went to take an order from a couple who had just entered the bar, and in his absence, Charlotte asked, "Do you think all that could be right?"

Wayne shrugged. "I don't know."

"Well, do you know this Trevor that was mentioned?"

"Oh, yeah, I know him. He's my brother."

"He's? Oh, I'm sorry. I didn't mean . . ."

But Wayne wouldn't let her finish her sentence. "And he'd no sooner hurt a man than levitate through this ceiling." Wayne pointed up at the foolish faux thatch that covered the bar's roof. "It was his partner who wanted to trade parachutes."

"But there *was* a trade?"

"Yeah," Wayne snapped, then said, "Do you mind?"

"Sorry," she said quietly. "I didn't mean anything by it." She took a sip of wine then twirled her glass stem, sending a square of yellow light skittering across the bar top. "Well, who else was there?" she finally asked, as if she couldn't help herself; how could any reasonable person stay off the subject?

"What do you mean who else was there?"

"Yoouu *know*," Charlotte said, tick-tocking her head, "who were the other jumpers? Like was Henry Lazar there or . . ."

"I don't know about any Henry Lazar." But Wayne realized he did. He'd read something in the paper about a Henry Lazar—the man had survived a shipwreck—and once, in the market, Wayne had heard some gossip about Henry Lazar, people saying he was pretending to be a duppy. He didn't know why he hadn't connected those stories with the surfer he'd met on the beach.

"I'm just wondering, if all the skydivers weren't professional, how were they all rounded up and . . ."

"Well, no," Wayne said. He had to get to a bathroom, his guts were exploding, "There was no Henry in the plane."

"That's strange, so, um, why wouldn't he . . ."

The bartender, back from taking an order, was busily shaking up a martini. At a break in Charlotte's questioning—there was, Wayne thought, something relentless about it—the bartender said, "Henry Lazar has disappeared."

"What?" Charlotte said.

The bartender gestured to a bearded man sitting behind them. "My friend Greg says that Henry Lazar has disappeared." Charlotte turned and, unaccountably, gave a little-girl wave to the bearded man. "Greg was playing poker with Henry the other night. Henry left in the middle of the game and never came back. Never went back to his house and never showed at his parents' anniversary party on Sunday."

Wayne laughed. "That hardly sounds like someone who's disappeared." His own brother, Trevor, could be gone for days in this fashion— at some woman's house, or passed out on the beach.

"Yeah, I suppose," the bartender allowed. "But," he held up his finger, as if something had just occurred to him, "it was forty days since he returned from his drowning, so you know what people be saying."

Wayne turned to Charlotte to explain. "A duppy is a ghost, and everyone . . ."

"Oh, I heard the rumor," she stopped him.

"Well, according to the folklore, a duppy haunts the living for forty days, then retires to his grave."

"So if he's a duppy," the bartender put in, "he's in his grave now."

"Or if he's a con man, he knew when the con was up," Wayne said. "Wasn't he using the story to get people to buy him free beers?"

"All I know," said the bartender, "is our island's got its very own Crown Heights."

"What are you talking about?" Wayne said testily.

"Our own little Crown Heights with a tropical twist. Greg says so."
The bartender pointed behind them, but the bearded man was gone.
"Some black folk messing with the parachute, because they'd finally had it
with the rich Jews."

"Excuse me," Charlotte said, as if trying to figure out if she should be
offended.

"Well, then, you're probably Jewish for all I know," the bartender said.

Charlotte gave him a slow look. "I am," she said, then turned to Wayne,
using her shoulder as a fence to close the bartender out of their conversation. The bartender must have recognized the gesture for what it was, for
he said, "No offense, of course," then abandoned his post behind the bar
to go to chat with the unhappy-looking woman by the oil pot.

"So is that an acknowledged source of tension on the island?" Charlotte said. "Blacks and Jews?"

"No," Wayne said, tired before he began. "That guy," he nodded to the
bartender, who was noisily burning his mouth on a hot fritter, "is what
people down here call a mockstick, an idiot. I wouldn't worry about him."

"Still, in light of what he's saying," Charlotte leaned her head to the
bartender, and she let her words turn more formal. They were clearly off
small talk and back to the question that had brought them together. "How
do you suppose the Jewish community would respond to your proposal
about the menorah?"

"You know," Wayne said, "that really doesn't matter to me. What matters to me is what is right." These were Frank's words from the other day,
and Wayne was almost surprised by his unwillingness to continue to try to
charm Charlotte. There was no reason, no professional reason, to antagonize her. In fact, there was no reason to antagonize a person whom—
Wayne had to admit—he still had a vague sexual interest in, even if it
wasn't based on the fabulous connection they were making over drinks.
Back in Boston, Deirdre had accused him of being irritable, sometimes
outright mean, to women who didn't return his affections. Wayne had denied it vehemently, since his relationship with Deirdre was comprised of a
constant playful bickering, but, of course, that only confirmed her theory.

Charlotte was quiet.

"We don't even know if this is an instance of anti-Semitism," Wayne
began.

"But if it were," Charlotte interrupted. She seemed to have an enthusiasm for the possibility.

"Think we niggers hate the Jews?" Wayne said.

"God, no," Charlotte said, drawing her hand back to her pale neck. "No, no, no, I didn't mean to suggest . . ."

Wayne shook his head as if to say it was all right. He recognized her apologetic manner; his liberal friends back in Boston twisted themselves in knots trying to make sure their language didn't offend, and it only made Wayne want to say something offensive himself.

"For a black person to use a swastika," Wayne started, then stopped. "You see, it's obviously a rumor, or you're talking about an anti-Semite with a rather large self-esteem problem."

"You know," Charlotte said pleasantly, "I'm kind of hating this conversation."

Wayne laughed. He was kind of hating it, too—the way they were both on the edge, he suspected, of slipping into the standard arguments. He didn't like the way Jews wouldn't recognize that their persecution belonged, primarily, to another hemisphere and an earlier decade; the way they wouldn't admit that by virtue of the whiteness of their skin they were privileged; the way they wanted to be thanked for "helping" the blacks during civil rights. Still, the whole black-Jewish conflict seemed like a decoy, a way to keep everybody arguing about the wrong thing. Wasn't Barbados evidence that talk could be sweet, people could run around saying, "All Bajans is one," the citizenry could have a reputation for extraordinary politeness, and wealth could still be distributed so unevenly that housing patterns mimicked South Africa, with whites in mansions and blacks in shacks?

"I'm sorry," Wayne offered now. "And, of course, if this were a genuinely anti-Semitic attack I'd be appalled."

"Well, me, too. I'm sorry, too. But basically, I think, we're on the same side. Or mean to be."

Wayne squirmed at this but kept his mouth shut. It occurred to him that lately he opposed whomever he was talking to. Frank and Trevor, earlier today. Just two days ago, in the plane, when Desmond was making fun of the Lazars and their guests, he'd been the defender of the Jews. Here the antagonist. He always thought of himself as so accommodating. When had he changed? He'd spent his boyhood taking on the personality of whomever he talked to. When he was still at Combermere, an anthropologist had come in and named his own behavior for him: code shifting. All the man meant was that Wayne talked in Bajan dialect at home, in crisp British tones at school. All he meant, Wayne thought now, since college had so thoroughly Americanized his speech and manner—why else would he be talking so easily with Charlotte?—was that wherever Wayne was, he was a fraud. "I'm not dead yet," Me-Self had said back in the hospital, but sometimes Wayne thought he was.

CHAPTER EIGHT

Charlotte Lewin

June 23–24, 1997

⤞⟶

I T WASN'T TILL WAYNE JOGGED HER MEMORY that she remembered
everything: how she'd seen him in the waiting room at Mass General,
but also in other places, slinking down the halls or hunched over a plate of
cafeteria food. She'd hardly forget someone that tall, especially since he
was a "wall walker," Helen's term for the hospital employees—invariably
your research-scientist types—who trailed, like spidery bugs, along the
edges of the building's wide corridors, trying not to be squashed. There
were other things: she remembered Wayne's reading glasses. They were
your classic nerd's glasses, rimmed in thick, black plastic, and he aggravated their effect by strapping them to his head with a wide elastic band.
It was cute, in a way, such a contrast to his overwhelming physical presence. He'd taken them off that time when he'd defended her against the
other man's slight. She remembered how surprised she'd been; up till that
moment, she'd thought—she felt some shame in admitting this, even to
herself—that Wayne and the tall, black patient were twins.

"It's been a pleasure meeting you," Charlotte finally said. "But you've
probably had a long work day, and I'm only extending it."

"No problem. It's good to get to talk about Boston."

Charlotte had started to slide off her stool when Wayne said, "Can you
give me an idea of what your plans for the menorah are?"

"No," Charlotte said, her butt hanging in midair. She did not want to
sit back down. "I don't have any final authority."

"Well, here's my number," he pulled out a card. "Business is on the
front. I'll put home on back. If you have any questions or can give me any
sense . . ."

"Of course," Charlotte interrupted him. "Of course." She took the card and straightened to stick it in the pocket of her dress. "Well," she added, apologetic, unsure if Wayne wanted her to continue talking over dinner. She hoped not, though she would have liked to ask him one last question; why had his brother been in jail? "I'd better get going," she offered instead and waved, the kind of baby bye-bye that she'd resolved, hundreds of times, to drop from her repertoire of hand gestures. "See you."

The phone was ringing when Charlotte opened the door to her hotel room. She felt hopeful—her mother? Lawrence?—either would be good, evidence that Charlotte's absence from home hadn't gone entirely unnoticed.

"Marty Berkowitz," the man at the other end announced, and Charlotte wanted to kick the phone. No one would call. Not Lawrence, not her mother, who had once said—she had actually said this—"Well, I love you both, but Helen is my favorite." The mail was a metaphor for everything: you waited and waited, and nothing came.

"Well, hello, I just saw you on TV."

"Yes, the local news," Marty laughed. "I'm famous! But actually that's why I'm calling. What with everything going on with the Lazars, I thought we could talk about the menorah. Save them from having to deal with this matter."

"Sure," Charlotte said. She was surprised that he even wanted to deal with it. "Do you think this is a good time?"

Berkowitz answered as if she were only inquiring after his schedule, "Absolutely, yes, I'm perfectly free. Why don't I come get you in the morning, and you can come out to my house for lunch?"

"Well, sure, if it's no trouble," Charlotte said, liking the idea of getting to see the interior of an island home. "If you were a ghost," Helen used to ask her when they were little, "where would you go?" The answer was always the same: into other people's houses.

"Absolutely, no trouble. Bring a bathing suit if you'd like. I'll get you in front of your hotel at nine tomorrow. Sound good?"

"Yes, yes," Charlotte said, but when she hung up the phone, she admitted to herself that it didn't sound good. When she'd left Wayne, only ten minutes earlier, she'd planned to call Howard and tell him about Josh and the murder assertion and her own sense that another week in Barbados was a mistake. Now she had to play things out for another day. Ironic, she supposed, that the very trip that was meant to get her away from tragedy was leading her right back to it, though how far away did anyone ever get? In high school, when she read newspaper accounts of tragedy, Charlotte used to think, *My death is right here with me*. Such portability, appallingly convenient. Everything else seemed to weigh so much then—her backpack with the day's homework, her body as it rounded itself out—but death was, contrary to all the imagery she'd encountered in English class, the lightest of things. Shuffle to the right or left, and it'd come along.

Of course, the circumstances of Josh's death were so different from Helen's that Charlotte knew she shouldn't be acting like it was all the same thing, part of the same tragedy. After all, it did matter *how* you died. She could picture Josh Lazar spinning to the ground. Evil—that's what he had to think about in his final, terrified moments. Evil—a word that looked storybook absurd, even when you spelled it, as if you didn't truly believe it existed, despite all the evidence to the contrary. And what *had* Josh done? Flapped his arms, as if he could save himself by flying?

"Don't," Charlotte breathed, a command for her psyche, as if death were a flame and she a child hovering about its blue center. And Henry Lazar, where had he gone to? But it wasn't her concern. It wasn't. She flopped back on the hotel bed. Some years back—when she was having trouble resisting her own black moods, her vaguely suicidal thoughts— her mother had told her that she should allow fifteen minutes, at the end of the day, to be sad. Otherwise, she should get on with things. There was no resolving certain feelings; they simply had to be abandoned for a stretch.

Charlotte clicked on the TV: pointless entertainment, a safe place to put her brain for a while. But somewhere after an announcement about Crop Over, and during a description of how to make callaloo, she lapsed into sleep. She woke once to click the TV off, then fell into a dream in which her sister was alive but hideously disfigured. Only Charlotte seemed to notice the transformation. Helen was so oblivious that she was dancing on the back streets of their childhood neighborhood. As she moved, the huge balloon of her head flopped about on a lollipop-stick neck. Around her, monstrous rhododendrons, their blooms a headachy pink, clogged the sidewalks. Gigantic bumblebees—wrapped in yellow-and-black shag carpeting—darted among spongy leaves, their green undersides emitting an acrid smell, as if of burning tires.

Charlotte woke abruptly from the dream and thought, methodically, as if she were the *Wildlife of Omaha* narrator for her own life, *I had a nightmare. It was terrible. Helen was dying.* Then, with the same twitch that woke her from the dream, the same sudden seizure as if the foot of the hotel bed were a mountainous precipice and she had jerked herself back from the edge just in time, *Ohmygod.* She *is* dead.

This waking moment, where her nighttime fears were realized, had happened so often that Charlotte was only surprised by her surprise. And that her unconscious put her through the shock again and again. What was this compulsion to animate the dead? Her interest in the duppy was part of the same desire. It was a fake desire, of course, because you didn't really want *the dead* to come back. You only wanted to want them back.

Looking past the hotel curtains, Charlotte thought about how much atmosphere there was between the island and home. All that sky. It was this sense of space that had prevented her from traveling as a younger woman. Distance scared her. Or used to. Now she didn't care how far she went from the familiar.

Helen had always been adventurous, though. Her junior year of high school, she had gone to London to study music, then traveled east to Vienna during the week of the Chernobyl nuclear disaster. And wasn't the disaster the source of Charlotte's dream? Why else would the vegetation be so outsized? Why else would Helen have been dancing to the tune—Charlotte only remembered it as she thought through the dream; was it a disco-era thing?—"I'm radioactive, radioactive"? When the Lewins speculated about causes for Helen's cancer—for there was no family history—this was what they came up with: the winds must have been blowing toward Vienna that week, the week of Chernobyl.

In the morning, Charlotte waited in front of the hotel. Two red wings of a sunburn heated the backsides of her arms. Somehow she'd missed putting lotion there. Each time an approaching car wasn't for her, she turned and gave the doorman an apologetic smile.

Finally, Marty Berkowitz showed up. He fairly jumped out of his gray

Volvo and instead of shaking her hand, called out, "Got your bathing suit?"

"No. No, I thought . . ."

"Well, run and get it. We'll wait."

Charlotte did as he said, though she didn't really want to go swimming and certainly didn't think it was something she'd want to do in the middle of a meeting.

Back downstairs, Berkowitz ushered her into the passenger seat of his car and enjoined her to call him Marty. In the backseat was a pretty, olive-skinned girl of about six.

"This," Marty said significantly, "is Tatiana."

"Hello," Charlotte said.

The girl didn't respond but reached through a white dress patterned with tiny flowers to readjust what was apparently the uncomfortable elastic of her underwear.

You were given, Charlotte thought, *one of these slightly pretentious, overly feminine names, and, soon enough, you had a personality to match.*

"How old are you, Tatiana?"

"I'm five," the girl said and held up the fingers of one hand. "I have a baby brother. He's two."

Marty said, "Will you forgive me? My wife's out of the country with our son, so I brought Tatiana along. And we have a favor to ask you, don't we?"

In the backseat, Tatiana, well-behaved, nodded. She actually didn't seem pretentious, but rather sweet. *You never did get over your grade-school urge to equate prettiness with meanness*, Charlotte thought.

"We have to buy a microwave," Tatiana said.

Charlotte laughed.

"It's true," Marty admitted. "Ours broke last night, so could we possibly trouble you to come with us to Cave Shepherd before we head home?"

"Sure, that's fine. Cave Shepherd's the department store?"

"You haven't been to Cave Shepherd yet?" Marty seemed amazed. "It's duty-free shopping!"

"Oh, I'm not much of a shopper," Charlotte said, as if apologizing for a lack, though she took this to be a virtue: *Charlotte Lewin treads lightly on the world. Only uses what she needs and remembers to recycle.*

"Oh, me neither. I hate it. Hate it, hate it, hate it. But, you know," he said, mocking himself, "those household needs."

They made the brief drive down the road to Bridgetown, past a street-side row of large red and white poinsettias. Charlotte didn't know why she hadn't noticed the plants on her walk the other day, especially given Bridgetown's surprising lack of vegetation. At the parking lot, Marty hopped out of the car and started walking briskly toward a crowded shopping area. *Men,* Charlotte thought with distaste. A woman would know to slow down for her daughter and guest. "Let's run," Charlotte said to Tatiana, and the two broke into a slow jog to keep up with Marty.

There were far more people in the streets than there had been two days ago, and the sun had a white, stark quality that made Charlotte nervous about the patches of sunburn on her arms. Outside Cave Shepherd, a ragged beggar was yelling into a bullhorn. The sound came out as gobble-degook, though occasionally a word emerged. It was the usual—Christ, blood, your sins—certain kinds of madness having, apparently, no trouble crossing cultures.

Inside Cave Shepherd, it was cool and quiet. A relief, but then Marty took an endlessly long time interrogating a salesman, and Charlotte's sandaled toes—she had a problem with the circulation in her feet—started to blue in the air-conditioning.

While Marty disappeared into a back room to look at some ovens, Charlotte asked Tatiana kid-type questions: "What's your favorite color?" "Do you know how to blow bubbles in the water?" "Have you ever seen *Sesame Street?*"

Tatiana liked yellow, she already knew how to swim, and she loved *Sesame Street.* When she was most sick, Helen took in hours of TV and had decided, finally, that *Sesame Street* was the only thing worth watching. At the end, in the hospital, the TV seemed always to be on, and always to be playing the same commercial of a young man dressed as Abraham Lincoln. He looked uncannily like a boy in college who'd given Charlotte chlamydia. As a phone number flashed on the screen, the actor rapped, "My name is Honest Abe and I'm here to say, five dollars will get you cable every single day." If someone asked Charlotte to draw a picture of the Grim Reaper, she'd have sketched this man and let his sloppily adhered fake beard be the sickle. "I heard a fly buzz" indeed. *Ms. Dickinson,* Charlotte would think as she walked the hospital halls, *I submit to you, Honest Abe.* And yet, she absentmindedly sang the cable jingle all the time. "Shut up," Helen once said, and Charlotte realized, with something close to horror, that she'd been singing out loud. Even in Barbados, the tune was at Charlotte's back—death again, it was right here with her, only now Helen's reproach was part of it.

Charlotte was asking Tatiana what the Cookie Monster's favorite thing to eat was when Marty finally finished.

"Listen," he whispered to Charlotte. "I just wanted to ask you one last favor. Will you sign the duty-free slip so I can get the discount?"

Charlotte hesitated. "I'd rather not."

"Oh, it's nothing. People do it all the time down here. Really. Just sign." He put the slip in front of her.

"But when I leave the country, aren't they going to expect . . ."

"No, no," Marty assured her, "just say you shipped it. I wouldn't ask you to do this if I thought there was going to be a problem."

Unconvinced, Charlotte nodded her head and signed.

As they walked back through the crowded streets to the car, taxi drivers approached Marty as if he were a tourist.

"Taxi, taxi," the uniformed men called.

One driver came right up to his face and said insistently, "Taxi."

"Is it free?" Marty said.

"No free. Taxi," the man replied.

"Oh, well, no then, we can't do that," Marty said and walked on.

"Well," Charlotte offered, feeling like she should say something, "we had a very nice chat about *Sesame Street.* We talked about Cookie Monster and who else?"

Tatiana said, "Oscar the Grouch. Da-dee, do you like Oscar?"

"Of course, I like Oscar."

"And Big Bird. And Maria. Do you like Maria?"

"Yes, yes. Everyone likes Maria. She looks like Mommy. Don't you think?"

"And Bob," Tatiana said.

"I don't like Bob."

"What's wrong with Bob?" Charlotte asked.

"He's too human."

Marty walked faster now, ignoring the taxi drivers as he weaved expertly through the crowd, Tatiana and Charlotte following in the space behind him. Suddenly, he stopped at a fruit stand. He lifted two avocados—they called them pears down here—and put one to his ear, and one to his mouth. "Hello, Ma-mee," he said into the lower avocado, as if he were talking on an old-fashioned phone. "Here," he said and passed the avocado at his mouth to Tatiana. "*You* talk."

"Hello," Tatiana said tentatively than quickly handed the pear back to Marty.

"Okay," Marty said, his tone turning serious, "I've kept you long enough. We'll hurry back to the car."

They pushed through the crowds on Broad Street and then over the bridge and toward the parking lot.

"Look!" Tatiana tugged at Charlotte's hand. A cellophane packet of hamburger meat was floating in the dirty water below.

"Yuck," Charlotte said, again for Tatiana's benefit, but sincere in her disgust. There did seem to be something disturbing about this particular bit of trash.

Marty swooped down to pick up his daughter. He lifted her under the back and knees, as if she were a bride. "What if I throw you in there?" he said, in a mock-monster voice. He swung her toward the river.

"No," she squealed. "No."

Marty gave another swing, up over the guard rail. Then he said, in a saccharine, baby voice, "Of course, I would never do that to you," and placed his daughter gently on the ground.

Charlotte's head ached. She wished she'd rented a car, so she could have skipped this morning's errand and driven out to Berkowitz's place on her own. Not that she thought, as Marty eased into traffic, that she'd be too skilled on these narrow streets, even with one of the toy-sized cars that most people here seemed to drive. Or too good with this driving on the left side of the street business.

Tatiana busied herself in the backseat with a Barbie doll, so Charlotte, feeling she'd more than fulfilled her prebusiness small-talk obligations, said, "Why don't you tell me what you're thinking about the menorah?"

"Oh, not yet," Marty said. "We'll get home, and I'll get my notes. Please. Enjoy the drive."

Last night, with Wayne, the nature of the required small talk was clear, but today she didn't know what to say. Marty was hard to get a line on.

"What do you do for a living?" Charlotte finally asked. The day of the week—for it was a Tuesday—suddenly struck her. Why wasn't he at work?

"Oh, I'm retired."

"But you're so young," Charlotte said, in a voice that turned her disapproval—for she didn't believe in retirement—into a compliment.

"Yes, well, I had early success in business, but it was a rat race, a rat race. Always trying to keep up with this one and that one. I had ulcers in my twenties. I'd been down here once or twice for vacation. I came for a third time and decided I was going to make my home here. I gave up everything for the simple life."

Charlotte said, "So you're not from here originally?"

"God, no," Marty said. "I'm from Toronto, but I was in London before that."

"And what kind of business were you in?"

"A little of this and that. Financial stuff."

This sort of answer irritated Charlotte. It reminded her of junior-high friends who didn't know what their parents did for a living. How was such a thing possible?

"And you've been here how long?"

"Da-dee," Tatiana called from the backseat. "Da-dee."

"Tatiana," Marty said. "Daddy's talking right now." He added, in that same mock-monster voice he'd used earlier, "I'm going to have to spank you if you don't behave. Spank and spank and spank." Then he turned sweet-voiced again, "But I don't know how to spank. Teach me how to spank."

Jesus Christ, Charlotte thought, and looked out the passenger window, as if that would indicate her disapproval.

They had pulled onto a main thoroughfare of sorts and were crossing to the east side of the island. The land along the road was dry, a series of razed sugar fields, separated by orderly rows of evenly spaced cabbage palms. Even the soil here, a potato-skin brown, looked poor and ill-used. They passed an old woman standing next to one of the upended orange crates that seemed to mark countryside bus stops. She was holding an umbrella against the sun; the red of it gave the air around her head a peculiar hothouse glow. There was something in the stony cast of her face that suggested a noble accomplishment: she had waited, she would continue to wait, for the bus, even though it had been rerouted decades ago.

"I do teach a bit," Marty offered finally, returning to their previous conversation. "To keep myself busy down here, I got a Ph.D. In my spare time. Now I do slave history and all that blah-de-blah. At the University of the West Indies." For a man like him, apparently, such endeavors were a lark. Why, he might pick up a handful of these Ph.D.-things!

"I started late. I come up for tenure this year. What a system, a guaranteed job! I tell them, 'This wasn't how we did things when I was in business.' And it's a business, education. Don't let anyone tell you otherwise."

"So," Charlotte said, "what are race relations like in Barbados?"

"Well," Marty said, his answer hardly professorial, "everyone gets along. That's what I teach her." He nodded to the backseat. "We're all the same." He swallowed, then called out, "Tatiana, what do we think of black people?"

Singsong, the girl said, "Most of them are good and some of them are bad."

"And what do we think of Jewish people?"

"Most of them are good and some of them are bad."

"And Christians?"

"Most of them are good and some of them are bad."

"There are Jewish people who are bad?"

"No," Tatiana said.

"I didn't teach her that," Marty said.

"They're all bad." Tatiana giggled.

"Hey, now," Marty chided.

"Soooo," Charlotte said slowly. "What you said on TV about what happened in the plane . . ."

"Well, you didn't ask me what *they* think of *us*."

Charlotte considered this. Hadn't she?

"The blacks think we've got some nerve, talking about ourselves like a minority, because we're Jews. They say we're not recognizing our white privilege."

"Don't they have a point?"

"When it comes to finances, sure, but other things . . ."

"And the news said that a swastika . . ."

"Oh, *that*," Marty said. "*I* told them that, but I wasn't serious. They didn't understand I was being *i*-ron-ic."

Charlotte didn't understand either. Under what circumstances would it make sense to be ironic about a swastika? "And you think . . . you really think someone on the plane killed Josh Lazar?"

"Oh," Marty said, "so you're curious about *that?*"

"Well, who wouldn't be?"

"Who indeed?" He smiled, then said, "We're getting close."

The car was passing though a small settlement of chattel houses. When he was trying to entice her into this trip, Howard had said that what was striking about Barbados was the friendliness and cleanliness of the people. By way of example, he'd cited the colorful, freshly laundered curtains that hung in the chattel-house windows. Even the poorest, Charlotte had been made to understand, took care to keep things nice. And there *was* a festive feel to the colors here, each house wrapped like a gift in exuberant paper, the blues, greens, and pinks of which were set against a rectangle of contrasting color at the windows. But as they crossed the island, it was the poverty of the arrangement, not the colors, that impressed Charlotte. The houses were no bigger than sheds surrounded by rusty tin fences, fruit skins, and sooty old newspaper. Corrugated cardboard had been used to patch holes, and bits of words—information about the contents of the original box—dotted the homes like inelegant spackling.

As they drew closer to Berkowitz's place, though, the houses neatened themselves up, tucked in their shirts, and snipped at the threads dangling from their skirt hems. The fences and garbage dropped away, and the houses seemed to position themselves along a grid and behind short driveways. Things looked almost suburban.

"Tatiana," Marty called, "I'm going to make someone drive in front of me." A red Peugeot appeared out of nowhere and barely missed scraping off the front bumper of Marty's car. "And now I'm going to make that car go in my driveway." Charlotte saw the same red car pull between two square white pillars bracketing a long drive. The car backed up. "And then make that person turn around and go away." The car turned down a separate road also bracketed by pillars.

"There's a hotel up that way," Marty offered, as he pulled down his drive. "The Imperial. People get confused all the time." Most hotels, he explained, were on the western or southern shores. Out here, there were only luxury places, the most exclusive of resorts.

Marty's home was an enormous, flat-roofed place. With its glass bricks, skylights, and odd angles, it reminded Charlotte of the cover of her college architecture textbook. Even the blue of the sky looked like the blue of that book—as if the photographer had overdone things, gone for a bit too much contrast in the darkroom. A thick white fence, overgrown with a delicate vine that sprouted tiny purple flowers, surrounded the yard.

Given the homes they'd just passed, it was impossible not to be disgusted by the grandeur, and yet there was a movie-set elegance to the home that made Charlotte conscious, for the first time all day, of the length of her legs and the stretch of her arms in her sleeveless blue shift—the same outfit she'd worn last night. She was grateful for the stylish cut of the dress, and for her relative slimness, as it was the kind of home that demanded attractiveness of its occupants.

"I have a house, too," Tatiana cried as the car came to a stop. "Can she see my house? Can she?"

"She has a name," Marty instructed. "What's her name?"

Tatiana clearly didn't remember but Marty persisted, "If you can't call her by her name, how can you invite her to your house?"

"I'm Charlotte," Charlotte said quickly. "And I'd *love* to see your house."

Tatiana pulled Charlotte to the end of the driveway then around to the back of the house. "See," she shouted, and there, by a ceramic-tiled patio, was a miniature version of the large house. Le Corbusier for Lilliputians.

"What's over here?" Charlotte asked the girl and wandered away from the toy house to the white fence.

"The sea, the sea," Tatiana cried, and once she was right up against the fence, Charlotte could see the girl was right. Water surrounded the house on three sides, as if the grounds were at the very corner of the island, though from Marty's description, Charlotte knew she was at a promontory farther north. "The air," Marty had said, "it's straight from Europe." Clean, he meant, fragrant and light, nothing to pollute it over the Atlantic, but it sounded like he was giving the air airs.

"How do you get down?" she asked the girl.

"There are stairs." Tatiana pointed to the right where the fence broke for a small metal gate. Near it, a white mermaid extended a clamshell tray upward, as if offering the sky a snack. "But you're not supposed to climb over, and you can't go down without Da-dee," Tatiana warned.

"Okay," Charlotte laughed. For some reason, she couldn't imagine wanting to descend. The formidable white house behind her certainly was doing a good job of keeping all worlds—the world of the poor and even the elements—at a distance.

"Tatiana," Marty called. "Come on. We're going swimming."

Charlotte saw Marty round the corner of the house with two Weimaraners. She tried not to react, though she was terrified of dogs. All dogs. Her earliest memory was of pushing a doll in a baby carriage and having the neighbors' mutt bound down the driveway and bite her left cheek. The spidery scar had mostly faded, but when she got too much sun, it emerged, like an asterisk, on her face. She'd had no other bad experiences with dogs but still cowered around them. She was as frightened, now, of her fear, the way her nervousness looked, as she was of the animals.

Marty beckoned Charlotte toward the house, then led her through an airy, white kitchen, dining room, and living room. Even the rugs were white. Just the sort of house people didn't have if they had kids. Tatiana followed, swinging her Barbie doll by the hair. The dogs, two leggy sentinels, kept to Marty's side.

Past several white couches, Marty deposited Charlotte in a dimly lit hallway. He disappeared for a moment, then returned with a towel. "Why don't we have a swim? It'll tire the little one out and then, while she's napping, we can have a chat."

Before Charlotte could answer, a door at the end of the hall opened, and a dark-skinned woman—perhaps she was Peruvian?—stepped out. Dressed in jeans and a black T-shirt, she looked about Charlotte's age.

"An-tee, An-tee, An-tee," Tatiana cried, with sudden despair. She ran over and hugged the woman's thighs tightly.

"I'm going shop-ping," the woman said flatly, and even in the darkness of the hall, Charlotte could make out the quick scowl she gave Marty. There was an edgy silence. Marty made no move to make introductions, and the young woman ignored Charlotte completely.

"Wellll," the aunt said at last, bending to give Tatiana a kiss on top of the head. "I'm going." She loosened Tatiana's arms from her thighs and said, "I'll buy you a treat for dinner."

"Ice cream?" Tatiana said hopefully.

"Yes, if that's what you want, ice cream."

When she was gone, Marty turned to Charlotte and let out an elaborate sigh. He flipped the electric lights on, and Charlotte noticed a vein pulsing in his eyelid like a metronome. She let it beat—one, two, three, four—before asking, as she knew she was expected to, "Are you all right?"

"Well," Marty breathed, as if this were all terribly difficult for him, "I think she'll always blame me for my wife's accident."

Accident? Oh, Christ, Charlotte thought, expecting scary music to start piping from the walls. *I think she still blames me for the accident, the blood drinking, the knife tossing, the sexual torture.*

"Um," Charlotte said cautiously, "what happened?"

"A kitchen accident. Carlotta, my wife. *Her* sister," Marty said and nodded on these last two words toward the front door. "It was years ago. She was browning some garlic in oil. I've always loved that over pasta, and she accidentally hit the fry-pan handle, and the pot went flying up and oil splattered onto her face. She had some bad burns, but she recovered. She's off the island now because she's having some additional plastic surgery. She'll be even prettier than before, and my wife was beautiful. She could have been a model. I always told her that. 'You could have been a model.' But, of course, it's been painful. A terrible thing, and she blames me."

"Your wife does?"

"Oh, no, of course not. *She* blames herself. Thinks this is her punishment for a lifetime of clumsiness, but her sister, who you can see is also vain about her looks"—Charlotte had noticed no such thing—"she thinks it's my fault for liking hot oil on pasta. Perhaps she has a point."

"Well," Charlotte said, "I don't quite see the logic of *that*. An accident, after all." ("If only," Charlotte's mother sometimes said of Helen, "we never let her go to London." But what was the point of that? Helen had loved London. It was—and because there were only twenty-six to pick from it was easy to make this claim—the happiest year of her life.)

"Yes, an accident," Marty mused, as if he were deeply grateful for and surprised by this possible interpretation, even though he'd called the whole thing a kitchen accident in the first place.

"I wouldn't be too hard on yourself," Charlotte said.

"Well, thank you. You're kind. I could tell as soon as I met you the other night that you were a kind person. And maternal. You're good with Tatiana."

Charlotte smiled. This was the sort of compliment she loved, since it confirmed something she secretly believed to be true: she had a talent for empathy, though that talent hadn't done her much good in romantic relations. There, it seemed to her, empathy might be beside the point. The point being—what? She couldn't quite figure it out, always dropped back on some easy generalization about what the culture made men think they wanted out of life, and thus others. Excitement, fun, sex, emotional freedom. Basically the qualities a pinball machine could offer you, especially if you were the kind of person (as Lawrence was) who seemed to hump the machine as you played.

"You want children?"

"I do. Eventually."

"And you'll probably breast-feed, right?"

"I . . ." Was this a normal question? "I suppose I'll see." She looked at the floor.

"Well, there's a room for you to change in back there," Marty said. "And some more towels. We'll meet you at the pool." He pointed out the hall and said, "Thread your way back through the bedrooms and the sitting room. It's at the side of the house."

They spent an hour in the pool, concentrating on Tatiana, having her swim between them. Charlotte felt completely irritated. She shouldn't have to do this. To take any suggestion of intimacy away from the situation, Charlotte focused on the child. Before she'd slipped into the pool, Marty had offered to rub lotion onto her back, and his line gave her the creeps. "Ah, no. I'll take care of that myself," she'd said, crisply, and swiped the greasy bottle out of his hand.

When Marty had decided they'd had enough swimming, he padded back inside with Charlotte and pointed to a shower. He said he'd meet her in the kitchen, they'd have a quick lunch, he'd put the girl down—the phrase made Charlotte think of killing an old racehorse—and then they could talk.

The bathroom was spacious, covered with a deep red tile. In the corner of the room was a clamshell-shaped shower. Groggily, Charlotte peeled off her bathing suit and picked a leaf off her stomach. She was still sunblind, so the room had a strange cast to it, as if it were a browning photograph. She faced the mirror and leaned in closely to study some new freckles on her nose. It was hard to get a clear sight of herself, though she thought the asterisk on her cheek was emerging, making her feel like some giant foot-note for a scholarly text, an extra point about—what? She wrinkled her nose. Her current chlorine-besotted feeling reminded her of girlhood swim practices. Back then, the combination of exercise and an hour's im-mersion in water always gave her the paradoxical feel of being hollow-bellied and drunk.

She moved even closer to the mirror to examine her chin. She had broken out, even here, even with all this sun. Maybe she was getting her period. She leaned forward to squeeze a pimple, though this would, no doubt, make things worse. Behind her, she saw something flash in the window. She turned quickly, but there was nothing there, only the white fence Tatiana had warned her away from and the blue of the sky. And yet, Charlotte felt Marty was watching her. She tightened her bath towel and looked about the room, as if it might offer up a previously unobserved camera.

Ridiculous, she thought. Of course, he's not watching me. This was the kind of bullshit thinking that came from growing up with a TV set in the house. Still, she skipped the shower and dressed quickly, leaving her towel on as she pulled her underwear up, only dropping it as she pulled her dress over her head. And she didn't return to picking at her face, as if a well-behaved woman owed a pervert this politeness.

In the kitchen, Tatiana was running around in a bathing suit, and Marty, a towel wrapped around his wait, was busily making tuna fish sandwiches. It was unclear whether Marty had a suit on under his towel. When she'd first seen him at the Lazars, Marty had struck her as an attractive man; he'd even reminded her of a painter who taught at the Museum School, a man on whom who she'd had a minor crush last year. Now she wondered how she could have thought there was a similarity. The man looked like a frog, only instead of a pulsing at his throat, there was that beating of his eyelid, a flap of skin that was beginning, she thought, to swell, as if the chlorine had aggravated a hidden cyst.

"Which knife would you use for bread?" Marty asked Tatiana, and she pointed to a serrated blade hanging on a magnetic strip near the sink. "And if you were going to cut cheese?" She pointed to a smaller knife and giggled. "And which knife would you use if you were going to be an obstetrician/ gynecologist?"

Charlotte grimaced.

"If you were going to cut your stomach to get out a baby, would you use this knife?" Marty pulled the largest knife off the wall.

"Jesus Christ," Charlotte cried. "Stop that."

Marty looked over, surprised. He put the knife back on the wall. "I'm just playing with her. She's just learned where babies come from." He turned to Tatiana. "How did Ma-mee feed you when you were in her belly? How did she do it?"

Tatiana shrugged.

"How did she?"

Tatiana looked confused.

Charlotte wanted to tell Marty to stop it again, but her situation—for now this definitely seemed like a situation—struck her with some force. She didn't know Marty's address. The neighbors were all far off, and who knew when the aunt would return from her shopping?

"Tell me how she did it," he said again, using the monster voice he had used earlier, "or I'll spank you."

"Umbilical cord," Charlotte answered sharply, suddenly realizing what he was driving at. How was the girl supposed to get it when it took an adult this long? "And I don't think you should make jokes about spanking."

"Oh. I've never hit her," Marty said. "It's just a bit of reverse psychology." He said this as if he were very clever, as if he'd figured out the true and only way to deal with the mischievous mind of a child.

"Well, let's eat," Charlotte said crisply, since Marty had finished laying the table with sandwiches and a salad. The three sat down, and despite herself, Charlotte ate heartily. Marty was polite and solicitous, and Charlotte felt vaguely guilty for having read him as such a sinister character. He was peculiar, no doubt, and it would probably take years of therapy for Tatiana to recover from the damage he was now doing, but he wasn't truly violent. Just as Charlotte was thinking this, Tatiana accidentally knocked over a bottle of salad dressing, and Marty went berserk.

"Look what you've done. Look what you've done," he cried at the mess of glass and French dressing that had managed to splatter itself over a good portion of the kitchen floor.

"It's nothing," Charlotte insisted, reaching for a roll of paper towels on the table. "Here. I'll clean it up."

"Don't step on the floor. Don't step on the floor," Marty almost shrieked.

Tatiana pulled her knees up to her chest, as if this were a game; the white linoleum was the sea, infested with sharks. Marty swabbed with his napkin at the mess of glass and dressing by his own bare feet and immediately cut himself. It was a tiny sliver, but he grabbed the pad of his forefinger dramatically, squeezed a single drop of blood from the wound, and said to Tatiana, "Look what you made me do." The girl looked genuinely terrified.

"Listen, why don't you both keep eating, and I'll clean up. I have shoes on," Charlotte said evenly.

"Yes," Marty said, his voice returning to normal, "*she'll* clean up." It was unclear who he was saying this to, for he didn't seem to be speaking to Tatiana.

Charlotte quickly did as she said she would, using the better part of the roll of paper towels to clean the mess up to Marty's satisfaction.

"It's okay," Charlotte said when she was done, and Marty, as if nothing had happened, asked, "Do you take tea or coffee?"

When the meal was finally over and Tatiana had been sent to her room for a nap, Marty changed into shorts and a T-shirt, then joined Charlotte on a side patio. While Charlotte watched salamanders run up and down Berkowitz's white wall, he explained his feelings about the island's Jewish community. He started off by saying that the Lazars, the standard-bearers of the community, were lovely people, but they were out of touch with the younger, more reform-minded members of the community. Without wanting in any way to offend the Lazars—"The king and the queen," he started to call them and seemed to expect Charlotte to find his sarcasm clever—he wanted to have a place where his children wouldn't be subject to the monarch's rule. "You see what I'm saying?" he asked and continued to punctuate his thoughts with that question, though Charlotte didn't see how there might be any chance for confusion.

"So the menorah . . ." Charlotte began.

"Yes," Marty said. "Well, obviously we have legal rights to it, so there's really no argument."

"But why not share?"

"A holy object. You must understand. You're a Jew yourself. Profane uses. And there's the principle of the thing. After all, Hanukkah commemorates a struggle for spiritual freedom and to say, 'No, what's ours is really yours and subject to your rule . . .'" He shook his head. "You see what I'm saying? It just doesn't make sense."

This seemed to be the whole of his argument. Why hadn't he just told her all this on the phone? A waste of her day.

"You can give it to me, since the Lazars are so . . . indisposed."

Charlote ignored this. "Do you think"—she paused to consider the appropriateness of her next question, then wondered why she cared, given who she was talking to—"that any of what you're saying about the Lazars and their handling of authority, what you were saying before about 'the king and the queen,' explains Josh's death?"

"Oh, still interested in *that?*" There was something vaguely lewd in the question. "Well, sure. You had a known drug dealer on the plane."

"Trevor?" Charlotte said.

"You know him?" Marty asked abruptly, apparently shocked.

"No, the news. You said his name on the news."

"Well, maybe Trevor was trying to extort money out of Josh. That would explain things, wouldn't it? There's certainly plenty of cash in those tight pockets."

Charlotte grimaced, remembered a chubby Jewish kid on her high-school bus. He talked constantly about money. And he'd never lend a dollar. Charlotte had always hated him for confirming the stereotype, hated him more than the boys who asked him, daily, for change for a candy bar.

"You know," Marty said, "it wasn't until I married and had children that I felt so strongly about all this. The Jewish stuff. I have a son by a previous marriage, and he visited here once with his wife and said, 'Dad, when'd you get religion?' And I told him that it was island life. You see what's important once you get down here."

"Do you have the . . . ?" Charlotte tapped her wrist to indicate the word "time."

Marty looked at his wrist and said, "Three. Oh, we have to turn on the radio."

"Excuse me?" Charlotte said, not bothering to keep the incredulity out of her voice.

A radio was sitting on the table behind them and Marty snapped it on. "I always listen to the business news at three." An advertisement for something called Dragon Start or Stout crackled on. "It po-wer-ful," one voice said. "And," added another lecherously, "it dif-fi-cult to control."

"Listen," Charlotte said.

"I can see that," said the voice on the radio, as if he'd just come across two Dragon Stout/Start drinkers fucking.

Charlotte blushed, despite herself. "I should have told you when you picked me up that I had a four o'clock appointment. I didn't know our meeting would last so long."

"Who with?" Marty said, and Charlotte started. He was using the same mock-monster voice that he had with his daughter.

"Mister Berkowitz," Charlotte decided she wasn't going to try to be polite anymore. "That's none of your business."

"Oh, ha!" Marty cried out.

"I'm sorry." Charlotte stiffened. "You've been generous to have me for the swim and the lunch and the last half-hour has been informative, but I'm going to have to ask you to take me back to the hotel."

"Oh," Marty said, using the creepy voice again, "you want me to take you to a hotel room?"

"You know what I meant," Charlotte replied, then fell silent.

"You want me to take you to a hotel room?" Marty repeated.

Charlotte was quiet. When was he going to turn sweet-voiced and deny that he would ever do such a thing?

"You want me . . ." Marty started.

"I'm not going to do this," Charlotte said steadily. "What I want is for you to take me back to the hotel and drop me off at the front door." She couldn't imagine a cab agreeing to come all this way for a fare.

"Before I was married," Marty said, in a normal voice, "I had a lot of one-night stands with younger women, but I don't think that kind of behavior is very fulfilling, do you?"

He's not real, Charlotte thought, and the perception had so much pull on her, it was as if, finally, there had been a crack, a fissure, in the scene before her and now something else—the true world—was pushing itself through. The man was a dybbuk. *That was it*, Charlotte thought. All day she had this vague sense that he reminded her of something, and it was of the play *The Dybbuk*. Marty was relatively normal and then some odd spirit entered him and demanded bad behavior. But he didn't seem to be suffering for it, as the character in the play—the girl who got possessed—had. Hadn't she been killed, in the end, by the thing that entered her?

"Do you? Do you think that's fulfilling behavior?" Marty demanded, this time in the monster voice, and before she answered, he said, in the normal voice, "It just occurs to me. Carlotta. Charlotte. You have the same name as my wife."

Charlotte looked down. *Tous les deux*, she said to herself. *Tous les deux.* She didn't know why.

"You know . . ." Charlotte said, standing.

"Those affairs, the ones I used to have were . . . like my students, that wouldn't be right, an abuse of power but . . . with women about your age." Berkowitz looked down her body as if she'd stood expressly to be examined.

Tous les deux Charlotte remembered—her mind was leaping all over the place now—was the refrain of a mother in Thomas Mann's *The Magic Mountain*. Both of her children—"tous les deux," as she would say to anyone who listened—had succumbed to tuberculosis.

I'm scared, Charlotte thought, and the thought seemed like the single beat of a drum; she didn't let it fill more than a moment.

"Excuse me, I have to go to the bathroom." She turned for the house, looked once over her shoulder to make sure Berkowitz wasn't following, then, as soon as she was out of sight, she fingered the pocket of her dress. The card from last night was still there. With Wayne's home number scribbled on the back. She was conscious of wishing—even now, even frightened—that it was from Henry. But, in truth, she was glad for any number, for she had no idea how to call information in this country.

The phone in the kitchen was too close to the patio, so she headed into the bedroom, the room in which she most didn't want to be found, and pulled out the card. She dialed quickly. When Wayne Deare's voice burbled onto the other end, she started to say, "Hello," but her words—this had never happened to her before—caught in her throat.

"Who is this?" Wayne said angrily into the phone's silence.

"Charlotte," Charlotte coughed out. "Lewin. The woman with the menorah. I need to ask you a favor. I'm visiting this man's house, and I think I might be in a little bit of a situation. He won't drive me back to my hotel, and I think I just might be," she stopped to laugh quickly, as if at her own stupidity, "I might just be a little frightened." She tried to speak casually, in case she had misread Berkowitz's strangeness, but her voice gave her away. It was high and breathy, as it always was when she was upset or sexually excited. "Could you possibly come fetch me?" *Fetch me*, she said, using what she thought might be the correct British word for the request.

"You need a lift?" Wayne said, as if he weren't quite clear on what she was asking.

"Yes, if you wouldn't mind." She was talking as fast as an auctioneer.

"Of course," he said at the same moment she admitted, "I'm not even sure where I am."

CHAPTER NINE

Charlotte Lewin

June 24, 1997

⌒

I N HER ABSENCE, THE DOGS HAD MATERIALIZED. And why not?
Dogs, later rats, they should all show up if this was going to be *her*
nightmare, and there should be boys, too, allowing, with great regret, that
Charlotte Lewin was awfully ugly. Herself a dog.

But when she sat back down on the patio, the animals *didn't* bound forward, gray gums bared for a juicy thigh. Nor did their inquisitive snouts
wander toward her crotch. Their good behavior a reproach: why, the world
wasn't dangerous, after all! They sat, frozen and regal, by Marty's chair,
statues at the entrance to the public library, as ridiculous—even without
ruffled collars or cone-shaped party hats—as any Wegman hound.

"Freshened up?" Marty asked.

"Yup," Charlotte answered tersely. A prehistoric-looking orange sala-
mander scampered by her foot. Marty turned back to the radio, and Charlotte almost said something provocative to confirm her previous impression
or to see how disastrously this might all play out. She was a tub of vanilla
fudge-swirl ice cream, and the chocolate ripples were her self-destructive
thoughts. They were there, all right, but mixed up with the whole thing.
They never took over, just influenced the flavor. But, of course, she wasn't
going to worsen her situation. When you fiddled with your darker urges,
you had to stay in strict control: know exactly which sleeping pill to stop
at, when to turn your gaze from the subway tracks and berate yourself for
self-indulgent melodrama. And, the most important thing: you had to
play by yourself. Others might not understand when things were supposed
to stop.

"I've called a cab," Charlotte imagined herself saying.

And the lie, even in daydream form, made her nostalgic. The old Charlotte, the pre-Helen's-death Charlotte, would have considered it, for before Helen got sick, Charlotte imagined she could eliminate herself without anyone minding. *I don't want to do this anymore*, she'd think during her twenties, and at first she supposed she meant graduate school till she realized she meant life. She wasn't thinking revenge as much as escape. It was when she could imagine that her family wouldn't mind—perhaps they wouldn't notice?—that she supposed offing herself wouldn't matter. Then a doctor put her on antidepressants. This was in the years when the drugs first became so fashionable, almost a joke to take them, though she didn't doubt she needed the prescription. Look down the list of symptoms for depression, and she had every single one. "Anti-bummer pills," she called them; it seemed right to make fun. Not a cure, of course. As the woman outside the Lazars' home had said the other night: *There weren't pills for everything.* Then Helen got sick, and Charlotte's internal opera seemed that much more untenable. By the time Helen died, Charlotte's anti-bummer pills had kicked in. Charlotte was grief-stricken but not depressed. The emotions were entirely dissimilar. But as soon as her depression departed, Charlotte sometimes longed to have it back. The delightful, hysterical extremity of it. The sense that when she was most sunk in it, she was the most herself, the most Charlotte.

"You're not interested in business?" Marty jerked his ear toward the radio. His tone was reasonable: anybody's uncle making polite conversation.

"No," Charlotte said and dropped her sharp tone, "it's only that I have an obligation." She'd have tapped the face of her watch if she still had it.

"Oh, yes, your date," Marty said at the same time Charlotte said, "A business appointment."

She quickly added, "But I'm sure it won't hurt if I listen to a bit of this show with you." She grinned at the radio.

"Hurt?" Marty seemed to be musing over the word, then he said, all in a hurry. "No, I don't think it'll hurt."

Charlotte considered her knees, the pattern of freckles there. She thought if she looked up she'd see that same vein pulsing in Berkowitz's eyelid. "Do you?" Marty asked, in a reasonable tone.

"Um," Charlotte cleared her throat and said vaguely, "Do I what?"

He slipped back into his monster voice. "Do you think it will hurt?"

Charlotte looked away, across the lawn to the mermaid. She seemed different now, like an escapee from a rococo painting, a sloe-eyed cherub, designed to float over frivolously wanton scenes.

"Do you?" Marty repeated, and Charlotte kept her eyes trained on the statue, as if she hadn't heard him. What exactly *was* Marty's relationship to the synagogue? He hadn't been on the Menorah Committee list, so who *was* he? On TV, yesterday, the reporter had identified him as a representative of the synagogue. What did that mean? That he'd gone to services, once, on High Holy Days? And why hadn't she thought to ask all this *before* she stepped into his car?

The doorbell rang out. It was one of those long rings, four elaborate two-belled chimes. Charlotte would have heard it on the patio even if her ears hadn't been straining for the sound. Marty made no move to stand.

"Your door," Charlotte offered, her hand fluttering over her shoulder. It couldn't be Wayne yet, could it? He had said he would check the phone book to find out where she was, so for the last few minutes, she'd been half-consciously imagining his progress across the island: picturing him slipping on his tremendous high-top sneakers, the three key turns it would take to start his car, the traffic that would stall him in Bridgetown. According to her calculations, he was thirty minutes away.

"Oh, I don't answer the door here," Marty allowed mildly. "You never know who's going to be out there."

"Well, then, let me." Charlotte grabbed her bag and turned toward the house and jogged through the kitchen and past the living room for the large white door she'd passed through earlier. She fiddled with a bolt above the doorknob, but it seemed to be sticking. Marty was quickly behind her. She could feel the sweat at his sides, could feel it as surely as if she were in his body.

"Hel-lo," Charlotte sang out, her voice mimicking the earlier chimes. "We're here," she called. "Can't get this door open."

"You know," Marty started to say and Charlotte turned. His face, with its tuna-fish breath, pulsing eyelid, and large red pores, was next to hers. She could smell the hair oil at his scalp, the hot, human scent of him. Charlotte hissed, "I'll scream. I swear I'll scream."

Marty drew back, shocked, as if she'd spoken a line that belonged to another play—a horror story when they were having a polite drawing-room comedy. Was she crazy?

"My Lord," he said quietly. "You're so upset. I didn't mean to upset you. Of course, I'll see who it is."

Charlotte swallowed the apology that rose to her lips. Could she have misinterpreted the whole afternoon?

"I'm sorry," Marty said evenly. "I didn't mean to upset you. This door sticks a bit." He pressed his hip into it, then swung the bolt and pulled the door open. A latticework-covered screen stood between Marty and the outside of the house. For a moment, Charlotte felt a dizzy reluctance to focus on the other side of the screen, for what if it wasn't help—or a FedEx delivery? What if it was the neighbor, who always stopped by around now to join Berkowitz for some afternoon molestation?

"Hello," she finally said, to the two people in front of her, their aspects decidedly benign. A slight, muscular black man and a tiny white woman in chef's whites and round, John Lennon-type sunglasses. The man had the soft, affable face of a child, but he looked sad, as if the heat of the day was wearing on him. His lower lip jutted slightly forward and was shel-lacked with spit.

"Let me get this," Marty was saying, as he struggled with the tiny baby tooth of metal that locked the screen. "There," he said and pushed the door open.

"Trevor Deare," the black man announced, emphasizing the Deare and giving Charlotte an almost apologetic grin. Wayne's brother.

"Yes," chimed the chef, companionably taking the crook of Trevor's elbow, "don't you think he's a *dear?*" She winked at Charlotte, and Charlotte—a determined nonwinker, a hater of winkers everywhere—wanted to lean over and kiss her. A dear. She got it. Trevor Deare was re-lated to Wayne. He was here to help Charlotte, because—

"So, so," Marty crooned, as if the two at the door were old friends. "Come in, come in." Charlotte was baffled by the invitation. Hadn't he called Trevor a murderer twenty-four hours earlier?

The chef let go of Trevor's arm, placed her clipboard by her feet, and bent down into a runner's stretch. First the left leg. Then the right. She jumped up again. "There, that's better." She looked at Marty and said, "We can't come in." She picked up her clipboard. "We're actually looking

for this one." She pointed to Charlotte. "Had to call her hotel and everything to track her down."

"I . . ." Charlotte started, confused.

"Oh, don't even try to deny it," the chef interrupted. The lines of her
otherwise youthful face were so deep that they looked drawn on, as if she'd
decided to go to a costume party as the old version of herself. "We've got
you listed right here." She jabbed the clipboard with her finger. "Charlotte Lewin. Taste of the Caribbean. Fees paid. Well, sure. But does she remember to come? She does not."

Trevor shook his head sorrowfully at this news, then stumbled toward
the chef, as if an invisible hand had shoved him into her.

"I've been cooking all morning, but what does she care?" the chef said,
as she righted Trevor. "*She* figures it's enough that she's *paid* for the cooking demonstration. But"—she stopped, so she could turn and direct her
words to Charlotte—"it's not about money. That's what you tourists can't
seem to understand. It's about art. The Taste, the Taste is . . . it's a belly-
ologist's dream."

"That's what I always say," Trevor added, rather flatly. He smiled at
Charlotte but seemed to miss her face; his eyes lingered somewhere above
her left shoulder. Could he be drunk?

"So," the chef said to Marty, "I have to take your guest away."

"Well, I'm afraid I can't let . . ." Marty began.

But Charlotte cut him off. "Yes, yes. I've been telling Marty I had a
business appointment and he . . . well, not everyone would look at a cooking class as business, but I've always had this fantasy of opening a . . . yes,"
she said. She felt transparent and stupid. This was hardly a good acting
job. "The time got away from me. Please, let's go." She started to push the
door open when Marty leaned over and took her wrist. "I've been looking
forward," Charlotte said sharply, shaking off his hand, the dead-mouse
feel of it, "to the class since I got here."

"But you have time for a drink, no?" Marty appealed to the couple outside. "Why don't you come in for something?"

"Whatcha got?" Trevor asked, stepping forward, but his tone was
lightly mocking.

"For you?" Marty started, and the question sounded like a threat.

The chef gave Trevor a flirtatious slap on the arm. "Thanks, Marty," she said. "You're a pal, but the class was supposed to have started already. She's caused us enough trouble." There was a brief pause, then the chef barked, "Well, come on, already."

"Yes, I'm sorry, I'm sorry." The relief Charlotte felt as she stepped onto the first round stone of the front walkway was immediate. She turned back to the door. "And thank you, Mr. Berkowitz, for . . ." She didn't know what she could possibly thank him for, then saw a bit of lettuce wedged between his upper teeth. "Lunch," she finished.

"You *ate?*" the chef called, incensed. She'd already started to walk toward a car in the drive but turned back for Charlotte's wrist. She gave a sharp tug and Charlotte stumbled after her.

"A pleasure, my man," she heard Trevor say, behind her.

They couldn't have been truly out of earshot, when the chef hooted, like a drunk boy at a soccer game, and said, "I haven't had that much fun in years." Trevor caught up to them, and she threw her arm around his shoulder and laughed. "That was, you have to admit, that was a fabulous performance." She quickly drew her hand back and turned to pull a few limes from a tree that edged the drive. "Need some of these for the ceviche."

"Thank you," Charlotte said, as she climbed into the backseat of the car. "That man was really frightening me."

"I say Hollywood. That's what I say." The chef gave her limes a quick juggle then slipped into the driver's seat. She called out the window, "The Taste! Here we come."

"You must be Wayne's brother?"

Trevor twisted around in the front seat, nodded, and smiled, almost shyly. "Yeah, he said to tell you it take him thirty minutes to get here, so I come help you out."

Wayne looked nothing like his brother. Trevor was at least a foot shorter. Trim, but soft-looking, with a round pumpkin of a face. Charlotte tried to make out the design cut into the gold cap on his front tooth.

"Well," Charlotte started, "this is . . . I really appreciate this."

But no one was going to listen to her gratitude or her story.

As she backed down the drive, the chef said, "Hey, by the way, I'm Trevor's boss. The Sow Pig." She laughed, a slightly hysterical sound that was disarming yet infectious. There was something about her that suggested cocaine addiction—she was altogether *too much* fun—and Charlotte felt ashamed for enjoying her broad manner. "He's harmless," the chef added, turning to cock her chin back toward the house.

"Don't know about *that,*" Trevor put in.

"Well, harmless unless you sleep with his wife. You didn't sleep with his wife, did you?"

"No," Charlotte said. Could it be that neither of them knew what Marty had said about Trevor on the news? "I didn't do that."

"Well, there you go, then. Let's get you something to eat."

Within minutes, the car was pulling into the parking lot of the Imperial Hotel, an elegant pink villa that branched off, in several wings, to hotel rooms. Here was a place, at last, with guests, though they were a dispiriting lot. Under the potted palms of the lobby, all the men looked like cadavers, all the women like Winston Churchill. Outside, by the amoeba-shaped pool, a flock of bald heads, a herd of droopy bellies. One man, facedown on a lawn chair, looked as if he were molting.

The sun ducked behind a cloud, and the bathers shivered in the sudden shade. Now that she was safe, Charlotte was getting the weather to match her experience. And the supporting characters: a woman, skin tightened into a grimace around her skull, pushed her wheelchaired husband up to the snack bar.

Trevor and the chef guided Charlotte past the pool and back inside, up a spiral staircase to a virtually empty restaurant. Bamboo chairs with pink cushions surrounded tables covered with white linen and adorned with pink, tapered candles. All the things people did to console themselves, all the people who would never have the money for even these sad efforts. Sometimes the world could feel like this for days—constructed entirely to stave off terror—and then something would shift in Charlotte, the dread-o-meter clicked off, and everything was okay.

"Wayne say he'll meet you here," Trevor announced before heading for the kitchen. The chef stayed with Charlotte, directing her to a table with a view of the coast. Charlotte sat, half expecting, as she looked out the window, to see a dark moor. Instead, there was an oddly eroded promontory that forced the ocean waves into playful geysers. A submerged giant might have been floating out there, just beyond the rocks, spitting up fountains of sea water.

Charlotte turned to the chef. Now, she thought, was the time to tell her story—she felt a pressing need to do so, as if she couldn't be rid of her fear till she'd narrated it—but the chef still wanted to talk about *her* performance. After fifteen minutes, though, even she had exhausted the subject. She was sitting with one leg tucked underneath her and chewing thoughtfully at the skin around her nails when Wayne found them.

"Well, *here* you are," Wayne called across the now empty dining room. Charlotte had been waiting, she realized, for the chef to ask her a question, and because she hadn't, the two women had lapsed into an edgy silence.

"We've had a little adventure." The chef waved Wayne toward a seat, seemed happy for the new excuse to talk. "God, you're tall," she added. "How tall *are* you?"

Charlotte could see Wayne bristle. He hated her. That was clear. "My brother found you?" he asked, as if the answer weren't obvious. Still, his voice was full of the concern that Charlotte had been wanting from Trevor and the chef. "Are you okay?" he mouthed, as he took a chair. Charlotte *liked* people who asked questions. The simple generosity of curiosity.

"Yes, *thank* you," she whispered back and felt like a gear, *some*thing had snapped into place. They meant more to each other than they had twenty-four hours ago. After all, a favor had been asked for, granted, and accepted. What could be more intimate?

"Wait. Before we tell you, I'll get your brother," the chef said and scurried off for the kitchen.

"Listen," Charlotte said, in her absence. She put her hand on the arm of Wayne's chair. "I can't thank you enough. I may have misread the situation." She stopped and pulled her fingers through her hair, still damp from the pool. "I know given the menorah this might seem like some manipulative sort of . . . but I had your phone number." She patted the pocket of her dress.

"Of course, don't worry yourself. We're old chums, remember? We go *way* back." As Wayne shifted in his chair to say this, his knees knocked the underside of the table. He slammed his palms down to prevent the whole thing from tipping over. "Sorry," he muttered angrily.

Charlotte picked up the toppled candlesticks and an unbroken glass as if she hadn't noticed what caused them to fall. "Well, that's nice of you," she said.

"I know you. I know your sister. I might recognize your parents if they walked in."

Charlotte let out half a laugh. "My sister's dead. I don't know if that happened while you were still visiting your friend."

"No," Wayne said, looking down. "I'm sorry."

"Oh, no, *I'm* sorry. I don't mean to . . . throw that fact in your face, it's only that when I meet strangers, these days, I can barely stop from introducing myself by saying, 'Hello, my sister just died.' So I figured I might as well . . ." She waved her hand to cover the words *tell you*. She meant all this to cement the sudden affection she felt for him, to atone for how crisp she'd been when they parted last night.

Wayne must have understood for he said, "I'm glad you did." He was quiet for a moment then asked, "Well, what happened?"

"She had breast cancer."

"Oh," Wayne said—he sounded apologetic—"I meant with Marty."

"Oh, sorry." Charlotte gave a theatrical grimace, then told Wayne everything, starting with the visit to Cave Shepherd and ending with Trevor and the chef at Marty's front door. Wayne nodded throughout, offering the requisite expressions of shock, interrupting once to say she should have called him sooner.

As Charlotte finished up, Trevor and the chef returned. Trevor put a plate of hors d'oeuvres on the table. "Oh, please," the chef said, as she curled herself back into a chair, "sit down."

But Trevor wouldn't. "Stuffed with . . ." he said, indicating the plate of slim ravioli, "ah, something that went bad in the kitchen."

The chef hit Trevor playfully then said to Wayne, "He calls me a sow pig, you know. He's the worst. The worst. Don't you think?" She focused her attention on Wayne. "Don't you think he's the worst?"

It wasn't a question that admitted of an answer, but the chef seemed to require one. There was a long silence, then Wayne said slowly, "Well, not exactly."

"Sure, he is. The worst."

"I was telling," Charlotte interrupted, "about what happened over there."

"Oh, yes. The *Taste*." The chef started to tell the story again. Behind her, Trevor used his right hand to imitate her yapping.

Charlotte, unwilling to hear the story again, turned to Trevor. "Do you know what that man said about you on TV?" He looked at her blankly. "That you were an ex-con? That you might have killed Josh Lazar?"

Trevor jerked his head back, smiled broadly. "He say that?" He laughed.

"Yeah, little brother," Wayne said. "No one told you?"

But Trevor didn't seem upset at the news. He thought it was funny that Marty should have made such an accusation. The chef seemed to find it similarly humorous, said that she'd known Marty for years—he and his wife were always coming into the bar for supper—and he wasn't anything to worry about.

"That man a bad man," Trevor said but laughed, again, as if the chef was right: he was nothing to worry about. "He involved in all sorts of shit."

"Like what?" Wayne asked.

"How would I know?" Trevor said, defensive.

Wayne stared at his brother. Charlotte thought the two might start to argue, but Wayne said, "Well, you know, I guess I *knew* something was wrong with him. At the party for the Lazars, I remember thinking that I'd heard something bad about him and his wife."

"Oh, ho," the chef cried, as if she had guessed what he was going to say next, but then Trevor shot her a rather withering look, and she clamped her hand over her own mouth and whispered, "Oops," from behind her fingers.

Wayne went on. At the party, before the accident, he'd seen Marty lean lovingly forward to croon into the microphone, had seen him use the microphone cord as an impromptu jump rope (all part of the show), and it was then that Wayne had remembered what he knew about Marty's wife. But it was one of those memories, elusive as any dream, that disappeared the moment he grasped hold of it.

"Then," Wayne said, turning to Charlotte, "you called and"—he clapped his hands together—"total recall."

The story, Wayne said, was simple: boy meets girl, boy gets girl, boy ruins girl. Which is to say, Berkowitz had married some knockout, many years his junior. She was colored, from a wealthy Trinidadian family. Wayne had actually seen her once, bent over the circulation desk at the university library. Wayne had been fingering his way through the soft, yellow catalogue cards, vaguely redolent of jam and soot: all the scholars' hands that had preceded him. His friend Jude came over—from R; *his* book report was on the Roman games—to cluck in Wayne's ear, "Tschk-tschk." He gestured with his eyes toward the counter. There was a woman whispering to the man behind the desk. She had long, thick hair, which she swept over one shoulder in a way that was both dramatic and pretentious. There was something between them—her and this library fellow. Wayne could see that.

And he could see why the library fellow might be interested. In black bike pants and a bright green top that stopped under her breasts, the woman was an MTV girl, sinewy and inclined to postures that displayed her cleavage. "Oh, my, my," Jude allowed, but Wayne guessed he was faking. (He trusted the latest Combermere gossip: Jude was gay; he just didn't know it yet.) But this woman, Berkowitz's wife. Jude knew all about her, said she had several sisters, all pretty, but none quite as . . . he'd waved his hand to indicate *hot,* as if he'd been burned by her looks. And the parents? he continued. Butt ugly. A degenerative bone disease had forced doctors to remove the mother's jaw, leaving her with the lightbulb-shaped head of a skeleton. And the father—a white man—had the liver-spotted, loose-jowled skin of a career drunk. Jude said the mother was crazy jealous of her daughters, but mostly this one. He jerked his chin forward. *She'd* married Marty Berkowitz.

"Well, what's that supposed to mean?" Wayne had said; he didn't know who Marty Berkowitz was, but Jude kept saying, "Sure you do, sure you do. The crazy white man who comes by the back gate?" The back gate at Combermere. At lunchtime, some grandmother sold fried chicken there. It was famously tasty. Now and then, locals even swung by to buy a drumstick and chips.

Months later, in morning assembly, Jude finished off the Berkowitz story, the boy-ruins-girl part: Berkowitz's wife was no longer beautiful, he reported, for her loco husband had thrown hot oil in her face. Burns everywhere, of course, and there would be scars. "Plenty o' disfigurement," Jude pronounced, then added that now that she was spoiled, he sent her on regular trips off the island, back home to her mother's, so he could carry on with whom he pleased. Still, she hadn't pressed charges. No one could figure out why.

"Which is why," Wayne turned to Charlotte to finish off the story, "I called my brother. I figured if Marty planned to heat some cooking oil and start tossing, I'd never get to you in time."

"Which is why he took me," the chef put in. "The famous Sow Pig. On the rescue mission."

Wayne was quiet. And who could blame him? This hardly made sense.

"For pro-tec-tion, brother," Trevor said. "Got it covered. I'm boo-ing. I'm down."

"Cut the homeboy shit," Wayne said.

Charlotte smiled weakly at the chef. She didn't like to be around family squabbles.

"Got it? Get it?" Trevor said, as if to demonstrate Wayne's profound stupidity, his inability to negotiate the real world. And Charlotte, for her part, got it. The Sow Pig was white, and she went in case, later, there was need for a witness.

"I get it," Wayne said, angrily. "Let's . . ."

"Why don't you sit down, Trevor?" the chef interrupted. He'd been standing throughout the story about Marty. "It wouldn't hurt you to, you know, actually look like you're *with* us."

Trevor said he'd sit down if Wayne would shut up about Marty and the Sow Pig would shut up about the Taste. Wayne nodded but slouched back into his chair as if he were above the whole group of them: his jerk of a brother, the motor-mouthed chef and . . . well, who knew how he'd characterize Charlotte? The chef agreed, too, but the concession seemed to deflate her. She said sullenly, "So what'll we talk about now?" There was a long pause, as if they had indeed exhausted all the available topics, but then Charlotte said, "I can't believe that guy is actually a professor."

"A professor?" the chef said. "Marty told you that?" She started to laugh.

"Yes, and he's coming up for tenure. A specialist in slave relations."

"Oh," she composed herself. "That might be true. At UWI, the University of the West Indies. Right here, at the Cave Hill Campus. I shouldn't laugh. But that man doesn't work."

"So . . . ," Charlotte began, but the chef sensed her question.

"He's the heir to some huge fucking fortune, but I guess the terms of the trust are that he has to have a job. I mean, tenure would be perfect, I'm sure, because then he'll have a job, but he can go on permanent leave. I can't imagine they'll give it to him. I don't know how he weaseled his way in there in the first place. But didn't we say we weren't going to talk about him anymore?"

"Oh, yes, yes. I'm sorry."

They were quiet again, and needing something to do, Charlotte reached for one of the ravioli on the table. It was wonderful, some sort of nutmeg wrapper filled with sweet potato paste. "Amazing," she told the chef.

"Yeah," the chef said, matter-of-factly, "I'm fabulous." Then she hit Trevor on the back and said, "Are you *honestly* going to tell *that* story?"

Trevor hadn't looked like he was about to tell any story, but he rolled his eyes heavenward and said, "Nah. Not in mixed company."

"Well, now you *have* to," Charlotte said.

"Come on, come on," the chef added, as if coaxing a cat out from under a bed. "He told *everyone* in the kitchen."

"Is just. I come into work the other day, and the Sow Pig sitting down, having a smoke, when all of a sudden, she jump up, scream, go running to the pool. Jump in with all her clothes. Come back and say," he gestured to her, so she could deliver the final line.

"Never," the chef leaned over the table to confide, "masturbate after cooking with a hot pepper."

"Well," Wayne said, a single word of reprimand, but the chef was laughing, and Charlotte found herself giving Trevor a vague, polite smile.

"I think," Wayne said, "it's time to go."

On the drive back—this time on a curvy road, through lush green hills dotted with chattel houses—Wayne apologized for his brother's story. "Oh, please, it's nothing to apologize for," Charlotte told him, but she saw Wayne thought it was, so she added, "Thank you." They passed a field with men dressed in cricket whites, a roadside fruit stand, a tent under which a predominately female congregation stood swaying and clapping. At one point, Wayne drove so close to the left side of the road that a broad-leafed banana plant reached through the window and slapped Charlotte's cheek. "Terribly sorry," Wayne said, and it took Charlotte a moment before she realized he was still apologizing for his brother.

"Really," Charlotte tried to assure him. "It's okay. I wasn't offended." But Wayne tightened his lips at this and shook his head, a child rejecting a spoonful of medicine. Charlotte's sister had been like this, prudish at times. Or maybe Wayne wasn't being a prude. Maybe it was only that he had already slipped into a role with her, that of protector. Charlotte was someone to be looked after. There was something luxurious and slothful about entertaining such a notion. But Wayne *had* saved her. He'd called his brother. He'd driven across the island to get her. Even if Charlotte had completely misread Marty Berkowitz, Wayne's kindness was undeniable. Charlotte told him so, then felt embarrassed. Was she being patronizing? Would she even wonder this if he was white? "Everyone's a racist." That's what people said, and Charlotte hated the line, but then, wasn't she? If racist meant (and she guessed it did) an unhappy awareness of what the color of one's skin might mean in a social situation? And there was another reason to be ashamed of her compliment, for even as she thanked and praised Wayne, Charlotte was thinking, I *must act aloof, friendly but aloof,* as if aloofness were still necessary given the menorah.

"There, there, there," Wayne shouted, all of a sudden, and slowed the car. He pointed off to the right. "Green monkey."

"Oh," Charlotte cried, but she couldn't see it.

"They're a terrible nuisance," Wayne admitted, as he sped back up, "but I never get tired of seeing them."

"I can't believe I missed it."

"I could take you up to St. Lucy—up where I'm from. You can almost always see one there."

"Oh, no, I think I'd better be getting back."

Finally, they reached the hotel. As Charlotte climbed out of the car— it smelled of something both sweet and unpleasant that she couldn't quite identify—Wayne called, "Wait." He got out himself and went around to his car's trunk. "I brought this for you. From a tree my father planted." He handed her a deep, almost bloody, red mango. This was the sort of thing, she assumed, a real lawyer couldn't accept. Small as it was. And someone helping a lawyer? But she was too tired to consider the implications. Of the fruit, or of the day. Instead, she said good-bye, went to her room, and collapsed on the bed. Then, still lying down, she put in a call to her grandfather. After all, the implications were his job. She was only trying to get some information.

"Charlotte." Howard sounded delighted to hear from her.

"How are you feeling?" She fingered the date book in her purse. She hadn't yet asked Howard to switch her plane flight back.

"I'm feeling great. Tell me about your vacation."

"Grand-pa," she said. "This business about the menorah. I've got into a situation down here. . . ."

"Listen, sweetheart, if it's bothering you, don't worry about it. You call up . . . hold on. I got a telegram the other day." His voice drifted away then came back. "You call a man named . . . wait, I've got it here . . . named Abraham Lazar, say you're the courier for Temple Sinai, give him the menorah and forget about the whole thing."

"Forget about the whole thing? What about the Bajan Institute?"

"You let them make their appeal to the synagogue down there. This has nothing to do with us."

"It doesn't?"

"Doesn't. Never did. We just wanted you to take a vacation."

"*Never* did?"

"Well, okay, sweetheart. It did a week ago, before we had a good look at the contract and a talk with a friend here who specializes in international claims. But there's nothing ambiguous about what *we* should do. What that synagogue down there does . . . well, that's another story."

"I have to tell you. I've made some . . . friends here, so I've done some things that might compromise a legal case, if it came to that."

"Just call Abraham Lazar."

"And I'm not working on any research for you?"

"No, you're not. You're on vacation."

Oh, Charlotte breathed, *I'm on vacation.* "Thank you," she said and felt completely relieved. And ridiculous. This was the gift Howard had tried to give her in the first place. She should have just taken it.

Hanging up after talking with him, though, Charlotte hesitated. It wasn't really such a cut-and-dried case, was it? The Bajan Institute did have a legitimate claim, and maybe she hadn't made that clear to Howard. Certainly the Jews had yet to tell her why *they* felt they had to have the menorah year-round. Perhaps, being Jewish, she was supposed to already know. The Lazars weren't going to want to talk about it now, and she wasn't having anything more to do with Berkowitz. To whom should she appeal? There were other names on the Menorah Committee list, but the idea of calling them, knowing that they might have been close to Josh Lazar . . . it was too much. Perhaps she should have explained all this to Howard. Howard, who had once said something so ugly about the shvartzers on the subway. What was it? Charlotte couldn't recall, only remembered her cringing shame at being related to him, and then her despair at hating someone who had been so generous to her. But her family's limitations were one thing, contract law another. She was off the hook. Charlotte wanted, *needed*, to be off the hook, and who was she to deny her people just because her grandfather had once said something offensive?

Before she could change her mind, she dialed Abe Lazar, even though she knew he'd be sitting shiva. She figured he wouldn't pick up the phone, and she could leave a message, saying she'd deliver the menorah at his convenience. Only Abe Lazar *did* answer. And Charlotte, expecting an answering machine, had to start with a fumbling apology: she was only on the island for a little while and sorry to call at such a sad time.

But Abe Lazar was willing to talk. "Oh, yes, we saw you the other night."

"I know, a terrible time to be bothering you with . . ."

"No, no," he said. "We need to get this taken care of. Why don't you come Thursday night?"

During shiva? she thought to ask, incredulously, but didn't.

"There'll be people here, then," Abe Lazar explained, his manner curmudgeonly and distracted, but not truly angry. It was as if the Thursday-night visitors would help him withstand her presence. "And you know how to get here."

She felt uneasy when she hung up, as she always did when she made an inadvisable phone call: a hello to an old boyfriend or an are-you-mad-at-me?-type question to a friend who, in fact, had upset *her*. But she pressed on—a task started must be completed—and called Wayne. An answering machine picked up. She heard Wayne say, "Trevor and Wayne. You know the drill. Leave us a message and"—here a cheery rise to his voice, "we'll call you back."

She kept it as brief as possible, saying she had no options, or so it turned out. The Bajan Institute could still present their case to the Barbados synagogue, but Temple Sinai had no power to decide where the menorah went. She was, essentially, through with the matter. This means, she wanted to add, we can be friends, but that sounded woefully schoolgirlish, so she said she hoped he'd be in touch.

Hanging up, she thought of the battles she'd had with Helen over answering-machine messages. Helen wanted silly ones: "We're not here right now and neither is our roommate," then Helen would splice in the voice of an announcer saying, "Elvis has left the building, Elvis has left the building," before finishing up with the usual request for a message and promise to call back. Charlotte thought it was funny, but she wanted an ordinary greeting. After all, the museum *did* sometimes call her at home. Charlotte won that argument but never felt good about it. Soon Helen wasn't going to have a life, why couldn't she allow her a dippy phone message? And as Charlotte thought this, it occurred to her that today, for whole minutes at a time, she had been too frightened to think of Helen. Too frightened. A worthless achievement, a regrettable one, but there it was: Charlotte's own life making its claims.

If she had any doubt about how burdened she'd been feeling by the case and her night with Henry and her day with Marty, she knew it now, from the low ache in her neck and upper back, her happy sense—she used to feel this way after she'd finished college exams—that all she had to do was shave her legs and do her laundry and she'd have wiped the slate clean. No more responsibilities. So she took a shower, plucked her eyebrows, spent twenty minutes with the bathroom's free soaps and lotions. Each morning, the maid left a variety, and now she sampled each bottle, even used the shower cap, so she could feel she was getting her—or Howard's—money's worth. When she was through, she felt vaguely like the greased watermelon that camp counselors had forced her to play with in the lakes of her youth. She stepped out of the bathroom and back into the bedroom, which was freezing now that she was wet. She saw her date book on the bed. She *hadn't* remembered to ask Howard about the plane ticket, but maybe it was just as well. She *could* take another week off work if she wanted. She could stay down here and do what he said: try to enjoy herself. It wasn't as if anyone were anxiously awaiting her return. And with that in mind, she called and left a message on her boss's answering machine: she was going to stay another week, if he had no objections. She knew he wouldn't—the year's programs had already been planned and the volunteers loved to be asked to shepherd the kids through the museum.

Hanging up the phone, she adjusted the room's air-conditioning, considered abandoning clothes for pajamas and maybe thoughts of Henry—absentminded masturbation for the rest of the night—when she noticed something by the door. A blue piece of paper. She didn't think it had been there when she'd walked in.

She made water footprints on the rug as she stepped over to it. It looked like a flyer. Something that had been folded in half and shoved under the door. She prayed it wasn't another invitation to a cocktail party. She'd gone to one of these Manager's Parties, early in the evening of her second night in Barbados. The remnants of a fort edged the hotel, and tables of liquor had been set up by a crumbling wall. It was a nice idea, she supposed, something to get all the guests together. But Charlotte had felt so awkward with her sugary glass of rum punch that, after studying the flowers that adorned the cannons and looking with no interest at the sea, she'd walked purposefully away, as if to find the companion who was waiting for her elsewhere in the hotel.

But the blue piece of paper wasn't an invitation to a party. It was a short, typed note.

"Ms. Lewin," it read. "Would you like to know who killed me? I'm downstairs in the hotel bar. If you come down, I'll tell you everything. Most sincerely, Josh Lazar."

My God, she thought, entirely spooked. What the hell was this? A prank, but why? Her room suddenly felt very remote—the single lighted office in a skyscraper. The hotel bar was, at least, a public space.

In the elevator on the way down to the bar, Charlotte struck up a conversation with two visitors. Visitors: the Barbados term; you were not a tourist but a guest of the nation. These two were Guyanese, a mother-daughter pair. Both were slump-shouldered with boredom. There was no one to flirt with here. They didn't say that, but it was clearly the problem; no narrative excitement. The women walked around, they went swimming. And that was all. In answer to Charlotte's questions, the mother allowed that her vacation had been "okay," an admission of defeat, since you were supposed to respond to all inquiries about your stay with a kind of hysterical enthusiasm. Barbados was fabulous! You were having the time of your life!

No one appeared to be having the time of his life (or afterlife) in the hotel bar. No one beyond the aggressive bartender from the other night. "I remember you," he called out as Charlotte entered the bar. "The usual?" he said and laughed. "Drinks are two for one tonight."

"Well," Charlotte said, slipping into one of the bar's low gray chairs, "a white wine," and he brought her two glasses, set them both down in front of her as if that's how the two-for-one deal went. Then he fetched a small plate of fritters.

"Has anyone been in here?" Charlotte asked as he set the plate before her. "I'm kind of looking for someone."

"Aren't we all?" the bartender said. *He* had probably sent the note. Another sicko. "But, nope, nobody here. 'Cept me." He took the chair opposite Charlotte as if he meant to join her for a stretch. "But I don't suppose *I* count."

"No," Charlotte said, more sharply than she intended, but she'd had her fill of this kind of talk today, "you don't." The bartender scrabbled to his feet. Charlotte added, more softly, "I'll wait a little longer."

He shrugged, as if to say it hardly mattered to him.

At length, two white women in bathing-suit tops and sarong bottoms sat down at the bar. *They* obviously hadn't authored the note; they took no notice of Charlotte whatsoever.

"Honey, when you going to visit *me*?" the bartender asked one of the women. Reflexive sexual banter. It had as little to do here as it did in the States with actual sex, so why were adults (Charlotte included; she was no better than anyone else) so drawn to it? Teenagers you could forgive, but adults? She didn't know how the Guyanese pair in the elevator had managed to miss out on the bartender's come-ons. She should invite them to join her down here: a whole vacation's worth of flirtation in under an hour.

Charlotte rose to see if anyone was waiting on the outside patio. But no one was there either. She didn't know why the whole thing didn't un‑ nerve her more, why she hadn't called the police as soon as she read the note. Perhaps she was only capable of so much fear, and she'd already used up the day's supply. When she came back, a small gray bird was eating off her plate. At an irritated wave of her hand, the bird flapped up then landed on a fruit display, giving one aggressive peck to a papaya before the bartender threw a rag at him. The women at the bar laughed in that way Charlotte used to laugh as a teenager—with a conviction that she was amusing, blessed by a singular ability to resist boredom, to see the world as unusual. The most common of convictions, she thought now, since every‑ where she saw teenagers speaking with stagey enthusiasm. ("We're differ‑ ent," Helen used to say. "We're different, and if you come along and act like me, you can be different, too.")

"Bye, now," Charlotte heard the bartender say.

"See you later," the women waved. They would be back, she suspected, when the bar heated up, but the bar never heated up. Something about this whole place made you feel that the party was elsewhere. The party would always be elsewhere.

She sipped her wine. The night was sibilant: the waves slapping the shore, the pronounced rustle of the ocean's invisible sleeves as it gathered water back into itself, and the cricket-like chirp of the whistling frogs, an insistent sound above it all. Her wineglass was cold against her palm. She took the card out of her bag and reread it.

"Ms. Lewin, Would you like to know who killed me?"

A joke? If so, it was an ugly one, so what was the card about? "If you come down . . ."

She hesitated, then it came to her: her passport. Of course. Someone had been trying to get her out of her room, so they could steal her pass‑ port. Charlotte paid quickly and hurried to the elevators. One was out of order, having apparently just broken. The other was infuriatingly slow. She pressed the 5 button over and over, as if that would make her rise faster. At her room, her hands fumbled with the key card: no actual keys anymore but these blank credit cards you poked into doors. Finally, the card clicked. She opened the door cautiously. But the room was empty.

She went first to the dresser. The passport was there. Nothing touched. Her underwear sat in an orderly pile next to the running shorts she'd failed to make use of this trip. Still she felt suspicious. *Someone* wanted her out of her room. She walked into the bathroom, threw the shower curtain back. Nothing there either. She checked under the bed, walked out onto the balcony. How silly. Did she think she was in an action thriller? Everything was as it had been before. And yet—she called down to the front desk and asked for hotel security.

"You hold the line a minute, please," a female voice said. Charlotte waited, and as she sat, tethered to the phone line, to the promise of something like official help, a quick broom sweep of sound drew her eyes to the door. A piece of paper—renegade, an escapee squeezing through the hole under the prison fence—inched its way into her room. She hurried to the door, chained it, then stuck her eye to the peephole. No one there. She pulled the paper from the door. It was a postcard, a homemade affair, with a note (typed again) that read, "Where were you? I was looking for you."

This time, the card wasn't signed. Nor was her name at the top. But right where an address would have been if the card had been posted, someone had glued a snapshot, one of those small photos that people use for passports, the kind of picture you might get from a curtained booth at Kmart. It was a picture of a man in his early twenties, dressed in a black T-shirt and army fatigues. Maybe this was Josh Lazar. In the forehead and sweep of dark hair over one ear, there *was* a certain resemblance to Henry, though Josh had darker skin and a vague, thug-like look, which was, no doubt, a result of his nose. It wasn't a bad nose, but it looked like it had been broken and then reset rather sloppily.

The postcard itself was a photograph of two children running down a dark alley, away from the camera. A shaft of light illuminated the backs of their elaborately rippled T-shirts. In the foreground were three banged-up metal trash cans, one tipped over, though nothing spilled out. On the message side of the postcard, where a professionally printed postcard would have a bit of information—the name of the image and the location of the museum in which it hung—someone had typed, "Medellin, Colombia."

Jesus Christ, Charlotte breathed. This seemed so threatening. She returned to the phone but in the space of time it had taken her to go to the door and back, she'd been cut off. Dead, she thought, the phone line severed, a goon with an ether-soaked rag ready to grab her if she was foolish enough to open the door. But the dial tone was working, and when she called again, she was put right through to a security guard, who agreed to come, with his partner, up to her room.

As she waited, she studied the face in the photograph. The man's lips were chapped, and he seemed to be broader-shouldered and heavier than Henry. Not fat, really, but wide. He had a dumb look, like whatever had hit his nose had also knocked his head one too many times. It was a look she vaguely associated with boys in her long-ago Hebrew school classes, the slack-jawed faces they had as they stuttered their way through a passage of Hebrew, their mouths grasping at each letter: *veee-aaa-hav-ta. Veahavta.* Charlotte never sympathized with their pained efforts. *Idiots,* she thought, *if only they'd practiced.* It didn't matter that the boys were reading prayers; she wanted to grab their shoulders, shake the pronunciation into them.

By the time the security guards arrived at her room, her complaint was vague, nonspecific. She didn't want—what? Postcards slipped under her door? The guards were confused, slow to offer concrete assistance, and Charlotte didn't know what to ask; they could hardly monitor everybody who got on and off the elevator. She explained, again, that the postcard was from someone who was dead, possibly murdered. (Postcards from the Afterlife. Missives from the Great Beyond. *Having a great time. Wish you were* . . . But they wouldn't, would they? Wish *that?*) The guards grinned uncertainly at Charlotte. *Don't you get it?* she expected them to say. *There is movement all the time between this world and that. This* . . . They'd stop to flick a forefinger at the postcard, *This is nothing to worry your head about.* Charlotte smiled herself, but persisted: shouldn't they take this card to the police? They said they would but seemed unalarmed. What, exactly, was the crime here?

CHAPTER TEN

Wayne Deare

June 24–25, 1997

↝

F ROM THE IMPERIAL TO ST. JOSEPH, there was a lumpy coastal road, bubbling up like black bean soup, ash gray and roiling. As they bounced over it, Wayne had the vague feeling that Charlotte, some sort of existential oyster shucker, was prying him open. She had a detective's approach to conversation. Once her first question was out and he'd answered, she'd ask another. Where he hesitated, she pushed further. What was *that* hesitation about?

Did he have any other siblings? she asked him now. No, he told her. And his parents? Dead, he said. His father of lung cancer. And his mother? Wayne waved his hand, as if to say it was a long story. "Sooo," Charlotte said, dragging the word out while (Wayne guessed) she thought of another question to ask, something to keep the conversation going. Wayne couldn't imagine her sitting in happy silence with a friend. She'd think something was the matter. "Really, what is it?" he could picture her asking, and the friend would finally lose patience, say, "Nothing! All right?"

Wayne was taking a scenic route back from the Imperial—past hilly vistas of palms and cashews and sad-faced cows. Along the road, there were even some late-blooming African tulips.

"So . . ." Charlotte repeated. "Um, how long ago was it? That you lost your mother?"

"My freshman year of college." He could offer more, but a full explanation involved his father's deafness, and the two houses the family had lived in—the chattel house up in St. Lucy and the current house in Pine Grove, a place his father had bought back in 1986.

Charlotte nodded at the information then looked out the window. "Pretty," she murmured, though Wayne wasn't exactly sure what she was referring to.

He tried to ask her a question. "Is my island what you expected?"

"Actually I didn't expect to take to it, to find things so interesting," Charlotte began, almost dreamily, then she stopped herself. "But, no, no, wait. Let's finish *this*. What—if you don't mind my asking—happened to your mother?"

"Marva," Wayne said. "We all called her by her first name." He was quiet for a moment then said, "My father bought us this house in a development. It was cheap, a good deal, and the reason was . . . there was a drug ring operating out of one of the houses on the road. Everyone moved out if they could afford to. But my dad didn't know about all this, and then we couldn't get our old place back. One evening, when everyone was out, some addict beat my mother up."

"He what? Oh, my God. He beat her to *death?*"

"Well, basically, yeah."

"Oh, God, Wayne. I'm so sorry."

"I can't tell you any more," Wayne said, though he kept his tone cheerful enough.

"No," Charlotte said, as if in agreement. The day had been too somber—with the scare she'd gotten from Marty and now this news. It almost seemed in poor taste of Wayne to have such a sad story to tell.

"Well," Wayne said, as if to wipe the fact of his mother's death away, and then, as if he'd timed the awkwardness of the conversation to coincide with the end of the drive, he pulled up to her hotel. Charlotte smiled—there would be no chance to interrogate her—and said, as she left the car, "Thank you, again. I can't tell you how much I appreciate your help today. You're really very kind."

Wayne drove home, thinking about what he'd left out of his story. He didn't imagine there was any part of the rest that he'd ever feel comfortable telling another person.

The addict had come to rob the Deare household and, finding nothing worth pawning, had beaten Wayne's mother till she blacked out, then he dug an infant almond tree out of the front yard, apparently in hopes of selling it. Wayne had been away at school when this happened. His father and Trevor had been out. Some neighbors found Marva. They called the hospital, and when they couldn't persuade anybody to send an ambulance, they put Marva in the back of a pickup and took her over to QEH themselves. Even so, the hospital wouldn't accept her, since there was no relative to sign for treatment. Finally, the neighbors found Wayne's father at a rum shop, but the hospital wouldn't accept his signature either. Wayne's parents had been together for almost three decades but never had enough money for a wedding. Technically, Wayne's father wasn't Marva's husband. No matter that this was how most of the unions on the island worked. So he took the bus home (this was before he had a car; this was the reason he finally bought a car) and called Marva's sister. (Called her on the home phone, the one that amplified voices, and in his darkest moments, Wayne let himself think that if his father hadn't been frightened of using the hospital pay phone, his mother might be alive today.) By the time his father reached Wayne's aunt, Marva was dead.

Wayne flew home from Boston as soon as he got the news. No one even told him about the beating until he arrived. He stayed on the island for two days after his mother's funeral and then, because there was nothing else for him to do—because he couldn't say, *Why didn't you make the phone call from the hospital?* or *How could the ambulance refuse to come?*—he flew back to school and resumed his studies. Lawsuit, he was thinking, the whole way back. He should sue the hospital, also the police who never found the man who'd done the beating, though there'd been plenty of neighbors to attest to who he was. But Wayne didn't have the heart for litigation; he was as defeated as his father. It wasn't until Deirdre visited his dorm room, took his hand, and said, "Wayne, sweetheart, your poor mom," that the tears came. He'd always held this belief: while a person was alive, you should do everything possible for them, but after they were gone, their death was a fact; their circumstances simply their fate. You shouldn't dwell on what you couldn't change. That night in his dorm room, Wayne wondered if he'd ever get back from where he was—crying and saying, "It's all right, it's all right," so Deirdre would stop patting his arm—to that belief.

But, of course, it wasn't all right. He thought of how Deirdre had finally allowed Wayne his way of looking at things, but then, with the kind of pure perversity that might make someone say "looking good" to a blind person, she spent the rest of the semester noting narcotics busts in the paper, or telling Wayne what people were smoking, snorting, and injecting at the parties she attended.

By the time Wayne got home to Pine Grove, he was despondent. This stupid house, he thought as he stepped through the door. He missed the old galvanize-gable that his family used to live in, though he remembered how delighted he'd initially been with the indoor bathroom at Pine Grove. Their old place had its charms—a lime tree where Marva tied a small cat and a breadfruit tree—but it also had an outhouse and Wayne, in his efforts to avoid the feeling that he was going to be sucked, butt first, into an endless hole of shit, had developed a case of childhood constipation so severe that once he had to be taken to the doctor to have the contents of his bowels manually removed. After that, his mother mixed him a daily concoction that Wayne found just as humiliating. The brown powder she dumped into a glass and mixed with water looked suspiciously like dried manure, and the jar in which the powder came clearly indicated the recommended dose for pregnant women. They were apparently the only people, other than Wayne, forced to consume the yeasty-tasting stuff. As a boy, Wayne had attacked the label with a pen before Trevor had a chance to read and employ this terrible fact against him.

Not that the WC in Pine Grove did the teenage Wayne any good. "You have bad-feels?" his mother would ask, employing her euphemism but not even waiting for the answer to start to tell him where she'd stored the powder, the sticky jar she'd transported, along with her spices, from St. Lucy. "No," Wayne would say, but the truth was he had a permanent case of bad-feels.

Now, Wayne wanted one good thing to happen. Something to put on the opposite side of the scale from his parents' deaths—not that he really thought such a thing existed, but something to make him feel that tragedy didn't always win out. The only event left for the day, though, was dinner, and he'd found himself awaiting it, even though he had no desire for food. He knew he should sit down and write job letters, but the task seemed impossible, and he gave the couch, with its newspapers from London, Toronto, and New York, a wide berth as he walked through the room. Trevor almost never slept at home these days, but Wayne wished he'd show up tonight. He didn't want to be alone with his thoughts.

While he was in the bathroom, the phone rang. Wayne waited expectantly for the answering machine to click on, in hopes that it would be somebody asking him out to do something, but it was Charlotte saying she wasn't going to give the Bajan Institute the menorah, after all. *Oh, shit,* Wayne thought. He should have pursued his case today, made a stronger pitch for the thing. He'd let a perfectly decent opportunity to convince her go to waste. But then he played the answering machine over again. Charlotte said she hoped he'd be in touch, and there was something in her voice—Wayne stood, for a moment, weighing what sort of invitation she was extending.

And then he decided he'd just call Deirdre, ask her what she thought about it.

Lying on the floor with a pillow (crimson with gold tassels; his mother had favored bordello hues) over his stomach and an ear pressed to the phone, he told Deirdre about his day. When he got to his departure from Charlotte, Deirdre snapped, "I hate when you do that."

"Do what?" As they'd talked, Wayne had silently, halfheartedly started to jack off, but her anger deflated him. He zipped his jeans and sat up, his back chastely against the wall. "Flacido," he wrote in the margin of a newspaper, "Flacido Domingo," then crossed the words out. In front of him, dark wiry strands of hair covered the wan, plushless carpet. *Shedding,* Wayne thought. "My carpet," he told Deirdre, "I think it's alive."

"What I hate is when you make your voice go all idiot wistful when you tell about someone complimenting you. 'You're really kind.' You'd think no one ever said anything nice to you in your whole life. It makes you sound so fuck-ing pitiful."

"Well, anger's a real normal response to someone being pitiful, I must say."

"Because," Deirdre huffed, "because it's so self-defeating. And because you do it more now than ever before. You weren't like this in college. You really weren't. Just giving you a reality check. In college, you wouldn't faint at someone telling you you were kind, which is only the most nothing compliment on the planet."

"Let's change the subject," Wayne said and hefted himself up on the couch. The inky smell of newspapers reached up to his nose. The re-proach of the classifieds.

"Un-less," Deirdre mused, "you're falling in love, in which case maybe you're looking for evidence."

"New subject," Wayne said, but then admitted he was thinking of inviting Charlotte to a Friday-night fish fry.

"Oh, yes," Deirdre started up, in the adolescent, needling voice she adopted whenever they spoke of affairs of the heart, "some-bodies in love."

"Yeah?" Wayne shot back. "Jealous?"

"Maybe I am," Deirdre said, her voice a challenge. But did she mean she was jealous of him (for having an interest) or jealous of Charlotte (for being that interest)?

"Well," Wayne said, "let's not open *that* can of worms," though it was the very can he'd been struggling with for years.

"Right," Deirdre said abruptly. "I gotta go."

"Well, okay," Wayne agreed slowly. His face felt hot, bloated with blood. He'd liked being able to accuse her, however obliquely, of interest, but now he just felt like a jerk.

"Yeah, bye," she said snippily.

"Hey, Deirdre," Wayne started, but she was already gone, and Wayne was secretly glad. Too many missed opportunities of this sort. They'd never get together now, and anything he said would only embarrass them both. It was good to turn his thoughts to Charlotte. A new prospect.

As soon as he hung up the phone, it rang. Deirdre, he thought, calling back to amend the conversation; she did that whenever she thought there'd been a misunderstanding, but it wasn't her.

"Phone's been busy all night," Trevor said, using the voice he em-ployed whenever he was well into a fight with Wayne, a voice so full of fundamental outrage that Wayne had a clear sense of how he must figure in his brother's dreams. And as if to confirm this thought, he remembered how a month ago, after a rare night home, Trevor had spit toothpaste over Wayne's shoulder and into the bathroom sink, then said, companionably, "I dream I yelling at you."

"I was talk . . ." Wayne started now, but his brother cut him off.

"I in duck's guts and you jabbing on the phone. I *trying* to call you."

Trevor was so upset that it took a moment to figure out what he was saying, one of those strange moments in which Wayne simultaneously heard
and accommodated himself to bad news: Trevor was at the Hastings police station, about to be remanded to the Glendairy Prison for the murder
of Josh Lazar. They'd found his fingerprints all over Josh's parachute.

"'Course they did," Trevor shouted. "Was my jacket before was his.
We switch. Enough people see." He let out a wailing sound of frustration.

"Right," Wayne said, pulling the phone to his chest and standing.
"Plenty of witnesses." What an asshole he'd been, thinking about women
when his brother was in trouble. How had he let himself believe nothing
would come of Berkowitz's TV interview? "Everyone saw," he added,
pushing his feet back into his sneakers. As he did, Wayne flashed on the
surreal night, toward the end of his father's life, when he and Trevor had
ground an overdose of morphine pills into their father's breadfruit. They
did this in silence, concentrating on the tines of their forks, pressing medicine into the tan-green mush. Then, at the same moment, they looked up,
registered each other's eyes and dumped the whole concoction in the
trash.

There was a knocking sound on the phone. "Still there?" Trevor called.

"Yeah," Wayne said. "*You* could have been the one that died. Didn't
you tell them that?"

"That's what I say. I say they should feel . . . I bless. Some angel come
and make that boy ask me to switch chutes. They say, 'Oh, you a religious
boy,' and looks like they want to smack me head."

"Christ," Wayne said.

"You a religious one, too," Trevor said and gave a little laugh that was
altogether uncharacteristic for him.

"The hangar," Wayne breathed. "That meeting. I knew we should have
stayed for the questioning. Now they'll say that looked suspicious."

"You have to criticize right now? You have to?" Trevor said, his voice
thick with self-righteous disbelief.

"I'm not . . ." Wayne stopped himself. "I'm just thinking," he said
evenly. "I'm just thinking what *they* must be thinking." Which wasn't
true; he was thinking that even when, *especially* when, his brother asked
for comfort, there was something aggressive about the request, an insistence on there being only one possible response—which was, oddly

enough, praise; he wanted to be praised, even now—and Wayne always reacted physically to the demand, his hands balling up, not for a punch, but because kindness was something he felt the urge to hold, tightly, in his fists and never let go.

"You got to help me. I can't stay here another minute."

"Of course, I'll be there. I'll come . . ."

"Yeah, come to Hastings. I knew they gonna accuse someone."

"What?"

"I knew someone gonna take the blame for that fall."

"You did?" News reports aside, Wayne still believed the death had been an accident, imagined others did, too.

"Sure, anyone could guess it be me. They have to pick somebody. They pick me."

Two years earlier, when Trevor had first been arrested, Wayne's father had gone to all the hearings, cried when the judge ruled that Trevor would actually do time. Wayne had stayed away. Not that he had a choice. He was at Tufts, and no one told him what was going on till it was over. That was the way things always worked with the Deares, and if someone complained, asked, as Wayne did now, "Why didn't you tell me?" they'd say, as Trevor also did now, "Didn't want to upset you."

"Well, it didn't work," Wayne said. "I'm upset."

"Okay," Trevor coughed, ignoring him. What difference did Wayne's emotions make? "You come to Hastings."

Wayne went, of course. The police station was right by the Savannah. Last week, any one of the police, outside on a break, might have looked past the station's flagpole and around the mess of construction for a broken culvert and seen a man falling to earth. From the station, it wouldn't have looked like a punishable offense. It would have looked like a fluorescent pink bag of trash, like any late-afternoon trick of the eye, a reason to invest in sunglasses.

Past midnight, Bridgetown traffic was sparse, and as Wayne drove toward the water, the city shut off the last of its lights, pulled the dark blanket of night over itself. Only the wind was up, still playing with the ocean and tree leaves. But then, as Wayne's car idled at a traffic light, a single white woman, sandals dangling from her fingers, appeared at the side of the road. She exclaimed to an invisible companion, "She stayed on the boat. She's balling him on the boat. Well, I don't want any part of that." And then the light turned and Wayne was past even her. Everything was so peaceful, he imagined that he would have to arrive to find his brother free, the officers apologetic for their mistake, quick to agree that finger-prints couldn't be evidence in a case like this. And by the time Wayne got to Hastings, Trevor *was* gone. "Oh," Wayne said, ready to be pleased till an officer behind the front desk—a man with a small gap between his front teeth, a dark space that seemed to announce the whole of his stupidity—walked forward to announce that Trevor had been remanded to Glendairy. "Well, how . . ." Wayne started to ask but the officer turned from him to tell another officer the plot of a "flim" he'd seen the previous night. "It was a good flim," he was saying as Wayne stepped back out of the station. "I always wanted to write a flim myself."

Trevor had been to Glendairy before and he was not going back. He said it to whoever would listen. It was the one subject on which he was garru-lous: his refusal to be reincarcerated. Wayne had pressed for details. Prison. Pri-son. It was impossible to imagine, and he'd wanted to know—things, but Trevor said little. "It was hard," he'd allowed, emphasizing the "hard." When you were in there, a single day lasted forever. His own four months ballooned into years, then decades. He'd left an old man. And, he'd confessed, there were a lot of gays. The old men liked the young ones.

"So," Wayne said slowly, "did you have to watch your back all the time?"

"No," Trevor said quickly. "It wasn't like that. Nobody force anything on you."

Wayne felt sure this abrupt denial could mean only one thing, but Trevor shook his head. It wasn't what Wayne thought. It *wasn't*. Glen-dairy. You could get thrown in for carrying a knife, and then when you were there, they'd give you an ax.

An ax, a table saw. If you happened to be in the woodworking shop. Otherwise, you were stationed behind a sewing machine, or put in a ditch with a bunch of cement. You were handed a rock and told to bang dried coconut husks. Later, you'd stuff the fiber into one of the slim mattresses prisoners slept on. This is if you were lucky. The place was overcrowded, so there wasn't enough work for everybody. You might just sit around the mess hall, playing chess or Monopoly. Maybe you worked your way through colorful puzzle books. First-timers tended to farm. Cows, pigs, baby chicks. Fly-ridden animals in their fly-ridden stalls. Only Trevor wouldn't be put in with the first-timers. He'd be in the front prison.

It wasn't what Wayne imagined; Trevor said that again and again. And still Wayne couldn't get the image of a lockup out of his head, even as Trevor described an old colonial-style prison. This time, Trevor's green-doored cell would open on a verandah where all the men hung out, looking down on the courtyard with its cocoa-colored dirt, its parched vegetables, fenced off for protection. (Like all food on the grounds, the withered crops were worth fighting over.) Only those on death row spent the day in cells. They came out, fifteen minutes each day, to play road tennis in a cage at the rear of the prison. They never wore shirts. Their shorts were in disarray, pulled too low over their hips or rolled at the waistband, and though everything else was strict in the prison—Trevor stood up and saluted guards whenever they passed—the men on death row were given this one sartorial freedom. Wayne could almost imagine them, their chests gleaming, for those fifteen minutes in the sun. They were going to die, sure, but they had what no one else had: the freedom to take off their shirts.

Wayne knew all this. And he knew that the one thing Trevor had liked about prison was working in the bakeshop, molding the yeasty-smelling rolls. He got to love their baby's ass smoothness, the round, neat way they sat on a tray before baking. Wayne was remembering all this as he waited in the open-air waiting room by the prison's gate. It was morning, the day after his trip to Hastings. He'd spent the previous night trying to drink himself to sleep. Glasses of frozen orange juice and vodka, at Deirdre's suggestion. It hadn't worked, any more than his repeated reminders that he couldn't free his brother simply by worrying, that he'd have to put his concerns on hold till morning, when calls could be made. But then he'd woken—his mouth sour with juice and his stomach in turmoil, the toilet bowl filling up with pus and shit—and he made his way to the prison, where there was no phone or bathroom. Only the small waiting room with a single occupant, a heavy middle-aged woman, sweet-faced but set-

tled into a posture—legs and arms crossed, eyes trained on the ceiling—
that suggested her profound unwillingness to engage in conversation. She
didn't even nod hello. *I am here*, Wayne wanted to shout like a schoolboy.
Nobody forget me.

Across the way was the prison wall. And the main door. Wayne had
actually never seen it before today. Or never seen the entrance with its gigantic yellow and white portico. He'd had glimpses of the prison's wall,
though, the gray limestone capped with twisted wire, suggestive of Dick-
ensian horrors beyond. The sky above the wall had always seemed to
darken when Wayne, as a boy, biked by. Back then, it gave Wayne the
sense that the place really was in gloomy London and that its prisoners
were kept in dungeons filled with devices ready to remove tongues and
fingers, to crush a man's balls or steal his heart. Now, as if to confirm his
boyhood vision, an old man with a wild, white beard hobbled up to the
yellow portico's tremendous green gates and started to pound on them
with a six-foot walking stick. He cried, "Lemme in. Lemme in."

"Papa Pawpaw," Wayne's companion offered and gestured with her
chin to the petitioner by the door before shaking her head in sorrow or
disapproval.

"You mean, that's that guy's name?"

"Un-huh."

A door was cut into the green gate. As Wayne and the woman watched,
a guard swung the door open and said—loudly, but not unkindly—"Okay,
now. Calm down. Calm down."

"Lemme in, lemme in," the man pleaded. "Forsake me not."

The guard stepped out of the prison, taking one comically elongated
first step, since the door was a few feet up from the ground. He tapped the
old man on the shoulder and pointed to a sign by the gate. It said something—Wayne wasn't willing to stand to find out—about all persons entering the premises. The old man responded to this information by pulling
a medallion from underneath his T-shirt. It was the size of a dinner plate.
He seemed to want the guard to read it, but the guard just shook his head
and stepped back through the green door. Something about the scene
seemed familiar. Then it hit Wayne: the Wizard of Oz. It was just like the
movie. The prison's green door slammed open and shut with the same
mirthful briskness of the entrance window at the castle of Oz.

"Yeah," the woman waiting with Wayne said, "Papa Pawpaw. And he calls that stick his staff." She gave a snort of a laugh, but there was no mirth in it. She looked down, then started to finger a cross at her neck. She didn't seem eager to talk, only obligated now that she'd begun. "He was in there, years ago. Now his son is in. He wants to visit him. That's why he's upset."

"You'd think they'd just let him."

"They did, but . . . you never been here before?"

Wayne shook his head.

"You know you only get fifteen minutes a month?"

"No, I didn't."

"Unless your friend hasn't been convicted. If he's just remanded, you get fifteen minutes a week, and you know he has to request you. He has to request a visit from you, otherwise you can't go in."

Wayne considered this. But, of course, his brother would have made the request.

"They ask for you and say what they want to receive." She pulled half a sheet of paper from her bag. "This is my boy's." On a form, someone had scrawled: "Cigarettes, snacks, long pants." At the woman's feet, a paper shopping bag, soft with reuse, was filled with packets of M&Ms. "That's the way it works. And you can't come on Sunday, and when you get in there, don't touch the wire, or they'll kick you out."

"The wire?"

"Like the screen, between you."

Wayne nodded. For some reason, he had been imagining talking on a telephone through glass. He had no idea why he thought the prison would have the high-tech accoutrements the rest of the island lacked.

Wayne was still waiting outside the prison at 11:30. Only by now he was starting to have his doubts. Perhaps Trevor *hadn't* asked for him? But at 11:45 one of the guards stuck his head out of the gate and called, "Deare, Deare." ("Yes, honey," Trevor had once trilled at a schoolmaster taking roll and had received a week's detention for his cleverness.) Wayne hurried to the door, stepped through, and found himself in a dark archway that led, via a gigantic barred gate, to the sunlit courtyard of the prison. Wayne took everything in fast. This seemed important: that he see as much as he could. This was his brother's life, at least for now, and love commanded that he know it. He could make out a sentry tower through the gate, but little more. To his right, guards checked under a van that had passed through the gates just before Wayne's name was called. On his left, he saw a tally board with the numbers of people out at court or the hospital, or still here in the women's prison, or the men's. There were 740 men, the chalkboard said, and 38 women, and one baby. The baby—he'd read about her last week. A woman had delivered within the prison walls, and the papers had printed a snapshot of her returning from the hospital. She was in a gingham blue dress, a matching scarf wrapped around her head. Ever since then, there'd been outraged articles in the *Nation* about the "baby inmate."

"Okay, sir," a skinny guard said. He had the stringy look of cured meat. Wayne took in the green band on his hat, the HMP on his shoulder, the wooden baton with a gold top that he smacked once into his hand. *HMP. Her Majesty's Pleasure.* Behind him, two male prisoners in faded blue shirts and short pants stood at the barred gate. One wore Teva sandals; another, women's cloth sandals embroidered with the map of Barbados.

"This way," the guard instructed and guided Wayne up two stairs that led to a room painted a pale, dirty green. Here, a tall, forest green partition gave way at waist height to wire mesh. Trevor—still in his waiter outfit from yesterday—was standing behind the central portion of the divider.

"Brother." Wayne stepped right to him, lowered his voice, though he didn't know why. He always made a point of speaking distinctly to his brother. "How are you? How are you in here?"

Trevor nodded his head. A fan clacked away behind him. "Can't talk about it. Or they can stop the visit." He gestured, with his basset hound eyes to the guard standing behind Wayne.

"Okay," Wayne said, "Okay."

Trevor began slowly, each syllable its own sentence, "I . . . didn't . . . do . . . no . . . thing."

"Look, I know. What about Desmond? If they thought someone did something, why didn't they pick up Desmond? He was the one making all the fuss in the plane."

"Ah, sure, he gone now. Jamaica. And police at the station say nobody can find him."

"My boss, my boss is a lawyer. First thing I leave here, and I'm going to get him to help. It'll be . . . you'll be out . . ."

Fifteen minutes. Wayne almost couldn't hear because those words—as if they were his heartbeat, amplified a thousand times—kept booming in his ear. He felt it was necessary to hear Trevor's heartbeat against the whoosh-thud of his own. If he could have done anything, he would have reached through the mesh to press his ear against Trevor's chest. The lonely fact of his own pulse. If he cried now, it wouldn't be for his brother. What was he supposed to do? He'd never hired a lawyer before. How would he know if he'd found a good one, and how would he ever pay for the help?

"So just tell me what happened," he said, his mouth managing all the confident authority his heart lacked. And Trevor told about how he'd been picked up, taken to the police station. He raced through the details: the downstairs bathroom where you couldn't even take a shit because the place had never had a roll of toilet paper; the room with the brown table and black chairs with the foam poking through the tears in the vinyl. No one cared about his explanation for why his fingerprints were all over the dead man's parachute.

"They say I have a record," Trevor added, indignant, and Wayne almost said, "But you do."

"I can't stay here," Trevor finished, nearly hysterical. "I can't. They check me parts. Understand? For scars."

"For scars?"

"They think I'm gonna escape and try to disguise meself."

A guard standing behind Trevor rapped his cane against the wall and shook his head. If the prisoners had complaints, they were supposed to take it up with the administration. "Ten minutes," the same guard called out.

"I got to tell this one thing." Trevor reached up urgently and touched the wire between them.

"That's it," the guard called. "Can't do that. Visit's over."

Trevor's eyes shot open. The guard behind Trevor stepped forward. "Wayne," Trevor said, and Wayne thought, *When have I ever even heard him use my name?* and Trevor grabbed at the wire with both hands and said, "I sleep with that man's wife." The guard's hands were on Trevor's arms, pulling him back to the door.

"It's okay," Wayne said. He hands were on the wire now, too. "It's going to be okay." And Trevor was shaking his head fiercely as if to get him to shut up so he could just say one more thing. "Mar-ty Berk-witz. I sleep with his wife. He did this. Someone do this. He did this, thinking he gonna get me."

"I heard you," Wayne said, because it seemed important to say this, and then louder, "I heard you, brother," as Trevor was pulled from the room.

Wayne turned to the guard on his side, "Can't I . . . ?"

And the guard shook his head, even before the question was out. No, whatever it was, he couldn't.

The panic Wayne felt as he drove to work bordered on pleasure. There was something almost good about knowing his needs were, at last, urgent enough for attention, for interrupting, for bad behavior. Emergencies. They were terrible, heartbreaking, and yet they provided a release. Finally, finally, he counted, but even as Wayne thought this, he felt the pure embarrassment of trouble, of how much he wished it would just go away.

As he walked from his car to the Bajan Institute, Wayne's feet hit the pavement with an insistent rhythm. The thump of his heart again, he supposed, but then realized that wasn't it, that wasn't it at all. He was walking to the chorus of a calypso song—popular last year, or the year before—to the words, "Listen to me, listen to me, listen to me."

How he wished he could simply lean back on the cushion of his parents, let them take care of all this. But even alive, Wayne's father wouldn't have known what to do, and Wayne's mother rarely roused herself from her protective focus on her husband to consider her sons. "Where *were* they when you were growing up?" Deirdre had once asked. And Wayne didn't know how to explain that his mother, at least, was always *right there* but also gone. The terror he and Trevor had felt on the night that they'd ground up their father's morphine pills was different only in magnitude from what they'd felt their whole lives: there was no one around who knew what to do.

Ever since before the Lazars' party, Wayne had been dreaming about falling out of planes. But two nights ago, the dream had abruptly stopped—a portent of today's troubles?—and Wayne had spent his sleeping hours pelting Frank with office supplies: a stapler, pencils, an empty trash can, till finally he heaved the old IBM Selectric off Janice's desk and sent it flying toward his boss.

Now Wayne stepped through the open door of the Bajan Institute, past the typewriter of his dreams, and into the maelstrom of bad temper that was a day at the office with Frank. "Well," Frank said and checked his watch, "arriving about six hours late for work. I'd say that's grounds for dismissal."

He wasn't joking. Frank was ready to believe the worst of people, had a tendency to speak of betrayals by former friends, of enemies as "evil." (Deirdre once told Wayne that her freshman roommate went around telling people that Deirdre had *hit* her during a disagreement. *Hit* her! Deirdre couldn't stop thinking about it; it was so crazy. A preoccupation Wayne never understood till he acknowledged his own interest in Frank's disapprobation. It was completely fascinating.)

"Listen"—Wayne coughed self-consciously but finished his sentence anyway—"to me."

"Un-hmm," Frank said and kicked his feet up on his desk. Wayne sat—bent forward in the characteristic attitude of the supplicant—and described his morning, his sense of his brother's situation, and Marty Berkowitz's responsibility for it. Frank listened attentively, the fury draining out of his face. He was mollified by Wayne's troubles; they almost seemed to cheer him.

"I don't," Wayne said when he was through, "know what to do." Frank was silent. "I can't," Wayne finally choked out, "do anything."

Frank nodded. Then he pulled at his chin, as if there were a beard there. It was true, the gesture seemed to say, Wayne couldn't do anything, but Frank could. Power. After all, Frank trafficked in it, and Wayne had always felt contemptuous of him for it: his life was "just" politics. But now Wayne saw how that could be everything.

Frank was smiling. It wasn't that he wished misfortune on Wayne—he wasn't *that* mean—but that this was an opportunity for resistance. Frank didn't have a talent for kindness—that was too personal for him—but he did have one for justice: morality played out on the big canvas. And the issues were clear, or clear enough for Frank.

"See," Frank said, shaking his head when Wayne was all through talking, "see how they treat us? As if we won't notice."

"Berkowitz?" Wayne said, tentatively, though he felt his body quicken to the suggestion.

Frank huffed. "I'm talking about the Lazars. Who do you think would have had Trevor picked up in the first place? You had—how many? You said twenty-eight witnesses on that plane? This isn't justice in anyone's system. A man dies. And everybody wants to blame somebody. There's nobody to blame, so pick on the black man." These were Trevor's words from last night—sort of: death isn't an accident but somebody's fault.

"So why not blame . . ." Wayne stopped. He wanted to say, *Somebody else*. There was a brief silence while Frank waited for Wayne to finish his sentence, and when he didn't, Frank seemed to imagine Wayne's thought through nonetheless.

"There was nobody else to blame on the plane."

"Desmond? The guy who was my brother's partner?"

Frank blew his nose noisily. "But you said he was unavailable for blame." This seemed a strange way of putting it. "He went to Jamaica?"

"Yes, yes," Wayne said, "but there were twenty-something other black folk in that plane . . ."

"Remember, my friend," Frank interrupted, "money whitens."

"But the others, they were just like . . ." Wayne threw up his hands. "Like me. I mean, I don't know what they were—surfers, Josh's buddies— but everyone was there *for* the money. They were paying us." Wayne held his tongue on the sum. On his first day of work, Frank made it clear he thought Wayne was greedy, since he'd bargained for an hourly wage higher than customary. "Well, I suppose it's all about self-interest now," Frank had said, as if he'd had a sudden vision of the dark, capitalist heart of Wayne's generation, and Wayne had said, nonsensically, "I've worked at Barbecue Barn."

"I mean," Wayne tried again now, "no one in that plane had money." Despite his words, part of him wanted to be convinced by Frank. He always felt a brand of excitement—it bordered on the sexual—about unequivocal racism, the full permission it gave him not to consider others, to hate right back. He wanted that menorah, he thought, with sudden ferocity. Bonus or no—he was going to get it.

"Friends of Lazar?" Frank said authoritatively. "They had money. I know those types. I've seen them. 'Oh, Miss Hattie,' they say and rub their forearm to say she's colored, as if they haven't had a good look at their own skin recently. Color's at the bottom of everything thought or done or felt on this island." Frank smiled, then pulled his feet off his desk, leaned over, and touched Wayne lightly, almost affectionately, at the brow. "That fancy schooling just gave you a touch of amnesia, so you forgot."

The heat of Frank's finger pads made him shiver. "And my brother's idea? About Marty Berkowitz? I've heard stories about this Berkowitz. Supposedly he threw cooking oil—I mean, hot cooking oil—in his wife's face."

"A domestic dispute doesn't mean you're going to frame another man for murder."

"Even if that man's your wife's lover?"

Frank waved his hand, as if to say, *That's nothing.*

"I don't know," Wayne said, "what I can pay you. I can put up the house. I'll put up the house but . . ." He felt Frank's fingerprint on his head and thought, *No one ever touches me except doctors.*

"Yo, Toni," Frank called across the office, "think we should make this Deare case pro bono?"

She laughed, so she had to have been listening all along, and said, "I don't think you're exactly in the law business anymore. I think you *have* to make it pro bono."

"Thank you," Wayne said, quietly to Frank. "I'll give you what I can."

Frank said, "I have two things to tell you. One is I don't want what you can give." There was a hint of his old derision in this. "Two is, she's right. I'm not practicing anymore, so all I'm going to do is make some phone calls for you, see what I can find out. But I can tell you that if your brother's not out in, say, forty-eight hours, we'll be"—Frank noisily cleared his throat, then coughed out the end of his sentence—"having ourselves a little protest." He blew his nose and then repeated himself in case his hacking had muffled his final words. "A little public dispute with the Lazars."

CHAPTER ELEVEN

Charlotte Lewin

June 26–28, 1997

᠅

F OUR DAYS INTO CHARLOTTE'S STAY, the morning paper started to
appear at her door, and she hadn't questioned the gift, had assumed it
was meant to be there all along. On Thursday, she pulled it in with her
toes, only to find she was stepping on Trevor Deare's nose. At her heel was
the story:

> A St. Michael man has been charged in the death of Josh
> Lazar, late of St. James. According to Police Public Rela-
> tions Inspector Harris Tull, charges have been brought
> stemming from an altercation that occurred just minutes
> before Josh Lazar fell out of a plane and to his death over
> the Garrison Savannah. "There was a lot of bad talk on
> the plane," Marty Berkowitz of St. Phillips told the *Daily
> Nation*. "Mocking of Jews." Parachuters at the scene con-
> firm his words as well as reports of a last-minute parachute
> exchange between Lazar and Deare. "Of course," says
> Berkowitz, "Trevor Deare knew it was faulty. He wanted it
> to look like an accident. I think I speak for the Lazar family
> when we way we're all shocked and horrified by this sort of
> brutality in our community." Late on Tuesday night, Trevor
> Deare was taken in for questioning, then remanded to
> Glendairy.

The phone interrupted Charlotte's reading. It was security from downstairs, returning her call about the safe. She needed to retrieve the menorah before she went out that evening, and they could accommodate her

now. Charlotte had spent the previous day at the National Archives, had returned dusty and sweaty but with no real evidence that Nigel Jones had made the menorah. Wayne was right about the forge, though. The menorah had come from Dundidge; the plantation's stamp was on the sole of one of the elephant's feet, and there was a bill of sale indicating that the menorah had been sold by Cornelius Dundidge to "Emanuel Hezakel of the Jews' Synagogue." Still, for all the records revealed, it might have been produced by anyone with access to the Dundidge forge. Not that this lack of paperwork made her so sanguine about handing the elephants over to the Lazars. After all, what sort of records did she expect slaves were allowed to keep? Still, she told the security guard that she'd be right down.

But first she finished the article. The newspaper followed Berkowitz's claims with a charge from Frank Elcock, the Director of the Bajan Institute. He denied there'd been *any* anti-Semitic banter in the plane. "In fact," he was quoted as saying, "the very Jews who are accusing this poor boy of murder have stolen a valuable piece of artwork from my museum." *The menorah?* Charlotte thought. *Could he mean that?* But, as she read on, it was clear he did.

His words made it that much easier for Charlotte to do what she intended: fetch the menorah, fold it in bubble wrap, drop it in her oversized bag and, early that evening, call a cab. What was hard was ignoring Wayne—*not* phoning to offer sympathy, or help, or an apology for ferrying the menorah to his brother's accusers.

That night, before she left the hotel, Charlotte stopped at the front desk to see if she had any messages.

"Not a thing," the desk clerk said.

"You're sure?"

The clerk shrugged, annoyed. "I *said* no."

"Will you just go check my box?"

"Okay," the woman sighed in irritation. She disappeared for a moment then returned and placed a handful of small white pieces of paper, folded in quarters, on the counter. "Here."

Charlotte rolled her eyes, then unfolded them. There were three messages: one from her mother, one from Howard, and one from the Guyanese visitors she'd met the other day on the elevator. The mother-daughter pair had been invited to a fête at a distant cousin's house and wanted to know if she'd like to come along. She would have loved to. "Call right away," the message said, but it was dated several days ago, as were the other messages, and the party had been last night. Charlotte looked up, almost said something, but somehow her anger, real as it was, felt as scripted as the clerk's lazy disinterest, and she let it go.

A cab took her inland, then up a hill through a crowded stretch of broken-down chattel houses. Yesterday, on a break from her research, Charlotte heard two women talking about a couple who sawed their house in half when they split up. Apparently, they'd carried the respective halves away to their new lovers. Now Charlotte heard the refrain of "Saw Da House in Half" thumping out of the taxi radio and wondered if she'd actually been eavesdropping on a discussion of the song.

Charlotte's cab seemed to be going too far to the east. She leaned forward in her seat to say, "You have the address, right? Ocean Way in St. John?"

"Oh, yes," the cabdriver assured her, "don't worry your head."

He turned, headed north, then west, back down toward the water. Charlotte had the sense they'd made a giant U. Perhaps the cabbie was trying to get extra miles out of the trip? Still, it was a nice drive. The night was pleasantly cool; the breeze through the window played with the skirt of her dress. It was a sleeveless white rayon with pale tan lines—her Agnes Martin dress, Charlotte told people at the museum. It looked, under the circumstances, less like a minimalist painting than a gaudy wedding costume. But it was the best she could do: a white dress and a gigantic straw bag for shiva.

It was fully dark by the time she reached the Lazars. As Charlotte handed the cabdriver the money—she had it already prepared in her hand, a habit left over from her brief stint as a New Yorker—he said, "Wait. How you getting home?"

"I'll call a cab, I guess."

"Well, you call me." He fumbled under his seat for something. "And you seen the island? I take you around the island."

"Oh," Charlotte said, "I think I'd rent a car for sightseeing."

"Why you want to take your life in hand like that? *I* take you." He found his business card and presented it to her. His photograph was glued to one side in the manner of the photograph on the postcard she'd received the other night.

"This," she said, turning it over, "is interesting. What did you do, just use some glue?"

"Oh, yeah. You like that? I give you another," and he started looking through a pile of junk on the seat to his right: old food wrappers and a copy of V. S. Naipaul's *A Bend in the River*. "I got it done at Cave Shepherd. They do one hundred for ten dollar. But you have to bring your own photo." He handed her another card: James Braithwaite. "You call me."

"Okay, I will," she said, knowing she would not and feeling a slap of reproach. Instinct warred with values on this island; she couldn't be a good person here, not even if she tried. And something about finally acknowledging this relaxed her, gave her permission to abandon the effort.

As soon as she stepped outside, a chorus of dogs started up behind a neighbor's high wall. Charlotte made her way to the Lazars' front gate, but it was locked. There was no bell, so she walked away from the dogs, around the left side of the house. It was a corner lot, fronting the beach, but there was no entrance here either. She tried the original gate again then walked hesitantly toward the neighbors'. As she left the street for the dark stretch of grass that ran between the two homes, the barking grew louder. Bougainvillea flowed over the walls to her right and left. The dogs went wild. She could imagine them hurling themselves against their side of the stone wall, teeth bared, willing to break their bones if it meant they could get to her flesh. Her eyes teared, blurring her vision. She could bonk a dog on the head with the menorah if she had to. She could do that. She took another tentative step forward. The barking exploded beside her. She rocked—forward and back, which way to go?—then saw a gate up ahead. She ran for it, not expecting it to give, but it did, it did, first admitting her into the Lazars' backyard and then clanging reassuringly shut behind her.

She straightened her dress, breathed twice deeply, in through the nose, out through the mouth. It was what the nurses told Helen to do, that last time in the hospital.

Even though the house before her was illuminated, the curtains were drawn for shiva, so the yard was settled into a greeny darkness. Nearby, the ocean slurped liquid back into itself. Charlotte couldn't quite see her feet. She extended her arms and patted the air before her, as if expecting to find a wall with a light switch. She hoped she wasn't stepping through a well-maintained flower garden, and just as she thought this, the smell of some perfumey bloom reached her nose, a reminder of all the things to which she didn't normally pay attention.

"Can I help you?" a voice from off to her right inquired, and Charlotte cried out, "Oh," her whole body jerking. "I just . . . I'm sorry. I wasn't trying to intrude. I couldn't find the door." She was yelling, she realized, over the noise of the dogs.

She could make out a large tree to her side and a figure sitting on a white wrought-iron bench wrapped around the trunk. The white shone in the dark, as Charlotte imagined she must, with her dress.

"I'll shut them up," the voice said—a man's—and he threw something—a rock, maybe?—over the fence. She heard it striking the neighbor's wall, then the man hollering, "Enough already," and the animals were quiet. In their stead, the night came alive with sounds—whistling frogs, the wind in the coconut palms, and a steady mechanical murmur, perhaps from an electric generator, farther back in the yard.

"Mutts," the voice said, disdainfully. "Stupid mutts."

"It's so dark," Charlotte said, and the man—suddenly closer, though Charlotte hadn't heard him stand—said, "Oh, it's you."

"What?" Charlotte asked then realized who it was. "Henry?" She squinted into the night.

"Yeah?" he said, and then he was next to her. "I'll show you." He turned toward the house. Despite his words, there was nothing in his manner to suggest he remembered *how* he knew Charlotte.

"I'm sorry," she said. "I'm so sorry about your brother."

He looked down, as if trying to compose himself, then said, "Come on," and started walking. She followed after. They came around the side of the house to the front drive with the white globes that Charlotte had seen a few days earlier. Henry stood over a globe, and the light flickered at his chin, the bottom of his nose. He hadn't shaved in a few days, and there was a musky tobacco smell to him.

"I'm not ready to go in just yet," he gestured to the house. "But you go."

"Do they . . ." She didn't know if he knew it was general knowledge that he'd disappeared after his brother's accident. "Do they know you're here?"

"Not yet." He sighed deeply. "So if you don't mind . . ."

"Oh, sure. I won't say anything." There was something intimate about this, she supposed; he was willing to trust her with a confidence. "Well, thanks," she said slowly, hoping he'd say something else. When he didn't, she turned and started up the path.

Then he said, so softly she wasn't sure, at first, he was speaking, "Hey, that was nice the other night, wasn't it?"

She waited for a moment then turned to say, "Yeah, it was." She kept her manner quiet, matching his.

"So maybe, when you're through in there," he waved again at the house, "you could come back out and we could talk."

"Oh, yeah, okay, I'll do that," Charlotte said. She had an urge to reach out to his arm, match the curve of its muscle to her palm.

"I'll be right back there," he pointed toward the circular white bench. "Where you found me."

Charlotte nodded, then continued up the walk, shifting, as she went, her hold on her purse, as if it no longer contained a canine defense system but Henry Lazar's eggshell heart.

A thin, black maid greeted her silently at the Lazars' door. Not the front door from the other night, but a side entrance to its right. Following Charlotte's eyes to her slippers, the maid whispered, "They're from Miss Perle." Charlotte imagined Perle had presented her old slippers as a gift, along with blouses permanently yellowed under the arms and towels worn thin with use. The maid led her through a small, dimly lit kitchen filled with bowls of rice salad, fruit, and chicken. It had been days since Charlotte had eaten a true meal—her diet had devolved into fritters, digestive biscuits, bananas, and white wine—and her interest in the food embarrassed her. Then Charlotte was in a large dining room/living room, its beige curtains drawn on the view. On the far side of the room, mourners gathered in a circle, reciting prayers.

Charlotte waited in the dining room till the circle broke up. Women embraced as men slid yarmulkes off their heads and into a straw basket that Abe Lazar passed around. Having collected the skullcaps, he came toward a bookcase near Charlotte. He stored the basket by a large dictionary, then looked up, a little lost, before he approached.

"Hello, again," he said, stretching out his hand.

"Yes," Charlotte said, "I'm so sorry. For your loss. And my timing."

Abe nodded.

Charlotte intuited his wish: that she not even try here. Still, she couldn't leave it at that. "I'm sorry I never got to meet Josh. I wish I'd had a chance to know him."

"Oh, you would have loved him," Abe said, as if he knew her well enough to claim such a thing. "Hannah put together a scrapbook. Would you like to see?"

"Oh, sure, yes." Charlotte followed him to the far side of the living room where some mourners were still chatting. A scrapbook lay on the center of a leather coffee table.

"I don't want to keep you from . . ." Charlotte indicated the others in the room who had drifted over to a stone table laden with food.

"Yes, I should," he said, "but let me set you up here." He picked up the scrapbook on the coffee table. "Hannah put it together."

"Yes, you said. Well . . ." She put out her hand. "I'd like to have a look."

Abe joined the others while Charlotte flipped through the scrapbook, saw a young boy slowly developing—a print in a tray of darkroom chemicals—into the face she'd seen the other night on the postcard. At first, there were pages of photographs of him: sitting in a crib; playing with a bigger boy (Henry, no doubt); wearing a large mask, then holding the mask at his side and giggling. There was a picture of him in a yarmulke, bent over the Torah: his bar mitzvah, no doubt. His hair, parted in the middle, was slicked to his head. In a later picture, he held a glass of pink frothy liquid and gave a wide grin. Charlotte sensed—she wasn't quite sure why—his misery. He looked skinny and pathetic. There were few pictures after that. But there were some documents to fill in the years: a letter admitting Josh to Harrison's Boys' College, a newspaper photograph of him on a surfboard. But the photograph might have been of a different person, for his body had suddenly fleshed out, the angles disappearing, muscles blooming on his frame. Steroids? Or a sudden devotion to a basement gym? The last photographs were of his high-school graduation. Perhaps he'd had a nose job and a chin job by then, because he looked dramatically different. Even his lips seemed thicker, and he had the vague, meathead look Charlotte had deciphered from the postcard. Finally, there was a transcript from a semester of classes at the University of the West Indies. Not something another parent would have saved: a B, two Cs, and two Ds. Charlotte wondered if he had been stupid. Or lazy. Or simply uninterested. He'd taken introduction to political philosophy, studio art, introduction to literature, meteorology, and algebra. He got a D in the math and philosophy classes, a B for meteorology. A boy who loved weather. Hannah, Charlotte supposed, would slip in his obituary after the report card. Only a mother could miss the scrapbook's final message: failing, failed.

"It's a shame," a woman said. Charlotte looked up to see the couple who'd been outside the Lazars' door the other night. Holding spartan plates of cut vegetables, they maneuvered themselves around the coffee table and joined her on the couch.

"Jody Rabinowitz," the woman said. She shook back her clunky gold bracelet and stuck out her hand. Charlotte took it. "And this is my husband, Jacob." Her husband leaned forward on the couch to wave a hello. He had a slight paunch but looked energetic, as if he had some sport— sailing or golf or something—to keep him attuned to his body. He was the only man who hadn't taken off his yarmulke.

"You're a visitor?" Jacob asked.

"Yes, I met you briefly the other night."

"Oh, I remember," Jody said

"The visitor with the menorah?"

"That's me."

"It's an interesting story, how that piece came to you in Boston. Do you know it?" Josh inquired, his tone professorial and warm.

Charlotte shook her head.

"Well, when our synagogue was deconsecrated, most of the belongings went to London, which made sense, but at the time, there was a young visitor who'd become quite smitten with the synagogue. It was almost like a love affair. He'd go every day to the synagogue. He thought it was terrible they were letting the place go to ruin. He'd get down on his hands and knees with a rag and wash the gravestones, pick the dirt out of the letters.

This was just for a week at first. He was a visitor, but then he bought a place here, and for a whole season, he was down at the government offices, trying to keep the synagogue open. Soon there wouldn't be any more Jews on the island, but this is what he wanted. Of course, it didn't work, but when they were deciding where the synagogue's effects should go, they must've thought, what the hell, and they gave the menorah to this man. Who took it, but he never felt like he should have it. It shouldn't belong to a person. It didn't matter that he had the piece just . . . how did they say it?"

"Until such time as the synagogue was reconsecrated," Jody said and smiled, perhaps at her legalese. Charlotte had the impression that Jody wasn't generally considered smart, that Jacob was known as the smart one in the couple. As if to confirm this perception, Jody shrugged apologetically and said, "I've read the contract."

"But this fellow, he kept the menorah till late in life, then he couldn't decide how to transfer ownership. He hadn't married. There were no children. It must have been 1960 or so, and he was maybe eighty himself. So he thought, 'Well, it's from the second oldest synagogue in the hemisphere.'"

"Is that true?" Charlotte said.

"I think so," Jody said, then called toward the dining room. "Abe, what's the synagogue? Second oldest in the hemisphere? Third?"

"I forget," Abe Lazar said, snappishly, and made an abrupt hand gesture, as if he were shooing away a bee, though he came toward Jody anyway.

"Whatever," Jacob said. "Whatever number it was. Let's say third. So he decided to entrust it to the third youngest synagogue in the hemisphere and that was this . . . what's your synagogue's name again?"

"Temple Sinai."

"Temple Sinai." Jacob slapped his thigh. "There you go."

It might as well have been Howard relating the tale. Jacob had that same eagerness to please through conversation. She could imagine him saying, as Howard often did, "Oh, listen, this'll interest you," as if he'd been saving some select morsel for her ears alone. It didn't matter that he'd repeat the story later, with the identical introductory line, to someone else.

Charlotte placed the scrapbook—in her hands, all this while—back on the table and relaxed into the couple's willingness to talk to her. "It's always been just the one synagogue here?" she leaned forward to address Jacob, then leaned back on the couch to include Jody in her gaze.

"Well, no," Jacob said. "A long time ago there was a synagogue in Speightstown, and there are still the black Jews. Their congregation is called the Heavenly . . . no, the Holy Temple of Sheba."

"Oh, them," Abe Lazar said, taking a seat opposite the couch. "Sheba. That's for handouts." He rubbed his thumb back and forth along his fingers then said, as if Charlotte didn't know the gesture, "For money. They're not legit."

"Really?"

"Well," Jacob said, "they have their ways and we have ours. There's no antagonism, but we don't worship together."

"The blacks," Abe said, "they like to say they're Jewish, because it means they're part white. You see?"

"I can't imagine *that's* true," Charlotte said sharply. The maid and a single black guest were on the other side of the room.

"This menorah," Jacob said, ignoring Abe's comment. "You know it's *copper*. And it just so happens that for the West African, copper was almost exclusively used for exchange. Or for rituals. Iron was the everyday metal."

"Actually," Charlotte put in, "the menorah is made of silver. With parcel gilt."

"Is it *really?*" Jacob asked. "So how did I get so misinformed?" He seemed genuinely curious, not at all aggrieved about being corrected. "Well, I apologize, shooting off my mouth like I know everything."

Abe Lazar stood, then, to give his seat to his wife, who had just joined them. But she did not sit. "Hannah," Abe said, taking her forearm, as if to steady her, "this is Charlotte Lewin. Remember? From Boston."

"Oh, yes," Hannah said and reached over the coffee table to take Charlotte's hand.

"I'm sorry for your loss," Charlotte said, standing herself.

"Oh, yes, yes." Hannah's eyes skittered away. "Will you have something to eat? We've got—I don't know what all. *Say* you'll have something to eat."

She seemed to require assent so Charlotte said, "Yes, in a bit."

"Oh, good. There's so much here. We don't know what we'll do with it. Really we don't." Hannah looked plaintively toward the dining room, then back to the group, but her eyes seemed to focus somewhere far behind them, as if the curtains were open and even in the dark she were able to see across the ocean to Montserrat, where orange worms of lava were snaking through the streets. "Jody," she called, tremulously, as if she'd only just realized her child had died. "Oh, God."

Jody stood and stepped awkwardly over the coffee table to take Hannah in her arms. "Okay," she said, patting her back. Hannah started to sob. "Okay." She pulled her to the wall, took both of her hands, and started speaking in a low voice.

"I'm sorry. You see . . ." Abe began.

"Of course," Charlotte interrupted. "Please, don't apologize."

Abe's heart started to ring. "What now?" he said and reached into his breast pocket to pull out a phone. "Right," he shouted into it. "Right. I'm coming." Then, forcefully, "I'll . . . be . . . right . . . there." He clicked the phone off. "My sister-in-law. If she'd only shut off the goddamn TV, she could hear me. But she's got that CNN on all the time."

"She's still calling the White House?" Jacob asked.

"Oh, sure," Abe said. "When she can advise the president. Apparently they all know her at this number she's found. She wants to talk to them about the extradition of Pol Pot."

"She calls the White House?" Jody turned from Hannah to say.

"You know all this," Jacob said and waved his hand, as if to indicate Jody should get back to the business of comforting Hannah.

"Well," Abe said, "for now, the important thing to know is she doesn't drive, so if you'll excuse me, I have to go get her." He called out to Hannah, as if she were far away, or hard of hearing, "I have to get Perle."

"Drive safe," Hannah said. Then, with the sure sense that disaster awaited him out on the roads, "Say you'll take care."

"Of course," he said, an edge to his voice, then turned to Jacob to add, "It's unbelievable where she lives. All the blacks walk in the middle of the street, and in the dark, you know, all you can see is their teeth."

Jacob scratched his head. "I guess I haven't ever been over by Perle's place."

"Why would you? A slum. She lives just like them in a slum. But it's what she wants. It's what she picked. Perhaps," Abe turned back to Charlotte, "we had better settle the business of the menorah now."

"Oh," Charlotte said, "I just need your address. Then we can ship it."

"Fine," Abe said. She expected him to be startled. After all, she'd told him she'd bring it with her. He pulled a card from his wallet. "Send it to my office," and then he turned abruptly, distracted already by the errand at hand.

"His sister-in-law's a bit of a chore," Jacob explained quietly. "A bit of a lunatic, in fact. When she forgets to take her lithium, that is."

Charlotte nodded at this, and he said, as if he were her ally in the conversation that had just transpired, "Let's get a drink. Don't you think we both need a drink?"

She poured a glass of wine then veered away from Jacob and made her way to the bathroom. She had a large swallow, then another. She wasn't quite sure why she was pretending she didn't have the menorah with her. If only Abe Lazar hadn't said blacks liked to claim they were Jewish, because it made them part white. Not that this was an impossible idea. She remembered a black friend in college—actually the man to whom she'd lost her virginity—telling her he wished he weren't black. And how startled she'd been, for she'd never wished she weren't Jewish. She'd always loved being in the minority—even, no, *especially* in the face of the occasional anti-Semitic remark. But—she knew, she knew—if she told him this, he'd say it was different, that she couldn't possibly understand.

Still, Abe's comment and then the line about blacks and their teeth. She could hardly hand him the menorah after *that*. Not that the whole community should suffer for *his* shortcomings. Although, as she thought this, something occurred to her. She weaved her way back to the kitchen and found the maid.

"Could I use the phone?" The maid pointed to a wall phone in the corner. "And do you have a phone book?"

"Right there," the maid mumbled. She was painfully shy, and Charlotte's mannerisms broadened to compensate for her lack of affect.

"Should I . . ." She put her hand to her throat. "Or maybe I'll be in your way." She fanned her hand out to indicate the kitchen.

"There's another phone. In the study."

Charlotte said, "Oh?" eagerly—this was what she wanted—and the maid led her into a small room off the kitchen. It was a mess of papers, open file drawers, and books piled into dangerous towers. Charlotte slipped into the chair behind an old wooden desk and mouthed a thank-you as the maid closed the door, leaving her alone in the musty-smelling room, its brown mess distinguished by lilac touches: an old throw pillow and a wall hanging of Noah and the Ark, with detachable animals nestled in tiny pockets along the purple fabric's surface.

She felt furtive as she located the number for the Holy Temple of Sheba. She didn't know who she thought would answer this late on a Thursday, but she dialed anyway. The phone rang twice, then someone picked up the line. There was no greeting, but a roaring sound, as if the phone were alongside the highway. Charlotte heard a noisy clatter and the indecipherable hubbub of conversation.

"Hello," Charlotte said. "Do I have the temple?"

"Wha'?" a man said. Behind him, an irate voice shouted, "Put my business out in the street? Out in *the street?*"

"Maybe I have the wrong number?"

"Wha'? Wha'?" the man said. There was a crashing sound, as if several tin garbage cans had been violently kicked over.

"I was wondering . . ." Charlotte started, then flashed on the turned-over garbage cans in the postcard she'd been sent and abruptly hung up. *So much,* she thought, *for that.* She took a lion from Noah's Ark, studied the thread of his mouth, then put him back, headfirst, in his pocket.

Henry outside. The fact of him tugged at her, but she had to stay a decent length of time at shiva, so she ambled back to the dining room, had a small plate of food, and listened to a conversation about a home for AIDS patients, a place right next to the island's old leper colony. Behind her, someone was recommending a restaurant to another mourner. "Oh," Charlotte heard a woman say, with such importance that Charlotte knew she was talking about Nancy and Ron, "the Reagans ate there." And a moment later, the same voice said knowingly, "Yes, the Reagans swam there."

After a while, she wandered back to Jacob's side.

"Do you like our island?" he asked her.

"You know what I like? Some sense of family I have here. Not my nuclear family, of course, but when I visited your synagogue, I felt surprisingly at home. In an almost historical sense, if that makes sense. I could see how I might fit in the calendar. I don't have that back at home."

"No?" Jacob said.

"I grew up in a WASPy suburb of Boston. I already know more about the history of this place than I ever did about my hometown. I suppose it's often that way when you travel."

"No, no, I don't think so. I think you're feeling something that *is* special about our community."

"Have you lived here long?"

"My whole life. The kids—people Josh," he grimaced, "and Henry's age—they move on. It's different now. They're people of passage. And they don't marry Jews. There are no Jews here for them to marry. I don't blame them, but it makes me sad. Here," he said and gestured to two stiff-backed chairs pulled away from the dining-room table, so guests could serve themselves food, "why don't we sit?"

"Do you mind if I ask you about something you said back there?"

"Not at all," Jacob said. "If it's something I can answer, I'll tell you." He tapped the rim of his wineglass with one finger. "You're in luck. After all, 'What a sober heart conceal, does a drunken tongue reveal.' It's an old Bajan proverb."

"Just about the black Jews and . . ."

"Oh," Jacob waved his hand. "It's not like Abe says. It's a real temple. They have services on Saturday mornings and everything. The style is different. It's completely different. Blacks come to our services, too. You should come. You'll see."

"So with this menorah . . ."

"Oh, the black Jews? Well, despite what I just said, they're not *technically* Jews, because they haven't converted, though they claim lineage back to the tribe of Judah. I don't think they'd even want the menorah, since it's not part of *their* religious history here. It's hard to explain. That rabbi . . . well, he has strange living habits. I don't know much, but there must be somebody who can tell you." He pulled a small black address book out of his pants and flipped through it quickly. "I just . . . hm . . . I don't know. I don't know who can help you."

"Well, that's okay." Charlotte pulled her hand through her hair. She wondered what time it was. "I read the newspaper this morning, and there was a fair amount of anger being expressed at the Jews. At least by the director of the Bajan Institute, who wants the menorah, too. It made me wonder if . . ."

Jacob nodded his head sympathetically then cut her off. "Yes, I know him. Elcock. A bit of a rabble-rouser. He has a point about the menorah. I'm not denying that, but really, a sacred object. He should understand." Jacob threw up his hands. "We worry about that here. If we make too much of a . . . if we're too much of a presence, people will hate us. So we try to lie low. And even so, this happens. It's a bad situation."

"Yes, I see."

"And what else? You can ask me anything."

"I should have met you my first day here! But, no, that's all." She laughed. "Actually, no, I *do* have a question. Tell me about Marty Berkowitz. What's his association with the . . ."

"Oh, him," Jacob said dismissively. "How do you know *him?*"

"He called me about the menorah and I spent . . ."

"Why would he call *you?*" Jacob pulled himself back in the seat, as if he expected to hear something startling.

"I don't know. I thought he was representing the synagogue, but then . . ."

Jacob's posture relaxed. He started to laugh and shake his head. "I gotta tell Jody this . . ."

"Oh, please, don't. I mean, it wasn't a big deal. He never quite got to . . ."

"All right," he said but beckoned his wife over nonetheless. "He's trying to consolidate his power in the synagogue. Oh, I shouldn't even go into it, but he wants . . . he probably thought if he could broker something with you, everyone would thank him for it, and he'd get voted president, which is what he wants. And which is never going to happen. The Lazars and he . . ." Jacob held up his two forefingers and drew them apart. "Once they were in together on some development project, but Abe says Berkowitz messed his end up. Acting the big shot, squandering money. Anyway, they don't get along."

"Oh, is the community very fractious?"

"Not really," Jody put in. "Just your normal back-and-forth."

"In fact," Jacob continued, " I wouldn't be surprised if Berkowitz shows up here tonight. He was planning to come. They don't get along, but everyone's polite enough. You know, the community is so small we have to tolerate everyone."

Jody nodded her agreement then said, "Marty's thing is that he thinks he's funny with all his tricks and jokes. He couldn't be more offensive, but he doesn't see it."

Charlotte nodded. She didn't want to be around if Berkowitz was going to show, and that seemed excuse enough to make her departure. She'd go back out to talk with Henry—that possibility had already charged the evening for her, though she didn't know what she supposed would happen, just that she felt the nonsensical anticipation that she associated with the moment before she read her merit reviews at the museum or parted from a date. It all came down to the same thing: someone decided to, or not to, kiss you. Literally, metaphorically. The moment of judgment—if you cared for the judge—was always terrible and erotic. You were wanted. Or you were not.

"Berkowitz, though." Jacob shook his head. "I'd keep your distance. He's the kind of guy who burns buildings for insurance money."

Jody slapped Jacob's arm. "Now, you don't know that about him." She turned to Charlotte and said, "We're just a bunch of small-town gossips."

"You're right, you're right," Jacob said. "I have no proof, but I'd like to know where that man gets his money. Of course, if he *did* burn a building, he'd tell you it was funny and that you just weren't clever enough to get the joke. Which, undoubtedly, we're not."

"Listen," Charlotte said, "I really should be going but thank you. Thank you for talking."

"Of course." Jody reached over to give her a hug, and Jacob did the same, as if they were not two people she'd just met but family.

Outside, her feet felt the way to the backyard. She grew steadily accustomed to the dark, could make out more now. The yard appeared to be covered with low, flowering trees. Behind them, a row of coconut palms provided some protection from the wind off the ocean. But she didn't see Henry.

"Um . . . Henry?" she tried, but that was all she would say. She wasn't going to go stomping about calling his name. She was conscious of feeling deflated but also of being unwilling to wait for him, like some girl at a restaurant, sitting long past the hour of a rendezvous, advertising her readiness to be disregarded. Still, she found the white bench where she'd seen Henry earlier and sat, for a moment, to fix the strap of her sandal. It had twisted and was whittling a blister into the back of her heel.

"So there you are," Henry called and suddenly he was beside her. "I thought you'd forgotten about me."

"No, I wouldn't forget." He shifted closer to her, perhaps trying to re-establish the intimacy of the other night.

"How is it in there?" he gestured with his head to the house. He smelled of mint—was he trying to cover up some drinking?—and of salt, as if he'd gone for a swim since she'd last seen him, then let the ocean dry on his skin. His hair was even wet.

"Umm . . . sad?" Charlotte said. Was this what he meant? "Where were you? I mean, where have you been the past few days?"

He looked away abruptly, as if this were an irritating question, but turned his head back to say, "Away. I didn't know . . . I didn't know about the accident till I came back."

"Where's away?" Charlotte wanted to ask but thought better of it, then thought better of *that*. Who the hell cared what she asked? "Where'd you go?"

"Oh, a charter boat, with some friends. That's what I do sometimes. For money. Or whatever. And I come back and my brother's dead." His voice took on a poor-pitiful-me quality that, while hardly undeserved, made Charlotte flinch. "And everyone wants to know what I had to do with it."

Charlotte pulled her head back. "No one thinks you had anything to do with it."

He nodded, then ran a knuckle back and forth against the chapped skin of his lips. Charlotte couldn't see the details of his mouth but could hear the decisive whisper of skin against skin. Even now, she had the urge to lean over and kiss him, to put her hand under the open collar of his shirt. "Well, I don't know," he said at length. "Not that I even knew. Like I said. I was just trying to get out of a party." He looked back at the house. "My parents' parties," he said, as if that explained it all.

They were quiet then, and in the silence, Charlotte wondered why he was what he was to her. Which was: someone she purely wanted. His

looks—and that was really it, the container of him—had some sort of authority, some claim on confidence, maybe even glamour, for which she
longed. It didn't surprise her that he was the first white she'd met here
who seemed comfortable among blacks, who was enough a part of their
lives that they'd have rumors about him.

Henry ran his fingers through his hair and sighed. He was in the camp
of the elegantly troubled.

"I lost"—she needed to make it clear that she was in the club herself,
the woefully wounded, though it made her a little sick to use Helen's
death this way, "a sister. To an illness, not an accident, so I know . . . I
mean I don't know, but . . ."

"No," he said, thoughtfully. "No, then *you'd* understand." His voice
took on a tone Charlotte recognized from back home; she was about to be
admitted into a confidence. "Ever since he died, I just . . . I can't stop
thinking that I'm going to die, too, you know? Do you have that?" It was
as if his brother's death were months, instead of days, in the past.

"No." She gave a half-snort, half-laugh. "I think everyone I love is
going to die. But I don't think *I'm* going to die. My punishment is going to
be that I'll outlive everyone I care about." She wasn't joking, exactly, but
she kept her tone light enough. She hated most of her other fears—was
ashamed of the way she flinched at dogs, started near ledges, held the bi-
cycle brakes all the way down hills—but felt there was something generous in this fear: it meant she loved others, didn't it?

"Well," he said. He stood, and, with that word, seemed to be shaking his
thoughts off, as if he shouldn't have tried to share them. He had a manner
that suggested tremendous forbearance. It drew her in—she supposed she
idealized the troubled—but then there was something too heavy-handed
in the sag of his back, his sheepish gaze at the ground, as if he'd italicized his
own emotions for effect when he should have left them in plain type.

Charlotte stood, too. It seemed their conversation was over.

"So," he said, as if this were what he meant to say all along, "should we
get involved?"

"What?"

"*You* know," he said and stepped toward her, so he could reach his
hand around her back, run it down her side and over the curve of her ass.

A crazy non sequitur of a gesture. He was too shaken, she supposed, to know what he was doing. Still, she imagined throwing away her life—the whole unsatisfying mess of it—pitching all her wool sweaters and moving to the island.

So she didn't step back when he kissed her, though it felt strange, stranger maybe than the other night when she had more alcohol to ease things. His tongue felt heavy, almost sandy, in her mouth. She started to pull back, but he put his arms around her and started to run his fingers enthusiastically through her hair. The energy felt inappropriate for the moment, so she reached up to take his wrists. In an instant, she was dizzy, unsure where her body ended and his started. But it wasn't passion that made her feel this way. She pulled his hands down and said, "You're wearing my watch."

Even in the dark, she could see it on his wrist—a woman's Timex with a slim black band. If she leaned in closely, she had no doubt she'd see the small blue squiggles that meant the watch was waterproof. If he hadn't shaken her hands away when he heard her words, her fingernails might have traced the tiny grooves from when she'd scratched the watch face on the pebbly wall of her parents' basement.

"You," she started and coughed a little—a piece of his hair, or her own, was going down her throat—"you stole my watch."

"Oh, yeah." He grinned. "I took it when we were playing cards." He held up his wrist, which looked surprisingly fey with the woman's watchband. "I've been wearing it ever since."

She stared at him. He seemed proud.

"I hope you haven't missed it," he said, as he unfastened it. She held out her palm, and he dropped it in. "I didn't know you'd come here, you see. So I took it. So I'd have an excuse to call you."

"Oh." Her shoulders relaxed. It was an explanation, at least. "You didn't need an excuse."

"Well," he smiled shyly, though there was something confident, even in this shyness, as if he knew it would charm, "I didn't know that."

She looked at the watch. "It's midnight?"

"Oh, no," he said. "Let me see that." She handed the watch back to him, and he held it to his eye, then his ear. "No, it's stopped."

"I guess I need a new battery."

"No, it's ruined. I always stop watches. That's why I never wear one. You'll have to let me buy you a new one."

Charlotte remembered the conversation from the other night, how he said he'd started a clock just by thinking about it.

"I'm awfully sorry," Henry said.

"Don't worry about it." Charlotte folded the watch into her pocket. "A cheap thing, anyway." She stepped back. Why would he take her watch if he knew he'd ruin it? "I need to call a taxi. I need to get home."

"You think I'm a bad man now?" he said, smiling, and Charlotte didn't know how to answer. He was one of those men on whom irony and honesty were indistinguishable. She imagined that when he was being most cutting, he was most earnest, and as if to confirm this suspicion, Henry said, "Did I ever say, Ms. Lewin, how much I admire your project here?" She didn't know that she'd ever told him about the menorah.

"What's the matter with you?" she said.

"Oh, come on. I'm teasing."

Never, Charlotte thought of a children's book that had puzzled her when she was a girl, *tease a weasel. A weasel will not like it and teasing isn't nice.*

"Let's sit again. Come on. Let's sit."

She did, reluctantly. "Honestly, I only took it because I wanted to see you again. I didn't know you'd have business with my parents. Greg— you remember the newspaper guy from the card game?—*he* told me. But after . . ."

"Okay, okay," she waved him quiet.

"I guess. I haven't been thinking clearly. Even more so, of course, since I got back." He sighed deeply and Charlotte felt ashamed for forgetting, however briefly, the grief he must be feeling. "I've got to go in there. I've got to go in there tonight."

Charlotte nodded, as if to say, "Yes, you do."

"Thinking I was responsible," he murmured and shook his head. "It's so crazy. It's always so crazy." And Charlotte realized—with something like shock—that he was on the edge of tears.

"It's okay," she said, meaning his emotion: it was okay to be upset. She stroked his back and when he turned to her and started to kiss her again, she thought possibly he'd engineered the moment of sadness to make her start touching him, but the kiss felt earnest—slow and mournful, if a kiss can be such a thing. Then he was unzipping the back of her dress and whispering, "You know, what I'd like to do . . ." and before he could finish, she patted his arms away from her, shook him off.

"I mean," she gestured to his parents' house, as if the death itself were embodied by the home.

"I know," Henry said, "I know," and then he leaned over to kiss her again. Charlotte went with it: his mouth on hers, his hand on her breast, but then he started to pull up her dress and said, "Just turn around. Let me fuck you from behind."

"What's the matter with you?" Charlotte pulled away from him again and crossed her arms over her chest. "What's going on?"

"What do you mean?"

"I mean," she said, her eyes opening wide and her arms spread as if to indicate the whole yard, "what *is* this?"

"I'll call you a taxi," he said, as if he suddenly couldn't wait to be rid of her. "You're right. You need a taxi."

"Are you all right?" she asked. And when he didn't answer, "This is a little . . . I *really* need to get home."

"See, I didn't think you'd want to see me again." But he didn't truly sound disappointed.

"That's not the issue." Something occurred to her. "You didn't send me those notes, did you?"

"I just didn't think you'd want to see me again," he repeated. It was hard to get a handle on him. She had the sense that inside Henry was another, smaller Henry, the true Henry, a boxer, bobbing and weaving, pleased to be dodging definition.

"So you used your brother's . . . God, what kind of person would use their brother's death like that when he wasn't even . . . " What did people say, *When he was still warm in the ground?* Which someone would always be, down here. "Didn't you think . . . ?" But she stopped herself. She actually—this was rare for her—didn't want to know more.

"What're you talking about?"

"The postcard."

"What postcard?"

"The postcard from your brother. Did you send that?"

"He's dead. There's no reason to make fun of me."

"On Tuesday, I got two notes. Slipped under my hotel door. From your brother. Did you send them?"

"Holy shit, no. What do you mean, 'from my brother'?"

"Never mind." But, of course, he wouldn't leave it at that, and she ended up explaining the whole thing, the strange notes under her hotel door, calling her downstairs for a meeting that never happened.

"Well, who would do that?" Henry asked, but Charlotte didn't trust his curiosity, for instead of waiting for an answer he said, "You look so good in that dress."

"Shouldn't you . . . aren't you even upset your brother died? I mean . . . that would make most people want to hold their horses for, say, twenty-four hours."

Henry stepped back, clearly outraged. "Of course, I'm upset. But I mean, my God, he tried so many times before, it's just . . ." He moderated his voice. "It's just, I did this already, and so many times in my imagination, that I already . . . I mean, let's see." He looked up at the stars. "When I was 15 and 18 and 21, and it's now, like, okay. What's different is this is the last time."

"He *killed* himself?"

"Well, he'd make it *look* like an accident."

"He *killed* himself?"

Henry said nothing.

"But they accused a man of murdering your brother!"

"They?"

"Your parents."

"No," Henry said. "They wouldn't do that. They'd know how it happened."

"Well, they must *know* about the accusation. It was in the papers. Don't you read the paper?"

"Only the *Times*."

Oh, la de da, she almost said. "Well, your parents must have read about it."

"Oh, yeah," he said, sarcastic, as if he'd intuited her unspoken thought, "where'd you think I got *that* habit?"

"I'm sorry, I cannot believe that your parents wouldn't read an article about their own son's death."

"Well." Henry shrugged, as if to say it was her right not to believe, but that didn't change the facts.

"I think you better call the authorities." And then, since he stayed quiet, she dropped her voice and said, "Why . . . did he?"

"To punish my parents, I suppose." Henry shrugged. "Or me."

"Well," Charlotte said, not meaning to make a joke, but unable to stop herself, "there's getting back at your parents and then there's getting back at your parents."

Henry gave a rueful laugh. "Well, he certainly made a statement."

"Why? I mean, what happened?" Charlotte meant, she supposed, what happened in the family, as if Henry could answer.

She expected him to snap at her, but he said, "You've met them."

She nodded her head.

"Well," he said, "wouldn't you?"

Kill yourself, she thought he meant. What a batty idea. And yet here she was, someone who wasn't a stranger to suicidal thoughts.

"Oh shit," Henry said, and pressed his fingers to the bridge of his nose, "I can't . . ." His voice broke. "You know, when I was on the life raft . . . you heard *that* story . . . I floated around for a couple of days then washed up here, all dehydrated. But I had time to think, and suicide's mean. That's its"—he stumbled a little, as if he weren't used to abstract thought—"its essential character. And to do it this way." He cleared his throat. "Talk about a fuck-you." There was a long silence before he spoke again. "I trust you," he said.

"Why should you? You don't even know me."

"But I can see . . . I can see you're a good person. I could see that right away." This reminded her of Marty. Hadn't he said something like this the other day? "If I asked you to do something, you'd do it, wouldn't you?" he continued.

"I would not," she said, guessing he meant sex and scaring herself, a little, by realizing she was still open to him, open to the idea of him. What was with her? She'd been so weirdly reckless since she got here, as if she'd checked her instinct for self-preservation—along with a spare case of produce—at customs.

"You would," he said, and she thought if he kissed her now, she wouldn't pull back—she was that foolish. Concubine for the sex maniac. A decidedly mixed-up girl.

"I've been carrying something around with me. You should probably give it to the police."

"Why don't *you* give it to them?"

"Well, that would be a hard thing to do," he said.

"Well, what is it?"

"It's a letter. Josh always writes these letters. Before . . ." He waved his hand, and in the flutter of his fingers, Charlotte saw the previous efforts, the razor blade to the wrist, the swallowed bottle of pills, the surfing during hurricanes.

"No," she said, "that's crazy. And they'll think it's crazy, too. A tourist bringing them your brother's suicide note?"

Henry was quiet for a minute, considering her logic. "But you'll explain it to them. How . . . I didn't want to hurt my parents. I mean, I'm going to go in there," he pointed to the house, "and tell them to call the police themselves, so you'll just be bringing evidence in case they don't call."

"Well, if you explain everything, why wouldn't they call?"

"My parents. You never know. They might want to save face. They might not want to believe it."

"Well, if there's any doubt . . ."

"There's *no* doubt," Henry said sharply. "The evidence of the world doesn't change *their* view of the world."

Henry turned toward a suit jacket lying on the bench behind him. He took something from a pocket.

"Please take it," Henry said and pressed an envelope into her hand, but she wouldn't, and the letter dropped, a white flag, between their feet. "You have to. To free an innocent man." A gust of wind tumbled the envelope across the grass, and they both went running for it. Charlotte stabbed the envelope with the heel of her sandal, tearing paper in the process. He picked it up, licked the flap to seal it, and then they both walked back toward the bench.

"I don't want my folks to read it," Henry said, quietly, then he pushed the letter back into her hands, as if it were a bomb only a stranger could defuse.

"Okay," Charlotte said, realizing that he was giving her a gift, a chance to repay her debt to Wayne and Trevor. "I'll take it to the police for you."

"Okay, and I'll get you a cab," he said. He produced a hand-held phone from his jacket, then motioned her out the gate. The dogs from before were gone, and the air was slightly chilly. "I'll wait with you," Henry said, guiding her back to the empty sidewalk.

"Thanks."

"Will you see me again?" Henry said as he took his hand from her.

"I think I'd better say no." Charlotte felt her cheeks and eyes tighten into an apologetic squint. She would be in Barbados for two more weeks and could see she'd spend the whole time longing to call him.

A car pulled to the front of the house, and Henry insisted on stepping back into the shadows, so his parents' friends wouldn't see him. A second car pulled up. Marty Berkowitz emerged from the first car, stuck his hand through the open window of the second, and shook hands with the occupant. He went back to his own car and leaned through a window. Inside, Tatiana fiddled with the car's backseat light switch, illuminating herself, then settling into darkness, then illuminating herself again. Marty gave her something—a picture book?—then as he turned to walk away, he looked back over his shoulder and called into the car, "Stay," as if Tatiana were a dog.

"He thinks he's funny," Henry said, "but what he is is an asshole." Charlotte liked him for the judgment: a man with a moral sense, after all.

A cab pulled up, and Charlotte stepped back onto the sidewalk. A hand emerged from the window of the cab and motioned her forward, but Henry caught her arm. "Let me visit you. Where are you staying?"

She smiled—it *was* flattering to be asked. "The Paradise, but, no. I'm sorry." She had the real sense he might be this ardent with half a dozen other women before the night was over.

He put his hand on her waist.

"Thank you," she said, automatically, as if she'd received a compliment.

Behind her, she heard Marty talking with the cabdriver, "Will you let me have your keys?" he said. "Will you let me have your keys?"

"No," the driver said. "What you want my keys for?"

"Because no one's ever given me a free taxi before, and then I can say I got a free taxi."

"Jerk," Henry said and leaned over to kiss Charlotte on the mouth. The taxi honked loudly. "Yes, yes," she cried and ran into the street. "I'm here."

She didn't say hello to Berkowitz, couldn't stand the idea of even a pleasantry. Instead, she stepped into the infernally hot taxi. Wind blew from the dashboard, as if the driver had the heat on.

"The nearest police station," she said hurriedly, and as the driver pulled from the curb, she heard Berkowitz call out, in the same tone with which he'd addressed the driver, as if he were terribly amusing, "Did you get my cards? I hope you got my notes."

Charlotte delivered the letter as promised, but on Friday and then again on Saturday, the papers gave no evidence that the police had been swayed by its contents. On Friday, the *Nation* didn't even report on the Lazar murder. The major news item concerned an upcoming fight between Evander Holyfield and Mike Tyson. There was a letter to the editor, though, a complaint about how the media was handling the Lazar story: far more attention for the murder of a white man than there would have been for a black man. The editors replied that murder—black, white, or green—was rare in Barbados, and always newsworthy. The next day, an angry reader wrote, "The editors refer to people 'either black, white, or green,' which implies that there are green people in the world. People all over this planet are either black, white, or yellow, there are absolutely no green people. Thus, it is fallacious to make a reference to such."

Charlotte wondered what to do. She'd spent Friday at the archives again, which she realized were located in the old leper colony that she'd heard someone mention at shiva. She had a renewed interest in finding a reason *not* to return the menorah to the Jews, but her research was getting her nowhere. She didn't know how to proceed, and the librarians had grown testy with her requests. Others used the archives to trace their roots, paging through old slave registries, antique tomes with spidery handwriting and pages crumbly as piecrust. "Jensen, Jensen," a woman who looked a bit like Alice Walker had crooned her family name as she scanned a scratched microfilm screen. Charlotte had liked watching her, felt how large her world might become if she stayed here, opted for a new life, altogether different from the one for which she'd prepared herself. Even her awkwardness—and she did feel awkward in her whiteness, no-

ticed how the librarians seemed to make a point of helping her last—
didn't pain so much as intrigue her; there were layers of things she didn't
normally consider, and the island was forcing her to those things.

On Saturday, Charlotte couldn't return to her research—this time at
the museum's library—without doing something for Trevor. A second
visit to the police seemed unlikely to help; why should they trust her version of Henry's story? So: call Wayne? call Henry? call the Lazars? What
she knew: a weight, burdensome as the menorah, that would lift on transfer. She needed to talk. Still, she allowed herself a few rounds of picking
up the phone receiver, then hanging it back up, before she finally dialed
the Lazars.

"He's not here," Abe said when she asked for Henry, and since he
didn't offer to take a message, Charlotte wondered if he ever had been. "I
didn't know you knew my son," Abe allowed, after a moment.

"I had a chance to talk to him the other night," Charlotte began, surprised by her own nervousness. "And something he said made me wonder
if you'd seen the *Daily Nation*, if you'd seen . . . I'm sorry . . . how they've
been covering the accident?"

"Of course, I've seen the papers," Abe said, a get-to-the-point brusque-
ness in his reply.

"So you know that Trevor Deare has been charged . . ."

"Young lady, my son is dead. I'm not particularly in the mood for small
talk." Abe paused, then called to someone off the line, "It's nothing."

Charlotte heard a receiver being lifted. A third person breathed on
the line. Henry? But no one said a thing. "Yes, yes," she actually stuttered,
her voice rising into its terrible girly twitter. "But if you had reason to believe it was an *unjust* accusation, since your son had a history of . . . " she
couldn't bring herself to say *suicide attempts*, so she finished off with the
word "depression."

Hannah's voice—from the other receiver—replied in a clinical,
knowing way, "Josh got down in the dumps sometimes, but I wouldn't call
that depression. Not in the capital D sense."

"Get off the line," Abe barked, then hissed, not over the line but
through the rooms of the house, "Have you *ever* had an unexpressed
thought?" A receiver clattered down, then Abe addressed Charlotte,
"How can you bother my family at a time like this? How can you? Where

do they *get* people like you? Where do they *find* you?" The implied answer: the worlds of the Kelipah, the Jewish realms of evil that Charlotte had never even heard of before last night, when she'd finally cracked the book on Judaism that she'd brought with her from Boston.

"I'm sorry. I'm terribly sorry. I'll go now," she said, and before he could respond, she hung up.

He'd rattled her, and she sat back on her bed, stunned. *He's a racist*, she reminded herself. And rude to his wife, his friends. But she knew, she knew. Her and her questions. People told her she could go on sometimes. It cowed her—the criticism—and then she got on her high horse. Curiosity was a virtue. Without it, how could you have love? Or justice?

She remembered, then, that someone—Wayne?—had told her that Henry and Josh had fought before the Lazars' party, and she wondered why she hadn't thought to ask Henry what the fight was about. And why, too, she hadn't simply stuck her head out of the taxi the other night, and said to Marty Berkowitz, "Why? *Why* did you send me those notes?"

And then, picking up the phone again, she had a final question—this time for herself—why hadn't she called Wayne and told him what she knew in the first place?

CHAPTER TWELVE

Wayne Deare

June 28, 1997

⁓

A DAY SPENT STAPLING POSTERS to telephone poles, tucking flyers under windshield wipers. Announcements of the evening rally. Busyness staving off worry. By late afternoon, Frank, Toni, and Wayne were exhausted—damp with sweat, dizzy with exertion—and the rally hadn't even begun. They conferred by the base of the Lord Nelson statue. Nearby, thick orange extension cords snaked away from a generator, down the street, and into a building where—even from here—Wayne could hear an exercise instructor calling out the steps for an aerobics class. "Over the top," a woman's voice kept saying. "Over."

Frank had rigged up a microphone to project his voice to the whole of Trafalgar Square, which was no square, but a concrete park, shaped like an exclamation point, an enthusiasm that separated the Houses of Parliament from the Careenage—an inlet of still water that ran under two small bridges and a tarred-over car park before it opened up for pleasure boats and eventually the sea.

It was Saturday evening, and Trevor was still in Glendairy. In four days, Wayne could have fifteen more minutes with him.

"Ready for oratory?" Toni asked Frank.

"You know I am." Frank seemed—it was strange to use the word in connection with him—happy. He reached up and slapped, for no particular reason, the knee of Lord Nelson.

"Well, let's have a little of that standpipe logic," Toni said and turned to Wayne to add, "He who talks the loudest gets to be right." The microphone crackled on.

"I hope so," Wayne said. In the past two days, he'd learned nothing about his brother's situation or why the authorities thought they had a right to hold him. Yesterday, Frank had called him with a new piece of information: the Lazars hadn't, as Frank had first supposed, made the charges against Josh. It had been Berkowitz, Berkowitz all along. He'd told the police he was a representative of the Jewish community, ready to speak for the Lazars who were, he'd insisted, too heartbroken for accusation. So Frank's new idea: Berkowitz did it. Only he hadn't meant to kill a Lazar. He'd meant to kill Trevor, his wife's lover. A black man, after all; entirely dispensable. But the last-minute parachute exchange had thwarted Berkowitz's plans. So, another idea for revenge. Pin a murder on Trevor. The theory. But, as the police were quick to point out, there was no evidence. Still, the Lazars—according to Frank—were happy to go along with Berkowitz's accusation. If there was no evidence against a Jewish man *and* no evidence against a black man, then clearly the black man was guilty.

"Don't panic," Toni had called Wayne last night to say, and she repeated her reassurances now, but Wayne was as agitated as he'd ever been, his stomach in a hard knot. When he'd stood up from the toilet this morning, its contents were half-shit and half-blood.

Frank had timed the rally to coincide with the final hour of a rare Saturday meeting of Parliament—some special session to consider the current controversy over the Greenland dump. (A sign that Wayne had been away from the island for too long: when he first returned, someone mentioned Greenland, and he thought they meant the island in the northern Atlantic.) Toni and Wayne positioned themselves against the concrete wall and railing that ran along the Careenage. If Trafalgar Square itself were a lady's fan, half-collapsed, then Toni and Wayne were standing on the fan's outer finger, just where the decorated silk started. From here, they had a full view of the Square and the Parliament buildings, as well as of Frank standing opposite the fan's fulcrum. At dusk, Frank called out, "Brothers," then coughed into the microphone and began to tell the story of Trevor Deare and the powerful white interests who had accused him. At first, it didn't seem anyone would take notice. None of the cab-drivers, who lined the far side of the park, came over, nor did any of the hawkers by the bridge, nor the last of the day's Rastafarians, still selling small statues to people exiting the bus station, half a block from the

Square. Tourists, beggars, even a goat crossed the Square without ac-knowledging Frank's words with more than a vague scowl in the statue's direction. Members of Parliament, finally through with *their* discussion, scurried to cars, eager to get home for dinner. The only truly attentive per-son was a bald woman in a pink housedress and man's straw hat. She sat cross-legged at Frank's feet. At intervals, she reached one hand up and doffed the hat, as if greeting a passerby.

Still, Frank persevered. There was nothing in his manner to suggest the absence of a devoted crowd, and perhaps for this reason, the bald woman was eventually joined by early evening revelers, then by some skateboarding teenagers, and finally a reporter who took notes on a nar-row paper pad. His interest seemed to attract others. The streetlights clicked on, and they gave Frank's hastily constructed podium the look of a stage set. Within half an hour, there was a respectable crowd—thirty or so—and by 8:00, the Square was packed. "A hundred," Toni guessed when the numbers seemed to have peaked. Wayne thought it might be more. Some vendors wheeled over, and people bought beers and maubys and sugar cakes. A nearby rehearsal for Crop Over had ended, and from 7:30 on, the gathering, dotted with people in costume, had a festive feel.

"Well," Toni patted Wayne's shoulder, "a confirmed success."

"Attendance," Wayne allowed, but he was losing hope. He'd never liked these sorts of events. They unnerved him. The seal-like response of the crowd, Frank's dumbed-down, inflammatory rhetoric: how would any of this translate into Trevor's release? But the phone calls, the phone calls Frank had made . . . they might. Or Wayne had to think they would.

After a while, he stopped listening to Frank, or he heard him but only vaguely, because he was thinking of things—stupid things—about Trevor, like a time when the flying fish were coming in to spawn by Oistins, and they had gone out into the water and grabbed them, thrown handfuls up to their mother onshore. Or another time, when they were fishing with their homemade poles by Cattlewash, filling up Trevor's backpack with the little fish they'd caught. They thought their mother would be proud of their haul instead of disgusted with them for ruining Trevor's backpack.

"You all right?" Toni said. She had gone off for a while and returned with a soda for Wayne.

"Yeah, I thinking about my brother and thing like that."

A man with a radio passed by and drowned out Frank for a second. "Your spleen," Wayne heard through the static, "your toenails, all very, very special."

Then there was Frank saying, "The Lazars have no interest in these discoveries. They say the claim to this menorah is historical, but they are—they have proven themselves to be—no friends of history."

In front of Wayne, a woman with silvery plaits that met at the top of her head like border piping shouted out, "Keep them big mouth shut."

And there was a chorus of agreement: the Lazars should be silenced.

"What happened to my brother?" Wayne asked. He hopped up onto the railing of the wall behind him. Below him the harbor water looked scummy, as if someone had been boiling beans in it.

Toni didn't answer but gestured with her chin to Charlotte, who was standing under a streetlight on the other side of the park. It was dark, but there were enough city lights to make people out. "That white girl is waving at you."

"That's her," Wayne said. "The one with the menorah."

"Cute," Toni said. "If you go in for that sort of thing."

He wasn't sure what sort of thing she meant. He waved back, but he'd already lost sight of her. "Thanks for this," he said and wiped the can's condensation along the back of his neck, before putting it between his legs so he could use one hand to crack it open. His clothes were plastered to him. Even the legs of his shorts were wet. It had taken a long time, up north, to get out of the habit of taking several showers a day. A girl in his dorm used to tease him about it, and he'd explained about the heat in Barbados, how dirty it made you feel, and she'd said, as if this weren't an insulting thing to say, "Oh, and I just thought you had a stick up your ass."

"Now she's there," Toni said and pointed to Charlotte who'd moved forward in the crowd. She was wearing a white and red halter dress and rubbing, as she walked, lotion into her left shoulder. She must have just put some on her face, because when she passed under a streetlight, Wayne could see a large white streak at her chin. Wayne waved, then whistled to get her attention. She put her arm up—Wayne thought she was acknowledging him—but she was actually raising her hand, like a schoolchild, to be called on.

"Miss," Frank called out. Apparently he was taking questions.

"I wondered if you could say something about your CBC interview," she said. "In particular, what you said about conspiracies."

Wayne jumped down off the railing. "What's she talking about?"

Toni cocked her mouth into a half-grimace. "Oh, I found out when I got the Coke." She gestured to his can. "Frank was on the CBC, and he said eight of the ten ultrarich who bought land on the northeast coast were Jewish and didn't care about some poor black kid, just as long as they had an explanation for Josh's death. He said these were the same people who were keeping a valuable piece of silver from the Institute, who'd take art from the hands of its makers. A conspiracy."

"He said that?"

"It was on the news."

"Oh, boy," Wayne said. "Even when he *knows* the Lazars didn't accuse Trevor?"

"I think he'd argue they did when they let Marty Berkowitz speak for them, but take heart. At least he didn't say, 'A conspiracy of Jewish money-lenders.'"

"But that's what people would hear. No? God, this," Wayne jerked his ear to the statue, "isn't about helping my brother, is it?"

She shrugged, "It might not be, but it might help anyway."

"I just . . ." His guts twisted painfully. He had this idea that something was ripping apart in there, that for the rest of his life, everything he ate would come out as blood.

Toni reached up and touched his forearm lightly. "It really might."

"Miss," Wayne turned from Toni to hear Frank say, "when you're lying facedown in the gutter and the Man has his foot on your neck, you don't ask him what God he's praying to. You just know that there's a foot on your neck."

"I don't think you're answering my question," Charlotte said, as if she weren't angry but confused. Still, the crowd responded with a low hiss.

"Somebody shut *her* up," the woman in front of Wayne called.

"Frank, my man," Toni said as if she were actually cautioning, *Easy, easy.* Wayne tried again to spot Charlotte in the crowd, but she was hidden from view, or maybe she'd started to back away from the rally. He wished she would.

"What we're looking for here," Frank called out, "is justice for our people."

"What we're looking for here," Wayne said, "is a political career in the West Indies." To his left, a woman clucked once loudly. He turned to her. She wore a large white shirt with a gigantic butterfly over her left breast. The yellow skin of her face was dotted with chocolate-colored skin tags. "That man," he said and pointed toward Lord Nelson, "is talking about my brother." The woman looked at him blankly and made a clucking sound again. Now that she was facing him, Wayne saw there was scar tissue at her throat. The sound wasn't a reproof, just a quirk, probably related to the operation that had produced the scars.

"Sorry," he mumbled and turned back to Frank and Lord Nelson. "It is," he remembered reading years ago, in a book about madness in Barbados, "a common affliction to think you're Lord Nelson." Meaning more than one patient at Black Rock suffered under this delusion. Lord Nelson: arrived in Barbados in 1805, died later that year in the battle of Trafalgar. He couldn't have been more incidental to any Bajan's life, though here he was in the Square and haunting the minds of madmen.

Frank started up a chant. In the same lilting way that Wayne and his Combermere classmates used to chant, *No guns, no war, U.S. out of El Sal-va-dooooor*, he called, *Trevor Deare, Trevor Deare, you betta let him outta there*. The crowd, and Wayne, quickly joined in.

"Well, look who's here," Toni said, as the crowd continued on. "I just knew he'd show." Toni pointed her finger at a man in a devil's costume who'd appeared in front of her. He looked more like a lobster with his large red hood and puffy, claw-like arms, but a yarn tail wound from his butt, and he was holding a giant pitchfork, spray-painted red.

Toni stepped to him. "Out doing your business? Gathering up all the good folk?"

"Now, honey, how could I be doing that if I don't have you?" the devil said.

"No, really," Toni smiled. "What's this about?" Wayne couldn't believe she was flirting.

"Crop Over," the devil said. "Dress rehearsal for a new calypso tent," and then he dug under his red shirt to pull a piece of paper from his red tights. An invitation.

"You gotta come," the devil said.

"Well," Toni twisted the paper into a tube and looked through it at the devil's smiling face.

"Do you mind?" Wayne said and stuck his hand out toward Frank.

"Eeew," the devil said and gave a mock shiver. He tapped his pitchfork twice on the ground. "Got one of these up the ass, do we?"

Wayne gave Toni a hard stare, as if the man's words were *her* fault, then he said, "I'm outta here," and started to move into the crowd, even as Toni said, "Hey, Wayne. I'm sorry." A stick up his ass. Why did people keep saying that to him? His brother was in jail, for Christ's sake. He wasn't supposed to be out partying. The evening had been a waste. Thinking Frank might help: what a horrible fuckup. "Excuse me," Wayne said. "Excuse me." The crowd parted reluctantly before him. And then, finally furious at everyone and everything, Wayne started calling, "Excuse me, excuse me, excuse, excuse, excuse," a string of words elided together, one long plea he was going to use to get out of here. It wasn't so hard now to imagine his father, as he stood in the hospital, years ago, and listened to an administrator tell him he couldn't sign the papers for his wife's care. He must have stood there for a moment, before he took the bus home. There must have been some time when he thought his will couldn't possibly mean nothing, that good would have to win out, that the doctors couldn't be so unreasonable. He was . . . he must have wanted to give his name, as evidence of something, before he allowed that Claude Deare meant nothing, and he dug into his pocket for change, walked out to the road, climbed onto a crowded bus, and heard the driver chant, "Sit in the back, sit in the back"—understanding the command as "sin in da back, sin in da back"— as he made his way home.

Trevor, Trevor, Trevor.

There was no way to stop anything. Wayne felt it now: the lie of his schooling, that he could do something if he wanted to.

But then Charlotte was upon him, breathless. "Finally," she cried. "I called this morning, but I couldn't find you. I have to tell you something. I think it's going to be okay for your brother."

The man in the devil suit bumped past them. Next to him, giant silvery spokes protruded from the back of a woman dressed in yellow. Sparkles covered her face. Perhaps she was supposed to be the sun. And behind her, from a distant galaxy or another circle of hell, came Frank's voice: "Let me tell you how this work was taken from us." He was return-ing to his principal subject after a detour to Trevor Deare, island history (with an emphasis on resistance: the Federation Riots, the riots of the hungry thirties), and the meaning—the true meaning—of Bussa's statue, a statue that every Bajan knew, of a slave bursting from his chains. It was in the center of Barbados's busiest roundabout.

"That man," Charlotte said, pointing at Frank, "is really pissing me off. He knows how repatriation works."

"My brother," Wayne said helplessly.

"Well, your brother's going to be fine, so if you don't mind, I'll be right back. And don't . . . you know, take what I'm going to say in the wrong way."

She started to push forward in the crowd. Wayne followed her. Didn't she know she shouldn't try to say something now? Charlotte raised her hand again, as people nearby shot her disdainful looks. Somehow they'd ended up in the dead center of the crowd. Wayne leaned forward and pulled Charlotte's wrist down.

"You know," she snapped, then patted her gigantic handbag, " I got my donor card from the ACLU in here. And Oxfam. My liberal walking pa-pers are in order."

One of the protesters, a woman behind square, Clark Kent-type glasses—so ugly they were hip—turned to Charlotte and said, "What you want? Congratulations?" She wore a royal blue jumpsuit, requisite wear for her shift at some factory for the super-fashionable.

"No," Charlotte said. "Of course not."

"They're punishing that man for being black and poor," the woman said, shaking her head. Braids cascaded from a spout at the top of her scalp and whipped angrily by her ears.

"Maybe they are. I don't know. I'm not talking about that. I'm saying this menorah issue is something different, and no one stole—"

"What you don't understand is that this society has proven time and time again that they don't treat us fairly, and your people are part of that."

"I don't know who you think my people are," Charlotte said, sharply, "but no, no they're not."

"Charlotte," Wayne cautioned.

Frank was now talking about the Israelites, *their* congregation in Ellstown. "Some of you will have heard them called black Jews," Frank called to the crowd, "but they are Hebrews, descended from the ancients."

Voices burbled out in the crowd. There was a cry to stop the whole Jewish banking conspiracy, a call for black men to take responsibility for their children, a woman saying black men and women didn't need to be opposed, that that was an idea that the media had constructed, not one that any people, living day-to-day, believed in.

"You," the woman in the blue jumpsuit repeated to Charlotte, "and your people are part of that."

"You know," Charlotte said, "I could say the same thing to you. And to Mr. Jewish Conspiracy. " She waved her hand in the direction of the voice in the crowd that seemed to be speaking for Louis Farrakhan. "About how *my* people have been treated."

The woman responded by giving Charlotte's right shoulder a shove.

"Hey now," Wayne said and stepped between the two women.

"Okay," Charlotte said gently, clearly shocked that the woman had touched her. "I don't want to fight."

"What's your name?" a man said to Charlotte, then scribbled her answer down on a small writing pad. "L-E-W-I-N?" he asked. Charlotte nodded, then turned her back so only Wayne could hear her.

"I'd better go," she said, "but I have to tell you. The Lazar accident was probably a suicide. Josh's brother, Henry, told me. Josh had been depressed. He'd tried to take his own life before. You just need to tell the police. Henry Lazar will back you up. There's a suicide note and everything. I didn't read it, but I delivered it to the police myself. Maybe they need more evidence or are checking on its authenticity. I don't know why they haven't let your brother go, but if we could call Henry . . ."

"Jesus Christ, why didn't they say something right away?"

"The Lazars? Who knows? Maybe the parents can't face facts, but . . . there it is."

"Did you *hear* this?" the woman in the blue jumpsuit, apparently an adroit eavesdropper, called to the man with the writing pad. Immediately, Charlotte's news swirled through the crowd, a shot of vodka in the cranberry juice, changing the composition of the evening.

"They *knew* my brother didn't do it, and they kept him in jail?" Wayne struggled to keep his voice low.

"Yeah, yeah, I guess so. So there's your Jewish conspiracy. An inability to face facts. But don't blame me. The messenger," she crossed her hands over her breast to indicate who she meant, "not the message."

"Okay, yeah, okay. I mean, that's great. I mean . . ." Trafalgar Square suddenly felt like a subway car stopping to take on more passengers. There were so many more heads now, below him. From behind, people pushed Wayne forward, and from the front, people pushed back, so Wayne was pressed to Charlotte, his pelvis grazing below her breasts. He tilted his hips back. He would shoot himself if he got excited. "I mean, it's great that I know this." He shoved his fists into his pockets, ballooned the cloth of his shorts away from his thighs. "Why don't you go?" he suggested.

"My thoughts exactly," Charlotte said, giving a little grimace.

"I'd come with you, but . . ." Wayne waved his hand in Frank's direction. Now, the crowd seemed tremendous, as if it had grown and flourished in the rich soil of his momentary inattention.

"No," Charlotte said, "of course, your brother. You've got to be here."

Charlotte pushed through the dense crowd to the yellow cabs that rimmed the park. Wayne watched as she ducked into a taxi. It started into the road, but before it could get very far, the overflow crowd from the rally pushed out of the park and onto the street, stopping traffic completely. One man hoisted himself onto Charlotte's cab's hood and walked over it. His buddies joined him, and the cab started to rock dangerously. Wayne tried to push his way over there. He heard Charlotte's driver shout, "Hey, hey!" to no effect.

There was more shouting from behind him. Wayne heard someone scream, "See how a white man kick a black man? See?" And then he was jostled forward. He lost sight of Charlotte's cab. And there was more pushing. A fight had broken out, and he heard people saying that Mike Tyson had bitten Evander Holyfield's ear off. There was a surge in the crowd, and Wayne was carried, with his neighbors, out of the park, into the street. "His right ear," he heard someone scream. And someone else called, "A madman."

Frank's voice, behind it all, seemed to be taking questions again.

"Wayne," he heard Charlotte cry, as if for help, and then he saw her, head out of the cab, ten feet in front of him.

"You in the back," Frank said, almost triumphantly. "Another question," and just as he was almost to Charlotte, Wayne started at Trevor's voice saying, "Thank you, sir. I out. All charges drop. For lack of evidence."

And in the confusion of the next few moments, as members of the crowd lifted Trevor on their shoulders and Wayne caught a glimpse of his brother, still in white tuxedo shirt and black pants, Wayne thought: *I forgot to bring him more clothes.* And then, as Frank tried to reorient his speech without thanking anyone for anything, Wayne flashed on his dream of the other night, the spray of blood from Frank's nose after the IBM Selectric landed on his face, and then, only then, did he feel the natural happiness of a brother for his brother.

"Was he released?" Charlotte shouted to an elderly man standing by the cab.

"Yessir, young lady," he allowed and took off his pale blue cap and, for some reason, bowed to her.

"Thanks," she said and pulled her head back into the cab.

"Lord Nelson," Wayne heard the man say, as if introducing himself, "at your service."

And then someone else said, "Are you his brother?" Wayne nodded at no one in particular, then he, too, was lifted—lifted by several men—into the air. His haunches were balanced on two separate men's shoulders, his arms raised above his head—less in the classic victor's pose, than because he was trying, like a novice unicyclist, to keep his balance. They carried him through the park, a joyous bounce to their step, as they took him away from Charlotte, past the devil and Frank and Toni, over a sea of clapping hands, then out into the streets, away from Lord Nelson and the Careenage, but no closer—not even when the excitement died down and people went looking for TVs to find out about the championship fight— to his brother.

CHAPTER THIRTEEN

Charlotte Lewin

June 29–July 4, 1997

◦

A FTER THE RALLY, THE MENORAH'S plight was public knowledge, and Charlotte's phone started to ring. Calls from a whole slew
of strangers, making their case. "It should go to the Jews. It's for Hanukkah, for Christ's sake," one man said.

"It should go to the museum. How can it go to people who have born
false witness. The Jews have that commandment, too, don't they?" a
member of Parliament asked, his voice, lilting and proper and unsure, as if
he truly didn't know. Charlotte responded neutrally to everyone—"Oh,
thank you, sir. Thank you for your thoughts." If pressed, she continued to
deny she had any power in the matter, said the decision was out of her
hands. All during the day and into the evening, the phone rang and rang.
Charlotte didn't return the phone messages left for her at the desk: not
the messages from the *Daily Nation* or the *Barbados Advocate* or the CBC
(which she gathered stood for Caribbean Broadcasting Corporation) or
assorted strangers. It was hard to embrace this sort of disregard. A woman
who paid her bills the moment she received them, who returned phone
messages while the machine was still playing the day's calls.

There was a Hegelian force at work—if not in the world, then in her
psyche, where self-assertion trumped shame, then embarrassment trumped
them both. At various moments, any argument might persuade—and not
on the basis of its own merits but of Charlotte's emotions. Ethnic pride,
Jewish self-hate, liberal guilt. She was longing for personal neutrality, a
clarification of the ethical. She didn't want to be persuaded. She wanted to
discover how to act.

The eighth and ninth day of her visit passed, the tenth and eleventh, and then she'd been on the island for two weeks. She had begun to appreciate the sheer effort it took to live here. Things were always decaying and being cobbled back together. Fences, roads, houses. In the city, buildings had scaffolding that no one seemed to mount, and Charlotte never heard hammers working away at the half of her hotel that was boarded up. Since everyone else went around with jobs half-completed, Charlotte did the same. She spent her days in the Barbados Museum's library or at the archives, nights curled up with her book on Jewish life and a glass of white wine. Endless lessons! The Baal Shem Tov, founder of Hasidism, had a big, generous heart. His most famous successor, the Kotzker rebbe, emphasized Truth. Mercy and Truth did battle—according to one story—and Truth lost. Truth was cast to the ground. It wasn't just that man didn't live with the Truth; his very nature was incompatible with it, and yet it was that to which he should aspire. But he didn't. He was content with self-deceit, and the Kotzker was disgusted.

There was something Charlotte still needed to learn. What? She didn't know, but she'd know it when she saw it. And then she'd do, she hoped, the right thing. The honest *and* loving thing. She'd combine the head *and* the heart. Charlotte Lewin: future debunker of Hasidic metaphysics, undecided though her departure date loomed less than a week away.

In the summer, services weren't held at the Bridgetown synagogue but at New Rockley, a suburban home converted for the purpose. Interior walls had been knocked down; a raised platform and podium placed in the center of what must have once been a living room. Congregants—their backsides headed dangerously for the floor—bounced on the blue-and-white webbing of the seating, a donation from one of the temple's members, an aluminum lawn-chair manufacturer. The elderly and those with bad backs opted for the wooden pews to the left of the reader's desk. Two large and noisy fans tousled hair, blew wrap skirts open. On the Friday after the rally, a week of research behind her, Charlotte arrived late. She joined a disheveled group, permanents sitting, like half-fallen soufflés, on women's heads, yarmulkes slipping silkily down shirt backs. At first, Charlotte tried to edge to the back of the room, stifling the crisp click of her sandals as she went. But Jody Rabinowitz, sitting in the front row, next to the Lazars, waved her to an empty seat by her other side. Charlotte followed her directive, but not before she quickly scanned the assembled group. Twenty or so people, if you included the children, but no Berkowitz, no Perle, and no Henry.

Jody's husband—at the front of the room, his back to the congregation—was leading the service, but Charlotte couldn't hear him over the whirring of the fans. Jody tapped her prayer book so Charlotte would know where they were. Still no one—Jody included—seemed to be following along. Children ran back and forth between their seats and a game of jacks that had started up in the corner. Oblivious, Jacob chanted on, turning only once to say there weren't enough men to take out the Torah.

"Count the women," Abe Lazar insisted, but Jacob wouldn't. "Mashoog-a-na," Abe pronounced with cartoony exasperation. "Absolutely meshuggeneh."

"Ah, Abe," someone put in, good-humoredly, "let it be."

Without the Torah reading, it was a short service. The usual: We're the chosen people. You're the Lord. Oh, praise you, praise you, praise you. Let us be worthy. We're the chosen people.

Charlotte's late-night reading in *Life is (Still!) with People* had brought her here. Now she remembered why she didn't go to services. The repetition, the xenophobia. Although she liked singing the Hebrew—if she didn't look at the translation, the words and melody felt holy. They came back to her as if they weren't something she'd once learned but part of a vestigial organ, rediscovering its original purpose. "Oseh shalom," Jacob began. Next to her, Jody sang tunelessly, noisily along. La-la-la-la-la. Each "la," a distinct emphatic sound. No words, though even your supersecular Reform Jew normally knew the end of the Mourner's Kaddish. "Laaaa," Jody finished off, then turned to Charlotte, smiled and whispered, "A-*la*-men."

When the service broke and a blessing over the wine had been said in a small kitchen out back, Abe turned warmly to Charlotte, ready to forget their exchange of the other day. Hands wrapped around small pieces of pastry, they'd both left the kitchen and were now standing near where they'd been sitting. Abe rested his wine on the reader's desk. "We're coming out now," he said. "Out of the house. It seems the best thing to do."

Charlotte counted backward in her head. How many days had it been since shiva ended? Five? Six? The other night, Charlotte had read that in some communities, mourners took a walk around the block at the end of shiva, to signal their readiness to resume life. Before her, Abe scratched the tip of his nose. Charlotte bit into her rugelah.

"You know," he said, as if just remembering what it was he wanted to ask, "the boy at the office told me we still haven't received the menorah."

"Yes," Charlotte said, wiping the cake crumbling at her lips. "I haven't sent it yet. I needed to consider . . . to talk to people from the Barbados Institute."

"Why would you want to do that?"

"Because . . . well, surely you know they've made a claim to the menorah . . ."

"Them!" he puffed out air. "Characters. We have a contract."

"*Couldn't* you share?"

Abe laughed, a tired sort of chuckle. "Share a menorah! What . . . we get four elephants, and they get four?"

"There are other ways of sharing."

"What're you talking about?" Jody said as she joined them. Jacob lingered behind her, talking to a woman wearing large red plastic glasses and a designer running suit, white patterned with red and green.

"The community's very angry at you," Charlotte said pleasantly. "For the accusation against Trevor Deare."

"I had nothing to do with that," Abe said, drawing back.

"But to share. And when it's not Hanukkah. When it's not in use, isn't it really just . . . just a thing?"

"But it isn't," Jody said. "If things were just things then why . . ." she gestured to her husband's prayer shawl, folded up on a table by the front door, "then why all of this. Everything is something else. This . . ." and now she gestured to the reader's desk to her right, "is my right to exist. As I am."

Both Abe and Charlotte started to respond at the same time. A muffling of words. No one heard anything.

"Speak up," Jody said, taking Charlotte's hand and patting it. "*That's* the only way to get a word in edgewise here."

Helen's criticism of Charlotte's consistently Christian boyfriends, brought home for Thanksgiving or Passover: "They start a sentence, they don't finish for half an hour. They just can't keep up." Milquetoast interlopers, defeated by the noise and gleeful interrupting of the Lewin household.

"But," Charlotte said, "can't you see how *they'd* see it? The Jewish community here has so much and the rest of the island . . ."

Jody nodded her head vigorously. An agreement: neither of them would use the words *black* and *white*. "We do what we can, but you see what I'm saying. We live well. We don't apologize for it. I enjoy it. I don't pretend it doesn't matter. Truly, I love what I've been given. And I've been given a lot."

Abe turned from them, whispered in Jacob's ear. Then Jacob edged into their circle. "Can I give you my argument for the menorah? If you can stand to hear another opinion?"

"Please," Charlotte said.

"There's a symbolic importance to having the menorah, which has to do with religious freedom. The holiday commemorates one of the first times our people fought for spiritual—as opposed to political—freedom. Nowadays, people think Hanukkah is some sort of compensation for Christmas, so our kids can have toys, but that's just not true. It's a terribly important holiday. You know the saying, 'If all the festivals were abolished, Hanukkah and Purim would never disappear.' Our insistence on the menorah is about freedom to worship, which we haven't always felt here in Barbados, despite our obvious economic comfort. You know, there was a time when all the Jews on the island had to make a Jew pie—a pie of gold—and give it to the authorities. And we have some version of that now—though we call it charitable donations—so people will let us be, let us go our own way."

There were a few black people at services, milling about with Dixie cups of Manischevitz. Charlotte wondered what *their* take was on the matter. "Well, that makes sense," she allowed, and then, because something else seemed to be required, she acknowledged Hannah, who'd just appeared, by saying, "Henry doesn't come to services?"

"Oh, Henry," Hannah said. There was something disconcerting about her. Her eyes focused just behind Charlotte, as if perhaps she saw something there that was hidden from everyone else. "He's such a *good* boy."

"A real good kid," Abe bobbed his head in agreement.

They'd been saying this, it was clear, for years. No doubt Josh had gritted his teeth against the refrain, been accused, for his anger, of selfish-ness. "It doesn't take away from you if we say something nice about Henry." Charlotte's parents had said the same thing about Helen—"a good girl, a real good girl." They didn't say it before she got sick. Then, they were often angry at her for her flightiness, for spending too much money, for shaving her head for a college theatre production. But her bravery in illness re-deemed her. She wasn't flighty but lively. She didn't spend too much money, she had great taste in clothes, really knew how to put herself together. And—well, they never forgave the bald head, even after Charlotte—heartless, heartless!—reminded her mother that she had once, during a fight about Helen's hair, said, "I wish you were never born."

And why had Charlotte reminded her? For the same reason that she had an urge, now, to say, "I think your son Henry is a whore." Sometimes you just wanted to rub their faces in it. As soon as you did, though, the truth seemed like an entirely unnecessary thing. Hadn't the medical jour-nals—last year or the year before—found that depressed people had a more realistic worldview than those who were happy? Self-deception was good for you.

"I'm just glad," Hannah said, sighing loudly, dramatically, "that he didn't see the accident. I'm just so thankful for that." Her voice broke, and Abe put his arm around her. Charlotte wondered how the sight could pos-sibly be worse for a brother than a mother?

"See," Abe said, "how much things do matter? A faulty parachute and all these lives are ruined. Ruined because of a thing." He was helpless with anger now.

Charlotte compressed her lips into a grimace of sorrow. Could it be that they *didn't* know their son had killed himself?

"Remember that story Henry used to tell?" Hannah had started to cry, copiously but noiselessly. She didn't bother to wipe the tears from her cheek. It was almost as if Henry were the one who had died. And perhaps she *was* still processing the stories of *his* death, even though they'd turned out to be wrong. "About when he was staying in Jamaica?"

Jody turned to Charlotte to say, "The locusts landed in his yard and ate all his green underwear off the clothesline."

Abe laughed. "That's good. That's a good story."

Hannah said, "I don't know why I just thought of that, of all things. Henry's green underwear."

"Where *is* Henry?" Jacob asked.

"He and Sari went sailing." Hannah wiped her face with the back of her hands, then she turned to Jody to say, "I don't know when they'll be back. Maybe next spring."

"Next *spring?*" Jody said, apparently shocked. "Where'd they go?"

"Maine. Sari's family has a house up there. Swan Island. Swan's Island. Something like that."

Charlotte felt a stab of pain, worse because she had no right to it. How was it that she'd become the kind of woman with whom you had sex but did not get involved? She was so patently *not* that kind of woman. And Sari—Charlotte could imagine her: bikini-clad and cheerful, good with sailboats, friendly to dogs, a chipper attendee of cricket matches and beer bashes.

"I thought Josh and Sari . . ." Jody began.

"So did we," Abe interrupted. "But no. Just friends."

"I can't say I know what moves him," Hannah said, and again it seemed like she was talking to someone just outside their circle. "I can't say I know what moves either of them," and then she turned and fell, as if she'd been pushed, into Abe's arms.

"We thought we should come out, but maybe we shouldn't have," Abe allowed.

"It's hard," Charlotte said, "to know what to do." The urge to protect them was strong now. She hoped they'd never know the truth about either of their sons.

A man came out with a platter of cookies from the kitchen. Charlotte took one. "Another, another," the man insisted, and Charlotte obediently scooped a second cookie into her napkin. "Marsha baked them," the man said, and there was a murmur all around. She was such a good cook. The man's voice—crusty, aggrieved—sounded familiar, and Charlotte wondered if he might have been one of the people who'd called her on the phone to insist on the return of the menorah. He wasn't insisting now, but then, without an introduction, how would he know who she was?

Worley, a black man, joined them just long enough to say, "Good Shabbas," before he stepped out the door.

"So," Charlotte said, stating the obvious, "there are blacks in the congregation, despite the other synagogue?"

"Why not?" Jacob said, almost defensive. "They're welcome."

"I'm just wondering," Charlotte said, "why you'd pick one congregation over another. I mean, are there any white people in the . . . I forgot the name . . . the island's black congregation?"

"The Holy Temple of Sheba," Jacob said, his manner softening. "No, I can't imagine there are, but their ways are so different from ours. Very holy, though, that's what I hear. Their leader is very holy. And Worley, he's from Ethiopia. He's the most religious of us all. Ties his phylacteries on three times a day."

"I always wanted to do that as a girl. It bugged me that it was just for men," Charlotte said.

"Worley orders kosher meat, I heard," Jody said, "from the States."

"You're not," Helen had once said, accusatory—it was a fault—"a joiner." True enough. Charlotte had never liked coordinated action: group sports, political rallies, the bunny hop. But she liked being at New Rockley, the familiar comfort of Jewish conversation. The inflections, even here, in a foreign country, were entirely clear, as was the sense of humor, the interest in the intellect, the fast, frizzy way one conversation cut into another and then another.

Abe and Hannah started to say their good-byes, Abe apologizing as they went. They shouldn't have come. They really shouldn't have.

When they were gone, Charlotte turned to Jacob and said, "What was Josh like?"

Hannah answered for him. "Troubled."

"Why?"

"Why is anyone troubled?" Jacob asked.

"Come on," Jody said, the edge of a reprimand in her voice. "It weighed heavily on him, being a Lazar. His privilege. He thought he should be special. Those kids. They were *reared* to be special, and then when they just had *lives*, you know, they felt they'd disappointed."

"But they don't seem disappointed in Henry."

"Nooo," Jody allowed. "Henry was always able to set himself apart. You know, he'd just refuse to go to a party or something, because it wasn't his sort of thing. I'm almost not surprised that he'd go off on a trip at a time like this. It's his way. But Josh would never do such a thing. He'd stay around and be miserable. He didn't have that necessary distance. He always said, 'I just have to leave here.' That's what he told my daughter, Leah. And Leah said she'd tell him to go, but he couldn't quite. I don't know why. *She* went away. She lives in Toronto. But he . . ." She shrugged, and Charlotte saw her eyes were wet. "Oh, God, I didn't expect to get upset."

Jacob said, "What else can we tell you?"

Good-byes were coming faster now; the synagogue was emptying out.

Jody craned her neck around and looked at a clock back in the kitchen: 8:30. "Come," she said. "We'll talk while I clean up."

In the kitchen, Jacob and Charlotte helped Jody box up rugelah. "Take this," Jody said, pushing a box of pastry into Charlotte's ribs. "The last thing I need," she slapped her stomach. "How do you keep it off?"

Charlotte looked down at her body. "Oh, it's there," she laughed in that companionable way of women—you were all in peril of being encased in fat. "I'm just hiding it."

"Now sit while I take care of this food," Jody insisted. "I don't want the two of you in my way."

Jacob grinned as he pulled out a kitchen chair for Charlotte. "Woe to he—or she—who disobeys."

"I always thought," said Jody, as she dumped wet coffee grounds into the trash, "that there were two kinds of mothers in this world: those who were good with little ones, loving, doting, and those who were good with older ones, who could let their children go off and do whatever, make their mistakes, grow up, really. Hannah's the former, very generous in her way, but not comfortable with expressing affection. And there's something in both Hannah and Abe . . . I don't know how to explain it, it has to do with needing to be in charge. They really don't like others to have authority, even the authority of . . . just an independent existence, and I think that's why the kids sometimes seem a little . . . confused. They're not bad people, of course. Just rigid. And frightened, I think. Very frightened."

Charlotte nodded her head. In their worst moments, her parents could be the same way.

Jody poured juice from a glass pitcher back into its cardboard container, then sniffed at the juice and dumped the whole thing in the trash. "I once heard them in the bedroom fighting with Josh, and it wasn't very pretty. Abe yelling at him, saying over and over, 'You're so crazy. You're completely crazy.' And then Hannah came into the living room, where I was, and said me, 'I'm so worried. He's so out of control.'" I assumed she meant her husband—yelling in that way—but she didn't, she meant Josh. Who was yelling, too, and he *did* sound hysterical, but all he was saying was 'I'm not going to let you talk to me that way.'"

Jacob finally spoke up. "Well, to be fair, after a point, your kids are supposed to get on with things, stop blaming you for all their faults. Which Josh never learned how to do."

The last of the congregants stuck their heads into the kitchen to say their farewells. Jacob went to turn off the fans and lights in the main room. The kitchen was fluorescent bright, but giving way to gloom, reticulating, like a cracked eggshell, letting the dark seep through. Now that everyone was gone, Jody let Charlotte help her. The two women moved efficiently through the kitchen, wiping surfaces, washing dishes. Jacob came back to dry, then Charlotte sat while they both departed—Jody to store some platters in the basement, Jacob to lock the front door. In their absence, the room grew even darker. Night puddled at the window. The gloom entered Charlotte, too. She had to go home in less than a week. And what was there to go home to? July in her infernal Cambridge flat, listening to kids play street hockey into the early hours of the morning. There was nothing for her there. No Helen, no partner. Only the false brightness that her parents and Howard would require on her return. *How was your trip?!* They needn't wait for an answer; the question implied the response. She *had* to be happy, her mother once said, because Helen had died. Not to make up for the loss, but because Helen's death made it so clear that this was all one had, *this* life. Without Helen and now Lawrence, what kept her in Boston? Certainly not the Mother Goose feel of traipsing kids past the Museum of Fine Arts' Egyptian sphinxes, encouraging them *not* to notice the copulating figures in the sarcophagi. Perhaps Josh *was* right. You had to leave. Get the necessary distance, which was hard in a Jewish family. WASPs had the distance built right in. They simply never talked to one another.

She counted the days till her departure. Seven. Then counted back. It was the Fourth of July. Independence Day. She'd completely forgotten the holiday, but then there was nothing down here to remind her.

"I guess that's that," Jody said, clumping back up the stairs, wiping her damp hands on the seat of her pants. "We can give you a lift home."

They left by a side door, feeling hesitantly for the steps, because there were no outdoor lights.

"We had an interesting discussion this morning," Jacob said, once they were installed in his car, "at my Bible group. We're doing Kings 2." He pulled into the street, entirely silent at 9:00 on a Friday night.

"Oh, big fun," Jody said. "Hit the air, why don't you?"

Jacob pressed a button.

"Yes, well, Sonja Marks was saying the book was starting to make her hysterical. She felt sure the author of the book would say that the Holocaust was the Jews' punishment for not upholding the covenant with God." Jacob interrupted himself to tell Charlotte, "Sonja's a survivor. She still has the number on her arm."

"Well, there are some Orthodox who hold that, you know," Jody said. "The Holocaust as the final breaking of the covenant. God punishing the chosen for failing."

"You think I should have told her that sort of mishegoss?"

"No, of course not. I was just saying."

In the front seat, they talked on, while Charlotte thought of Judaism coming to a halt. Even those Jews who attended services tonight hardly seemed like believers. Except maybe Worley, who tied on the phylacteries every day. And then she thought of the Lewins, that variegated tribe, and how they, too, might peter out, come to an end with Charlotte. Sometime last year, Charlotte's mother had gone to the U.S. Archives to do the Lewins' family tree—a wild branching, the most colorful of leaves. A peddler who sold jewelry on the installment plan, a child who succumbed to diptheria after an inadvisable dip in the lake, a flag maker, a bookworm with no bookcase, a typist for Neky Sewing's Complaint Department, a man who fooled around with the models in his dress business. Austrians and Germans and Poles. Bankers, movie-theatre owners, printers.

"What do you want more," a father said to his prospective son-in-law, the bookworm with no bookcase, "a bookcase or my daughter?"

"A bookcase by far," the boy said.

"And near?" the father said.

All those stories that Charlotte had heard so many times, they might all end with her. Her parents had been only children. No son would carry on the family name, and now there was only one daughter left to pro-create. The true end of the line.

"Where are you staying again?" Jacob asked.

"The Paradise," Charlotte said.

"Paradise. Lucky girl," Jacob said. "Unfallen, untouched by sin."

"Now, Jacob," Jody said, "that's not a compliment for a modern girl. It's good to be a little touched. Right?"

"Absolutely," Charlotte said; she was a champ at sociable agreement—she was a little touched.

Jacob's car passed a pink hotel, and Charlotte heard a tinkling of music. They were out of the suburbs and back on the main drag that led to the Paradise. "Did you ever hear that story," Charlotte started up, "about how Henry was a duppy?"

"We heard something about it," Jacob allowed.

"Well, what was *that* all about?"

"Oh, I have a theory," Jody began. Charlotte leaned forward to hear. "You know the papers made such a big deal when a son of the Lazars died, and then when he *wasn't* dead, people needed some story."

Perhaps that, too, explained the lack of intensity in the Lazars' grief. It wasn't just that their younger son had a history of mental illness. It was that they'd just mourned Henry's demise, however unnecessarily, and something of the horror of *that* death impinged on the horror of the true tragedy.

"Also," Jacob put in, "Henry's always had a certain charm, a cer-tain . . ." He struggled, seemed to be repressing the word that might ap-propriately modify "charm." Charlotte started to offer *snake oil*, but Jacob cut her off by saying "charm" a second time. "If people were going to tell those stories about anyone, it would be him."

Charlotte nodded, then settled back into her seat. Maybe he *was* a ghost. There were the dead—again according to the book she'd been reading—who didn't know they had died. They *seemed* like real people but had no substance. They roamed the world with no goals. There was a story told by the famous scholar Abraham Joshua Heschel about the Kotzker rebbe and Reb Bunam, the Kotzker's predecessor. The two were out walking. Reb Bunam gestured to a nearby peasant and said, "You think he is wearing clothes, don't you? Well, he's not. He is enveloped in a shroud. He belongs to the world of phantoms." And they were everywhere, apparently, these beings. "Wherever there is turmoil," Heschel wrote, "you find them. They talk and are counted among the living. . . . They take sea voyages, trade, make and lose money, never realizing that they are living in a world of phantoms." A metaphor, Charlotte understood: these phantoms were a metaphor for the kind of people who didn't understand that there was no substance to the world of getting and spending, that true meaning lay elsewhere. Still, she'd liked finding out that these apparitions took sea voyages, liked that now two traditions suggested Henry wasn't real.

When they reached the hotel, Jacob and Jody both stepped out of the car, told Charlotte that she had to call when she next came to the island, and that they'd all have dinner, a real visit at a happier time. They embraced her. "Just, in case," Jody said, "we don't see you before you leave."

A letter Helen had written just before she traveled from London to Vienna: "I leave for . . . Vienna and Budapest! for ten GLORIOUS days! We (Fiona and me! I mean I!) may also take a quick trip to Salzburg, too. Yippee! I love going to new places, seeing new things, and being lost in a foreign language I can only pronounce because I sing Schubert and Brahms. Ah, happy life . . ."

Of course, Charlotte realized, she'd give the menorah to the Jews, the old tug of blood. The head and the heart didn't even enter into the equation. You did what you could to let your people continue.

Ah, happy life. You ran forward and embraced it, and it killed you.

CHAPTER FOURTEEN

Wayne Deare

June 30–July 5, 1997

ᴥ

W HEN HIS FEET FINALLY FOUND THE GROUND, sometime late on Saturday night, Wayne learned that the parachute had never been pulled, that both Marty Berkowitz and the Lazars had been told so by the skydiving outfit—not right away, but on Wednesday, when Trevor had been picked up, and they made no effort to pass this information on to the public or the police. Nor did they divulge what they learned on Thursday: someone had dismantled the parachute's safety. Frank was out-raged and Wayne, for once, was similarly indignant.

And so was the *Daily Nation*. And the *Barbados Advocate*. And Berko-witz was indignant at their indignance. So the chute hadn't been pulled. What did that prove? Josh Lazar might have been knocked on the head, then thrown to his death. Plenty of people could testify about what was said in the plane. In the papers, Berkowitz talked on and on: Of course, Josh's anti-Semitic enemy would have dismantled the safety. Murderers were clever; they'd know a parachute had a safety. But the police said the matter was closed. And the Lazars, unwilling to talk to the press, released a one-sentence statement saying they had no interest in pressing charges against anyone. A terrible accident that they intended to grieve pri-vately. As for the other Jews on the island, they didn't seem inclined to debate the tragedy. Or maybe the problem was one of reporting. Neither of the island's two papers seemed to find anyone other than Berkowitz to interview.

So the debate turned to the menorah, which, thanks to Frank, had be-come a well-known controversy. And now—bonus or no—Wayne cared as much as Frank about the piece. He wanted those elephants, could already imagine his fingers stroking their golden flanks, payment for what the Lazars had put the Deares through.

Frank had a new plan, and the evening after the rally, he arranged to meet the brothers at the Purple and Orange, a rum shop near the home of a woman with whom Trevor had been spending time. Trevor wouldn't tell Wayne her name, wouldn't actually admit to her existence, but from Trevor's familiarity with the shop—when Wayne and Trevor arrived, he walked behind the counter and helped himself to a Banks from the cooler—Wayne guessed it was the affectless clerk. She was about Trevor's age. Maybe twenty. Pretty but working to conceal it: hair tucked under a net, an oversized maroon T-shirt and black sweatpants hiding her body. Aside from the heavy, heart-shaped gold loops at her ears, she seemed aggressively unadorned.

Wayne and Trevor stood at the counter, sipping beers, as they waited for Frank. The Purple and Orange offered a riot of supplies, one of everything: a ginseng soda, a paintbrush, a bag of Italian-flavored plantains, an inhaler, a box of Tampax. And more: tomato paste, cake mix, Fisherman's Friend lozenges, Nature Valley granola bars, tinned fish, WD-40, spray paint, soy sauce, Bajan seasoning, Ramen noodles, hair grease, corn flakes, eggs. Above all this, a sign, under a dirty piece of plastic, said, "The Best of Business Is to Mind Your Own Business. If You've Got No Business, Then Make It Your Business to Leave Other People's Business Alone."

Outside, a horn gave a two-note beep, and Wayne turned to see Frank step out of a minivan and start trudging up the short hill that led away from the bus stop. "Hey," Frank said to Wayne, as he stepped through the door, then he turned to the woman behind the counter. "How's business?" he asked with real concern. "You doing okay?"

The clerk, apparently puzzled by Frank's question and intimate manner, tapped the sign.

Frank took no notice of its sage advice. Instead, he started talking with an elderly customer about how Crop Over was getting too flashy. He told a little boy Coke was his favorite drink, too. He worked his way through the entire shop—finding a quick way to connect with everyone—and when he was through, he pulled a stool outside and indicated that Trevor and Wayne should join him.

Once both brothers were perched on their stools, backs leaning against the rum shop's orange façade, Frank explained that he wanted the menorah as compensation for the false accusation. He wanted the menorah and an apology and Berkowitz's ass. That's what he'd come to say, but the day had been a scorcher, and after Frank made his intentions clear, even he lost his zeal for purposeful dialogue. He leaned against the shop's façade, then briefly closed his eyes. Wayne was disappointed in Frank. But what could he say? To a napping man?

"Shit," Frank finally offered, a general condemnation of the world, though as it spread out before them, it didn't seem such a bad place. Under the hazy sky, the hills fell away, so many green veils dropped, to the gray-white of the ocean. Across the road, the tree hibiscus had darkened from their morning yellow and afternoon copper to a deep red. There was, in the thickening of the air, the promise of rain and perhaps some cooling winds. It was nearing sunset.

Frank finally seemed ready for persuasion. He pressed his hands to his thighs and turned to Trevor to say, "Here's the idea. We take them to court with you as our star witness."

"He won't go," Wayne interrupted as if Trevor weren't sitting there.

"Won't," Trevor echoed, then got up to go back inside the rum shop.

"He's deaf," Wayne said.

"What are you talking about?"

"He hides it pretty well, but he can't hear much, and he won't do anything if he thinks he's going to be humiliated."

"Well, I'll prepare him."

"You can do what you like. I know my brother. He's not going." Frank went into the shop and bought Trevor a beer. The two men came back outside, and Frank explained how easy the testimony would be, but he didn't get anywhere. Trevor, Frank insisted, had to feel some anger at the Lazars and Berkowitz, some desire for justice, but rather than acknowledge this emotion, Trevor just said, "I done with the matter." So Frank tried to make him feel guilty. After all, he'd helped free him, but Trevor insisted he'd gotten out on his own good name. Then Frank talked about doing it for reasons of black self-help and to make a political point.

Meanwhile, a domino game was getting started in front of the shop. Someone had dragged a wooden table out from the TV room, and their laughter distracted Trevor; he'd always found Wayne's friends boring, and his boss was no exception. Finally, he turned to Frank and said, in a manner that suggested he was dismissing his companions, "Thanks, man, thanks for the beer. Let me buy you one." It was as if he'd only just noticed, now, in the dark, after the men had spent the evening together, that Frank hadn't been drinking.

"No, thanks," Frank said.

"Uh-oh, you a member of the Alcoholic Anonymous Party?" Trevor drew back, as if offended.

A man from the domino game chimed in, standing to declaim, "Is da rum shop government here, and I is de terror of de rum shop." He slapped his own chest. He was far gone, stumbling as he spoke. "Eh keep me mout shut fuh too long." He suggested that members of the Alcoholic Anonymous Party might want to congregate elsewhere.

"Give he a break, huh?" Trevor called over to the man, but Frank slipped off his stool and said no, no, he had to be going anyway.

He pitched a stone lazily at some goats tethered to a stick nearby, then said, "Mr. Deare." Wayne stood to shake his hand.

"Tomorrow," Wayne said by way of apology, and meaning he'd see Frank at work tomorrow. Frank looked uncharacteristically tired. His dress shirt was sticking to his back. He unbuttoned and rolled up his sleeves, as if it had only just occurred to him that this might help with the heat. "Well, gentlemen," he said and scooped up his briefcase—which was not really a briefcase but an old leather doctor's bag—and walked down the street to Da King and Da Queen, which was what everyone called the mural, painted on an abandoned shack, where the minivans stopped.

Once Frank was out of earshot—and thinking better of his question even as he uttered it—Wayne said, "What's the big deal? Why not help him out?"

"Don't tell me what to do."

"You don't mind what they did to you?"

"You think I need you to tell me what to do?" Trevor hissed, quickly accelerating from zero to one hundred on the anger speedometer.

"Okay, brother," Wayne said evenly, "I just wanted to ask." Then, as matter-of-factly as possible, "I'm going to settle up."

Ducking into the low-ceilinged shop, Wayne tripped over the legs of a boy slumped on a stool. A copy of *Jet* lay open on the counter. The boy bent over it, whispering words as he read. His manner was almost prayerful. Wayne glanced over his shoulder to see what he was reading, but it was nothing: a page of celebrity photos, actors and singers caught on their way into Los Angeles parties.

The young clerk from before was gone. Wayne imagined Trevor would be departing soon, too. Nights of love, that's what he imagined for his brother. Endless passion while Wayne was home whacking off. Now, a heavy woman with a scanty, steel-wool beard manned the counter.

"I've got to settle up," Wayne said.

"Your friend pay for it all."

Wayne gave her a look. "I think he just paid for my brother."

"I won't say no to your money, but he pay for it all."

Somehow this seemed far too much. It was one thing to be beholden to Frank for legal services rendered. Quite another to let him pay for a night's worth of beer. "Think he Lord of the Manor," Wayne's mother would have said; she never read gifts like this generously. And Wayne wasn't inclined to either. The gesture meant only one thing: that he owed Frank, that he should run down the hill, offer to give him a lift back to town.

Which is exactly what he did.

And as they drove to Bridgetown—in silence, both men's capacity for talk having re-exhausted itself—Wayne felt almost sorry for Frank, sorry that he was going to have to drop his case, and with it, perhaps, the fight for the menorah. There would be no apology from the Jews. There never would be, as if it didn't matter if you put a man in jail for the better part of a week. Black men could, after all—*did*, after all—take it. But it wasn't even this that disappointed Wayne. He had to admit, as his car dropped over the final hill to the sea, that his sorrow was a brand of jealousy. After all, Trevor had done what Wayne never could; he had defeated Frank.

"You like Trevor to look bad," Wayne's mother had once told Wayne. " 'Cause it make you look better."

"Oh, please," Wayne had snapped. "That's crazy."

And it was. Wayne wanted to see Trevor do well. He just didn't want to see him do well through his own stubborn stupidity.

As if he had heard this conclusion but applied it to the wrong brother, Frank cleared his throat and said in a manner so solicitous one might have guessed he cared for Wayne, "My friend, you should do something with your life."

Taken aback, Wayne whispered, "I *am* doing something with my life."

The two men were silent again, then, in the minutes before they arrived at Frank's home, Frank shook his head, as if burdened with the truth, and said, "No. No, you're not."

Back home, as he sat in the bathroom, another attack of bloody diarrhea upon him, Wayne tormented himself with Frank's charge. He felt, he thought, like shit. Pun entirely intended. He reviewed his food consumption for the day, for the previous day. The beers were probably a mistake but he hadn't had any cheese or fried food. There was undoubtedly something else Wayne needed to give up, but he couldn't guess what it might be.

Later, as Wayne was stepping out of the shower, Trevor called to tell him he had left his wallet at the rum shop. Wayne knew he should drive back to get it, but he felt—as his gut problems sometimes made him feel—worn out. He was hyperaware of his eye sockets—he always was at times like these—and he imagined all his exhaustion placed there. Sometimes, when his stomach was particularly bad, he'd instruct his bowels, actually say, out loud, "Okay, now, calm down." Or he'd imagine the part of himself that was working smoothly—no pain from mouth to stomach, stomach to belly button, and then an explosion below—and he'd try to convince the healthy part to press just a little farther into his system. He couldn't imagine there was another person on the planet who was this governed by his shit.

"I'm too tired," Wayne told Trevor, hoping his brother would offer to take the bus down the hill and deliver the wallet.

"Okay," Trevor said, failing to ask Wayne why he was so wiped out.

And even though he'd never been in the habit of sharing his worries with Trevor, Wayne said, "I've got a stomachache." And added, "This always happens. I get tense, I shit blood."

"Shit blood? You been to the doctor?"

"Oh, yeah. I've been and I've been. It's nothing, they say. Nerves, I guess."

"Well, I bring the wallet."

"Don't bother. I'll come get it tomorrow."

"No," Trevor said. "The woman's vex with me for talking so long. Who need it? I just come."

Wayne lay facedown, his head smashed into a pillow, his fists balled into his stomach. He had slept this way for as long as he could remember. Something about punching himself like this made him feel better. "Oh!" he groaned. Not in pain as much as defeat. He was as incapable as Trevor of negotiating the unknown. He didn't know how many more months, or even years, would pass this way if Frank, with his parting words, hadn't made him understand this. He *wasn't* doing something with his life. He was treading water, waiting for a sign to tell him which way to go.

School had been different. School hadn't involved choices, beyond the decision to go to the best one available. He'd have gone to Harrison's if it was an option, but it wasn't. Ditto Harvard. Now, he had a sinking feeling about his ambition. It was not true that he could succeed—if he put his mind to it—at law school or business school, for he simply couldn't put his mind to it. He'd lost some necessary urge. But he couldn't let this continue. The results were bound to be disastrous: the encroaching poverty of his childhood, the tedium of Trevor's days, or the thing he'd always wanted to avoid: permanent residence in the West Indies.

Something like terror finally made him stand, go into the living room, crack the papers on the couch, and circle ads. The same feeling made him leave a message on his old college advisor's office answering machine; it made him type up a letter to Tufts' career services office. "Dear Sirs," he began, "I am writing to inquire . . ." but he felt sure that they would read past his typewritten words, that they would see in the way the "h" of his machine jumped over the line of type—no computers in the Deare household—something more. They'd picture the letter he meant to send, as if it were sitting to the side of the typewriter, as if there, on a sheet of lined paper and in a frantic longhand, Wayne had scribbled a plea. It was his self-inflicted punishment for laziness, for letting his life slip away: to copy out these words, impossibly histrionic, over and over again, till he had filled the paper, "Help. Help me."

◦

And someone did.

First, Trevor.

He came that night and rested the back of his hand on Wayne's forehead. Wayne flashed on himself as a boy, emerging from the cave of sleep to see his mother doing the same thing. He'd been dreaming that his parents were boiling him and a bunch of greens for callaloo. That's when his mother felt his head.

"You're burning up," Trevor said. And then angrily, "What kind of doctor tell you it okay to shit blood?"

Wayne didn't want to explain that he'd gone to a GI doctor, back in Boston, that he'd had a tube shoved up his ass and everything was normal. "How much did we drink?" he asked Trevor instead.

"Drink? You didn't drink noth-thing. You sick. Look at you. You skin and bones."

Wayne had stripped down to his boxers in the hour before Trevor showed up. He hadn't lifted weights since he'd returned to the island, though he sometimes ran, when the weather cooled, and he had gone windsurfing a few times.

"I'm a little out of shape," he allowed.

Trevor puffed out air. "Let's go to QEH."

"What?"

"You need a hospital, man. Any idiot can see."

Wayne looked at his brother. "I always get these stomachaches."

Trevor smiled, ignoring him. "It true. Any idiot can see. And I any idiot, so give me the keys."

Wayne protested but handed over the car keys. Trevor's satisfaction at taking them was palpable. *The pleasures,* Wayne thought, with something like admiration. *The pleasures his brother was capable of.* And then his gut twisted painfully, and he cried out, "Oh, shit."

Trevor smirked.

"Fuck you," Wayne said.

They drove to the hospital, but it felt as if they were heading for a party. There was that much joy in Trevor once he was behind the wheel. He tooted the horn at passersby and slapped the outside of the car in time to the radio. He accelerated into a roundabout then continued to drive like a drunken teen, taking delight in his recklessness, as if it weren't a thrill but a dare to any cop who might pull him over when he had a brother to care for.

The doctor berated him. You didn't ignore a symptom like blood in the stools. Didn't he know that? Trevor bobbed his head, said happily, "That's what I tell him. That's what I tell him."

Wayne shrugged. He'd been to the doctor, he explained. The doctor in Boston. Twice.

"Yeah?" the QEH doctor raised a furry eyebrow. He was a large, dark-haired, white man with a manner halfway between pompous and hillbilly. "Well, you're a mess."

"Is that your clinical diagnosis?" Wayne asked.

"Oh," the doctor said and turned to Trevor. "He's a clown. Well, let me tell you, sir, my daddy back in Virginia was a clown. A real clown. Not everyone can say that, so you don't faze me."

"A real clown?" Wayne asked, interested.

"Went to clown funerals, buried a buddy in a coffin shaped like a hot dog. The whole nine yards. So I know how to deal with clowns."

Twenty-four hours later, Wayne had had another tube stuck up his ass. It wasn't like Boston—it was screamingly painful this time—and then he had a diagnosis (ulcerative colitis) and an IV in his arm and a series of drugs to purchase. He had his grad-school health insurance, he kept telling himself. He'd be screwed now if not for that. But he let himself—enjoy himself. At least until the doctor detailed the complications of the disease. He wasn't one of those people who secretly likes a stay in the hospital, so it wasn't that, but the promise that the stomachaches might not continue, might not be a permanent feature—as he'd thought of them—of his personality. That promise winged about his bed, a bird he watched: wasn't it pretty?

But then, on Wednesday, the hillbilly doctor came to visit, tapped his clipboard, and said, "Has anyone ever suggested to you that you might be acromegalic?"

"No," Wayne said, panicked. The lining of his intestines was going to dissolve into pus, and now he might just be a real, live giant.

"Well," the doctor smiled, eager apparently for an interesting case, "we'll run some tests on your pituitary."

⁓

Trevor came back, two days later, for a visit.

"Did you drive here?" Wayne asked. He had no idea his hospital stay was going to last so long, and he'd begun to feel edgy with inactivity.

"Yeah. You not using the car just now, are you?"

"Isn't that a little problem with . . ." Wayne stopped himself from saying the word *license*.

Trevor seemed to sense his concern. "Oh, I using yours, so I don't worry about *that*."

"Oh, well," Wayne said, as if to some third party in the room, "*that's* a relief."

Trevor pulled the white curtain around the bed, to shut the brothers off from the eyes of the room's other patients.

"Here," Trevor said, "I brought you something." He handed him a slim brown paper bag. In it, there was a porno magazine devoted to pictures of hunky white patients, presumably bedridden by a paper cut, and their eager-to-please black nurses.

"Great," Wayne frowned. "This'll pass the time."

Trevor grinned. The brothers had run out of things to say.

"Any messages?" Wayne finally asked. "On the machine."

"Oh, yeah, I brought it." From another paper bag, Trevor pulled out the answering machine. "You can hear for yourself."

There were plenty of messages: from his old college advisor, from Frank and Toni and Charlotte and Deirdre. From Grantley Edgehill, who was living in Canada but back in town for a week and wondering if he was free to get together. It wasn't so bad, staying on the island, Wayne thought. He had a life here, of sorts. Family and friends.

He called the advisor first—collect, he couldn't help it, since he was in the hospital, but she accepted the charges and his apologies and offered her own: it wasn't really urban planning, she was sorry to say, but there was an antipoverty agency looking for a caseworker, someone to attend to housing issues, which meant fuel assistance and shelters. And it was in Malden, which wasn't New York, or even a very—she paused; Wayne heard her swallow over the line—integrated city. And it paid poorly, but if he was interested. Her voice rose into a question.

"How poorly is poorly?"

"Twenty-five. Well, and health insurance."

Wayne calculated: the money he'd have if he sold the car and the house. Fifty percent of whatever that would bring. Or he could stay in Barbados. He saw that. Maybe sit for the Civil Service exam or try to get into education. He used to fantasize about being the principal of Combermere, about giving morning addresses to the students, about being the first head of school who made it illegal to discipline students by hitting them.

"It sounds great," he said. Was this really a good idea? "It sounds perfect."

He called Charlotte and told her where he was. "Oh, no," she said. And then in the same breath, "Can I come visit?" So that Saturday—five days into his hospital stay, the charm of checking off juices and Jello for meals having decidedly worn off—Charlotte arrived with a strange assortment of gifts: a blue stone, a box of chocolates in the shape of seashells, and— something she must have had in her bag—a pen from Saratoga Springs, New York. A jockey floated in water in the pen's shaft. Tip him one way and he won the race; tip him the other way and he fell off his horse.

"Oh, hello," Wayne called when she first stuck her head into his room. The hospitalization had already so altered his sense of time that she seemed part of another world, a life he'd long ceased living. So much lay between the hospital room and last week's rally: the puffy face the steroids might give him, the colostomy bag he might wear if the illness progressed, the colon cancer that might overtake him. All those mights to settle into. The world, though, had been rotating on its usual axis for her. She pulled her thick brown hair over one shoulder. "Melt in my mouth," commanded one of the nurses in Trevor's magazine. He'd slipped it under the covers when Charlotte walked in. Now, she chattily brought him up to speed. All week, people—black and white, Jewish and otherwise—had been calling her to make their case for the menorah. It was all Frank's doing. It seemed the whole island knew about the menorah now. She'd given up answering her telephone. Last night, she'd gone to services at the synagogue and kept her identity, more or less, concealed. She'd had it with petitions from strangers.

Wayne readjusted the pillows at his back. "I think you should give it to us. After everything they put us through. By way of atonement."

"Atonement. You know, I've been thinking that this year on Yom Kippur I should fast for two days, because I've been extra bad." Wayne gathered he was supposed to laugh. When he didn't, she said, "It's not a personal matter, you know, between you and them. The object has a history."

"Everything's a personal matter," Wayne said, but he allowed himself to drift away from her response. She was wearing black pants and a sleeveless tan shirt that gaped at the chest, so Wayne could see the webbing of her bra. If she were a denizen of the magazine at his hip, she'd oblige him by leaning over his bed, slipping his cock between her lips.

"What I wanted to tell you then," Charlotte was finishing up a thought, "was what I told you on the machine."

Wayne had no idea what she was talking about.

"I just wanted to say in person that I was sorry about the menorah. That it was all out of my control. Legally, you know."

"Oh," Wayne nodded vaguely, "right."

"So how are you feeling?" She'd taken up a chair by the side of the bed but then stood to reposition a glass of water on Wayne's hospital tray.

Okay, Wayne thought crankily. *I get it. You know hospitals.*

"Well?" she asked, when he didn't answer.

"Better, better." He gave her a look as if he were trying to ascertain just who she was, then he clapped his hands together. "Charlotte"—he remembered something he had to tell her—"I'm moving back to Boston. I'm quitting my job and moving back to Boston. It's been decided."

"It has?" She seemed confused. "By who?"

"Well, me."

"Oh, yes, of course." She smiled blankly. "Well, what's going on?"

She talked too fast. It was only now that he was feeling lousy that he saw it; she was a female Woody Allen. "I took a job," he began slowly. "In Malden. Housing. It relates to what I've been studying. I'll be there . . . soon. Sooner than you, maybe. When . . . how long *are* you here for?"

"Oh, another week," Charlotte waved. "The date keeps changing. At first it was going to be two weeks, now it's three. They're going to fire me if I'm not careful. The museum at home. Then maybe I'll never go back." She laughed. "I could stay here and die of sun poisoning. I could rent your flat."

"It's a house. And it's yours to rent if you're serious."

"But I'm not. Though it's an idea. Can you see me?" She laughed again.

"Well, why not?" Wayne said. "I've always lived abroad." But before she could answer, Frank walked in and Wayne, buoyed by the new job possibility and perhaps by Charlotte's presence, said, playfully, "It da boss." Frank smiled tightly. He was in his standard dress clothes, large wet spots decorating his underarms.

"Sir," Frank began sarcastically, "how are you?"

There was power, Wayne thought, in finally being below everybody. He liked looking up from his bed to see the underside of Frank's chin, instead of gazing down at his infuriatingly smooth pate.

Charlotte stood to give Frank her chair. He looked offended, said, "I don't take a woman's chair."

"I just thought . . ." Charlotte began.

"I know *you*," he said harshly, "the one with the menorah."

Her hand fluttered up in protest. A police officer's tentative palm, halfheartedly instructing traffic to stop.

"You're with the Jews," Frank continued.

"Well, I'm Jewish but . . ."

"So tell me about this Berkowitz fellow."

"What do you mean?"

"He a friend of yours? This Mar-ty Berk-o-witz." The syllables were an accusation in themselves.

"No," Wayne jumped in. "They're not friends."

"Would I be *here*, if he were a friend of mine?" Charlotte said.

"We can't charge him, you know, with this business." Frank waved the back of his hand at Wayne.

Wayne said, "No, I'll testify that he's responsible for my bad stomach. I'd be willing to do that."

"You're funny," Frank said flatly.

Wayne wondered if he'd tell Frank off before he quit, or if he'd just type up a polite, regretful letter, saying how sorry he was that he couldn't give more than one week's notice.

"So what is he to you, this Berkowitz?"

"He's a creep to me. What's he to you?"

Frank smiled, rubbed his hands together, and turned to Wayne to say, "Oh, I like that. She's got spunk."

Charlotte turned to Wayne, too. "Spunk. I like *that*. Makes me sound like a chipmunk." Then her tone softened, "But that Berkowitz. Did I tell you about the cards he sent me?"

Wayne shook his head no, and after Wayne quickly told Frank about Charlotte's weird day with Berkowitz, Charlotte told both men about receiving mysterious postcards from Josh Lazar. Special delivery from the other side, shipped right to her hotel room. They'd frightened her, she said; she'd even had the hotel call the police. Then, a few nights ago, she'd bumped into Berkowitz, and he'd called out to her, "Did you get my cards?"

"That's perfect," Frank said.

Charlotte looked at Wayne. "What's he talking about?"

"Oh, *he* doesn't know," Frank barked, dismissively. "I'm talking about your menorah." He motioned so Charlotte would sit back down in the chair, then squatted down by her to say, almost conspiratorially, "Why does this Berkowitz want it so bad?"

"Well, supposedly he's hoping to consolidate his power within the Jewish community, though from what I can tell, from the phone calls I've been getting, the Lazars are trying to disavow all connections with him. Once it became clear he pretended to be their representative." Now Charlotte gestured at Wayne. "The Lazars' version of an apology, I guess." She seemed to want Wayne and Frank to accept that small effort and move on.

"What kind of reason is that? That's no reason for wanting something," Frank declared. "You need to look at the files in the Barbados Museum. To determine who this menorah belongs to, you need to look at the files."

"I've looked at the files," Charlotte said defensively. No one was going to accuse her of failing to do her homework.

"And you've been to the Lazaretto?"

Charlotte faltered, then snapped back, "The old archives? Of course, I've been."

"It's such a pain, no?" Frank said, chummily, as if in apology for offending her. "The way you have to sit there and read everything. You can't take material out. They charge too much for copies. The fans blow all the papers around. This is at the archives. And then the museum. The air-conditioning freezes the sweat right on you."

"Yes," Charlotte allowed with half a laugh, "it's like that."

"Because people were walking off with material. They couldn't trust people. It wasn't like that before. It used to be you could go to the archives, take an old slave registry, go out into the courtyard, sit under the baobab tree, and imagine yourself a leper."

Here, Wayne interceded. "The archives," he explained, "used to be an old leper colony."

"Oh, yes," Charlotte nodded. "I think I'd heard that."

"Someone even stole one of your files, one of the Jewish files," Frank said.

"I wouldn't call them *my* files."

"Well, your people," Frank said, accusingly.

Wayne was irritated. Frank was leading up to something, but wouldn't say what. He wasn't speaking; he was laying out a case, point by point, getting Charlotte to consent along the way. Wayne felt a desire to protect her. Not a sudden desire—he'd been wanting to protect her since the day she called about Berkowitz—but a ferocious desire. He wanted her to be distinctly apart from all this. "Just say it," Wayne said. "Whatever you're getting at, just say it."

So Frank told them that he'd found a folder—long missing from the museum—in Berkowitz's home. A legal-sized folder, moldy in one corner, covered with coffee stains. It was stuffed with old newspaper clippings and a registry from the Speightstown synagogue, a place that had been destroyed long ago, and there was a little something in this folder that might concern Ms. Lewin, a little something about a menorah, a strange-looking thing. A line of elephants linked trunk to tail.

"Wait," Wayne said, "how did you get hold of this folder?"

"Broke into Berkowitz's home."

"You *what?*" Wayne said.

"I was trying to help your brother," Frank said, unapologetically. "I was looking for evidence."

"That's great," Charlotte enthused, as if completely unaware of the implications of such an act. She pointed her finger at Frank as if he were her student. "I've got to congratulate you. That must have taken balls."

Wayne cringed. He never liked it when women talked like this.

"Those elephants?" Frank said, eagerly now. "That's not usual in your tradition, is it? A menorah made of elephants?"

"Frank," Wayne snapped. "I'm not well. Just get to your point."

And so, finally, Frank did, telling Charlotte and Wayne what the documents in the yellowing file had told him. First, he'd found a letter, dated 1815, from John Coussins, attorney for the Jews' Synagogue, commissioning a charity, or *tzedakah*, box, to be made of silver by Nigel Jones of the Dundidge forge. Then, there was a second letter to Cornelius Dundidge, dated 1816, asking him to accept the Synagogue's regretful cancellation of the commission for the charity box now that Nigel Jones, responsible for the congregation's "much beloved menorah," had been lost to "the recent disturbance within the native population." The attorney went on to say that the congregation had a "profound affection" for Nigel Jones's handiwork. Apparently, they didn't think anyone else at the forge had comparable talents.

"Wow," Charlotte said.

"Gee whiz," Wayne echoed, but then felt mean for making fun of her.

Frank ignored them both. "A discovery like that would be worth something, wouldn't it?"

"Of course."

"It would. Thus Berkowitz's interest."

"Because?" Charlotte asked, but it was as if she was only prompting him. Wayne could see that she was ready to agree with whatever Frank might conclude. "What? He'd want the fame of the discovery?"

"Fame, of course. What else does a rich man want?"

Charlotte nodded her head, apparently unable to think of the other obvious answers: more money, women. But then she said, "No, Wayne, that's not it. Remember the Sow Pig, that day in the restaurant? Remember what she said about Berkowitz?"

"That he was harmless."

"No, that he's coming up for tenure, but she knew the university wouldn't give it to him."

"And he's a specialist in slave relations," Wayne said for Frank's benefit. "At UWI."

Frank made a sputtering sound, a few beads of spit flying out of his
mouth. "And Hitler's their chair of Jewish Studies."

"Well, maybe *that's* not fair," Charlotte said.

"The hell it's not."

"Fine," Charlotte said, her eyes shooting up to the ceiling, as if she
might find a more reasonable adversary up there. There was a brief silence.
"But the thing is . . ." she began slowly, "he's *not* a rich man, not without
tenure. He needs a job to get his money." She turned to Wayne. "Don't
you remember the chef telling us that? Those are the terms of his trust
fund."

"Oh," Wayne started. She was right, but Frank interrupted him.

"Perhaps you'll consider the Barbados Institute's request for the menorah in a new light now." The statement felt like a command.

"Of course," Charlotte said, crisply. She was all business now, and
Wayne guessed she'd been lying all along when she said she had to return
the menorah to the Jews, that she had no power to do otherwise. "Of
course, I will."

He opened his mouth. He wanted her to know he'd caught her in the
lie, but he could already hear the soprano notes of her protest: "Oh, when
I said *that*, what I meant *was* . . ." He didn't care. Now he was the one who
was no longer involved in the matter. After all, he was on the verge of
quitting his job.

He didn't like her anymore, he thought. It was as sudden as that. She
was promiscuous. Her behavior with Frank was evidence; something
about the loose way her breasts moved under her clothes made him think
she would compromise herself sexually just as easily as she'd compromise
herself professionally. She'd give herself to anyone who offered approval.

And Frank was offering now, fairly entreating, as he told her how
much it would mean to him to have a look at the menorah himself. And
she was grinning back, as if she were as excited about this bit of history as
he was, as if she was ready to let Frank have whatever he wanted.

CHAPTER FIFTEEN

Charlotte Lewin

July 5–6, 1997

✦

F RANK HAD NEVER ACTUALLY SEEN THE MENORAH, only photos of it, so an hour after Charlotte left Wayne's bedside, she and Frank were in her hotel room, she pulling the menorah from its box and Frank opening a bulky leather satchel he'd carried in from his car.

"It's all here," Frank said handing her a file shaggy with oversized newspaper clippings and Post-it notes. They were hunkered around the room's flimsy wicker table, which rocked when either one of them put the weight of an elbow on its surface. Charlotte flipped through the pages of the folder as Frank examined the elephants. "The stamp!" he cried when he found the forge's imprint.

"Mmm-hmm," Charlotte mumbled. She'd come to the pages Frank had been talking about at the hospital.

"See," he reached over and tapped the document in front of her. "No doubt about it. The menorah was made by Nigel Jones."

"I don't like," Charlotte looked up to say, apropos of nothing, "your attitude about the Jews." Now that she was up close to him, Frank didn't frighten her.

He put a mint in his mouth, said, self-righteously, around it, "I don't have any attitude about the Jews. I have an attitude about evil behavior, about false accusation. I don't judge people by the god they worship."

"You seemed to be . . . at the rally, and on the news."

"Well, then, you weren't paying good attention."

Charlotte surprised herself by mimicking him, like a bratty adolescent, "Well, then, you weren't paying good attention."

He laughed, said, "I like you. You know that."

He was not, she had to admit, the person she'd taken him to be at the rally. On the brief ride from the hospital—Charlotte pressed into Frank's tiny MG (just out of the shop, he said, though it stalled at every light)—they'd ended up talking, without rancor, about repatriation. In the abstract. Then as she'd climbed, awkwardly, out of his car, doing something of a bellyroll to right herself, he'd said, "They're troublesome issues, aren't they?" Not that this admission made her warm to Frank. The words only made her suspect him of being a Jesse Jackson type, altering his style and views as the occasion mandated. A man, in short, who knew how to play to his crowd, Charlotte being the crowd of the moment. It was later, in the hotel room, that she decided she liked him, too. Perhaps because he dropped his combative demeanor and excessive formality.

"I hope seeing this document makes you realize who really owns this menorah. I hope you see . . ."

Charlotte patted the air in front of her—a two-palmed basketball dribble—to stop him from finishing. "I know," she said, "I know."

"Well, then," Frank insisted, as if he expected her to make a decision right there.

"There are still some other things to consider. You know that," she said, almost sharply, and Frank seemed to accept the reprimand. At any rate, he was quiet as she continued to study the file. She found a notice announcing the closing of the Dundidge forge in 1816, the same year Nigel Jones disappeared. Also a list of items available from the forge: everything one might need for high tea—pots and creamers and sugar bowls. Then she flipped through documents about unrelated matters: the repair of a laver, the hiring of a cantor for High Holy Days. "Wish there was something in here about what happened to Nigel Jones." She turned a few more pages. "Escaped, I hope."

"Unlikely," Frank said. "Few did. There's really nowhere to hide on this island."

"I wonder how you could find out. You'd think there'd be something."

Frank rubbed his finger over the bits of colored glass on the elephants. "I think we should take this back." To the safe, he meant. Frank had already persuaded Charlotte that Berkowitz's postcards were a ruse, something to get her out of her room, so he could search the place for the

menorah. Berkowitz, Frank was convinced, would have no problem simply swiping the thing.

"I guess I'm done." Charlotte closed the file.

"Well," Frank began. He seemed ready to make his departure, but then
an idea came to him. Charlotte could see the thought brush his face, like
wind over water. "Do you have any more free time today?"

Charlotte waited for him to explain why, but he didn't. Instead, he
launched into a brief history lesson.

"Bajans have been considered complicit in their own oppression because of their good temper. Their placidity. Not like our Jamaican neighbors." He jerked his thumb over his shoulder—toward the window and
the ocean beyond. "We've been charged with being insufficiently rebel-
lious. But that was *never* so, that idea was planted by our masters. A way of
saying we *liked* being slaves. We weren't so unhappy. If we were, wouldn't
we have rebelled?"

Charlotte couldn't quite gauge where he was heading with this. She
looked down, considered the red polish of her toenails—her one concession to girldom.

"Well," Frank said and slapped his hands down on his thighs, as if now
he finally meant to go.

Downstairs, Charlotte followed the hotel clerk back to the safe. She
wanted to make sure she saw the thing locked away.

"Any messages come for me?" Charlotte said while out of Frank's
earshot. It was the same woman who had been so sullen earlier in the
week.

"Oh, sure," she chirped today. "I go check." She returned with a yellow
envelope. "Ms. C. Lewin," scrawled in purple pen on the front.

"What's this?" Charlotte said.

The woman shrugged. "Two letters. Come," she walked back toward
the front desk, checked something there—a calendar?—and said, "A week
ago. I think. Well, one of them come a week ago."

"Why don't you give me these things the day they arrive?" Charlotte
snapped, finally willing to be angry, but Frank was still standing by the
front desk, so she bit off the rest of what she had to say.

"My jacket," Frank said. "Did I leave my jacket in your room?"

"Were you wearing a jacket?"

"I had . . ." Frank calculated. "I guess I did. In your room. Or maybe the hospital?"

"Well, we can check."

On the way back up, Charlotte said, "It is frustrating, not having that information about Nigel Jones. Knowing you'll *never* know what happened to him." Charlotte pushed her key into the hotel door. "It just makes me so sorry."

She expected Frank to snap, "What do *you* have to be sorry for?" as if he thought *sorry* was always an apology instead of an expression of sympathy. But Frank laughed and said, "You are, aren't you? *That's* why I like you. I can see: you're as dedicated to the past as I am."

Charlotte nodded, though this was hardly the case. She'd already turned her mind to the envelope in her bag. What might *it* be? Still, she liked to be thought capable of broad historical concerns.

"It would be fun to know, wouldn't it?"

Fun. She supposed. There was something maddening about the number of times this trip that things *hadn't* revealed their riches. Those strange notes from Josh were just a disturbing joke. Her research had proved pointless. And her duppy. *Hers,* Charlotte thought. Henry was *her* duppy. Only he'd turned out to be an oversexed guy with no access to the mysteries of the Great Beyond. The envelope in her bag—probably a receipt, the hotel's listing of her weekly phone calls. It wasn't a surprise—you wanted a fortune when you opened your cookie and you always got some dumb maxim—but still it disappointed. Shouldn't the world break open at points? Shouldn't you have glimpses if you looked hard enough?

"Well," Frank said, quickly scanning Charlotte's room, "it's not here. Mind if I give Wayne a call?"

He twirled his car keys around his fingers as he waited to be connected. "Un-huh," he said, after he'd asked about the coat. "Maybe my car." He put his hand over the receiver to tell Charlotte the obvious: "Not there." Then he hung on, listening to Wayne. Finally, after a long silence, he started to bob his head up and down and say, "I understand, I understand. Well, you have to do what you have to do." Charlotte hoped he'd turn his back, so she could open her envelope, but he followed her movements about the room, held up his finger to indicate he'd be just another second, and Charlotte thought her absorption in her own business would look rude. Then, she heard Frank say, with something of an edge to his voice, "By the way, fine reading you're doing in the hospital. *Ex*-cellent magazine selection, the slave girl coming to her white master." There was a pause and Frank said, evenly, politely, "Fuck you, too," before he returned the receiver to its cradle.

"What was *that* about?" Charlotte asked, gesturing to the phone.

"Trust me," Frank said, and he picked up his leather satchel, "you don't want to know. What you *do* want to do is come with me."

"Excuse me?" Charlotte said, hugging her arms to her chest.

"No," Frank shook his head. "Let me rephrase that. I have something I think you might like to see, at the Barbados Museum. It won't take long. It's not even a mile from here."

She knew, she said, sharply. She'd been to the library there many times. "To do research," she emphasized.

But he didn't seem to be listening, just asked, in a manner that verged on the courtly, "Will you come?" And as much as she didn't like the idea of reassuming a supine position in his low-slung car—a seat that arranged (perhaps this was the manufacturer's intention?) all passengers for lovemaking—she said yes.

At one time, the museum had been a military prison. Past the entrance, there was a central courtyard, which led to a second, smaller courtyard. A covered verandah abutted the buildings and provided a walkway around the open space. Frank hurried along this corridor, leaving Charlotte to trot behind like a lapdog. Off the verandah, former jail cells featured exhibits of the Zouave uniform and old bush medicines.

Once he reached the far courtyard, Frank motioned Charlotte through a door with a "No Admittance" sign. He crossed through a hall of offices, then led her outside again, to an even tinier courtyard, also surrounded by a covered walkway. There was some greenery here, but the courtyard itself was an unlandscaped stretch of dirt. An occasional tree root eddied over the surface. Large white plastic buckets were scattered about, and the red petals of a shedding flamboyant tree dotted the land like bloody snowflakes.

A white man with a pale blond beard followed Charlotte and Frank into the courtyard. Frank turned to see who was at his back, then cried, "My friend." He grasped the man's right hand with both of his own. "Simon McGowan, Charlotte Lewin, a visitor from the States."

They shook hands. A young white woman, wearing shorts and the same Gap tank top as Charlotte, came in and addressed Simon, "Should I take the car back?" She had the flat intonations of a Midwesterner.

"No, don't bother. I'll visit with these blokes, and then I'll do it."

"Cool," she agreed and retreated into the hallway.

Simon had a British accent, but, in answer to Charlotte's questions, he explained that he was an American citizen. He'd first come here ten years ago, on a Fulbright. Now he was back with a group of undergraduates from UCLA. He was leading a dig. They'd just found a skeleton in the southeast part of the island, over near—he said the name of something and Charlotte cocked her head, confused.

"A hotel development," Frank interrupted to explain.

"On the coast," Simon added, "somewhat controversial. Because of our discoveries."

"But," Frank said, "that's neither here nor there. I've brought her to see Mama's Boy. If it's all right?" Frank turned to Simon.

Simon gestured to a sheet of blue plastic behind some white plastic buckets. "Please, be my guest."

Frank pulled back the blue tarp, which Charlotte now saw was a lining for a wooden box. In it lay a small skeleton, a man rolled on his side, huddled up, as if against the cold. His hips were wedged into stone, but the shank of his right leg, ribs, right arm, and skull had been fully extricated.

Simon picked up the skull and turned it over. It was filled with dirt, and the top part was gone, but the jawbone, the hole where the nose had been, and the left eye socket were all there.

"Alas, poor Yorick," Charlotte said, then laughed. "Does everyone say that?"

"A surprising number of people," Simon admitted, putting the skull back down.

"God," Charlotte said and leaned in close. "Talk about your pangs of the grave."

"Say what?" Simon asked.

Charlotte felt stupid. Why had she said that? So she could prove her own Jewishness? Declare, *Hey, everybody, I've got a culture, too.*

"Oh, it's a Jewish idea." She tried to be offhand. "From the Kabbalah. Supposedly after you die, you go through something called *hibbut ha-kever*, the separation from the body." In truth, Charlotte had learned all this only last night. Yet another discovery from her reading. "It lasts for three to seven days, the whole time people sit shiva, which is . . ."

"No need to explain," Simon said. He reached down to scratch a bloody bug bite on his shin. "I have a Jewish wife. I know what shiva is."

"Well, the separation from the body. Supposedly, it's very painful. The time when the dead try to release themselves from the world. Thus the pangs of the grave. Only the dead get confused sometimes, try to come back to their body or talk to their loved ones." She spoke authoritatively now, as if she held these beliefs. After all, she could guess where they sprang from: the way a body will shudder, after it's dead; the animating dreams of mourners. Still she was glad she hadn't known this while sitting shiva for Helen. Hope being stronger than belief, she'd have collapsed into superstition, tried to help Helen back into her body, or she'd have closed her eyes extra tight at night, as if against a vision. And then she'd have been ashamed. It was Helen, after all, only Helen. She couldn't be terrified of her.

"It's like the duppies here," Simon said.

"But *our* duppies," Frank noted, almost proudly, as if competition in this matter weren't absurd, "haunt the living for *forty* days."

Charlotte ignored him. "I always thought shiva was for the mourners, and it always made sense as a coping mechanism. But shiva is for the dead, too; it helps them realize they're dead."

Of course, there was nothing comforting about imagining Helen confused, wandering (as the tradition had it) back and forth between the grave and their Cambridge flat, as she accommodated herself to death. So much emotional terror to go through, and after such a long illness, such a horrible death. And how could she cotton to the idea of Josh Lazar watching his brother make out with some foreigner in his parents' backyard?

"So, Mama's Boy?" Frank prompted her. Apparently this was the nickname for the skeleton.

"Yes," Charlotte finished, "so when the seven days pass, it's . . . like this fellow. The soul and the body are definitely apart."

Only, she thought, you couldn't say this skeleton's soul and body *were* completely separate, because there was something touching about his bones. After a moment, she realized why. Or, to be fair, she registered the reason, since the first thing she'd noticed was the skeleton's posture. She asked, "Why is it all huddled up like that?" The skeleton's knees were up against its ribs, the arms wrapped around the shins, as if cringing back in terror. It was—this was what had moved her—frightened.

"Yes," Simon said, apparently pleased by the question. "In fetal position."

Charlotte nodded. Of course, *that's* what it was.

"There are two ideas about it," Simon said. "We found this guy in a posthole. He probably was buried in the corner of the kitchen. The romantic idea is that he's in this position because it's a back-to-the-womb kind of thing. You should go out of this world as you first encountered it, in your mother's belly. But the other idea, and this is probably the real reason, is that he was buried this way because it's a small space. Less of a hole to dig."

"Oh," Charlotte said and continued to study the form while the student from before returned to ask Simon some questions about the excavation site. Her thoughts drifted. She'd bought the *Life is (Still!) with People* book, because the man at the Israel Bookstore, back in Brookline, had said it had an excellent chapter on Hanukkah in general and menorah designs in particular. But she'd wandered into the chapter on Kabbalistic views of the afterlife. Last night, it had been a decided surprise to learn what (some of) her people believed. To wit: After the pangs of the grave, the soul went to Gehenna, a sort of purgatory, for a year of punishment and emotional purification, then to Lower Gan Eden and Upper Gan Eden, different levels of heaven, which brought the worthy, ascending soul closer and closer to the Infinite, till finally a soul might arrive at a state of "being with God," in "the storehouse of souls." Then—depending on what ancient text you consulted—the soul was prepared for rebirth. No one ever talked about any of this back at Charlotte's Hebrew school, never suggested that the world existed on levels, that the universe was created because God concealed himself, that there was, nonetheless, an interpenetration of dimensions, that man's good acts—the *mitzvahs* the rabbi always spoke of—actually had the power to create, *literally create*, angels, while bad deeds produced subversive angels. Man's behavior made a cosmological difference. You did a good act and thereby put more good in the world: a belief, Charlotte thought, she could get behind, a belief she could love. Thinking of all this, she had an urge to go back to the Barbados synagogue: a metaphoric representation of the universe, that's what the book said, but she had never sat in a temple and considered it this way.

She wanted something to occur to her as she looked at the skeleton, something significant. She stared harder, as if she could find the truth by dint of effort, as if close concentration was all it took to see ultraviolet light or atomic particles—everything that is there but won't reveal itself. The skeleton only started to look like a pile of chicken bones on a greasy plate, and Charlotte turned, feeling a little sick. When she looked back, Simon was saying, "Good night, Mama's Boy," and wrapping the blue sheet over his find.

The student left again and they talked on. Charlotte said she envied the students, the chance to come down here and do this sort of work.

Simon asked Charlotte about her job, and she explained what she did with kids at the museum. "Brilliant," he kept saying, but flatly, as she described it. "Oh, yes, that's brilliant." Frank's eye wandered about the courtyard. He seemed impatient to go.

"Shall we . . . ?" Charlotte finally offered, and they said their good-byes. Only when they came out to the front of the museum, Frank didn't head straight for his car. There was a large group of uniformed schoolgirls swarming around a cannon by the front walkway.

"School's not in session, is it?"

"Oh, camp," Frank said and lit up a cigarette. "They go to camp."

A teacher clapped her hands and motioned the girls into rows. She wanted to take their picture.

"I brought you here for a reason," Frank said, and Charlotte thought, *Oh, here it comes.* She started to protest, but he cut her off. "I'm wondering if you'd like a job, if you'd like a job with the Barbados Institute. We've just lost our PR person, and we're looking to hire someone who has more of an art background this next time around. Someone a little more tenacious.

You're obviously qualified . . . and hard-working. You care about history. I could see that in there." He directed his cigarette back to the museum. "And you ask good questions. You don't back down. I like that."

Charlotte smiled, even though his compliment struck her as remarkably paternalistic. (*A real busy bee of a worker,* he might well have gushed.) "I don't have . . . citizenship or . . . I mean, I have a job." She couldn't think why he'd want to hire a foreigner, and a white one at that, unless he thought there was some political advantage to having such a person involved.

"Tell me you'll think about it."

"Well, sure. Sure, I will." It was such an absurd idea. She looked over at the girls. They were cute, with their pressed uniforms. She couldn't imagine living among them, and for that very reason, the idea attracted. Why not? She didn't have to live the way she expected to, did she?

"It's good," Frank said, "to have someone who cares so much about history."

I don't, Charlotte wanted to say. *I don't care at all. I just care about the dead.*

Frank obliged her by dropping her off at the synagogue instead of back at the hotel. She wandered, like any dead soul, about the graveyard before she remembered: the envelope in her bag. There was no place to sit, so she headed inside. At the door, Perle—stationed behind a small wooden desk piled high with pamphlets—stopped her.

"Welcome," she said, somewhat mechanically, "this is Barbados's oldest synagogue." She heaved herself up, then arced her arm stiffly around to indicate the room. "You'll see it's an old Sephardic-style synagogue, built in 1833, after a hurricane destroyed the original building in 1831." She almost sounded as if she was reading from a book. "Recently restored, the outside of the building looks much as it did in the 1830s."

"Perle," Charlotte said carefully, as if she were trying to wake her from a trance. "Hello. We met last week, when I was here." Perle put her hand to her brow, to block out the sunlight.

"Oh, dahr-ling," Perle crowed. "Forgive me. I didn't recognize you. I'm so sorry."

Charlotte stepped further into the building, "Of course, it's been a hard couple of weeks . . ."

"And you never came for dinner. Wasn't I going to have you for dinner?" She seemed genuinely confused, as she slid back into her chair.

"You were, but . . ."

"Oh, I'm a terrible cook. Did someone tell you?" There was an edge of paranoia in her voice.

"No, of course not."

"Well, you have to come. But you're young. You won't want to visit with just me." She leaned forward over the table, her hands pressed together, prayer-style, then bobbed them in Charlotte's direction as if to indicate she was thinking. "A couple came in here from New Jersey. Just walked over from the cruise boat. I could ask them."

"Well, I don't know. I really can't . . ." She couldn't imagine a more painful evening.

Perle studied Charlotte's face, then started to nod, as if she'd figured something out. "Did the rabbi say something to you? Did he tell you I couldn't cook?"

"The rabbi? I thought the congregation didn't have a rabbi."

"Oh, sure . . ." She laughed and then her laugh turned into a long, wheezing cough. When it was all through, she said, "Not the rabbi for *here*. The black rabbi for the Holy Temple of Sheba. In *my* neighborhood. He's very religious, wears tallis and yarmulke and everything. He came over and brought a sack dinner. It might not be that he thinks I'm a bad cook. He has a little thing for me, you know, but I don't keep kosher. You can't on this island. It's impossible. They did a study—a sci-en-ti-fic study and decided it couldn't be done."

"And the rabbi?" Charlotte said slowly. "What's he like?"

"Oh, he's a char-ming, world-ly man," Perle said, emphasizing the adjectives as if Charlotte might prove reluctant to trust this characterization. "Well-spoken. He lives right near me on Rowans Road. Sometimes I think he has," she dropped her voice to a whisper, "a little crush." And then, in case Charlotte didn't get it, "On me." She pursed her lips and made a little farting sound, as if to say how ridiculous this was.

"Maybe *he* could come to dinner?" Charlotte said, hoping this wasn't terribly rude. "I'd like to meet *him*."

"Of course you would," Perle said, as if this had all been decided long ago. "So you'll come tomorrow."

"Yes, how do I get to you?"

"No, no," Perle said. "I'll send my driver. Where are you? The Sonesta. That's right." She scribbled the word *Sonesta* down on a piece of paper in front of her.

"No, the Paradise."

"Paradise." She didn't bother to scratch out her previous note to herself. "Then it's done. He'll be there at seven."

"Okay," Charlotte said, not completely trusting that a driver *would* show up at the correct hotel at seven. "I'm just going to sit for a while." She gestured toward a pew at the room's far corner.

"Yes, sweetheart. Stay as long as you like. There's an exhibit on the back wall. All about the restoration."

Charlotte nodded and walked, backward, to the pew she'd selected for reading.

Finally, the envelope. She ripped it open. It contained two items: a folded-up note and a smaller yellow envelope which had been mailed from the police to "Charlotte Lewin, visitor, Paradise Hotel." Inside *that* envelope, there was a letter from Police Inspector H. Tull, explaining that he was returning a piece of evidence to her, but that she should be aware that a copy of the enclosed would be kept in police files. The enclosed was Josh's suicide note, of course. The police had sent it back, still in the envelope Henry had given her, only now that envelope wasn't sealed.

As for the other piece of correspondence, it was from Henry, written on Paradise Hotel stationery.

> Dear Charlotte:
> No news in the paper yesterday about Trevor Deare,
> then no news again today. (Am a reader of the dailies now,
> thank you.) So did you? Josh's. Will you? When you can,
> soon as you can. And me, if you say you'll see me again, I'll
> appear. If not, vanish. I'm waiting, trying not to disappear,
> even now. So call. 648-9214. Till then. Ciao.
> HL

But he'd already vanished, was back out on the high seas. An un-drowned sailor. Perhaps he had called the police himself when the newspapers made it seem that Charlotte hadn't delivered the letter. That might explain why Trevor had been let out of prison but not immediately. The police needed more evidence: a call from Henry along with the note.

She turned to Josh's letter. As soon as she realized it wasn't sealed, she knew she would read it. How could she not? She was no more likely to respect the Lazars' privacy than to walk out on the final scene of a movie or skip the last chapter of a novel. She looked up for a moment. She was trying to remember what the *Life is (Still!) with People* book had said about synagogue design but could only remember that the screen—she supposed that meant the curtains in front of the Torah—was the symbolic representation of how God creates by withdrawing. Or something like that.

Charlotte pulled two sheets of white paper from the envelope. So strange to hold the whole of someone's despair. She unfolded the sheets and began to read:

> Again, these days, too many of them. Walking down the street and can't decide what next: keep walking, just stop, sit down on the curb, like a hawker, with nothing to sell, or head for the nearest hotel room with the bottles. Makes me feel safe to have them, to know if I need, I have enough to get out. They package them in such small containers now, but I know what to do. Store to store, buying single bottles, laying in a stash. You don't want to under-do things and end up a vegetable.

But here Charlotte stopped. She couldn't, for the moment, read more. It didn't feel like inclination that made her look up, and it wasn't that the water in her eyes had blurred the paper, though she had started to cry. She felt like a hand had come down from above and gently lifted her chin.

In Charlotte's bedroom, in a plastic file case, there was a folder of all the letters she had ever received from Helen. It would be years before she reread them. She might never reread them, though she knew that she'd carry that folder with her, from apartment to apartment, to a house if she ever settled down. She'd look at it, consider reading the contents, whenever she finished some large project at work, when everything—the housecleaning and the taxes and really absolutely everything—was done.

She'd consider reading them, but she wouldn't do it. She'd find something else to scrub. She'd update her address book. Still, sometimes she'd glance in the folder. Look at the paper there. Helen had gone through a phase of lilac stationery. Then started to use a computer-generated letterhead. And she'd always sent birthday cards: broad drawings with jokes about overeating. Or *The Far Side* cartoons: cows having cocktail parties; the devil, standing over a caption that read "Aerobics in Hell" and shouting, "One thousand leg lifts on the right side."

Sometimes Charlotte would imagine the day Helen bought that lilac bulk stationery in Baltimore. She'd found a pen with plum-colored ink, and in her chubby handwriting had scribbled out letters. Charlotte remembered a few of them. A missive for Jonathan, Charlotte's graduate-school boyfriend. Helen had written to introduce herself. "Well," she'd scribbled to Jonathan, "you must be wondering about ME!" Maybe Charlotte would wait till she married to reread those words, only to find she'd married (on purpose?) a man with so many of his own losses, he'd be incapable of saying, "Tell me about her." Or, "*I'd* like to read those letters."

At some point, Charlotte sensed she'd have to make an accounting. To Helen. Explain why she never got around to the letters. And at that time, Helen would hold up Josh Lazar's letter by one corner, as if it was something worthless, cheap toilet paper, and she'd say, "But you could read this?"

And the answer was, yes. Suicide was fascinating, cancer a bore. More unfairness: the meager afterlife of the brave and uncomplaining, the ghostly grandstanding of pill swallowers and ledge leapers. Bad behavior always won the prize.

She turned back to the letter.

> How it was with me was always strange and hard to say.
> Your blood is blue till it sees oxygen. You know it's so, but
> you never get the evidence firsthand. Ditto me. No way to
> be. No way. Couldn't be H. Though who'd want to be?
> Henry and his conquests. Or Dad: "Ooooh, you! You've
> had such an unhappy childhood, poor you." That's him.
> And H. His list: Sari Schapiro (MY Sari), Cate Barnes,
> Jennifer Schultz, Lydia White, Lashley Teka, Janet

Connell, Jossette Payne, Margaret Sealy (our old maid, remember her?), and that woman who stayed with us—what
was her name?—that summer the folks went to Paris. Also
Mark Herbert. Why limit yourself to one sex? And me. Me,
me, me. Not literally, but he fucked me all the same. Old,
good boy Henry and his layabout brother. That nut, Josh
Lazar. NEVER sleeps anymore. NEVER and that's what he
really wants to do. To sleep. For a good, long time.

Charlotte rubbed the back of a knuckle against her eye. She was pretty
tired now herself. She folded the letter back into its envelope and looked
up, sniffed once. She felt, on some level, a kinship with Josh, but she
didn't feel sympathy. Not really. If there was a Platonic form for a chair
and goodness, then there was one for her angst and here it was: Josh's letter. A toxic thing. Dangerous to touch. Its fury might rub off on her. And
that list of Henry's women. And the man. Charlotte was connected with
them now, too. All that potential infection.

"Well," she said, out loud, standing. She approached Perle, the letter
extended. "Could I give you something to give to your nephew? To Henry
Lazar?"

"Sure, sweetheart." Perle seemed to have forgotten who Charlotte was
again, but she took the letter. "His brother died. Did you hear his brother
died?"

"Yes," Charlotte nodded gravely, "I heard about the accident."

"Oh," Perle coughed, and gestured with an unlit cigarette to the corner of the graveyard where Josh lay, "*that* was no accident." And then,
after a beat, "Everybody knows that."

CHAPTER SIXTEEN

Charlotte Lewin

July 5, 1997

⚭

B ACK AT THE HOTEL, SHE FOUND HENRY, sitting on the floor by
her door.

"Hi," she called tentatively from down the hall. "Weren't you going on
a trip?"

"Yeah," he said, standing as she neared. His sailor's tan had faded dramatically, so he looked diluted, a watercolor with too much water. "I *am*
going on a trip."

He was up by the time she reached him, and though she didn't think
either of them had offered a signal of intentions, they immediately embraced, kissing with sloppy, puppy-dog enthusiasm. Charlotte—one hand
to her skirt pocket—pulled out her room key, opened the door and, still
ardently making out, they pushed in, Henry kicking the door shut with
the heel of his shoe.

Charlotte missed the transition to the floor. *It was just boom, down,* she
thought, offering herself a play-by-play of events, as if she might be called
upon to report later, though who did she think her audience would be? On
top of her, Henry felt distinctly lighter than she remembered, though he
didn't look as if he'd lost weight. He tugged her skirt up. She started to un-
button his shirt but lackadaisically, stopping when he leaned over to kiss
her belly. It was like before. He was willing to make her body the center of
attention. Henry seemed to like to be in charge. Still, feeling greedy,
Charlotte lifted a shoulder and rolled Henry over. She straddled his hips
and started to undo his belt, and as she did, something clicked off in
Henry. It was dramatic, a refrigerator hum abruptly silencing. A complete
power outage.

"What?" Charlotte sat up on his thighs.

"Just . . ." Henry brushed her hands away from his belt. He struggled to his elbows. "Just this wasn't what I came here for."

"Oh, sorry," Charlotte said, hand to the base of her throat, and pulled herself quickly off him. Still kneeling, she straightened her clothes.

"No, don't be sorry," Henry said. "It's just . . . can we?" He cocked a thumb over his head toward the room.

"Oh, yeah. Oh, sure." She couldn't remember when she'd been more embarrassed. She pushed to her feet, crossed her arms, then said, as if he'd just entered, "Please, come in."

Despite his words, he didn't take a chair but stretched out on the room's bed. He lay down on his left side, head propped up in his hand. "Join me," he said and patted the floral pattern of the spread.

She did. Facing him, she mimicked his pose, but this arrangement didn't feel intimate. Given their brief history, a bed was entirely too prosaic.

"What I came here for was my brother's letter. I went to the police, and they said they'd sent it back to you. So, I realized—first off—that you *did* give them the letter. So, thank you. Really, *thank* you."

"It was nothing," Charlotte said. She felt uncomfortable. She re-arranged herself on the bed, sitting back on her heels. A posture from yoga class: she'd missed six sessions since she'd been in Barbados. "But I'm afraid I gave the letter to your aunt Perle. No more than an hour ago. I asked *her* to give it to you."

"Oh, shit," Henry rolled onto his back, pressed the heels of his hands to his eyes.

"I'm sorry. I didn't think I'd see you again, so I thought she . . ."

"No, no, no," Henry said and reached over to squeeze her hand. "You did the right thing. It's just. Well, maybe she *won't* read it. *You* didn't, after all."

"Well," Charlotte admitted. "Actually, I *did*."

"You did? And still you . . ." Henry pointed to the floor by the door. "Huh," he added. "I wouldn't have thought."

Charlotte was quiet.

"I don't come off so well in that letter."

"No," she agreed. "You don't." And then because he was quiet, "Is it true? What he said?"

"Oh," Henry heaved a great sigh, "more or less, I suppose." He sat up and rubbed his hand over his face, then stood and retucked his shirt. His eyes flickered over the room. "Very neat," he remarked, as he took a chair that faced the bed.

Charlotte scooted to the bed's edge and perched primly there.

"So, how did you know I was going on a trip?"

"With Sari."

"Right. With Sari."

"I went to synagogue. Your folks told me."

Henry nodded gravely, then made a face, as if he'd bitten an unripe persimmon. He smiled, but only because he wasn't talking, and she was looking at him.

"Can I ask you something?"

"Sure," Henry said, half-distracted. He slumped deeper into the chair, as if suddenly even sitting up was too much work.

Charlotte waited for a moment, considered the wisdom of her question. There was truly something about Henry that wouldn't come into focus for her. If a friend back home asked her what he was like, she didn't know how she'd answer. If anything, he seemed less clear to her now than he had when she'd first met him. "Well," she began slowly—she didn't want to be cruel—"I heard you and your brother fought before the party and, you know, his jump. I wondered what you fought about."

Henry picked up the TV remote control, lying on a desk near him, and fingered the small plastic squares there. "That isn't," he said, not looking at her, "any of your business." But his tone wasn't sharp.

"True enough."

"Okay," Henry said abruptly, "who gives a flying fuck?" He stood up, shoved his hands in his chino pockets, and started pacing the room. A theatrical gesture that, Charlotte thought, a woman would never stoop to. "First, this parachute thing. That's what we fought about first. I said, 'No fucking way. I'm not jumping out of a plane and dancing around with a bunch of other goofballs.' Josh is like, 'You have to.' And I said no, and then like it's the most important thing in the whole world that I do it, he threatens to tell my folks about . . . about this." He flapped his hand back and forth between himself and the bed.

"About *us*?"

"Well, not *you*."

"What?"

"Just me and that little tally Josh had going about my partners. So I said he could go right ahead for all I cared, if he was going to try to blackmail his own brother. And he tried to back out of it. No, no, no, he'd never do such a thing. He was just mad. And I said—and I was, you know, sarcastic—'Well, I'm feeling a little pissed myself. I think I'll sleep with Sari.' Sari's this woman he's always had a thing for. Only she doesn't even *like* him. He said, 'Go ahead.' And I said, 'Well, thanks for your permission 'cause I already did.'" Henry stopped walking and sank back into his chair.

"And had you?"

"Yeah, I had, but that's not the point."

"It's not?"

"No, the point is he said, 'If I find out you have . . .' A threat, you know. And I said, 'What? What will you do? Kill yourself? You're not going to kill yourself.' He said, 'Just you watch me,' and I said that I wasn't going to even *come* to his stupid party. And you know I figured he *was* going to say something to my folks, which is why I took off. I didn't want to be around if he *was* going to tell them. My parents going . . ." Putting his fists to his heart, he raised his voice into a high mousy squeak, "'Oh, our Henry? Not our Henry?'" He dropped his head, briefly, into his hands—a cartoon version of parental despair—then sat back in his chair. "So I take off. I'm on a boat with some friends, and one of them gets a call from his folks, hears about what happened at the party. So . . ." He brushed his hands through the air, as if he were a magician, saying, "Ta-da!"

"So why are you going away now?"

"Because . . ." But Henry didn't finish his thought. He seemed stumped. Apparently, the question didn't have an answer. "It's what I do," he offered at last. Then, he said, "And Sari. Sari wants to go."

Charlotte gave a small laugh at this.

"You probably think I'm heartless. Of all people, how could I do her? But Sari. She knew Josh, so we're in this together. And no one ever *causes* another person's suicide. I mean, if we all killed ourselves when we were betrayed, we'd all be dead."

Charlotte didn't know what to say to this.

"I'm sorry. I just don't want you to think I got you involved in all this on purpose." He seemed to have a rather urgent need for her to say it was okay, that he wasn't a bad person. Of course, no one ever thought they were the bad guys. That was the problem: a *universal* conviction of innocence.

"I just don't want you to think that I . . ."

"Don't worry," Charlotte said. "You and I . . . we're fine. And I'm glad we didn't . . . you know. I wouldn't want to complicate things with you and Sari."

"Yeah," Henry said. "That's a consideration." But he didn't say this with any conviction, as if Sari would be unfazed by infidelity.

"Well," Henry said, his mind already elsewhere.

"Good-bye," she said, wanting to beat him to a farewell. A foolish bit of one-upmanship.

"Yeah," he said vaguely, though he didn't stand. This felt anticlimactic. She wanted something more from him. But it wasn't going to come. She could feel that. Her mother had once told her—when she'd been complaining about some old boyfriend, about some failure of generosity on his part—that Charlotte couldn't expect him to act better. It was like asking a man who was five feet ten inches to be six feet; it just wasn't going to happen.

Charlotte stood and said, though it wasn't true, "Well, I should get back to work."

"Yes," Henry said, "work," as if he didn't quite know what that was. He stood himself, then leaned over to give her a chaste kiss on the cheek. "Bye."

"Yeah, bye-bye." They walked to the door. People always compared themselves to their siblings. It wasn't competition exactly. Brothers and sisters: they offered a yardstick. If Henry was the brother who went away, who was he now that Josh had—forever and ever—usurped his role? "Well," Charlotte said. This was starting to feel ridiculous. How many times could you say good-bye? "Farewell, so long, hasta la vista."

Henry laughed, so she kept calling, as he went down the hall, "Ciao. Shalom. Mañana. Later, baby."

Henry got on the elevator. He lifted his hand, offered a funny little wave. A grand twist of his wrist. Almost like British royalty. But there was so little of him in the gesture, so little of what she remembered from her first night in Barbados (Will: her duppy, demon lover, incubus), that she might have been watching a phantom.

Perle lived, as her brother-in-law had complained, just "like them," in a chattel house, notable on the outside only for being more run-down than the neighbors' homes. Otherwise, it featured the same stone front step, the same piece of fabric hung over the front door, and the same cheerful paint: turquoise with orange trim, in Perle's case.

Inside, though, the home could hardly be typical. All the walls had been knocked out. Instead of four tiny rooms, there was a single medium-sized one, window shutters closed, floors painted burgundy, walls faux marble. Putti clustered at the door frames. Behind a fainting couch and two overstuffed chairs sat a large table, covered with blue, green, and black graffiti. The entire place smelled of rotting fruit. In the corner, a large-screen TV was tuned to CNN. Some young woman had been trying to blackmail Bill Cosby. Tomorrow, she'd go to trial.

Perle's driver had, surprisingly enough, picked Charlotte up at the appointed hour. Fifteen minutes later, Charlotte was handing Perle a bouquet of cut flowers. The gift seemed to puzzle Perle as much as Charlotte's appearance on her doorstep. She didn't seem to be expecting guests but waved her into the house just the same.

Perle didn't have a kitchen, exactly, but along one wall were a sink and a single slim, brown table, laden with bottles, moldy bread, and two hotplates. Tiny fruit flies hovered in a cloud above a bunch of black finger bananas. Underneath the table sat a small refrigerator, the kind Charlotte associated with college-dorm rooms. A black-and-yellow cord snaked out the back door.

"What do you want for dinner?" Perle said, and Charlotte shrugged.

"Well, you have to decide," Perle replied, somewhat impatiently, and motioned for Charlotte to follow the bumblebee cord to the backyard. There, in a small space cordoned off with galvanized tin, sat a tremendous, horizontal freezer. In college, Charlotte had once spent the holidays with a Midwestern roommate whose parents had such a freezer, full up with deer parts. So now she averted her eyes as Perle fiddled with the padlock on the freezer's door. She half suspected a doe's mournful brown iris to greet her when the lid was flung open. Instead, a puff of white steam billowed out, and Perle leaned into the cloud and said, "Well, pick something." Inside, it was the Zabar's of the tundra. The entire case was packed full of white plastic containers marked in a round hand: Roasted Red Pepper Soup, Jambalaya, Potato-Leek, Chicken-Rice-Andouille.

"Anything," Charlotte said. "It all sounds wonderful."

Perle decided on chicken-rice-andouille.

"And is the rabbi coming?" Charlotte asked. Surely this wouldn't appeal to someone who kept kosher.

"Of course. I said so, didn't I?"

"You did. I'm sorry."

They went back inside. Perle slid the frozen blocks of soup into a pot, then placed the whole thing over the hotplate. To her right, the table was covered with fancy condiments: hot sauces and olive paste and bottles of tamari. A snapshot was propped against an open jar of capers: a Mr. T doll extended a fireplace match to the last candle on a fully illuminated menorah.

"What's this?" Charlotte said, pushing aside an empty cigarette pack and picking the picture up for a closer look. It was an ordinary menorah, much like the one she had at home.

"Oh," Perle said. "Dat's Mista Tee, the Macc-a-*bee*. The kids gave it to me."

Charlotte guffawed. "That's great. That cracks me up." She waved at a fly buzzing about the capers.

"Crop Over," Perle said. "There are always a lot of flies after the sugar crop."

"Is there anything I can do?" Charlotte offered.

"You want breadfruit, too?"

"Oh, yes, I've been wondering what it tastes like." But the fruit Perle picked from the table was covered with fungus. It gave, like an overripe melon, to her touch.

"Actually no," Charlotte said quickly. "The soup will be plenty."

"You know what we need to do . . ." Perle began, then seemed to lose track of her thought.

"Set the table?" Charlotte guessed.

"Yes, that's it." Perle handed her three bowls and some plastic spoons. She gestured to the table, which looked like a New York subway car, with its loud, angry graffiti. "The kids come in and do this. They did the table. I think I'm going to let them do a wall next."

Perle watched Charlotte taking in the "Motherfucker" that ran down one table leg and explained, "I let them do what they want. They know I accept them, that this is a safe place to come."

As if on cue, a boy stuck his head through the front door and asked if there was going to be any painting tonight. She said, "No, not tonight," and pressed a dollar into his hand. In quick succession, three more boys came with variants on the same question and ran away, giggling, when they each had their dollar.

Charlotte didn't know what she expected the rabbi to look like, but she must have had some firm idea, because she was so surprised by the man who finally came to the door. He was a large black man with tree trunk arms and legs, more substantial than fat, though his protuberant stomach merged with his chest for that distribution of flesh that gives a man a forceful or pompous look. His hair—a sheet of tiny braids under a tan hat—hung past his shoulders.

"Shalom, shalom," the rabbi said as he entered the house. He wore, as promised, a tallis, over a burgundy dress shirt and tan suit jacket.

"Are you hot?" Perle said. "It's so hot." She gestured the rabbi to one of the overstuffed chairs, encouraged Charlotte to take a seat by him, then plugged in a window fan and placed it by the front door. The fan sent the curtain flying and cooled, Charlotte imagined, the front step. The room's hot air barely stirred.

"Let's turn off the TV," the rabbi suggested. Perle found a remote control under the black bananas, and Bill Clinton's face disappeared from the room.

"I'll tend to dinner," Perle said, "and you tell her everything. How we met and everything."

The rabbi laughed, a knowing rumble. "We're involved in the welfare of this street. For a while, we headed an organization for after-school activities, trying to keep the kids out of trouble." His voice was surprisingly soft, and Charlotte had to strain to hear him over the fan.

"And tell her about your congregation." He nodded, as if he were about to do so, but then Perle shouted, with considerable outrage, "It's cold."

Charlotte looked up. "I think you have the pot on the wrong burner."

"Dahr-ling, you're right." Perle shifted the pot over to the red coils and said, "Where's my head?"

"Well," the rabbi began, "shall I tell you?"

"Oh, please."

"We're descendants of Ethiopian Jews."

Charlotte flashed on a news story from a few years ago: something about the shameful way Israeli officials had been treating Falashas, the Ethiopian immigrants who made *aliya*.

"You may not know about us. We descend from the lost tribe of Judah."

Charlotte nodded her head as if she knew exactly what this meant. Rastafarians thought this, too, didn't they? That they were descendants of ancient Israelites?

"And our congregation is very old. We have been here for almost twenty-eight years. There are about fifty families in our congregation, and as I say, most of our members are very old. We observe all the festivals of the Jewish faith, and I teach Hebrew to anyone who wants to learn."

The rabbi was sitting at the edge of his seat. Perhaps his chair, like Charlotte's, was slightly damp.

"And what's your relationship to the Bridgetown synagogue?"

"We are brothers, all right."

"But you don't . . . you don't worship together?"

The rabbi leaned back, rested his crossed hands on the top of his chest. He spoke slowly and his words had a musical lilt. "It's nothing to worry your head about. We are well-acquainted. A difference of style. But we are all Jews."

"And in terms of practice?"

"Everything is the same. There is no confusion."

"Could I come? To services?"

"Oh, yes. You're entirely welcome. We have two services on Saturdays, one for seniors and one for juniors, but the young people, they shy away from it."

Charlotte was about to express her regrets; she was flying home next Saturday, but she suddenly didn't want to admit she traveled on the Sabbath.

"I'll show you how to get there." The rabbi pulled a piece of paper from his coat pocket and drew a map. Handing it to her, he pointed to an X on the sheet and said, "It may not appear as a synagogue to you. The building is shaped like a chapel. Sometimes visitors are doubtful, but you'll find a Star of David in the center of our building. People come and do enjoy our services."

Charlotte took the paper and nodded. She wondered what he'd think of her when she failed to show.

"So what"—she hoped he wouldn't be offended by this—"what sort of training have you . . . ?"

He cut her off and answered—not angrily, but defensively, as if she needed to be convinced of his legitimacy. He embarked on a long explanation that she only partially followed about his ordination and the lineage between West Indian rabbis and Addis Ababa. When he was through, he said, "But tell me about you. Are you enjoying your holiday?"

"Dinner," Perle called.

The rabbi followed Charlotte to the table, then said, "You'll have to excuse me. I can't stay for the meal. An obligation at the old-age home. But I'll sit with you while you get started."

Perle pressed him to eat, but he agreed only to a glass of water.

"Actually," Charlotte started, then leaned over for a spoonful of soup. The broth was boiling hot, the chicken cold in the center. "I'm not exactly here on vacation."

"My dear," the rabbi said, checking his watch. "Forgive me. Such a short visit." He stood, ready to take his leave.

"Before you go," Charlotte said and reached out to toward his hand. "I'd like to give you . . . excuse me." She went to the chair where she had left her bag. "I think you should have this." She started to unzip the straw bag. It was a cheap Kmart pocketbook, something she'd bought only because she thought her brown winter purse would look strange with summer dresses. The purse's fiber had jammed the zipper. She struggled with it, then finally took a knife from Perle's table and cut a slit in the top of the bag. She pulled the bubble-wrapped menorah from her bag and handed it to the rabbi.

"I have a mission"—she smiled at her word choice; it sounded so silly—"to return this to the Jewish community of the island. So if you would . . ." She extended her bundle, but the rabbi didn't take it. "Please."

"Oh, no," the rabbi said, stepping back, "it's too much."

"Please. For your congregation. It doesn't belong to me. It belongs to the Jews of the island."

"But you'll want to give this to the Bridgetown synagogue. . . . In the paper, I saw that they . . ."

"No." Charlotte cut him off. She wanted, she thought, to give it back to the Sephardic Jews, the ones who had first come to the island, but they weren't here anymore. "If you want to give it to them, you can, but . . . please." She pushed it away from her. She was sick of having the piece in her care. Howard's remonstrance rang in her ear. "Didn't I say to give it to . . . ?"

"The Jews," Charlotte would interrupt, "the Jews. *That's* what you said."

Ignorance, she knew, was no defense. She'd heard Howard say this a thousand times. "Just because you don't know a law doesn't mean you're not subject to it."

"I said to give it to Abe Lazar," Howard would say, and Charlotte would answer, "Really? You did?"

Ignorance was no defense, but maybe, this one time, ignorance could be a mitzvah. Maybe angels—even now, as the rabbi said, "Thank you, my dear," and the weight of the elephants lifted from her palms—would materialize. Perle might sleep tonight (it suddenly occurred to Charlotte that there was no bed in this house) under their beneficent wings.

"Peace be with you," the rabbi said.

"And also with you," Charlotte offered automatically, and he was gone, as fast as he came.

Perle turned to Charlotte and gave her a wry smile. "You can see how he looks at me," she said. "But I'm too old. Too old for romance."

CHAPTER SEVENTEEN

Charlotte Lewin and Wayne Deare

July 6–12, 1997

✦

A ND THAT WAS THAT. NO MORE MENORAH. End of story. Only not quite the end, not of Charlotte's story, for she wouldn't fly home till Saturday, still almost a week away. So she rented a car and spent a day sightseeing—headed up north to the most rural part of the island. She stopped first at River Bay, a pretty little cove where Wayne said he'd gone swimming as a boy, then went over to the Animal Flower Cave, where she walked into the earth. Literally. She joined some other tourists and descended steep steps—it felt a bit as if they were ducking under a manhole cover—then slid over the cave's slick rocks in order to look at the "sea flowers." They were actually sea anemones in tide pools, but Charlotte couldn't quite see them, though the others appeared dutifully amazed. Then she crossed to the east side of the island, driving round the grassy drive of an abandoned resort hotel, a great dinosaur of a place, poised on a cliff, as if waiting for the final wind that would drop it into the sea. Here was a place for ghosts if ever there was one. They could run along the balconies, carrying gossip from room to room, or bring invisible highballs down to the patio. Against the gray-white of the building and the cracked concrete of the walkways, they'd be—even disembodied—the most colorful thing for miles around. And then Charlotte was past all this, driving towards a tiny village.

At a crossroads, four boys came running toward her car. They clustered at her window. "I'll give you directions," one of them offered eagerly.

"I'm not lost," she said and smiled, perhaps knowingly, for the boy continued, "You can smile if you like, ma'am, but the reason I want to talk to you today . . ."

"I'll find my own way," she interrupted. Soon after, Charlotte left the village for dirt roads and the farmland beyond. She passed by the stone base of a defunct windmill and saw a baby mongoose following its mother across the road. She slowed her car, and when she did, a skinny black girl stepped from the windmill's arched door. She took advantage of Charlotte's pace to stick her hand through the car window and say, "Hello, I won't hurt you. My name's Melody. How you doing?"

She was a slim, pretty teenager, with the round, flat face of a chestnut. Her hair must have been very long, for she'd formed a ponytail simply by gathering it all up and tying it into one big knot.

"Beautiful day, isn't it?" Melody said. She wore a purple muscle T-shirt and a pair of low-slung blue jean shorts. The frayed edges hung past her knees. The clothes looked well-worn, and Charlotte suspected she'd been in them for days.

"Well," Melody said and clapped her hands, then pointed off to the north. She started to describe a stretch of land that lay past the fields. Melody seemed to think Charlotte intended to go there, and she offered to take her if she wished.

"That's okay," Charlotte said.

"It's very magnificent." There was a silence, then Melody added, "I'll walk up and meet you there. I wouldn't have to come in your car if you didn't want."

"Well," Charlotte said, hesitantly. "All right."

The girl said she should drive off the road and over the empty cow field. Just past the trees at the far end of the field, she would find the sea. Charlotte started to do so but then felt too awkward. How could she not take the girl? She stopped the car and leaned over to open the passenger-side door.

Melody ran over and got inside. The small rental car lurched uneasily over the field's hardened waves of mud. "It won't hurt the car, I promise," Melody said, and there was something funny about such a young girl, a girl who probably wasn't old enough to get a driver's license, offering this reassurance. Melody directed Charlotte off the field toward the water. "Here it is," she said and pointed toward two coconut palms, where she wanted Charlotte to park.

The two got out of the car. They had come to the very tip of the island, a windy spit of exposed land. "Nothing from here to Africa," Melody said, and the air, cool and clean, seemed to confirm this. Up and down the coast, there was no one out, as far as Charlotte could see. And this made sense: both sea and land were too rough for boats or buildings.

Melody guided Charlotte to the edge of the nearest bluff. Steep paths led from it to a small beach. "We used to catch turtles down there," Melody said.

Charlotte nodded as she looked down on the bay's coral reef, entirely visible through the water. "You can't get turtles anymore?"

"No, you can still get them."

Charlotte followed Melody's eyes up to a white cliff in the distance. "It's very magnificent," Melody repeated, flatly, automatically.

After a while, Charlotte wandered to the other side of the bluff. Here, when the waves crashed at just the right angle, water spurted out of holes in the rocks like so many whale spouts. "Oh," Charlotte cried and clapped her hands, girlishly, the first time it happened.

"Well, take a picture," Melody commanded, as if wondering what Charlotte was doing. Obediently, Charlotte darted back to her car, pulled out a camera, and pointed it toward the white cliff in the distance. "And now I get you a coconut," Melody said as if this were the required next stop on the tour.

"Oh, that's all right."

"You don't want a coconut?" The girl seemed offended.

"Sure," Charlotte said, "a coconut would be great." They got back in the car.

"Are you from here, Melody?"

"It's not Melody," Melody said. "It's Melody."

Charlotte nodded as if this made sense. Was there something wrong in her pronunciation? Or was she mishearing the girl? Melody directed her through a grove of Australian pines—planted to prevent erosion, she explained—then over to a stand of coconut palms.

"And you have family here?"

"Yeah."

Charlotte tried some more questions. She found out that coco jelly was good for a man's back and that a ninety-one-year-old woman lived in the nearby village. She was as healthy as a woman half her age. But these facts didn't quite add up to a picture of Melody.

Charlotte and Melody got out of the car again, and the girl looked up, quickly surveying the possibilities. "This one," she said, picking a palm and walking to it. She put her hand around the trunk, like someone cupping a lover's head, then put her other hand around the trunk and started to walk up the side of the tree. When she got to the top, she bent down a leaf and grinned. She was posing, for the photograph she was sure Charlotte would want to take, but Charlotte refrained from ducking back into her car for the camera. The girl tossed down some coconuts, then descended.

"You're so strong—to get up the tree so easily!"

Melody shrugged then bent her left arm, as if Charlotte might want to reach over and feel her muscle. "It's good exercise," she said and pulled a jackknife from her shorts. She cut a spiral on top of the young coconut and handed it to Charlotte, then cut another one for herself. Charlotte drank the juice. It tasted sweet, almost carbonated.

"I drink one of these every day," Melody said. But it was the last bit of personal information Charlotte could drag out of her. Melody answered— but minimally—the questions Charlotte put to her as they got back into the car. Had she always lived in this area? (More or less.) What did she think of tourists? (People who *didn't* like them were racists.) Was she still in school? (No, she wasn't.)

Melody directed her back to the windmill. Charlotte stopped the car, then said, "I'd like to give you something for showing me all that." She took a bill from her pocket.

Melody held up her hand. "Naw, you don't have to do that."

"Well, I'd like to, if you don't mind."

"Naw, naw, that's okay . . ."

"Well, if you're sure . . ."

Melody said, "Yeah, no problem," then waved a good-natured fare-well. Charlotte started to drive away, but after 100 feet, she pulled over and stopped. She felt strange. Perhaps Melody *had* wanted her to insist about the money? Charlotte parked then ran back to the windmill. What she'd say to Melody was: "No, *really*, I wouldn't have seen all that without you; I *want* to give you something." But when she stepped into the windmill, Melody wasn't there. Which was impossible. Charlotte had *seen* her go in, and if she'd left, she'd be out in the field somewhere. The windmill was just a single round room—maybe six feet in circumference, empty save for two dried coconut husks that lay on the dirt floor. If there was a trapdoor, or a second floor, Charlotte would have seen it.

"Melody," Charlotte called, but the sound of her own voice echoing off the rock spooked her, and she hurried back to the rental car and drove on, checking, as she did, for Melody in the rearview mirror. But the girl never appeared, and soon Charlotte was back on a paved road, heading, she thought, south for the hotel, but when she passed by River Bay again, she realized how turned around she was. She'd been driving west for miles. By the time she found her way back to the Paradise, it had been dark for hours.

Not long after her return, the front desk called to say a message had been left for her. Someone named Pat wanted her to know that her flight had been canceled. She needed to stop in with a travel agent to reschedule. In the background, she could hear a woman calling out, presumably to another employee, "Go tell that red man the phone want he." A command which Charlotte turned over, along with the experience with Melody, for half the night, as if by concentrating, she could determine where her perception was off, what she'd missed that she was supposed to understand.

There were several small businesses, a travel agency among them, that bordered the walkway by the hotel's entrance. The next day, Charlotte went down to reschedule her flight. Only when the agent asked her to settle on an hour for departure—did she want the morning flight or the afternoon one?—Charlotte hesitated. Morning, she said; no, afternoon; no—would he excuse her? She got up and wandered out of the office, out to the almond trees behind the hotel shops, then farther, down the street to a fast-food restaurant. She needed a Coke, she thought. Low blood sugar had made her confused. But when she returned later that day, it was the same story. Only this time, when she stood, no decision made, and told the travel agent that she felt a little light-headed, he gave her a queer look, as if she were part of some complicated plot to defraud him.

Back in her hotel room, it occurred to her what the problem was. Not the flight time, but the going, for she supposed she'd genuinely been considering Frank's job offer. He'd called twice to give her the details, then he had his curator, Toni, call. Director of PR, $40,000 a year, which improved on Charlotte's current salary and offered that most desirable of things: a job where no one would feel inclined to put gum in her hair.

And as soon as Charlotte acknowledged her interest, she went back down to the travel agency and said the one o'clock flight on Saturday would be fine.

⇝

"So did you like our island?" Wayne asked. He was sitting with Charlotte on a concrete bench by one of the airport's kiosks.

"Everyone asks that here."

"I suppose we do." And what was wrong with that? Wayne thought. It was a reasonable enough question. Still he stopped himself from telling *her* so. Wayne had had an aggressive sense of his normalcy ever since the doctor had told him that he *wasn't* an acromegalic, that he was just—as if Wayne didn't already know this—tall. Since he'd left the hospital on Thursday, Wayne saw how his sudden confidence in his ordinariness might make him a jerk.

"I didn't expect it to be so Anglican," Charlotte allowed.

"More English than England she-self," Wayne said. He pulled out a handkerchief, mopped his forehead, then folded the cloth back into a tight square.

"Yes," Charlotte said. "I think I read that somewhere."

"So is it true Frank offered you my job?" Wayne asked.

"*Your* job?"

"Well, you know," Wayne said, "my old job." He'd already told her about his new position and what he knew of his future: he'd fly to Boston as soon as he had enough money for a ticket. In the meantime, he was using what cash he had to ship some boxes to Deirdre's. He'd stay with her until he found a place to live.

Earlier in the week, Deirdre had finally reached Wayne at the hospital. She was worried, motherly, as he knew she might be. But he wouldn't let her linger on his illness. He was already feeling better. His fever was gone, as was the IV. He'd been eating solid food and feeling—fine. It was the strangest thing: to simply feel fine.

"I'm coming back to Boston," he'd told her, "just as soon as I find a place." She immediately offered hers, and he'd said, "Well, wouldn't that be uncomfortable?"

She huffed angrily then said, "Well, we have to talk about that, don't we?"

Wayne said, "I don't know. Do we?"

And Deirdre said, "You asshole." There was a long silence then Deirdre said, "I'm not saying I don't want anything to happen," and Wayne snapped back, "Well, I'm not saying that either." And so there they were, thousands of miles apart, both not saying it. Wayne couldn't think when he'd been happier.

Now Charlotte said, "It didn't exactly sound like *your* job. I thought you worked part-time."

"He's offering you full-time work?"

Charlotte nodded then said, "Are you thirsty? Maybe we should get a drink."

"Fucking asshole." Wayne held up his hand and said, "Just don't tell me what he's offering you as salary." And he didn't want to know. He was done with it now, so he cleared his throat, then returned to his question, "So did you like our island?"

⌐

And what she thought was that it wasn't so much that she liked it as that she didn't want to go home, back to her old life. The baby-sitting at the museum. ("Don't color my dress, sweetie. There's paper right here.") Or her mother (who'd call her regularly at work and when she said she didn't have time to talk would say, "What do you mean? You can talk to me," before heading into some lengthy anecdote about her garden, leaving Charlotte with the understanding that Helen had been the kind of daughter who always had time for a mother.) Or Lawrence, her ex. (The painful details of getting her car back. She could imagine them sleeping together, right after he gave her the key, then both saying, "But it's still over, right?") Or her apartment, with Helen's room, and her memory of making the bed after Helen died, making it so everything would be in order for her when she came back.

"What time is it?" she asked Wayne.

"Twelve-thirty."

"Well, I better go to the gate."

"Oh, I'll come with you."

"Don't they only let people with tickets in?"

"No," Wayne laughed. "We're not so strict here." He heaved up her bag: one weighty carry-on, nothing to check through.

"Don't carry that, you," Charlotte said. "You're sick."

Wayne ignored her, slapped at her hand as she went to take her bag back. "I'm healthy now."

"Well, thanks," Charlotte said as they headed to the gate area. When they got there, he dropped her bag on a seat.

"I'm going to get some presents," she told him, "so really, you don't need to wait with me." But he insisted he wanted to see her off and sat quietly while she filled a bag with molasses and rum.

When she was almost through, she clapped her hand on his shoulders and said, "One last favor. Help me pick a CD. I need advice on what to buy."

The airport's small CD shop featured mostly mainstream pop music, but Wayne found her what she was looking for: a CD by a calypso singer named Red Plastic Bag.

"See," he said, "if you stayed longer, I could take you to the best calypso tent." She was missing it, she knew, her chance to go to one of the elaborate Crop Over celebrations, the highlight of a July or August vacation. She'd thought to go to one of the events, particularly after her day of touring the island, but she'd stuck close to the hotel on Thursday and Friday. She had suspected she was coming down with a cold, though whatever it was passed, and when it did, she felt an obligation to exercise. She swam in the ocean. She even took an aerobics class at a place near the hotel and cursed herself for not doing so sooner. She liked the friendly women in the class—all locals, not the spoiled tourists she was imagining. Or maybe what she liked was simply having a day that didn't puzzle her.

Melody. Maybe she'd been trying to say her name was Melony.

∽

Wayne only offered to take her to a calypso tent because he knew he wouldn't have to. All he wanted to do right now was make eight hundred dollars. Three hundred for the ticket, five hundred toward a deposit on a new apartment. He already had two hundred, but that would disappear soon enough. Still, things were about to get easier. He felt sure of that. He'd already told Trevor that they had to sell the house, or start renting it out; that they could both live (although this was most certainly over-stating the case) on the income. And Trevor didn't object. He wanted the money as much as Wayne.

But Wayne couldn't find a renter, or imagine a sale, till he made enough money to get out of the house himself. Yesterday, he'd gone for an interview to be a grocer's cashier, but he hadn't gotten the position. If sugar season weren't over, he could head canes for a while and make some cash with that. Tomorrow, there would be more want ads in the paper, and maybe he'd find something there. Or he could try for a loan.

"Did you know," Charlotte said, "that Frank doesn't have any mirrors in his house, because he can't stand to look at himself?" She was slumped over the black bag on the seat between them, hugging it like a pillow.

"Where'd you get that?"

"That woman, Toni, whom you worked with? She called to talk to me about the job . . ." Charlotte sat up, then mumbled the rest of her sentence, as if she were ashamed to have been caught in dialogue with Frank or Frank's co-workers. "Anyway, *she* said."

"Well, I don't love my own face, but I don't expect to get sympathy for it."

"I don't think she was trying to make me sympathize with him, just, you know . . . so I'd have a sense of where he was at."

"I don't like to look at his ugly mug, either," Wayne said, just as Charlotte added, "And you have a very nice face."

A voice announced that Charlotte's flight would be delayed by fifteen minutes.

"Really," Charlotte said, waving her hand in the direction of the sound from the intercom, "you don't have to wait with me. You know how this can be. It could be fifteen-minute delays all day."

"So take the job, why don't you?" Wayne asked, semisarcastic, because he knew Charlotte wouldn't. "You know, you got a place to stay in my house. I'm looking to rent it out."

⌒

"Don't think I'm not tempted," Charlotte laughed. "Yeah, you get on the plane, and I'll drive your car home." But, of course, she couldn't leave Boston, because what if Helen came back, looking for her? And found someone else in the apartment, his strange shoes and umbrella by the hall door? And what could Charlotte do? Shout—from some small concrete home in Barbados—"Don't worry, Helen. I'm right here"?

"Well, I can't give you my car. Trevor took that. He's had it since I was in the hospital, and . . . whenever I ask for the keys, he pats himself down and . . . I got a feeling he smashed it up or traded it for . . . who knows, but I'm guessing it's gone."

"I don't want you to give me your car."

"Well, I *do* want you to give me your plane ticket."

"It's yours." She handed her boarding pass to him.

"Yeah, right." He pushed it back.

"I'm serious," she said, but she was laughing. "We'll switch. It'll be like trading lives."

Or parachutes, she thought. Someone was bound to go smash. That's what happened when you didn't just ride with what had been given you. But that was stupid. There was no reason it had to be that way.

"So," Wayne said. "I'll draw you a map to get to my house." But he wasn't serious. Charlotte could see that, though he used the back of an envelope to draw her a picture. A voice crackled onto the intercom again. Flight 278 direct to Boston will be boarding in just a moment. "And here's the key," Wayne said. "And you'll need to know your own phone number." He scribbled some numbers down on the envelope. "And my number, at my friend in Boston's, so you can send the rent."

"Well, how much is it?"

"Seven hundred. With water and electric."

"Seven hundred Barbados?" That was three hundred and fifty U.S. dollars.

"Yes, of course," Wayne laughed. "What you think? American?" He drew her a little diagram of the floor plan. Two and a half rooms. "Fully furnished, though I'd want to come down, some vacation, and clear things out." He was quiet for a bit, then said, "There used to be problems with drugs in the area, but that's gone now. A suburban sort of place, not all run-down."

"I'll do it," Charlotte said evenly. She felt edgy, as if she were running, as fast as she could down a road, though she was sitting here, perfectly still.

"Oh, you will, will you?"

"Yeah, I will," Charlotte declared, more firmly now. "And you can have my place. It's seven hundred and fifty. American dollars, I'm afraid. And only water's included. Fully furnished, too, but I'd want to come up, some vacation, and . . ."

"I get the idea."

"It's North Cambridge, so it's not so," Charlotte rolled her eyes, "white bread. There's Italians and Hispanics and blacks on the street." She was copying the address of the place down and making a map herself. "I'll call and warn my landlady." They'd been joking, because that was the only way they could talk about it, but now they were serious. A wave of fear passed over her, and for a moment, she thought she might pass out. Such an enormous thing to do.

Flight 278 was boarding. First-class customers first. Wayne looked down at Charlotte's boarding pass.

"We should be," she said, "so lucky."

⟿

Of course, someone would need to tell Trevor. That was an obstacle. But Wayne had shipped most of his clothes already, save for a handful of things that were too light for Boston. He'd have to get . . . well, a new razor and toothbrush. He'd already closed out the bank and all the money he had in the world was sitting in his back pocket. Frank owed him one last paycheck. And he had to pee. He didn't know why excitement always made him feel like peeing.

"But I can't . . . I couldn't accept this, even if you were serious." He shook the boarding pass.

"I showed them my passport when I checked in, but . . . you know, it's a shitty system. Just because I show them a photo ID when I check in doesn't mean I'm the one who'll use the ticket."

"It's too much," Wayne said.

They were boarding the back of the plane.

"I'm not *giving* it to you," Charlotte said. "You can pay me back. Or no . . ." She stopped and tapped the ticket, "This is my first month's rent.

And you'll pay my landlady the rest of what you owe me. She lives on the first floor."

Charlotte wriggled a key off her key chain. Then she pressed her fingers to her temples and started saying, more to herself than to him, "But I need to . . . well, no, it doesn't matter. We'll talk on the phone. We'll figure it out." She looked up at him and said, "This is so crazy."

A voice came over the intercom. Rows twenty and back.

"That's you," Charlotte said. And then added, as if she were relieved to find an obstacle, "But you don't have a passport with you."

Wayne put his hand to his back pocket and slapped his wallet. "I've got it." He shook his head. "I can't believe we're doing this."

"Well," Charlotte said, but she looked a little dazed herself, "neither can I. I might change my mind in a month, so no promises on the apartment, but go, go, you don't want to miss it."

Wayne stood up. "Are you serious?"

"I guess," she smiled and reached out, gave him a hug, "I am."

◦—

He said he'd call when he got there, then he waved one final time and went through the gate. She thought of all the things he'd see in her apartment: the gurgling cod pitcher, the large stuffed panther on Helen's bed, the big photo of Helen and Charlotte and their parents sitting in a tree. The wildly expensive stereo system that her parents had bought for Helen. What would he think of *that*? But she didn't truly care. She turned toward the road, then realized she'd have to change money if she was staying. And she had to figure out her bank back home and call—oh God!— call her parents. It was all so overwhelming.

On her way to the money exchange, Charlotte almost walked into a man in a wheelchair. Half his right leg was gone. Phantom limbs, Charlotte thought, and remembered a person might experience shin splints even though he had no legs. Helen used to say she had a phantom boob. It itched, even though it was gone, and the feeling was so real that sometimes Helen scratched the air and Charlotte would say, "Don't itch. It will only make it worse."

"Sorry," she smiled at the man in the wheelchair. She tapped her forehead. "Not paying attention to where I'm going."

Back outside, the sun bleached everything. The field across the way looked like an aging photograph of itself.

"Taxi?" a man called.

Charlotte nodded her head as she searched her purse for sunglasses.

"This your first trip to our island?" the driver asked.

"Sort of," Charlotte allowed, then showed him the back of the envelope Wayne had given her. "I'm going here." She pointed to the address.

"Oh, you're going to love our island," the driver burbled as he held the taxi door open.

The end of the story, Charlotte thought, as he took her back over the road that had first brought her into the island, *was always the same. You got over it. You moved on,* but Charlotte wasn't going to move on. It didn't matter that she was driving away from her old life with every mile the cab covered. Helen might as well have been sitting on her lap, bouncing her head on the cab's ceiling each time the driver hit a pothole. So, her mother had been right: Charlotte held onto things. She dwelled. What could the possible end of her story be?

Life is haunted, and it would be so diminished if it were otherwise?

Could *that* be it? *Could* it?

And she saw, as the cab angled down to that first startling glimpse of water—part of the same sea she'd gazed into with Melony; it was all part of the same thing—that it could.

DEBRA SPARK is the author of the novel *Coconuts for the Saint* and editor of the anthology *Twenty Under Thirty: Best Stories by America's New Young Writers* (Scribners). She has been the recipient of several awards including a N.E.A. fellowship, a Bunting Institute fellowship from Radcliffe College, and the John Zacharis/*Ploughshares* award for best first book. She currently directs Colby College's Creative Writing Program and teaches in the M.F.A. Program for Writers at Warren Wilson College. She lives with her husband and son in North Yarmouth, Maine.

This text of *The Ghost of Bridgetown* has been set in Goudy, a typeface designed by Frederic Goudy and issued by Monotype in 1928.
Book design by Wendy Holdman.
Set in type by Stanton Publication Services, Inc.
Manufactured by Friesens Corporation on acid-free paper.

Graywolf Press is a not-for-profit, independent press. The books we publish include poetry, literary fiction, essays, and cultural criticism. We are less interested in best-sellers than in talented writers who display a freshness of voice coupled with a distinct vision. We believe these are the very qualities essential to shape a vital and diverse culture.

Thankfully, many of our readers feel the same way. They have shown this through their desire to buy books by Graywolf writers; they have told us this themselves through their e-mail notes and at author events; and they have reinforced their commitment by contributing financial support, in small amounts and in large amounts, and joining the "Friends of Graywolf."

If you enjoyed this book and wish to learn more about Graywolf Press, we invite you to ask your bookseller or librarian about further Graywolf titles; or to contact us for a free catalog; or to visit our award-winning web site that features information about our forthcoming books.

We would also like to invite you to consider joining the hundreds of individuals who are already "Friends of Graywolf" by contributing to our membership program. Individual donations of any size are significant to us: they tell us that you believe that the kind of publishing we do *matters*. Our web site gives you many more details about the benefits you will enjoy as a "Friend of Graywolf"; but if you do not have online access, we urge you to contact us for a copy of our membership brochure.

www.graywolfpress.org

Graywolf Press
2402 University Avenue, Suite 203
Saint Paul, MN 55114
Phone: (651) 641-0077
Fax: (651) 641-0036
E-mail: wolves@graywolfpress.org

Other Graywolf titles you might enjoy are:

Celebrities in Disgrace by Elizabeth Searle
Central Square by George Packer
And Give You Peace by Jessica Treadway
War Memorials by Clint McCown
Anna Imagined by Perrin Ireland
The Wedding Jester by Steve Stern